THE
LICTOR
OF
MAGIC

Also by W. J. Cherf

The Manuscripts of the Richards' Trust

Bow Tie

Recovery

Children of Ptah

Imhotep

Maat-ka-ra. Memoires of a Time Traveler

The Adventures of J.J. Stone

The First Soul

THE LICTOR OF MAGIC

THE ADVENTURES OF J.J. STONE

BOOK II

BY

W. J. CHERF

FBP
FOXBAT PUBLISHING

Foxbat Publishing
ISBN: 978-0-9989318-0-7

DEDICATION

Editors. Truth be told, writers are lost souls, who without an editor to guide, goad, correct, and encourage them, would never make the grade. Such an editor makes the book better, the writer more succinct. The result enhances the reader's experience. Keith and Mia are two of those marvelous resources, and without their help, this book would never have seen the light of day.

Beta readers. They are the brave ones who generously share their time on oftentimes flawed manuscripts. They then are faced with the task of telling the writer the hard truth, the happy news, or some awkward combination of both.

Finally, there is always Sweet Sue. Somehow she puts up with all of my madness. This one is entirely for you.

A GPS Adventure Book

How many times did you wish you could go where the story took place? That mummy's tomb? That Caribbean pirate ship? Normandy Beach or the Alamo?

For Harry Potter, there is Platform 9¾ at King's Cross Station, the Reptile House at the London Zoo, Leadenhall Market, and the Tower Bridge. Universal has an entire Wizarding World devoted to the famous J.K. Rowling series.

But did you ever read a book that told you where to go? To actually see what inspired the writer? Or where the action took place?

Well, now you can. Sleuth out any of the following GPS coordinates of J.J. Stone's first adventure. Be sure to have a USB adaptor handy that is appropriate for your device.

Good hunting!

1: GPS: Lat: 40° 45' 31.89" N. Long: 73° 58' 36.65" W.

2: GPS: Lat: 40° 45' 36.41" N. Long: 73° 58' 34.29" W.

3: GPS: Lat: 39° 51' 33.56" N. Long: 79° 49' 30.98" W.

4: GPS: Lat: 35° 38' 59.32" N. Long: 105° 48' 00.08" W.

5: GPS: Lat: 39° 37' 01.27" N. Long: 104° 47' 54.88" W.

6: GPS: Lat: 35° 39' 11.93" N. Long: 105° 57' 41.37" W.

7: GPS: Lat: 35° 39' 53.87" N. Long: 105° 58' 20.78" W.

PROLOGUE

The venerable senator signaled the first-speaker to address the assembled. Having received a nod of assent, he levered up his arthritic bones with a groan off the marble bench. He shuffled his way the needed sixteen paces, arranging his toga en route so its purple hem didn't drag upon the smoothed limestone pavers.

While the old man made his way, a rustle of shifting bodies, robes, and scraping sandals spread throughout the chamber.

One senator quipped to his neighbor, "Publius, harken. The old farmer wishes to lecture us yet again."

"Decorum!" demanded the first-speaker.

Finally reaching the semi-circular chamber's acoustic sweet spot, the distinguished senator faced his peers.

"Colleagues, I wish to address the shocking cost of common bread I noted today in the marketplace. Given our Egyptian grain shipments are unaccountably late, the market shortfall has been fulfilled by the expensive grains from ..." a rough cough interrupted the august senator, "our neighbor to the south—Libya.

"I find it sinister that, with their vile grain, another far more dangerous import has made its presence known within our city. I speak of human sacrifice, the most abhorrent of superstitions, and one this august body should outlaw forthwith," the grizzled veteran farmer spat.

"Just two days ago agents of the Republic discovered yet another burnt offering, another sacrificed infant. With one hand, the Carthaginians steal from our pockets with their costly grain, while, with the other, they steal our infants to appease their abominable gods.

"This will not stand!

"This must not stand!

"Carthage must be destroyed!" the stomping, red-faced senator raged.

As Senator Marcus Porcius Cato made his way back to his seat, many knowing glances were shared, hidden smiles covered, all accompanied by a low murmuring.

"It seems old Cato can find both a conniving *and* blasphemous Carthaginian lurking under every rock," one voiced while snickering to his neighbor.

Another senator quipped, "No matter the subject, he always finishes with that line, *Carthago delendum est*! He nags us like my damn mistress."

The Roman Senate acknowledged the threat Carthage represented, In fact, of those present, fully one fourth backed Cato's plea. Better, they had a plan.

Later that very evening, a group met at an empty storehouse in nearby Ostia, the port of Rome. Cato had requested their presence.

"Friends," Cato began. "I believe we must form a faction to protect and preserve the *mos maiorum*, our traditional ancestral customs. I propose that we, together, vigorously act against any superstition which practices human sacrifice and any other abhorrent foreign practice. Are we in agreement?"

All nodded in assent.

"I am most gratified, friends, for your support. So also, may I suggest we refer to our faction as the *Consilio ad Conservationem de Iure Naturali*, the

Council for the Preservation of Natural Law? This we can refer to in public as the CCIN."

A hand raised to be recognized, and the career military officer Publius Cornelius Scipio said, "Cato, I wish to make suggestion."

"Certainly," Cato encouraged.

"If we further abbreviate our name to simply CCI, 'the two hundred and one,' I believe the nature of our purpose will remain far more hidden."

"Two hundred and one, I like that," Cato said with approval. "And it holds a militaristic ring to it, all to better shield its meaning. So shall we be called."

All grunted in assent.

Another asked, "Cato. You mentioned we must 'vigorously act' against human sacrifice and other abhorrent practices. What did you have in mind?"

Cato wolfishly grinned. "We must appoint one of our number to act independently against the abomination that is human sacrifice, and against any other abhorrent superstitions which might harm our most sacred customs, in order to preserve our fair Republic's relationship with the gods.

"This sacred duty will be closely held. There will be no record made, no inscription cut, no celebration for the appointee of this sacred purpose. Yet, among our number, this heavy responsibility should be honored with a special title. I propose that designation be the *lictor magicae*."

So it was agreed.

As the assembled disbursed, Cato signaled one to remain.

"Scipio. I wish you to accept the mantle of *lictor magicae* and destroy the source of these abhorrent sacrifices. Will you so swear?"

"Yes, venerable one. I do so swear."

* * *

Shortly after this historic gathering, Cato died. But three years later, he got his wish as the mighty legions of Rome dealt the city of Carthage a mortal blow. Sacked, its population either massacred or sold into slavery, and its soil salted, Carthage had been leveled. The victorious Roman general, Publius Cornelius Scipio, earned the title *Africanus* as a result of this campaign. As much as Scipio relished the title, he had done so to fulfill his oath to Cato as the CCI's first *lictor magicae*.

CHAPTER 1
The Chairman's Oracle

They met in an upscale family restaurant on a cobble-stoned side street in Tivoli, a convenient location for both. Usually, their table conversation remained civil, sometimes even cordial, but not today.

"*Signore* Presto. Over thirty years ago I warned you about this *l'uomo potente*. You scoffed at my warnings, and what did you do? You dialed your phone and contracted a mercenary to do your dirty work. He failed miserably. Later, you contracted another, with the same result. *Twice* you shirked your responsibilities both to your *famiglia* and our Gathering.

"They, both, failed ..." The bristling oracle emphasized with a sneer, daring to get a rise out the seated figure opposite—the chairman of the most powerful paranormal organization on earth.

"And still, to this day, you ignore my portents, choosing instead to busy yourself with your race cars."

The chairman wanted to lash back, but was prevented by an extended open palm in his face—yet another slight.

"Well, *Signore* Presto, two days ago, this *l'uomo potente*, this American called Stone, participated in the murder of one of our own, a powerful adept, in Afghanistan."

Now gouging her forefinger into the table's fine linen tablecloth, "This wizard, Charles Smithers, fell before the American Stone and his own twin brother, Peter Smithers, the president and Lictor of Magic of TIIIS.

"Do you, *Signore*, know what that means?"

The oracle's challenge was met with silence as the chairman instead examined the glittering facets of his cufflinks against the table candle's flame.

As he continued to admire them, Giovanni Presto replied, "*Signora* Costa. I know of this Charles Smithers. He and our Gathering parted ways over a decade ago. So, if anything, his brother did us a favor by ridding the mortal landscape of a deranged adept. Do you wish me to send TIIIS a Thank-You note?" He concluded with an ingratiating smile.

The Oracle, Valeria Costa, who traced her lineage from the Vestal Virgins of ancient Rome, could not believe her ears. Annoyed beyond words, the attractive, middle-aged *strega* flicked an errant strand of her still raven-black hair behind one ear and sipped from her red wine. That pleasurable distraction somewhat blunted her dislike for the dolt opposite. She rallied again, as if dealing with a child, this time using verbal Crayons.

"*Signore*. Does it not occur to you as strange that Peter Smithers needed assistance in the fratricide of his own twin?

"*Signore*. Why do you think Peter Smithers chose Jonathan Joseph Stone join him?

"And, in case you haven't noticed, *Signore*, this nascent alliance, between Peter Smithers and the American, is a clear indication that the carrier of the First Soul of Creation came to the aid of the most prominent member of TIIIS.

"*Signore*. What do you conclude?"

With a mild shrug of his shoulders, "I see this as Peter Smithers' way of ridding himself of his wayward brother.

"On the other hand, the involvement of Stone in this family matter, I do find curious. What are *your* thoughts, *Signora*?"

Encouraged at this glimmer of intellect, Valeria said, "*Signore* Presto, Stone's 'involvement' means that TIIIS recruited him. And, given the age of Peter Smithers, this makes Stone the most logical choice for the next Lictor of Magic.

"Consider *Signore*, for one moment, what it would mean for TIIIS if the carrier of the First Soul was also their Lictor of Magic."

Warming to her subject, Valeria leaned forward and continued.

"The Americans have an expression for situations such as these; they're called 'game-changers,' *Signore*. It is long past time that you kill this *l'uomo potente* while you still can, and above all, before he joins with a ley line. As a blood-bound *amica* of your *famiglia*, and treaty-bound ally in-good-standing of our Gathering, Stone represents a frightening nexus of power and talent that the Gathering cannot allow to mature." The oracle concluded while wagging her finger in his face.

"Stone must be dealt with now." She emphasized with a closed fist. "You must crush him like a snake."

"You know, Valeria, you look magnificent when you're passionate about something. A flush comes to your cheeks that I find quite irresistible."

While the Chairman of CMES did not realize it, with that remark, he and his family just lost the services of the most reliable oracle alive.

Valeria for her part, sat back in her chair, took in his presence, sipped again from her family's fine wine, and vowed that she would see him replaced. With the coalescence of that thought, *Signora* Valeria Costa, Oracle of the Temple of Vesta, already knew who would be capable of permanently removing her dim companion.

CHAPTER 2
Heart to Heart

Nestled within a Pennsylvania old growth forest stood Old Oaks Academy. Founded in 1813 following the sack of Washington by the British, President James Madison made funds available to ensure the future home of the paranormal society whose motto read: "light triumphs over evil." The society's avowed purpose was to provide for "the education and training of the defenders of light." After the burning of the Capital by the British, many felt that sentiment as one well worth investing in.

By the twenty-first century the Academy's campus had expanded far beyond Old Main's solitary tower and sacrosanct cruciform foundations. Today, Old Main is encircled by magically augmented structures, each constructed in their own architectural style, be it Egyptian, Greek, Roman, Gothic, or Bauhaus aluminum, glass, and steel.

Interspersed between these impressive edifices, the first faculty had planted numerous flowering gardens, complete with their taxonomic identifications, which scented the air with their fragrances. Several student organizations have since cared for these pampered jewels of nature, openly and forever in competition with each other, over whom nurtured the beds the best.

Four blockhouse structures—actually truncated limestone pyramids—served the student body as their dormitories. Self-contained with their own cafeterias and auditoriums, each were precisely aligned along magnetic north. As a consequence, their official names were North, South, East, and West. But as with all things, rather fanciful nicknames took their place. Currently, the student body favored Never Never Land, Stalag 13, Eden, and West World, respectively.

Housing for the college's president and faculty dotted the campus' periphery. All were stucco, two-story bungalows with abundantly flowering gardens and generous front porches, where professors often held impromptu office hours, lemonade socials, tutorials, and wine tastings.

The campus as a whole is situated within a bucolic canopy of sun-dappled oak leaves, known for its early morning fog, which usually burns off before noon. Meandering amidst the whole snakes a crystalline stream known as the Jordan River, where first semester freshman are ritualistically dunked during the autumnal, campus-wide, hazing ceremony. Part good-natured fun, this activity, in which the faculty sit as witnesses, is meant to impress upon young minds the importance of clear, clean water in the vanquishing of evil, and the virtues of common hygiene.

The students and faculty, who look like any other university population, are devoted to developing themselves far beyond the norm. They come from all walks of life. The single criteria for admission are three recommendations from members-in-good-standing within the TIIIS paranormal community.

Following tradition, the international president of the society always has at his disposal a modest office within Old Main's tower. Because of its infrequent use, its confines smelled like a stale and musty book repository. It is kept locked and set aside for use at the president's pleasure, today was just such a day.

*   *   *

"Mr. Stone," the white-haired, tall nonagenarian president began without preamble, "I want you to familiarize yourself with your personal file." Smithers said to the seated rugged, blond-haired giant in his mid-thirties, a man in the prime of his life, while he patted the thick gray binder with a slightly tremulous hand covered with age spots.

"Within you will find why I selected you to succeed me as our society's Lictor of Magic. There are details that will trouble you, so allow me to explain."

Removing the first plasticized sheet from the portfolio's open ring binder, the president spun it around for me to read.

"This is the first notice our society received regarding your birth on 3 June 1973. Ignore for the moment the document's title of *Infant Insurance Policy Application*—that's just camouflage to distract an outsider.

"Note here," the president continued, pointing with a bony finger, "that your IPAR shows '10' with an SN of '1.' Now let's compare these with those of your parents. Your mother, Constance, for instance, has an IPAR of '1,' and your father, Andrew, a '3.'

"Based on these Innate Paranormal Ability Ratings, your parents are gifted sensitives. Such scores occur in only two percent of the human population. Your father, with an IPAR of '3,' is considered quite high, and, if he had ever received any rudimentary training, could have readily achieved a Fourth Class Adept status."

"Just like Mr. Henry Horatio Johnson," I said with widened eyes.

"Indeed."

"But, sir, genetics aside, how did I rate out as a '10'?"

"That, I suspect, is because of your Soul Number of '1.' You carry the First Soul of Creation. That has to amount to something, don't you think?"

"My God …"

"Indeed, again. In sum, there is far more to you than you realize. As a consequence, your upcoming training will push you very hard."

"I understand, sir, and thank you for sharing this with me. This explains why I could see and read auras from such a young age."

The president nodded in acknowledgement.

"Mr. Stone, there is much more in this file that you must read," the president said as he returned the page and took out two stapled bunches.

"These reports, for instance, chronicle two CMES attempts to assassinate you. The first occurred shortly after your birth. The second involved a tragic truck accident."

"What?"

The president sighed deeply.

"Mr. Stone, CMES has wanted you dead for some time," he said as he returned the field reports to the dossier, closed it, and pushed it over to me.

"Familiarize yourself with your file. I guarantee that CMES has an identical one in their archives." He handed me a bulky manila envelope. "And, take these. They are throw-away smart phones. Go over to IT and Security and they will explain the entire procedure. As of this moment, I want you off the grid—completely."

At my puzzled look, the president continued. "As

of this moment, you, me, your parents, friends, and colleagues, are all potential targets for CMES. Let's make it as difficult as possible for them."

After a wide-eyed gulp, I gathered up my file and the weighty manila envelope of five phones.

*　*　*

Later that day President Peter I. E. Smithers had another appointment, this time with a rising star within the society.

"Governor Betsy Silver Moon," the president warmed in his Cambridge accent, "as you know, I have extended our society's position of Lictor of Magic to Mr. J.J. Stone. Before we establish his initial training regimen, what I need from you are your impressions of the man. Frankly," he confided while examining his fountain pen, "I do not know him, even though he did perform well under duress while assisting me with the execution of my brother, Charles." He concluded, embarrassed.

"While I am current with his file, only you, governor, have scanned his mind. Every man has his baggage, and for a position as important as the Lictor of Magic, I need to know Stone's."

"Peter," the petite middle-aged Native American Indian woman with raven black hair said, "I will answer your questions as best I can. First off, Mr. Stone possesses qualities that no Lictor of Magic in recent memory has ever had, and I say that meaning no offense to present company."

A smile and a nod. "None taken."

"That fact alone is our society's greatest advantage. Consider: He carries the First Soul of Creation, which enhances his survivability. His service in the U.S. Marines is one of distinction. His command abilities are beyond question. He is a seasoned battlefield warrior with an agile, tactical mind, who can act independently."

"Stone is the sole person that I have met who has experienced long term possession and, somehow, someway, retained his sanity. In fact, he managed to capitalize on that extraordinary event and has become a published scholar in ancient Sumerian demonic texts."

Examining her hands, the governor continued. "Stone has been in contact with a primordial being, who explained to him the Cosmic Order and his role and responsibilities within it. Peter, that conversation alone confirms the veracity of *The Knot of Eternity*."

"How interesting. Please continue."

"The man possesses uncommon drive and focus. Over all, his Christian upbringing forms his sense of right and wrong. His service in the Marines transformed him into a true warrior, with a warrior ethos, something that modern civilians do not comprehend. In sum, Stone is the real deal and I whole-heartedly support his candidacy as our society's next Lictor of Magic."

The governor paused and raised her index finger.

"However, when I read Stone's mind, I saw that the man suffers from a central flaw—his empathy. Here is a man who communes with nature, understands its rhythms. Yet, because of the gruesome loss of a much-loved one in his youth, he once harbored a tremendous amount of guilt. And because of that loss, Stone enlisted into the military to lose himself, to forget, and perhaps seek out a dire punishment he believed he deserved. But, Peter, he fought through all of that. He's gotten past it. Nonetheless, scar tissue remains.

"Then there is this. Since Stone carries the First Soul of Creation, he enjoys divine protections. Fine. But on the other hand, he knows that anyone he associates with will eventually become targets of CMES or their minions. They know that they can't kill him. But they will try their damnedest to drive him mad by attacking his family and friends, making him a pariah in his mind, all to drive him to suicide. To date, they have not succeeded.

"As a consequence of his lost adolescent crush, and that since Stone once was an integral part of an elite military cadre and its mindset, he instinctively shuts himself off from civilians, does not make friends easily, and is socially inexperienced."

"Do you think that he's still a virgin?" the president asked.

"I think that it's a strong possibility.

"So, if there is a chink in Stone's character, he is susceptible to emotional manipulation and guile. Any meaningful relationship in his mind means inevitable pain and guilt. In fact, he has learned to suppress his emotions to the point of being almost robotic."

While the president listened to the observations of his governor of the Southwestern Region, he painted in his mind the image of a loner, a tortured soul.

"Do you know, Betsy, whether Stone has made contact with the First Soul?"

"No. I do not."

"Well, while we have him on campus, let's encourage to do that before we give him his training schedule."

"Understood. I'll see what I can do."

"And Betsy," the president added while pointing to his desk's top, "this schedule is only the beginning. Assuming he succeeds with his special conversation, he must be pushed, and pushed hard. Physical trials, magical self-defense, and lecture work will be undertaken together. I want complete immersion. I want him to recognized the possibilities of their integration. Furthermore, I will not put that man out there without rigorous testing. To do so, would be criminal."

"I agree. But if I might ..."

"Yes."

"May I suggest that Stone also train against some of our combat witches."

"Why?" the president asked with curious tilt of the head.

"Because, Peter, we have to reprogram Stone's social thinking. Right now he believes women are fragile objects that are only fit for worship atop pedestals. I want to change that. He has to learn that women can be as formidable a threat to him as men."

*   *   *

I felt that it was high time to seek some advice about contacting the First Soul. So, per President Smithers' suggestion made during my initiation into the society, I sought out Governor Silver Moon, and as luck would have it, I found her sitting alone at lunch.

"May I join you, governor?"

"Why, yes. That would be delightful."

As I settled in with my tray mounded with food, she prompted, "Is there something particular on your mind, Mr. Stone?"

"Yes, governor, there is. I need to initiate a

conversation with my soul and President Smithers told me that you would know how to go about that."

"You don't say," Governor Silver Moon deadpanned as she took a slow sip of her hot, black coffee.

Pushing her finished meal aside, she folded her hands on the table and said, "Mr. Stone, for the record, allow me to set the record straight on several issues. First of all, and counter to most western religions, we mortals provide the physical containers for immortal souls. Second, souls choose to reside within us at birth with the expectation of perfecting some aspect of their spiritual development en route to the ultimate goal of transcendence. Their selection of a mortal carrier, therefore, is never a trivial one."

My face must have showed the conflict that I felt. The governor asked, "Mr. Stone, what car manufacturer do you prefer?"

Surprised by the sudden shift, I blurted out, "Chevys."

"Now, Mr. Stone, think of a soul's choice of mortal carrier as a matter of brand choice. I am not being frivolous here. Likes do follow likes. A soul's past experiences figure into the equation. It often takes time for a soul to select its next mortal carrier, based upon its developmental needs and, yes, its preferences."

"But what about us?" I blurted out, motioning to myself. "Isn't what you just said reduce us to mere physical throw-aways?"

"Yes, it does. Get over it. It is the way of things." The governor said without qualm.

"We fragile mortals are indeed just … throw-aways, as you crudely put it. But keep in mind, we mortal carriers are not *unimportant*, in fact, we are *necessary*, because no immortal soul can perfect itself without having experienced what we experience. They need us, because we were created to teach them things like love, forgiveness, and understanding."

Precious moments passed while I thought about those words.

"Governor, what about my soul? By design, it's not like other souls. It's stuck, doomed to incarnate throughout eternity, without any chance for transcendence."

Nodding with grim appreciation, the governor said, "Yes, Mr. Stone, your soul cannot transcend. As the oldest, it has experienced the full gamut of what mortal experience can dish out."

With a wistful, almost dreamy look, she continued. "And still, the First Soul persists and soldiers on. Can you imagine its frustration?"

With a shake of my head, "Must be unimaginable."

"And, please note that it chose you within one day's time. Your birth notice said so—an astonishingly quick incarnation. That should tell you something, Mr. Stone. You and the First Soul must have much in common to cause it to act with such decisiveness."

"So, governor, what can I claim as me?"

"Your personality, your physical self, your intellect, and inherited genetic traits, all remain unique to you. Those facets make up who you are, what you can offer your soul. You are the sum total of your upbringing, your environment, your time. Those experiences are of tremendous value to your soul. It can and will learn from them. On the other hand, your soul has experienced many lives, many times. That can be of value to you. And, never forget, The First Soul has already, numerous times, helped you. You just didn't realize it."

"Yeah. I know what you mean—a push here, a quick side-step there. But how, governor, do I go about contacting the First Soul?"

She sighed.

"The usual approach is through some form of meditation. I know you can do that. I urge you to reach out. You just might be surprised at what you find."

After several more moments, the governor concluded. "Mr. Stone, be advised what you're going through is not unusual. Self-aware individuals have communed with their souls throughout time. However, such dialogues are not a preoccupation of Western cultures, who have not emphasized this relationship. In fact, I'm willing to bet that if you took a poll in this very cafeteria, few could even define what a soul is, because most self-absorbed westerners think in terms of their own personal qualities."

"Governor, I just had a thought. What is the role of organized religion in all of this?"

With a secretive smile, she leaned forward and answered. "The place of organized religion has always been to establish societal taboos, which become norms, and eventually codified law. Organized religions provide a medium to explain the unexplainable, as nowhere else can a structured discussion of the divine take place. Above all, we mortal carriers yearn for hope and seek answers to our questions. It's in our nature to do so. Each religion, in its own way, offers answers to those questions."

"Now wait a minute. Nowhere in my religious

upbringing was mention ever made of the interaction, much less existence of, the dark, light, and mortal realms; that we are just soul carriers. Why is that?"

"Because the organized religions of the West, mortal institutions all, positioned themselves from the start to be intermediaries between the mortal and divine. They wished to explain the unexplainable with religious tenets, which must be accepted on faith, and faith alone. As you yourself have discovered, in your conversations with an emissary of the Ledger Keeper, those tenets are nothing more than educated guesses.

"The only source that does discuss this cosmology is a work called *The Knot of Eternity*. When you begin your training, you will receive a translation of it. This work represented a dangerous voice, a heretical alternative to organized western religion. The contents of that book threatened, if not refuted, the established tenets and authority of Judaism, Christianity, and Islam."

I stopped to take a bite of my cheeseburger, not to silence my growling stomach, but as an excuse to stop, think, and consider.

Moments passed before the governor continued.

"Mr. Stone, it is time. I've taken the liberty to reserve to you a quiet place on campus to meditate in. It is not your favorite grassy, upland pasture in the Santa Fe National Forest, but it will have to do. I'll meet you there. Here are the directions," she said as she scribbled a note.

"In the meantime, calm yourself. Summon the First Soul. Discover what it wants from this existence, and most importantly, from you."

With that, she left me alone with my thoughts.

*   *   *

I closed my eyes and settled in, imagining myself sitting in fragrant spring grass under a cloudless New Mexican sky. My back warmed in the sun. Bees buzzed and the sound of their passage sent pleasurable chills up my spine. My breathing slowed to a crawl. I began to psychically poke about looking for the First Soul.

The process called to mind research that I had done into whether others have had conversations with their souls. An ancient Egyptian papyrus once described a lengthy philosophical discussion where a man and his soul argued over his intended suicide. While my reason to contact the First Soul went in an entirely different direction, I found it reassuring at least someone else had conceived of such a bizarre conversation.

I started by creating a mental tableau wherein such a discussion might take place. I imagined the First Soul sitting opposite me, cross-legged on the ground, with a low, slab-like rock between us. There sat—I imagined it as a he—a seasoned, heavily scarred, and wizened warrior. I further added broad shoulders, a darkly tanned, weathered, and wrinkled face, with long graying hair pulled back in a war knot above his neck. His leather armor possessed the patina of many years of hard use and just as many repairs. His calloused hands, much scarred and battered, lay open in his lap.

My goal was simple—forge an understanding. What did the First Soul want from this existence? And, how could it, with its long experience, help me with mine.

The First Soul spoke, his voice like gravel:
Curious.

While you are not the only mortal carrier who has desired congress with me, this is the first time I have done so in the guise of a warrior. I like it.More often than not, I am imagined as a bright light, a shapeless cloud, or even as a radiant woman. But you have managed to capture with your mind's eye a far truer sense that reflects my current incarnation's purpose. I am indeed old, much-battered, but still full of fight, soul carrier.

Surprised by The First Soul's candor, I choked out. "Why did you choose me?"

My question split that craggy face as he examined his open hands.

Never before have I joined with a soul carrier with your natural abilities. I did so purposefully, perhaps even guided by the Creator, because of the fragility of the Cosmic Order. It was I who guided you to join the military, all to find Nergal's soul container. Much was at stake. Yet you succeeded in healing the rent in the darkness' boundary by assisting with Nergal's quest. Verily, I cannot express sufficiently my joy, after all this time, to have my purpose finally come to pass at the hour of greatest need.

His deep green eyes now looked into mine. *You no doubt sense, soul carrier, that the balance of the mortal realm is also at stake. For far too long has the darkness' influence been abroad, unleashed for centuries by the open rent. This, too, requires our attention. It is time to root it out and set things again in balance. You, soul carrier, are at your base a reluctant warrior, who seeks justice and not vengeance. With this I can abide. But you might find that your reluctance can become a hindrance. Be mindful.*

"But what about you, First Soul? What can I provide to assist you?"

At first, he remained silent as he considered my words. Finally, with a grunt, a shifting of weight, *I wish to root out evil, soul carrier. That is the truest answer to your question. Our hunt will be brief, ferocious, as evil will surely seek us out first—and soon.*

I blinked in surprise.

Soul carrier. Remember—we are one until death. Have faith in yourself as I have in you. There is much in me that is you. Even your image of me, is but a reflection.

Verily, soul carrier, I have guided you many a time—most recently, the crushing of the evil one's skull as it tried to cast a death spell. That would have caused needless harm.

So he'd done that! I realized with elation. It was he who'd guided my impulse to crush the evil Charles' skull.

Soul carrier, your mortal course is destined to protect countless innocents. Follow it. Nurture it. In so doing you teach me, as have countless others—many whose memory I hold with great fondness and regard.

Remember, soul carrier, we are a team, first and always.

With that the First Soul vanished from my mind's eye. Meanwhile, I returned to the here and now, sitting on the floor of an empty office.

I was elated, fulfilled. Never before had I felt this complete, confident, and sure of myself. Not in a foolhardy or egotistical sense, but rather secure in my convictions. "Centered" would perhaps be the best way to express it.

Then Governor Silver Moon broke my moment of reverie. "So, Mr. Stone, were you successful?"

At first spooked by her presence, I blurted out, "Yes, yes indeed, ma'am," my dry voice cracked. "In fact, I'm ready to begin training right now!"

The governor just sat there, stone-faced. She handed me a stapled schedule on four sheets of paper.

"What's this?"

"Your training regime. It begins tomorrow."

"Great!"

"We'll see, Mr. Stone. We'll just see."

CHAPTER 3
Mother Rome

A Roman villa stood atop a hillock of limestone and barren sand where nothing grew. From the air, its faded red tiled roof embraced a parched gravel and terrazzo enclosure surrounded by shadowed porticos. This desolate façade veiled a myriad of underground passageways and chambers that honeycombed the bedrock of this stoutly defended outcrop. Stark and forbidding, this was the home of the most powerful paranormal organization on the planet—CMES, *Consilium magorum et sagarum*—The Council of Magicians and Witches. Its membership reverently referred to this hallowed ground as *Romae matrem*, "Mother Rome," since its founding in 30 BC.

Within sat six in a renovated high ceilinged chamber, an airy space which was once a grand dining room. Now transformed into the CMES chairman's office, its inlaid flooring surrounded an island of oriental carpeting and gilded high baroque furniture from another time.

Five regional directors, who thought of themselves as kings in their own right, grudgingly paid lip service to their chairman's pride of place. Despite the chairman's obvious primacy, the lone oddity to this paradigm was the status of the North American regional director, based in New York City. That entity disproportionately nurtured over sixty-five percent of the paranormal organization's assets. As a result, many considered the NYC regional directorship, a position of immense clout, as the chairman-elect.

*   *   *

Giovanni Presto became chairman at the age of twenty-two. His bloodline, aristocratic and Roman, once provided ancient Rome with more than its fair share of magistrates and high priests. Presto was himself a powerful telekinetic practitioner, who thought nothing of exercising his skill with cunning ruthlessness.

Presto sat at the head of a conference table thirty years later dressed in a midnight blue silk suit and a starched white dress shirt open at the collar. Fit, tanned, and with a shock of salt and pepper curly hair worn boyishly long over the ears, the Roman's presence dominated a room. Normally, this meeting would have annoyed him, as it took time away from his hobby, a Formula 1 racing team and its upcoming preparations for the Belgian Grand Prix. Indeed, Presto was an Enzo Ferrari wannabe. But on this day, the chairman had a lot on his mind, and one individual in particular.

Looking around the conference table he said, "This quarterly meeting is now in session. Let it be recorded, Regional Directors Victor Alexandrevich Volkov of St. Peterburg, Zakia Owusu of Mombasa, Feng Bai of Hong Kong, Mukhtar El-Najjar of Baghdad, and William Alexander of New York, are all present."

Presto paused as he internally bridled at the time-consuming formality of having to announce everyone's name, title, and attendance. His manicured fingers drummed with impatience.

The telepath, Zakia Owusu, and second oldest regional director at one hundred and twenty-seven years, dared to interrupt Presto's annoyance.

"Mr. Chairman. Excuse me," said in a deep basso

voice. "The formal declaration of the regional directors, by name and title, is a time-honored act of respect extended to the Gathering's regional leadership. To not do so might be construed as an insult. Do you wish to foment civil war?"

Presto glared at the elderly blue-black African while berating himself for not remembering to raise his mind blocks beforehand. Meanwhile, the other regional directors glanced around among themselves wondering what the exchange was all about.

"Regional Director Owusu," Presto coolly responded to the African oracle's polite reproof. "You are correct to remind me of our traditions. But as with so many things, change is in the air." Presto floated his fountain pen before the man, pointing it unwaveringly at bridge of the shaman's nose. While the other directors watched with more than a little fascination— the chairman's pen was rumored to be quite poisonous—Owusu's left eye involuntarily twitched.

Presto's eyes had turned dark. His voice soft. "Please accept my apology, regional director, but never again lecture me on the content of my unspoken thoughts."

Owusu bowed his head in submission and the fountain pen returned to Presto's outstretched palm. As it did, the African's numerous ritual scars across his high forehead rippled in irritation. Owusu had survived four previous chairmen. He harbored few doubts that he would outlive this arrogant youngster as well.

Presto paused to sip from his water glass.

"Let us begin," he said folding his hands. "What is the status of that meddling dream reader, the one who dared to elevate himself to ambassadorial status?"

"Dead, Mr. Chairman," the ruddy-faced and massively built native of St. Petersburg—himself a former Olympic Greco-Roman wrestler—stated for the record.

"How?" Presto pressed.

"Dismembered by an Assyrian griffin demon." The Russian's eyes glinted with satisfaction from beneath heavy eyebrows.

"Messy, but entertaining. Did the miscreant recant his diplomatic mission?"

"No, Mr. Chairman, Paul Anderson did not. Although he had been granted sufficient opportunity. As for his clan, ACME, a treaty-bound organization, they are not pleased with his … sudden passing."

"Not pleased …" murmured the chairman slitting his eyes. "Since when do we entertain such prattle from the treaty-bound? Anderson's actions constituted outright treason," he said as he tapped his fountain pen on the weathered red leather of the conference table.

"I want an apology from ACME," the chairman spat. "If they cannot control their own membership, I will take steps to do it for them. Make sure, director, that they understand the gravity of Anderson's crime and their precarious status. Remind them that the protections granted by treaty can also be annulled."

Regional Director Volkov's eyes widened as wrinkles formed on his shaved head. Owusu studied his chairman. Feng's face was immutable. El-Najjar dared to smile into his hand. Alexander, head down in boredom, examined his latest manicure.

Presto moved on. "What of the others, regional director? Your report mentioned three others. What of them?"

"Dead, Mr. Chairman. No one talked. Not one mentioned the existence of any secret alliances, much less a coup."

"Well, I am pleased to hear that. What else do you have?"

Volkov sighed.

"Mr. Chairman. My region has financially flat-lined due to a variety of internal economic issues. Be aware, however, I am addressing them all, and by next quarter I will have far better news to share. Regarding my region's membership, it is up three percent. While I am not happy with that number, I can accept it. Today's youth are a fishy bunch.

"What does trouble me, however, besides our finances, is our membership's losses on the many battlefields that have proliferated. Allow me be clear, I believe whole heartedly in our external policy, but there must be a better way to weaken our enemies than by sacrificing our own."

Folding his hands before him, Presto asked, "And how would you better project our policy of 'power and dominion,' than through *Blut und Eisen* (blood and iron), Regional Director Volkov?"

Volkov's broad shoulders fought containment within his tailored suit, said with a snarl, "If we must sacrifice our own, it should be done with some semblance of tactical restraint."

"Thank you, Regional Director Volkov, for your report. As for your call for 'tactical restraint,' when in our history have we shown any restraint whatsoever in the execution of our external policy? The answer is never. Nonetheless, I will take your concerns under advisement."

Turning in his chair, Presto next asked, "Regional Director Feng, what do you have to report?"

Feng Bai saw the world differently through his heavy eye folds. Impeccably dressed, compact, and round-faced, the Regional Director of Hong Kong possessed tremendous influence because he made it a point to speak in many languages. As a result, his tentacles reached out far and wide throughout the Pacific Rim. Besides, he liked that kind of broad situational awareness, and being fifty-three, considered himself a prime candidate for ascendancy to the chairmanship. Furthermore, he viewed the current hardline policy of dealing harshly with non-aligned paranormal organizations a distinct opportunity for his future advancement.

"Mr. Chairman," Feng reported, "I can report our region's financial health is stable and has realized a six percent increase to its portfolio. Also, our membership remains stable and is modestly growing at an annual rate of four percent. Thank you, Mr. Chairman."

Presto listened, nodded his approval, and moved on with deference. "Regional Director Owusu, do you have anything else to report?"

"No, Mr. Chairman. Our financials and membership status remain the same as last quarter's— growing."

Chairman Presto's eyes now panned to Mukhtar El-Najjar, "And you, Regional Director, what have you to report?"

Ahmad El-Najjar, the regional director of Baghdad, by birth had inherited the Islamic banking system built from the ground up by his father, Mukhtar. Learning at his father's knee, El-Najjar expanded upon what his father had created, and now his family's banks had spread throughout the Near East. Young and educated at Oxford, the junior El-Najjar looked every bit the international banker—tailored silk suit, open-collared shirt, and handsome with dark hair, eyes, and long eyelashes to match. He represented an ambitious threat to Presto.

"My war torn region is an administrative nightmare, Mr. Chairman, and yet it will rise like a phoenix. I say this with confidence, for our membership is up nineteen percent. Our coffers, while small, are growing due to the seizure of several oil resources. Out of this chaos our Gathering will rise to dominate all of Western Asia. It is Allah's will," he concluded.

"Thank you for your report, Regional Director El-Najjar." Presto smiled as if praising a child. "But if your vision is to ever to come to fruition, it will be because I willed it, not Allah."

Now finished with those he characterized as "the bull," "the sleepy head," "the stick," and "the kid," Presto now turned to his last regional director, an entity he dared not grant a private nickname to, because his telepathic abilities remained unknown, even with full blocks in place.

"Regional Director Alexander, what do you have to report?"

William Alexander began his existence in Renaissance Venice. Whispers within the Gathering estimated his age at over five hundred years. Yet, there sat a slight man with smooth, wrinkle-free, and ivory-colored skin, and flowing and luxuriant light brown hair cut fashionably long over the collar and ears. He didn't look a day over thirty. Dark magic can do marvelous things for the complexion, even if it makes you mad.

As the rest of the conference members turned to listen to Alexander's report, each did so, not out of pious respect for the man's great age, but rather out of sheer, raw, fear. Each suspected what lay behind the man's longevity, this thing which managed to traverse centuries of time. Each knew Alexander had amassed a prodigious corpus of curses and spells the likes of which no one could imagine, yet had seen in action all too often. Each also instinctively sensed this man thought of them as no better than lab rats.

"Mr. Chairman, I bare good news. Our finances, I am pleased to report, are up twenty-three percent for the quarter. We are at a point where my advisors wish to realign our portfolio away from our current liquid position, toward one more balanced, with the acquisition of several strategic fixed assets. If an appropriate opportunity becomes reality, I want us to be prepared for that delicious eventuality.

"As for our membership, we remain few, but influential in prominent urban locations along the East and West Coasts of the United States. I have even recently convinced a pivotal Washington politician to become, how should I say, most agreeable to our wishes."

All recognized what that euphemism meant—forced demonic possession.

"In addition, Mr. Chairman, I am now in a position to share with you the results of, let us just say, a side project of mine. U.S. membership has always been biased to the two coasts and its capital. My project is beginning to address that situation."

"What project is this?" Presto asked.

"Mr. Chairman. This membership project remains experimental in nature. Dare I say, provocative. I did not wish to report on it until I had results to share."

"You mean to tell me, Mr. Alexander, that you used the Gathering's resources for the benefit of your region without first asking me?" A vein pulsed on the chairman's forehead, while his fountain pen began to stir.

The regional director remained calm.

"Mr. Chairman, allow me to be clear," Alexander stated. "This membership recruitment project I funded entirely out of my own pocket. Not one cent has been spent from our Gathering's portfolio."

Mollified, the chairman probed. "So tells us about this project"

"Gladly. I purchased a multi-media production company in Las Vegas. To date, its revenues have tripled my original investment."

The rest of his colleagues leaned forward at that detail. Alexander noted this with pleasure.

"I am sure all of you are familiar with subliminal imprinting. I am now taking this technique to a new level with my multi-media productions. The process is selective. I want to attract only the very best candidates to enroll into our Gathering."

"So, what are your results?" the chairman asked.

"Mr. Chairman, as you are no doubt aware, Las Vegas is an international hub of travel, entertainment, and commerce. As a result, two hundred and seventy-three new members have joined, who now support our purpose of world domination and power."

"So few for such a large investment?" the chairman snorted.

"Those numbers represent only our first month of operations, Mr. Chairman."

"Whose membership rosters have been impacted?" the chairman wanted to know.

"Mine, Mr. Chairman."

Silence.

Everyone around the table knew what Alexander had in mind—the building of a powerbase loyal to himself and himself alone.

The chairman cleared his throat. "Most creative." He paused.

"Lastly, gentlemen, I wish to have addressed by one of you a persistent problem. The First Soul has incarnated within an American, who, since his birth, has managed to avoid elimination. His parents have eluded our agents as well. This individual, named Jonathan Joseph Stone, is now an adult. I want him dead."

The African raised a long, bony finger.

"Yes, Regional Director."

The lanky, near seven foot Kenyan said. "Mr. Chairman. Regarding this individual, I have to report a tangible shift in the current paranormal climate. This shift emanates from this Stone, a strong one, who enjoys the divine protection of the Most Ancient One. Nearly a year ago, he, and he alone, sealed the rift in the darkness and returned the Cosmic Order to its rightful path."

Unconsciously, all leaned in to listen to this shaman. Several paled in recognition of the Kenyan's statement. All had felt the lifting of the psychic overpressure, removed by Stone. Consequently, no one noticed Presto's shock as he remembered the words of his own oracle, *"l'uomo potente,"* the powerful one.

Owusu continued. "This powerful young one, not of our Gathering ... is formidable, a proven warrior, who has killed many times. He also is a man of God. Our chairman is correct, we have tried to kill him, yet he persists like an elusive hyena in the night. This Stone, we must deal with *him*, before he dictates terms to *us*. I agree with our chairman that we must act soon."

A silence gathered as furrowed brows weighed the Kenyan's words.

Presto broke the silence. "Regional Director Owusu. Do you know when and if he will act next?"

"No, Mr. Chairman, I do not, but I do know that last month he participated in the assassination of a well-known practitioner in Afghanistan."

The mention of that territory, adjacent to the regions of two directors, caused them to look at one another in alarm, as this was news to them.

"Regional Director Owusu, you said that Stone 'participated in the assassination.' What do you mean?"

"Stone aided Peter Smithers, the TIIIS president and Lictor of Magic, in the fratricide of his twin brother, Charles.

"Stone must be stopped, now, Mr. Chairman." He emphasized with one boney finger that stabbed the table top. "TIIIS cannot have among its membership such an individual, all the more since the First Soul chose to be carried by this warrior."

A rivulet of sweat ran down the middle of Presto's back, staining his starched dress shirt of fine Egyptian cotton.

"Interesting. You believe that Stone is in league with TIIIS."

A quick nod.

"Not good news." The chairman observed. "I believe that you have made your point, regional director."

"Now, who among you wishes to have the honor of dealing with this, Stone?" the chairman asked.

"Mr. Chairman," Alexander quickly said, "I seek your blessing to remove Stone from the paranormal landscape."

Alexander's words widened his eyes. Rarely did the New York regional director seek permission from anyone. Why did he now? His colleagues wanted to know.

Presto, also intrigued by Alexander's expressed desire, and seeing an opportunity to perhaps kill two birds with one stone, granted his permission with a simple nod.

Bene fortuna, Signore Alexander.

CHAPTER 4
Physical Training

The training schedule that Governor Silver Moon gave me called for a month of intensive hand-to-hand combat, lethal magic, and serious studying. A typical day began with a morning brief and several grueling hand-to-hand, self-defense sessions in the gym. After a debrief, I often made a visit to the infirmary for some aspirin or to stitch up a wound. In some ways the sessions harkened back this thirty-something's agonies during summer, two-a-day, high school football drills. But these sessions were far more intense—as in life and death.

After my third day things got progressively more difficult. I had my lip split twice, both eyebrows mended, dislocated some fingers, and earned colorful bruises in layers. My opponents, the TIIIS security staff, took me on in tag-teams of two and three. Today, it dawned on me to read their minds, recalling my dojo training with John Running Deer while in Santa Fe.

On day four, the game changed, as my instructors inserted personnel who could block their thoughts. In response, I resorted to watching for subtleties in their stance and posture, and as a result, began again beating them at their own game.

Again my instructors caught on to me, so I began reading my opponents' auras, and saw that they changed during a fight, reflecting an individual's moment of attack, level of fatigue, or stamina. I remarked about this revelation during a debrief and was told to practice seeing auras from one eye, in essence, forcing my brain to process both views of reality at once. I was told to look out for false auras. Apparently, some practitioners can obscure their true signature behind a spell—a trick that can be defeated by increasing one's auraic focus.

One twist devised by my instructors got my attention. During my third week I showed up at the gym at the usual time, which was ten minutes early so that I could stretch out prior to the usual briefing. While occupied, four women jumped me. Initially, I couldn't believe it. Sheer habit had told me that the training session had yet to begin, but here I was getting the hell beaten out of me.

They bloodied my nose, which got my attention, but had become a commonplace. These four hit like sledgehammers. So I went to work and took the offensive. It worked, but at a price—two more dislocated fingers and several bruised ribs.

I learned several important lessons from that session—do not give into habit, expect the unexpected, and that women can be surprising deadly as they use dissimilar tactics than their male counterparts.

But this exercise had another component. When these four attacked me, they were all pretty redheads. That was how they got the drop on me, I just sat there on the mat gaping, open mouthed, because they all looked so much like my beloved Grace from my high school days. Now here's the real kicker—at session's end, all four revealed themselves and none of them looked at all like Grace. It had all been magical camouflage and I had been sucker punched. That jarred me to my core. In a live situation, that clever distraction would have killed me.

So went the escalating cycle of challenge and response. By the end of the month, I had blended my gym training with my exercises in lethal magic to become an instinctual, multi-dimensional, hard-bodied brute. Now physically lighter, my reflexes improved, as had my personal choice of tactics, repertoire of attacks, and defensive ploys. Hand-to-hand combat had slowed to the point that I practically waited for my opponent's next move.

*   *   *

Near the end of my third week, my instructors led me to the Academy's Armory. Once inside and past a security post, I found myself in a laboratory setting, where they introduced me to this short, stocky guy named Mr. Gregory Loomis.

"Hi, I'm J.J. Stone." I said, gingerly extending the fingers of a recently mended right hand.

"I want to thank you for that Kevlar suit you made for me. It fit great."

Mr. Loomis took my hand with a firm grip, but I refused to wince.

"Why thank you for the compliment, Mr. Stone. But to be honest with you, that suit was an off-the-shelf item," Loomis replied with a thick Scottish burr as he eyed me up and down.

The man scrunched up his face, tilted it, and pinched his lower lip.

"Is there a problem?" I asked.

"We'll soon see." Came his curt reply. "And I didn't know that you had injured your hand." Apparently, I had winced.

The armorer led me over to a dressing room and

had me put a suit made of an airy, see-through, white-tan material.

"What is this stuff?" I asked as I paraded before him, feeling, and looking naked.

"It's muslin. Tailors have used it for decades to mock up suit coats and slacks."

As I stood before him, he pulled at this, tugged at that.

"Now, bend over with your knees straight and try to touch your toes."

This I did to the point of flattening my hands on the flooring thanks to all the stretching I had been doing over the past three weeks. However, Mr. Loomis made no comment of this near-yoga like move, and instead made some notes.

"All right, you can get dressed now, and take care taking off that muslin. It's fragile."

When I came back out with my muslin, Mr. Loomis had something else for me to try on.

"I am very sorry, but this composite mail just arrived. I need you to take off your blouse."

Blouse? I stared back with a quizzical look.

"Your shirt, sir."

I did. But I needed help putting on the confusing bunch of black interlocking rings. Mr. Loomis helped me pull it over my head. Once on, I understood what he meant by mail. It fit loosely, but followed my every contour. Armless, with a rounded open collar like a tee-shirt, it extended beyond my hips to form a short skirt.

Again, Mr. Loomis, once the mail settled in place, began tugging here and there, and again asked me to bend, stretch, the works, as with the muslin.

"So, what is this?" I asked.

While taking some notes, Mr. Loomis responded, "This will be the core structure of your new UCS, or Urban Combat Suit, Mr. Stone. All of these tiny rings are made of nano-carbon fiber, which are exceptionally strong yet light as a feather. We sandwich the mail between a foam interior and an exterior cross-weave of Kevlar fabric embedded with a silver mesh, to give the mail support. Then we take that and bond another layer of padded Kevlar on the inside. The resulting matrix should blunt a bullet or the point of a thrown knife. I say 'should,' because the technology behind this is bleeding edge."

Then the wily armorer told me about his intended additions that included—extra padding on the forearms, knees, elbows, and shoulders for absorbing blows; a holster on my right thigh, reversed, for my left-handed draw; sleeved pockets on my hips for ammo clips; a knife sheath on my left thigh for my favorite Bush knife; slit pockets along my waist for mask filters; a form-fitting hood with Kevlar face mask, ear guards, microphones, and an encrypted radio. Last, two oval ventilation units over my kidney region that modulated the UCS' internal temperature through its gazillions of air passages.

"By the way, what color will this be?"

For the first time the man smiled, put his hands on his hips, and said, "Mr. Stone, the surface material we're using the U.S. Defense Department hasn't even heard of. It's called No-See-Em; it's my own design." He finished with an even broader grin.

"What does No-See-Em look like?"

"Here, I'll show ya." After rummaging around his work desk, he held a square of a thin-looking material about the size of his palm and placed it across his bare arm. It disappeared! I kid you not. He placed it across his desk top. Again, it disappeared, blending in perfectly. Its presence betrayed only by the slight difference in the desk top's surface thickness.

"So how does it work?" I asked.

"Ah, Mr. Stone, that's proprietary."

"Oh, come on. I might need to know in an emergency. What if it fails in the field? How do I get it to work?"

This caused the man to think, scratch at his left ear, and pull on his lower lip.

"Okay, Mr. Stone, here's how it works …"

I almost forgot, the gloves, or gauntlets as Mr. Loomis calls them, are a pugilist's dream. Made of a sandwich of calfskin, Kevlar cloth, and No-See-Em, there are tiny pockets between those layers filled with silver grains. When I make a fist, the grains move around to support my knuckles and fingers in such a clever way that the end result is a near solid object. My armorer supplied me with a pair of silver knuckles.

Bottom line, the entire suit weighs in at twenty-eight pounds when loaded up with gear. The gauntlets weigh in at two pounds each.

*   *   *

A week later Mr. Loomis surprised me by saying that instead of gym work, President Smithers wanted to put me and my new UCS "through its paces." It seems that the president wanted to see both me and the armor in action.

The suit's trials took place on a tree-lined athletic field at the Academy. To my surprise, John Running

Deer, my first combat training instructor, was flown in from Santa Fe to observe. Unknown to all, hidden throughout the surrounding oak trees, were perched the tiny chipmunk-like *Argenti,* who observed the trials as well.

On that day, I faced twenty of TIIIS' security force. All were decked out in SWAT-like attire with helmets, face shields, and full body armor, but as I looked more closely, each had subtly customized their kit. For this "warm-up exercise," they all carried nightsticks, since this session was deemed a non-lethal, hand-to-hand test.

Some "test." I was unarmed. I was expected to acquire a nightstick or two. As far as I was concerned, this looked like an all-out gangbanger's delight. Key for me was to remain out of their grasp, otherwise, with five or six of them holding me down, I'd quickly become mincemeat.

I learned that after this "warm-up exercise," the president had scheduled additional, more lethal, combat scenarios. This, I was told, is how a new Lictor of Magic was tested, where expectations were perforce off the chart.

Immediately prior to the "warm-up exercise," I was allowed to hydrate.

How nice of them. I sourly thought.

So while I guzzled my water, I focused my mind on that special place, mind-blocked, and yet open to pick up my opponents' stray thoughts. Time slowed as I allowed my senses to focus with both eyes. As I half-finished my fourth paper cup of water, head tipped back, I reached out into the surrounding circle of awaiting security forces, found one that was not paying attention, *and attacked.* He was down before my crumpled paper cup had reached the ground. I grabbed his nightstick and got to work.

Afterward, John Running Deer said that it was a good thing that the "warm-up exercise" had been videotaped because during its opening seconds the former U.S. Marine and bar bouncer in me had taken out five of the security force before anyone else had moved a step. Armed now with a nightstick in each hand, I hacked and pummeled my way through them, advancing, attacking, ignoring the occasional blow that made contact, having managed to block or side-slip most.

In all, it had taken me just moments of brutish barbarism to reduce the security force to an unconscious, or semi-conscious, groaning mass. Upon examination, four required immediate transfer to the Academy's infirmary.

As for me, I stood in the center of the human wreckage, breathing hard, soaked to the skin in sweat, but comfortable. I think I had received three, maybe four, vicious strikes from their nightsticks, but the suit absorbed them. That impressed me.

Apparently, so were several others. John Running Deer smiled, shook his head, and glowed with a teacher's admiration. But President Smithers frowned when he heard the chorus of *Argenti* tittering and whistling from the surrounding oak trees.

"Brood Mistress!" he barked at the trees. "Attend to your brood! This is not sport intended for your entertainment!"

"What a bloody brawler!" I overheard Mr. Loomis' thick Scottish brogue.

Then, turning to the videographer, he asked,

"Laddie, did you get all of that?"

"Yes sir, on all four cameras." replied a shaken voice. "Although," he added, "Mr. Stone was such a blur I don't know what the video managed to capture. Fortunately, President Smithers asked me to set the video on high-speed definition."

* * *

Before the next session of trials were to begin, President Smithers called them off, saying, "I have seen enough. I see no need in maiming any more of our security staff."

Looking at me, he stated for the record, "I judge you lethal, Mr. Stone."

Turning to face Mr. Loomis, the president said, "Well done, Gregory. *Very* well done. While Stone was a blur, he was a near-invisible one."

* * *

After the president's cancellation of the UCS trials, Mr. Loomis approached me.

"What's up?" I asked.

"Well, Mr. Stone, the president and I have been giving your new duties some thought, and so I went ahead and made you a proper tool for the job. Follow me."

As we walked in silence back to his armory, I wondered what he meant by "a proper tool."

I soon found out when the man went to the corner of his laboratory space and picked up a long and narrow cardboard container, the kind that could house a rolled up flag or even a Callaway driver. Opening one end, he poured out this ever so slightly curved rod-like object that was coated in his No-See-Em material.

"Mr. Stone, I still need to attach her harness, but if you examine her, I think that you'll get the idea quick enough."

The object was a sword, which rested on the table in its narrow and graceful sheath. As I drew the blade from its oval scabbard, I gasped at its bone-white color.

Mr. Loomis warned, "Ya know, Mr. Stone, be mighty careful with that blade. Her edge is horrifically sharp, sharper than even fresh knapped obsidian. Her odd color comes from a metallo-ceramic coating that is made up of silver and titanium elements embedded in a ceramic matrix. She won't corrode, but her edge can be sharpened far beyond that of naked steel." The Scotsman said this with clear pride in his voice.

"She has a backbone of Damascus steel for strength and resilience. As for her guard, that simple oval is milled titanium. Beyond that, Mr. Stone, this sword, well, she'll soon become a one-of-a-kind. You see her double-handed grip that's now covered in plastic? When I remove it, she'll fix upon the energy signature of your aura when you first take a hold of her, even through the leather of your gauntlets. As a result, your very being will become a part of her. Every time you wield her, her grip will absorb a wee bit of your auraic energy. Every time you tap into a ley line, you'll charge her up even more. If I were you, I'd imprint her right quick, and while you're at it, give her a name, before she decides to name herself."

"What?"

"You heard me right, Mr. Stone. Blades like this can develop strong personalities. I tested this beastie's blade against ice blocks, and she remained flexible and her ceramic coating stout. You can bash an opponent's helmet or armor without care. Now for the question of the day, Mr. Stone, how do you wish to draw her? From across your back or from the hip?"

"You mean my 'Bone Sword,' Mr. Loomis?" I said as I stripped off the plastic sheathing from the grip and took hold of "her" with both hands. I squeezed and a slight tingling sensation tickled my fingers and palms.

"From across my back, so I can draw her with my left hand."

Smiling, the Scotsman shook his head and said. "Henceforth, Bone Sword she'll forever be, Mr. Stone."

He paused a beat.

"But before I can allow you to take possession of her, you'll have to go through training."

"That makes sense. God knows how much the Marines had trained me when they issued me my weapons. What am I in for?" I asked, not having a clue of the quicksand I was about to step into.

"There are basic sword fighting elements, but it's the mastering of them that'll take you a lifetime, that is of course, if you're lucky enough to last that long." The Scotsman darkly said.

"But, Mr. Stone, those elements include such things as proper breathing and relaxation, footwork, balance and body positioning, focus, and of course, the strike and parry. All of these you must learn and practice if you wish to survive your first encounter."

"Well, who should I see about learning these elements?"

"That would be me, sir." the man said with considerable sadness, "I'll only have you for two days.

On the plus side, I've seen you in action. You know your body. You have balance and strength, and know how to gather yourself while in the thick of it. But ya need to learn respect for the blade, and when and how to best use it."

*   *   *

"This stout wooden post, Mr. Stone, is a pell, and this heavy wooden sword is what we call a waster. We use these to teach technique and test endurance. Now take four swings against that pell," Mr. Loomis said, "slowly building them up in force."

This I did, hitting the pell with a upward two-handed blow, the whacking impacts echoing off the nearby oak trees. I went with a lefty's baseball swing, starting with my legs and lower body and finishing with my forearms and hands. By the fourth blow, I had the pell vibrating like a tuning fork.

"Ah, Mr. Stone, fine job. I had forgotten that you Americans like your baseball so. Sometimes it's the hardest thing to explain—how to get your body into a strike, but you've got the idea already. What did you notice the most?"

"The vibration on impact."

"Indeed. Now I want you to give me another four strikes, but this time allow your hands to relax. Don't choke the waster so tightly."

Moments later: "That was much better, Mr. Loomis. The vibration didn't rattle the fillings in my teeth that time."

"And, Mr. Stone, I dare say that your strikes were swifter as well. More of a slice than a bash."

"How?"

"Because when you let your hands relax, your forearms and shoulders do as well. You allowed those muscles to release into the pell far more smoothly."

And so went the lesson as I bashed the waster into the pell, seeking that perfect fluid motion of release at impact. After fifteen minutes, my shoulders were fatigued, my hands numb from vibration, and strangest of all, my buttocks had gotten a real workout.

"Well, Mr. Stone. You look right ragged. But that's good, because when we get tired, we slip into bad habits. Now give me just one more solid strike."

I wacked the pell a good one.

"*Stop!* Look down at your feet, man. While you think that you made a good strike, you lifted your right foot off the ground, which upset your center of gravity. If you were facing a pro, that strike would tell him two things: you're tired, and even worse, an amateur. Never tell your opponent such things. Hide them with sound technique.

"So, let's begin again. Step into your strike, but this time slide or glide your right foot forward. Keep balanced. Keep your feet under you, and don't lift that foot like a damn baseball player swinging for the fences."

Coil, glide, and strike. Coil, glide, and strike. That became my new mantra, and damn if it didn't work like a charm.

*   *   *

On day two, after stretching out a stiff upper body and God knows how many aspirin, I was raring to go. This time, however, Mr. Loomis did not introduce me to the pell, but rather to himself.

"Mr. Stone. So much for bashing the hell out of a mindless stationary post. Today, you'll have me as a far more challenging target," he said while pointing to his chest with his callused thumb.

"I will provide you today with a moving target that's dangerous as hell. But first, put on these training gauntlets, take up yer waster. Tis time to see if you remember anything from yesterday's walk-in-the-park."

Without so much as a howdy-do, I began blocking the man's slow moving, well-measured strikes. Some came at me horizontally, others as diagonal blows meant to decapitate. He speeded up his attack.

When I sensed an opportunity, I jumped at it, and forgot everything the man had been trying to teach me. I lunged and swung for the fences, even to the point of lifting my foot. This strike Mr. Loomis easily deflected and side-stepped. To add insult to injury, he deftly swept my planted foot out from under me.

I hit the ground hard, but spun away and regained my footing.

"That strike, Mr. Stone," Mr. Loomis critiqued, "while well-timed, was foolish and clumsy. That snap roll, however, might have saved yer life." On he attacked again, and again, and again.

Quite often, my heavy gauntlets prevented bruises to my hands and wrists. Mr. Loomis narrated. "Yer're too close, Mr. Stone. I'm cutting off your hands! Swordsmen need their hands! Back off a bit and give yerself some room to work!"

So it went for the next four hours. Just how Mr. Loomis kept it up marveled me. Tired, and just trying to survive, I again recalled the hand-to-hand combat drills that John Running Deer had put me through. I made a point to breathe. That helped some. I began listening in on Mr. Loomis' thoughts, and began anticipating his moves. I found myself becoming a whirl-wind on the offensive with the Scotsman defending himself for all his worth.

"Stop!" He called. "Enough. We need a breather." That was the first time Mr. Loomis had ever called for a time out.

"Hydrate yerself, Mr. Stone, before you *and* I fall over." He admitted with a half smile.

*   *   *

"This Bone Sword of yours is a rare beauty, Mr. Stone. Always be mindful to draw her away from you in a wide arc. Can't have you unnecessarily cutting yerself, now can we.

I slowly drew her out in an exaggerated manner.

"Okay, well done. That scabbard's guard will help prevent you from removing your fingers when you put her away. Now, take a few strikes against that hanging roll of bamboo. Tell me what you think of 'er."

This I did, staying within myself, firing off my stroke from the hips and upper legs, both feet on the ground, gliding forward, and finishing with my arms extended and hands relaxed. The effect was devastating. I sundered the entire twelve inch thick roll with my first strike.

"My God." I whispered.

"Indeed, Mr. Stone. What did you feel?"

"Surprising lightness. Wonderful balance. Virtually no vibration. Extraordinary cutting power. I just blew right through that bamboo as if it wasn't even there. I'm stunned."

"Yes, that Bone Sword is indeed all that and much more. Grip it with yer hands and extend its pommel away from yer torso. Now, twist it so."

Snick!

Out came a twelve inch long shiny spike from the pummel's end.

"And that surprise, Mr. Stone, you can use to gore a close-in opponent with the end of yer grip. It's Damascus steel, just like yer blade's backbone, but plated in silver. I canna let some nasty demonic beastie sneak up on you, now can I?"

*   *   *

Just before I packed up my truck to return to Santa Fe at week's end, Mr. Loomis appeared.

"Laddie, ahem, I mean, Mr. Stone. There has been a change in plans."

"What do you mean, Mr. Loomis?"

"I just got word from President Smithers that he's made arrangements for you to stay put at the Academy. How long, he didn't say. Just that Professor Glass has been informed and that you should plan on continuing your graduate studies here. The president also said that Mr. Good will to serve on your thesis committee."

"Oh."

"Buck up now, Mr. Stone." The armorer said as he slapped my back. "The Academy is a fine place to stay. Its selection of beer is exceptional. And besides, look at it this way, think of what a better swordsman you will become?"

CHAPTER 5
The Venetian

Everyone has a story.

Guilelmo da Ziliolo began his existence in Renaissance Venice on the wharf as an feverish child. With uncertain prospects, his impoverished family abandoned him to the Church, who thought that if he survived, he should best become a priest.

At the age of three, young da Ziliolo liked to trace with his fingers along the sharply carved letters of the church's foundation stone, which he reproduced with charcoal on the pavement. One of the priests saw this wonder and informed the bishop. Thereafter, da Ziliolo began to learn his letters under the tutelage of the cathedral's archivist, a monk of some repute, well-known throughout the region for his fine manuscript illuminations.

Time passed. da Ziliolo, now a young boy of eleven and still with a questionable constitution, could read Latin as well as any jurist in the fair City of Canals. In fact, the archivist had begun teaching him Greek with a mind of grooming him for his position. But also on the monk's mind was the boy himself, whose innocence he used for his own personal pleasures.

By the age of fifteen, da Ziliolo read with ease both Latin and Greek, and had already produced several manuscript copies for the cathedral's library, which his mentor illuminated with great care. Together, they made a productive team, but da Ziliolo chaffed at the callousness of his teacher's personal whims and at the snickers whispered behind their back. "Indeed, the pair work together like a hand in glove." It did not take long before the many innuendoes became more and more overt, creating within da Ziliolo a growing hatred of his curly headed mentor with the big brown eyes, and by extension, the Roman Church that had turned a blind eye to the situation.

A year later, da Ziliolo discovered a hidden manuscript written in Latin that described the mixing of ingredients into interesting and tempting concoctions. Reveling at the secular, and non-liturgical, nature of the work, da Ziliolo read and compounded in secret several of its mixtures. One was for relieving a headache using the fresh blossoms of the willow tree. Another employed a known poisonous tuber, with which he began dosing his mentor.

As the monk's health declined, the apprentice purloined a small amount of the gold leaf and added it to his meager savings. He went into the marketplace with a mind to secure a loan and open a small shop. da Ziliolo's plan was to continue with his studies in alchemy, but to produce perfumes and body lotions.

Many laughed at da Ziliolo and his dreams, but in the end, he secured a usurious loan and walked away from the Church, and its hurtful rumors, and entered the world of commerce.

By the year 1484 da Ziliolo had just reached his twenty-fifth year. Lean of build, with gray eyes and light brown hair, the alchemist now manufactured perfumes, scented bath oils, and ointments, took pride in his small shop, and his products. Somehow, someway, he always managed to keep one step ahead of his creditor. As a consequence, he always looked for anything new, wishing to help people appear healthier and younger looking. Himself plagued with a poor constitution and a chronic cough since childhood, this desire took him far and wide, and more often than not, his scientific mind rejected many claims as utter gibberish.

Given his lot, da Ziliolo's own health caused the man to consider whether a manufactured potion could improve his bodily humors to the point of realizing better health and youthfulness. The alchemist often scoffed at the marketplace rumors about the existence of a fountain of youth. The legendary Asiatic kingdom ruled by Prester John was said to possess it, but no one knew where, or even if it was true.

Undeterred, da Ziliolo asked himself, could such a potion be manufactured? He began haunting the manuscript merchants, looking for anything that might assist him in Latin or Greek. Impassioned, the chemist made no bones about what he sought after—alchemical treatises.

An itinerant merchant with contacts in Old Constantinople claimed to have access to an ancient manuscript collection from that fallen Byzantine city. After much discussion, the merchant produced a manuscript catalogue, which the Venetian eagerly pored over. After some thought, da Ziliolo selected a manuscript that looked promising.

One month later, per agreement, it arrived. The scroll, penned by the first century Roman physician Celsus, described treating various illnesses via a host of medicinal herbs and other like ingredients.

While interesting and useful to a physician, da Ziliolo, sought a treatise that focused upon the ingredients themselves and not upon healing per se. So, feeling cheated, the alchemist expressed his displeasure to the merchant, and among other things, accused him of being dishonest. Flustered, the man produced another list, one of anonymous works in the field of medicine, and other, more esoteric and questionable fields of inquiry.

Among them, da Ziliolo's eyes fell across one title that intrigued him. An Arabic treatise translated into Latin entitled *In Vivacitas, On Longevity*. Once again the fee for the procurement of this document stung da Ziliolo's purse. Once again, one month passed and the parchment roll exchanged hands. This time it arrived not by the usual courier, but rather by a bald, dark-skinned man with unusually light blue eyes, an emotionless wooden smile, and a strange accent da Ziliolo could not place.

"Why did this particular manuscript catch your attention?" the man with ice for eyes solicited.

"Did you know there are other, far more remarkable works available, works which are not approved by the Roman Church?"

While the Arabic/Latin treatise *On Longevity* proved quite useful for the making of common bath oils, creams, salves, and ointments, it fell far short of what da Ziliolo had in mind—a potion that would extend health and youthfulness.

At this point, in a rush of enthusiastic blindness, da Ziliolo became a buyer of condemned and forbidden texts, many which described dark ingredients used for nefarious purposes. Because of his fragile build and constitution, da Ziliolo threw himself into the project, heart and soul. As it turned out, it would be the surrender of the latter, his soul, that got him what he desired. Thus began da Ziliolo's slow transformation from Christian to heretic, and from heretic to pagan, and from pagan to something else altogether.

*   *   *

The first time the man with the haunting light blue eyes arrived with the prepared infusion, da Ziliolo bubbled with excitement. The innate alchemist within surmised repeated "treatments" would be necessary as time passed in order to bolster and renew a person's healthy and youthful state. The question remained, however, what might constitute such treatments?

The alchemist studied the swirling liquid within the stoppered glass globe. Brownish in color, da Ziliolo couldn't divine its composition, but had his suspicions.

"Signore," the man said, "this infusion is to be swallowed immediately. Otherwise, its strength will degrade."

The Venetian, against all discretion, did so, winced over the biting sourness of the draught, followed by a coppery aftertaste, which confirmed some of his suspicions.

The strange man, seeing da Ziliolo drinking down the infusion, smiled for the first time in a way that unnerved da Ziliolo to his very core. He said, "In three months' time, I will return with the second infusion. Its price will again be the same, *Signore*, six gold ducats."

Then he paused and looked into the Venetian's eyes. "In the meantime, *Signore*, you must avoid the touch of clear, fresh water, must not drink it, and shun all sunlight."

The prohibitions stunned da Ziliolo. "These will require consideration, *Signore*, as they will interfere with my business, going to market, my daily habits, and the like. Are you sure of these prohibitions?"

"Positively, *Signore*. And keep in mind, we are discussing your eternal youth and health," the man said accusingly. "For anything of great value there is always an equivalent cost that sometimes goes far beyond the price of a thing."

*　　*　　*

With all contact with water made anathema, da Ziliolo took to his ancient roots and used olive oil for bathing and wine for drinking. Likewise, he avoided direct exposure to sunlight. He now wore appropriate raiment, in the form of flowing Near Eastern robes or bulky monk-like attire, including a shadowed hood or head covering suitable for travel outside and visiting the markets.

After his first month, the Venetian began to see dramatic changes. All dead skin, calluses, and age spotting diminished, replaced with skin smooth and clear as a newborn babe's. His hair and beard became luxuriant and glossy, returning to their coal black luster. His chronic fatigue and cough disappeared. Common aches and pains became things of the past, his eyesight improved, even his finger nails grew strong and healthy, as they no longer chipped or broke. In every way, da Ziliolo had become a new man.

The Venetian's customers, in the main being women of means, were the first to take notice of his new look. They coveted his smooth and blemish-free skin. His glossy hair of long ringlets they found irresistible. When asked how he had come by his striking appearance and improved health, da Ziliolo passed a hand over several of his products and smiled. "*Mia Signora*, I produce only the very best in oils, lotions, and potions. I never sell what I do not personally use.

Business boomed, as did his *amore della vita* in the bedrooms of discreet and select customers, who first hand enjoyed his "youthful stamina."

Then came the arrival of the second infusion, which the Venetian drank without qualm. Since his business had become so brisk, the amount of six gold ducats, more than three years' pay for a common day labor, seemed but a trifle.

But when the time came for the delivery of the third infusion, his mysterious colleague told him he had to henceforth formulate it on his own. da Ziliolo, reading the formulation presented to him, recognized most of the required ingredients. However, the last ingredient on the list turned the alchemist's stomach and revolted his conscience—the liver of a male infant. Outraged at such a thing, the Venetian vehemently confronted the man with the light blue eyes, who, shrugged his shoulders and said.

"*Signore* da Ziliolo, I don't care what you do. You have paid me and I have revealed to you the secret of youthfulness and health. I have upheld my end of our little bargain, and now you even know how to prepare the secret elixir yourself."

Now exploding with anger, da Ziliolo retorted, "Well, it's simple. I will not make the potion. I'm not a murderer of innocent infants."

Laughing in his face, the other said, "Fine, good. I

already have your money in my pocket. But if you do not drink the elixir within four days' time, you will be a dead man. And, I might add, a dead man who has forfeited his very soul."

*   *   *

The same day the Venetian found ample evidence the man with the icy blue eyes now owned his very soul. As proof of this, da Ziliolo's own reflection in a mirror now contained a second image–that of his soul's owner. That hateful visage, always seen smiling, stood malevolently behind him. The image leered at him lecherously … possessively.

Convinced he had lost his eternal soul, da Ziliolo decided he would produce his own infusion, come what may, as to deny, out of sheer spite, that hateful devil's final possession of his soul. The first victim he purchased at the docks from an overseas merchant with too many mouths to feed. The babe, in a wretched flea-bitten condition and near starvation, expired with a quick and merciful twist of the neck. Thereafter, the preparation proceeded without incident. The disposal of the eviscerated corpse, which had presented a challenge, was solved via a ravenous clowder of feral cats.

With nothing else to lose, da Ziliolo threw himself into his business like never before, and even expanded his offerings beyond a shop of oils, salves, and scented lotions to include delicate silk scarves and shawls. But after ten years his time in Venice had become a dangerous liability, as during that period the cyclical disappearance of male infants became known. Some said that a pestilence had arrived. Other rumors suggested a far more accurate cause—a night demon stole them. No longer willing to risk his discovery, da Ziliolo chose to relocate to another city, one with a larger population and not as cramped as Venice.

*   *   *

da Ziliolo chose an inland city called Paris to re-establish his perfume and unguent business and in the process changed his name to Rene le Venetian. In the year 1492 King Charles VIII of the House of Valois reigned supreme. The move proved to be a masterstroke, for it preceded the French military intervention into Italian politics by almost two years.

Rene's perfume shop did very well among the royal court, where he was a frequent guest. His laboratory worked non-stop to keep up with their incessant demands. As for Rene, he too tried to satisfy his lady clients' other needs as well. The attentions of Rene *Le Taureau*, "the bull," soon became legendary and later influenced an aristocratic author to write about them, the Marquis de Sade.

As the decades went by, Rene would again change his name, move his shop to another borough, and begin anew, but this time as his own son, while the last of his "father's" clients died off. Few seemed to notice, much less care. However, the ruse once was discovered by an aging matron. After a simple demonic conjuring from one of the Venetian's forbidden texts, she took a deadly swim in the Seine the next day.

Time passed and the Venetian weathered it well. For periods he would live in poverty or seclusion while waiting for a generation to die, before reemerging with a new name and storefront. During such periods, he often traveled as an antiquarian in search of forbidden manuscripts that dealt with demonology. His collection grew.

While the French Revolution and its Terror came and went. The Venetian continued to provide his perfumes, changing his identity, and the locations of his laboratories on a periodic basis.

After several more name changes, the Venetian founded one of the oldest *parfumeries* of France. While the passage of the two world wars did have an impact on his business, he already had amassed immense wealth.

The construction of the Venetian's first modern laboratory began as Nazi Berlin fell. Now with modern facilities available, he tried many times to artificially synthesize the elixir, all to no avail. The Venetian, nonetheless, had never been concerned about a sufficient supply of infant male livers, not with the abundance of abortion mills and organ transplant markets throughout the world.

Today, if glimpsed on the street, the billionaire Venetian would appear a middle-aged man of medium height. Day after day, year after year, he has lived on, determined to cheat death, and forestall his damnation. He swore he'd reclaim his soul—though after over five hundred years, even he doubted if much could be left of it.

CHAPTER 6
Lethal Magic

During "Hell Month," my afternoons were divided between one-on-one tutoring in lethal magic and lectures that covered a wide variety of paranormal topics.

The office of my personal tutor in defensive and offensive lethal magic, Mr. Dexter, was on Old Main's third floor, nestled in the building's southwestern-most corner. Rapping on an aged wooden door, I heard *"Entrer,"* and so I did.

I stepped into a two-story, eighteenth century French library with floor to ceiling book shelves that intruded into Old Main's attic space. Its upper levels were reachable by a tracked wrought-iron ladder on wheels worn shiny with use. A period-piece Louis XIV desk and matching visitor's chair, and several odd rock-hewn candle bases of various heights added to the decor. Behind Mr. Dexter stood a magnificently carved wooden book stand, stressed under the weight of its many open burdens, haphazardly stacked one atop the other.

When I entered this bookish abode, its wooden floor creaked under my weight. Mr. Dexter, a tall thin man, stood. I judged him to be in his mid-fifties with thinning brown hair, a large beak-like nose, thin lips, and shallow cheeks. He was clean-shaven and smelled good of something clean, yet spicy. I guessed that his sallow complexion hadn't seen sunlight in years.

"I am honored to meet you, Mr. Stone. Much has been circulated about you, but in person, you seem somehow, so much more ..." he said with a tilt of his head and the wave of his hands.

"Don't let my aura fool you, Mr. Dexter. I'm just like anyone else around here."

"Ah, please be seated and make yourself comfortable."

Given that there was only one available "seat"— more a gilded high-backed throne in my opinion—I did so, and found it to be quite comfortable. Sitting back into it, the chair seemed to suck me in.

Hands folded before him, Mr. Dexter began. "Mr. Stone, thank you for being punctual. That's a quality I appreciate.

"And no, you are not at all like everyone else around here. Of that, I can assure you."

Then, after a brief pause, "Mr. Stone, do you know why you are here?"

"Yes, sir. President Smithers stated that I needed training in 'lethal magic.' While I am not sure what that is, I am here to do my best at mastering it."

"'Mastering it,'" Mr. Dexter murmured. "How ambitious ... Well, Mr. Stone, before we begin, let us establish an *accord*, an understanding. First and foremost, I am your teacher, and as your teacher, my greatest wish is for you to succeed. I am serious about this.

"On the other hand, you are my student, and my job is to push you beyond your perceived limits. I can guarantee that you will not like this process, this fiery crucible that I will subject you to, but it is necessary. You must find your limits and exceed them.

"Do we have an understanding, Mr. Stone?"

"Yes, sir."

"Bon." He said with a nod of acknowledgment.

"Let us begin by recognizing that lethal magic is neither white nor black. Rather, it is the application of the lethal magic that gives it, its … flavor, so to speak. Lethal magic used for evil is far easier to conjurer. The opposite is true for lethal magic used for good, which is why the forced exorcism of a demon from a mortal is taxing on the exorcist. It's an uphill battle."

I nodded my head in appreciation.

Seeing this, Mr. Dexter inquired, "So, you are familiar with what a forced demonic exorcism is like?"

"Yes, sir. Each time I was physically and emotionally drained. I needed to hydrate, eat, and recover."

Another interested tilt to Dexter's head told me that he drank in my words.

"And were you successful?"

"Yes, sir."

My candid affirmation caused Mr. Dexter to sit back, while his salt and pepper eye brows squinted. "What was your means? Your methodology?"

"I used laying-on-of-hands and prayer, augmented with the use of consecrated silver. That combination destroyed the demon, yet preserved its victim."

My answer caused the man to pause, turn in his chair, and his gaze became piercing.

Then I felt it. He was probing my mind, and like a thunderclap, I shut him down. His reaction was a sudden blink.

"Mr. Stone, who taught you your mind-blocking technique?"

"Governor Silver Moon and John Running Deer, sir. Why?"

"Both were once my students." He said with a thin smile of remembrance. "Fine, fine students. But who taught you about silver? I'm curious."

With my mental blocks in place, I said, "Initially, a primordial entity. That is, until one of Mr. Good's lectures."

This revelation caused the man to place his free hand over his mouth in wonder. His eyes drifted off toward the high ceiling.

Then, he whispered, "*Très intéressant.* You are in contact with the other side."

"Yes, sir."

Mr. Dexter, now leaned forward in his chair, and seemed to restart my interview anew.

"Mr. Stone, while working with you, I will introduce you to the several levels of lethal magic. Think of the entire suite of spells as an onion with many, many layers. Further, there are additional elements of telepathy and focusing tools, and above all, the exercise of one's common sense. One does not smash an ant with a sledgehammer, when a mere fingertip will do."

At this point, I interjected, "In other words, that onion is a three-dimensional construct, where spells, telepathy, and focusing tools are the axis."

By the annoyed look on his face, I could tell that he wasn't used to being interrupted. This I logged into my "Don't ever do that again" file. But when he thought about what I had just said, he nodded, and said, "*Précisément. Très bon*, Mr. Stone."

*   *   *

For the next four weeks, we met daily at two in the afternoon, for *précisément* one hour. To be honest, that was about all that I could take. Along the way, I picked up a handful of colorful French cuss words as we sparred back and forth. That development alone let me know I was making headway and holding my own.

* * *

"*Monsieur* Dexter. How is our pupil performing?"

"Mr. President, he is frightening in his sheer will, mental strength, and stamina. His mind, in many ways, is a mirror of his magnificent physique."

"And his grasp of lethal magic?"

"Time will tell. However, his memorization of the spells is quite good. After one week we have already begun intermediate level conjurings. If we had a solid three to six months, he would be *trés formidable*."

"*Monsieur* Dexter, he doesn't have that luxury. Push him."

"Understood. On Monday we will begin the advanced series."

* * *

My second through fourth weeks with Mr. Dexter could only be described as brutal. Never before had I so wished for my UCS, as bruise after bruise appeared on my exposed arms, neck, and shoulders. In comparison to the impacts delivered by the evil conjurer Charles Smithers, Mr. Dexter's telekinetic blows were far more precise, despite the fact that my blocking spells had been catching most of them. I found myself always playing defense.

Then, once again, John Running Deer's combat drills clicked; I read my attacker's thoughts, and when that strategy failed, I read Mr. Dexter's aura. That strategy turned the tables, putting me on the offensive, even when Mr. Dexter attempted to think one thing while doing another. That subterfuge Running Deer had schooled me on, many, many times before.

"*Mon Dieu!* Wherever did you learn that?" Mr. Dexter exclaimed.

"From one of your former students. And, I just realized, sir, that there exists a direct relationship between physical combat and the casting of spells. Your three dimensional onion, of spells, telepathy, and focus, requires a merging of body and mind. The imperative is that my brain must perform the same in all cases in order to avoid pain. Rules that govern one have application with the other. Is this making any sense?"

Again that tilted head, half-closed eyes stared back at me, and finally a single nod that I took for approval.

"Mr. Stone, you are a remarkable man. What you have just enunciated, the merging of body and mind, and the borrowing of lessons learned from each, is something that cannot be grasped by most, much less integrated as well as you just did. *Très bon.*"

The next day the intensity of our one hour session had reached what I thought of as critical mass. The Frenchman, ever more devious and stealthy in his castings, forced me to realize that lethal magic, either offensive or defensive, had a lot to do with one's frame of mind, attitude, and sheer will to dominate. In my mind, I reverted to my old high school football days as an offensive lineman, when I would not just block an opponent, but would put him on his back. Once I got that notion in my mind, Mr. Dexter's spells were blocked, obliterated, and rendered meaningless.

To my surprise, my last session was a gracious one filled with anything but magic. Instead, Mr. Dexter, ever the mysterious one, presented me with three bottles of red wine, each of considerable age.

"Mr. Stone, kindly select a bottle."

So I did, the center one. As he opened its, he explained while he filled two tall wine glasses with generous barrels.

"You made a fine selection. Today is a graduation of sorts. Allow me to toast to your hard-earned accomplishment. You completed in four weeks what most need far more time to achieve."

Now sitting back into his chair, he swirled his wine and said, "Wine, and the proper drinking of it, is like magic. A poor selection of a spell will not fit the situation. If you do not prepare the spell well, it will fail. But, if you do choose the correct spell and conjure correctly, you will succeed, and like a fine red, that accomplishment will warm your heart."

Then with his forefinger in the air, "Always remember: it is barbaric to eat a steak with a glass of milk. Such a glorious repast requires a full-bodied red, much like this one, and nothing less. Even more distasteful is the pairing of a white with a bloody dish. Many do in rank ignorance. But not you, *mon ami*, for today I am making quite sure that you know the difference."

CHAPTER 7
The Dark One

The long journey from modest shopkeeper to fragrance mogul told only half of the story. The alchemist murdered four innocents per year, which amounted to over two thousand sacrificed. A count that didn't include the inconvenient eye witness or mother who had second thoughts after having received payment for her infant. This reckless and selfish pursuit took a mighty toll on the Venetian's mind, but ensured his youthful physical appearance, ongoing health, and near immortality.

Madness incrementally overtook the Venetian year by year. Some argued that the stress of the infant sacrifices bent his mind. Others, however, sympathetically pointed to the unnatural grind of such an extended existence, the many names, emphasizing the sheer insanity of living a lie for such a long time. Regardless, the Venetian's co-workers knew that "look" their master occasionally wore and recognized it for what it was—stark, raving, insanity.

Besides the madness, over the centuries the alchemist changed. Time and experience does that. After his first year of preparing the elixir, his initial squeamishness passed ... replaced by a callousness and precision that would have shocked a hardened murderer.

Convinced that the reclamation of his eternal soul was a lost cause, the Venetian took matters into his own hand and began to amass a collection of dark spells and curses. Like businessmen throughout time, it began a ledger, within which he recorded his growing library.

The collection included the most despicable magical spells and curses imaginable. While several spells did allude to the potential recovery of a damned soul, a good number dealt with the manipulation of demons. Listed by category, purpose, strength, weakness, and description, the alchemist brought together a wealth of information on how to summon, command, and banish a denizen of the Underworld. With the decoding of cuneiform in the mid-nineteenth century, a cascade of ancient languages—Persian, Akkadian, and Sumerian—surfaced, and with them, more ancient spells and curses came into his possession.

Early on he came to realize the intrinsic utility of this collection. He deployed demons as handy business partners, who removed competitors or threats to his business or person—like the elderly matron who took a fatal final swim with his conjured demon.

Along the way the paranormal community became aware of the Venetian's presence by reputation alone. Who he was they did not know, just that his conjuring possessed a distinctive signature. As a result, the Parisian paranormal community assigned this rogue practitioner a name, *"Le Méchant,"* the Dark One, which connoted considerable respect, mixed with equal parts of pure, unadulterated fear.

Tools require a storage box, and when the Dark One conceived *The Book of Spells*, he made one to contain his demonic incantations. Up until the deciphering of Egyptian hieroglyphs by Jean-Françoise Champollion in the 1820s, he recorded his spells using a rudimentary Greek code. Around 1834, while the intellectual industry of Champollion triumphed, the Dark One converted his Greek code into Egyptian hieroglyphs in the belief a crude hieroglyphic transcription made a far better code than a Greek one, which could be read and broken by any educated individual of the times.

Since the ancient Egyptian language expressed itself in consonants, the Dark One invented his own vocalic glyphs, thereby preserving the precise pronunciation of a demon's name. Thus, the Venetian doubly encoded *The Book of Spells* as only he knew the sound values of the invented glyphs. This soothed his natural paranoia that someone, somehow, might steal his collection.

As best as the Dark One could tell, his collection reflected the magical wisdom of many ancient cultures—Near Eastern, Egyptian, Greek, Roman, and early Christian, along with a handful that defied attribution. How he came across these profane texts is unknown, but suffice it to say, many died revealing their secrets during his interrogations. Fantastical stories abound amidst the paranormal community about them. Torture played a role with those who refused to share their knowledge. While with others, the Dark One handsomely paid for a frank evening's conversation.

Four hundred years in the making, the compilation contained fifty-two spells, each which named a specific demon, for a specific purpose. The book itself was large and heavy. Bound within were fine velum sheets, each almost translucent, numbered ninety-two folia in all (rumors suggested he manufactured the folia from the skin of infants). These folia lay bound between sturdy oak covers with three hinged bronze clasps. The front cover, engraved with beautiful golden hieroglyphs, said—*The Book of Spells. Instructions for Summoning Those from the Netherworld.*

As a final safeguard, the Dark One permeated the oaken covers and its folia with a poisonous oil of his own design. Simple contact with naked skin meant a swift and horrible death.

The Dark One's enormous financial holdings explained his preeminence within the international business community and granted him the ability to buy considerable influence through the normal channels of human weakness—greed, bribery, and extortion. Whenever those avenues could not provide the results he required, he would not hesitate to employ demons of every kind. Such methods left his opposition either ruined, dead, or far worse.

In spite of his vast wealth and influence, there remained individuals and institutions beyond his reach. The Roman Catholic Church and their sharp-eyed exorcists vexed him the most. They seemed to shadow his very footsteps as they cast back into the dark void any demons summoned to do his bidding. In many ways, the Dark One saw himself in the guise of a demonic arsonist, while the agents of Holy Mother Church followed after him like exorcist firemen.

* * *

Throughout the years, decades, and centuries, the Dark One realized that to defeat the Roman Church's agents, he had to attack them from within their own institution by discrediting the entire sacrament of exorcism. He cared not one wit that some demons might be sheltered within the mortal realm as a consequence. The Dark

One passionately wished to defang the Vatican and reduce it to a powerless institution that would no longer be a threat *to him*.

This agenda the Dark One promoted at opportune times, often with the assistance of others with similar desires. It was at this point, in the late nineteenth century, that he emerged from the shadows, embraced CMES, and formed an alliance with them based on shared common goals. His reputation, already well known within the paranormal community, catapulted the Dark One within CMES to a high status. Their membership greeted him as one of their own, a foreign experience for him.

The Dark One quickly rose to become the Tribune of Alexandria. This post he jealously held until the mid-1980s. Now well ensconced within CMES, the Dark One pursued ruining the Vatican's exorcists with a patience born from long experience. The strategy succeeded during the Second Vatican Council, where a thorough revision of the seventeenth century ritual manual of exorcism took place. The final product, a shadow of its former self, stood ineffective against demon-kind.

But not for long, as the Dark One's victory over the exorcists was a hollow one, because not everyone accepted the revised text, seeing it for what it was—a gutted carcass. As a consequence, Father Gabriele Amorth, perhaps the greatest exorcist of the Roman Catholic Church, and his followers and students, chose to not employ the revised manual.

These individuals, these members of the Society of St. Paul, the Dark One despised, because it was they who had relentlessly hunted him throughout the centuries. But as a further vexation to his ire, Cardinal Antonio Garibaldi, through no fault of his own, resembled the lecherous and perverse librarian who had abuse him as an innocent.

These elements, when blended with the Dark One's ever-mounting insanity, created an anti-Roman Catholic sentiment of vast proportions.

In 1982, the Dark One was elevated to the Regional Directorship of North America. When he took up residence within its headquarters, a structure that was erected in the 1950s, one of his first agenda items included a thorough going-over of the structure's magical defenses. When a security officer questioned him as to why the roof had no such wards, the Dark One invited the individual to the roof, and in a mad fit, threw him off.

To the rest of the security staff, he ranted, "Now who else thinks that this roof is a security liability? Who are you expecting? King Kong?

"Besides, I don't want my roof smelling like a chicken coop! Can you imagine all those dead pigeons? No? Well, I live in the penthouse, and I'm not about to!"

CHAPTER 8
Serious Booking

After my physical training sessions, lunch, and Mr. Dexter's exercises, more times than not, I hobbled to my lectures. These courses ran the paranormal gamut—laws and materials, cosmology, and demonology. I filled ring-binders with notes, and at times thought my head would explode with information, for my teachers were masters of their disciplines. Best of all, they knew how to pitch their material using real world situations.

*   *   *

Professor Garfield, an informative lecturer, but more lawyer than paranormal, taught "Laws & Materials." Tall and well turned out, he exuded certitude. He reminded me of my first gunnery sergeant. By the time I staggered in, the only seat available was in the back of a packed lecture hall.

And there I sat—the lone thirty-three-year-old in the house. My colleagues took notes on their electronic devices, while I collected my notes the old fashioned way, long hand, on yellow legal-sized notepads attached to my leather zippered briefing case.

"A demon's banishment or destruction is always predicated on something uncommon to their place of origin. This illustrates well the *Law of Opposites*, for this law says that which is contrary, is powerful. For example, demons from desert environments tend to be harmed by water in all its forms—rain, snow, ice, sleet, and heavy fog. Meanwhile demons originating from cold or wet environments react poorly when exposed to fire, heat, and even sunlight. At the same time, demons born in the dark cannot tolerate light or appear blind. One caveat when applying the *Law of Opposites* to demonic behaviors—do not assume anything. Only hard-earned experience can be trusted when dealing with demons.

"Another law that I wish to tell you about is the *Law of Complimentary Mixtures and Compounds*. This law states that when certain elements are mixed or compounded together, their magical influence is increased geometrically, and not arithmetically. For example, we know a glass of pure, clear water can eventually be an effective remedy for demons or demon-possessed individuals, if applied in sufficient amounts. But if we pour into that glass of water pine pollen, that mixture will outright destroy a demon with one dousing.

"Perhaps the best known law is the *Law of Consecration*. Let us consider for one moment what the act of consecration is—it is a spell performed to better a condition. That act of 'betterment' has power. Anything consecrated is more powerful in some way. For example, imagine, how effective a mixture of water and pollen would be against a demon if it was consecrated. The melting images of the Wicked Witch of the West come to mind.

"But what if you find yourself in a pinch and need something powerful, but don't have consecrated water? Fall back upon the *Law of Complimentary Mixtures and Compounds*. Honeyed water, if mixed in generous amounts, can be quite powerful."

A tentative hand rose.

"Yes. I see a question." The Professor Garfield acknowledged.

"Ah, does that mean, professor, that mead can be an effective liquid?"

Several snickers broke out, but one brief glare from the lecturer silenced them.

Pinching his lower lip in thought, he said "Now that is a most novel suggestion. If you investigate that notion, I would be most grateful to hear your results. In fact, query Mr. Good about that, for I am sure that he would be interested as well. Good question. I'll get back to you."

Making a marginal note of the exchange, the professor continued.

"Since the paranormal world requires balance, therefore a *Law of Damnation* must exist as well. The act of damnation is the most used during exorcisms. This too is a powerful spell—one performed to worsen a condition. For example, the saving of a mortal by damning a demon back to the Underworld."

Does this guy ever breathe? I wondered, my hand cramping.

"As one might imagine, many materials are valuable when dealing with demon-kind. In general, always remember that Nature produces the best defensive materials. For example, in an ironic twist on the *Law of Opposites,* fresh smells and scents do not exist in the Underworld as they are the products of living, growing, healthy things, the very signature of Nature itself.

"Fragrant herbs, spices, and flowers repel demons. Notable in this regard is the genus *Allium*, which includes onions, garlic, leeks, and scallions, but just as effective is the genus *Mentha*—mints. For example, while the chewing of spearmint and peppermint leaves may have distinct social advantages, that spit is a harmful acid to demon-kind. Spit, impregnated with garlic and onions is just as effective, even if socially odiferous.

"As mentioned before, tree and flower pollens are fatally corrosive to demon-kind and that is why fragrant pine and balsam forests are not frequented by them. In springtime, when these trees relinquish their pollen in veritable clouds, such events, with external contact or ingestion, cripple and destroy demon-kind. Is it any wonder that ancient European cultures had such interest in their great pine forests?

"Another deterrent to demon-kind is silver in all of its forms—solid, liquid, and gas—as are any of its nitrates. The corrosive effects are quite instantaneous and marked. For example, weaponry impregnated with this element become more effective against demon-kind, leaving behind ulcerous wounds that cannot repair or mend. Ladies and gentlemen, silver is your friend. Use it.

"Another item, honey—the byproduct of pollen, is a devastating demon destroyer. Smear that sticky substance on demon-kind and watch them wither and die. If you are ever chased by a demon, make haste for the nearest bakery, and buy several honey-coated pastries! Baklava is wonderful in this regard. Plus, you get to lick your fingers afterward!"

Laughter broke out, but quelled when Professor Garfield raised his index finger in the air.

"Nature itself has provided an apex predator against demon kind—the honey bee. This industrious, organized, and protective organism is their most deadly foe. Consider—the bee collects pollen, creates nectar, and converts it into honey. All three are poisonous to demon-kind. When the bee stings an intruder, it commits a sort of hari-kari. This ultimate sacrifice can destroy any demon."

The professor paused to let his statement sink in.

"Ladies and gentlemen. It is not the venom of the bee sting that destroys the demon. Rather, it is the ultimate expenditure of a single bee's life force, Nature's own life force, that slays the demon.

"As a result, in your *TIIIS Survival Manual*, note that we routinely inoculate the possessed with the bee sting of a particular Africanized honey bee, *A. m. scutellata*—sometimes called the killer bee. Why? Because it is the most potent.

"By the way, has anyone noticed the growing ecological concern regarding the global decline of the bee population? Well, I have noted this, and I have a suspicion that CMES is the cause."

*   *   *

"Welcome. I am your instructor Professor Jonathan Winter and this is 'Cosmology.'"

Winter had all the stereotypical characteristics of a professor—disheveled salt and pepper hair that defied gravity and defined random, a wrinkled gray pin-striped suit, chalk-dust sprinkled sleeves, and comfortable brown loafers. His lopsided and misshapen bow tie and breast pocket handkerchief, both shaded a deep crimson, completed his ensemble.

"While Western religions possess a vague notion of the supernatural, they all lack an understanding of its true nature and landscape. Fortunately, we have a source that addresses this need called *The Knot of Eternity.* All of you have a copy on the flash drive each of you received yesterday, along with several other ancient texts in translation. Read them."

Only six of us populated the cavernous lecture hall, as apparently the subject matter was considered too basic.

"Here are the basics as we understand it," Winter began. "At Creation, an entity began its cosmic tinkering that resulted in the creation of a primordial overseer, the dark and light realms, and demonic caretakers for each. Next, he created the mortal realm and the first two souls to inhabit it.

"The dark and light realms, distinctly separate locations, received at a mortal's passing, the soul that it carried throughout its existence. First arriving in the dark realm, the soul is presented with a choice: to rise toward the light realm and pass into it, or, at its peril, to remain in the dark realm.

"The ability of a soul to rise to the light realm is a function of its sense of contrition, hope, and capacity for love. The overseer of this realm is called the Teacher. If a soul lacks, or worse, ignores these fine attributes, it is doomed to remain in the darkness, to descend, and ultimately meet its destruction by a ferocious demon called the Devourer of Souls."

A hand rose.

"Yes, Mr. Miller."

"Professor Winter, if a soul first chose to remain in the dark realm, can it ever change its mind and get another chance to incarnate? Or, does it just stay there until it is destroyed by the Devourer of Souls?"

This question caused Professor Winter a moment of thought. "Mr. Miller, salvation is always available, is always an option. It is up to the soul to make that commitment."

*　　*　　*

At the Academy my dream instructor, no offense to the others, was Mr. Theodore Good, who held high court over a series of lectures devoted to "Demonology." He rocked. Short, portly, with a silver gray peace wreath for a hairline, an absolute bundle of energy, boy did this man know his subject inside out. As I sat in his presentations, I drank from a fire hose turned on full blast and still couldn't get enough. Given my first-hand experience with the subject, I was always sure to grab a front row seat in his packed lectures.

"Ladies and gentlemen," Mr. Good began, "today's topic will be of vital importance to each and every one of you. I, of course, speak of demonology." Mr. Good enthused rubbing his hands together in genuine excitement.

"Demonology includes the theory and mechanisms behind the summoning, control, banishment, and destruction of a demon, not to mention their many classifications.

"By the way," Mr. Good expanded, "there are no vampires or werewolves. Such creatures are the imaginative product of superstition, myth, the writings of Bram Stoker, and Hollywood. Demon possession explains away both. Aberrant behavior is part and parcel of demonic possession. Sheer blood-lust explains vampirism. Wild, animal-like behavior the same for werewolves.

"As to when demonology began, no one knows, except that because of its close relationship to religion and magic, it's probably the second oldest profession. As to the first, I'll leave that up to you to decide."

Snickers rippled throughout the auditorium.

"A definitive catalogue of demons has yet to be compiled, there is no phone book listing their hidden names, no *Demons for Dummies* handbook. But," Mr. Good emphasized, "it is rumored that someone on 'the other team' might have such a document."

Serious looks were shared around the room.

"Can you imagine how dangerous such a 'book of spells' might be in the hands of an unscrupulous one? What a threat to humanity it would represent?"

Mr. Good answered himself. "An incalculable source of power and influence."

He paused.

"So, how would one amass such a collection? Gather all the sources needed? It would take decades, if not centuries. Not to mention all the hard-fought personal experience gained in the field. Throughout, extreme care is required.

"Some say no one conjurer could manage such a monumental task. What hogwash! In our business, knowledge with a capital 'K' equals power with a capital 'P'—pure and simple.

"So, ladies and gentlemen, that leaves us with one possibility. If such a collection exists, as I believe it does, then only one individual could be responsible for its creation. That means this particular individual has lived a very long time, as in centuries. Unfortunately, such an individual exists, and even has a name—The Dark One."

* * *

"The origin of demon-kind remains a murky subject. Consensus pleads that since thought and emotion are powerful forms of psychic energy, the first demon must have been their result. Coincident with this line of reasoning, the oldest, most ancient of demons should relate to the ancient cultures that first recognized them. Their names, qualities, powers, and weaknesses should all relate back to their cultural place of origin.

"Always remember, demon-kind manifest because something or someone granted them the energy to do so through their conjuring. The more energy an adept can project, the more powerful the demon.

"What else do we know? We know demons are self-aware, capable of learning, to a certain extent can evolve over time, and they never forget, ever. Think on that one for a moment.

"Conjuring the same white demon with a B-classification, for *benignus*, multiple times, for the same task is, perhaps, the safest use of them. But to summon an unknown demon, especially a dark one of the M-classification, for *malus*, even if you know how to banish it, requires delicacy, preparation, and proper safeguards. Quite literally, one false word spoken, or the lack of proper preparation, could turn a demon upon its conjurer. One final word: only the experienced should conjure a demon. Only a master adept can successfully manage several kinds.

"To emphasize this very point, an advanced student of this academy recently exercised some poor judgment. We're not sure how he had got himself possessed, but possessed he is."

Then, Mr. Good gestured to two guards by the double-door exit to his right. When they opened the doors, a gagged and disheveled-looking young man entered bound to a wheelchair. In a scene right out of *The Silence of the Lambs*, the young man's helplessness made me shiver for several reasons.

"Ladies and gentlemen," Mr. Good stated for the record, "this is an object lesson in what happens when you muck it up and don't follow the rules," as he removed the man's drool-soaked gag.

"I cannot make the point more clear. We have rules. Rules must to be followed. Don't follow the rules and this could happen to you.

"If you are able, note this mortal's current aura. For those of you who cannot, his aura is a dark, muddy, brownish-black—the mark of one possessed.

"By its aura, we know this demon. It renders its host susceptible to suggestion. Now watch this unusual demonstration of human physiology. I believe some of you will find it a valuable advantage in the field."

Mr. Good held his index finger before the bound victim's eyes like a doctor would during a common physical examination. Mr. Good horizontally panned his finger to the right of the unfortunate's head, whose eyes followed transfixed, but only so far as his neck refused to turn in that direction. Switching hands, Mr. Good performed the same test to the left and the possessed eyes and neck turned, tracking his finger, tracking, tracking until the unfortunate's head had turned almost a full one hundred and eighty degrees!

The audience gasped.

Then, Mr. Good panned his finger back so that the possessed once again faced the crowded auditorium.

"Ladies and gentlemen. What you have witnessed is the fact that the possessed cannot turn their heads to the right, but can to the left. The lesson here is, if you are stalking a possessed individual, do it from their right rear quadrant. But enough of such parlor tricks."

Reaching under his podium, Mr. Good produced a plastic bottle of drinking water.

"Now, watch what happens when I dribble some clear, fresh water on his head, always being mindful that if consecrated, the effect would be enhanced. The number of dousings, I will signify with the fingers of my hand. Why? You soon shall see."

As soon as the first droplets of water hit the top of the poor guy's head, his eyes got wild-looking, his body jerked this way and that, and he screamed his head off using atrocious language. Spittle flew in all directions.

Now with two fingers indicated, another stream trickled forth, the din continued, and had elevated, somehow. The shaking and struggling of the wheelchair required one of the guards to steady it in order to prevent injury to its occupant.

Then, with three fingers shown, the remainder of the water bottle flowed over the poor wretch's head, which now aimlessly lolled from side to side.

"Now, note his aura. It is light blue-green. The demon, an ancient Near Eastern variety, because of the *Law of Opposites*, has been banished with the thrice application of fresh, clear water."

At this point, the young man began to stir. Mr. Good asked from one knee beside the wheelchair. "Mr. Hughes, can you hear me?"

The slurred response said it all. "Oh, Mr. Good. Thank you so much! The Underworld is terrifying.

Thank you for saving me!"

"You're very welcome, Mr. Hughes. Now go to the infirmary, take several aspirins, and get some ice packs for your neck. It's sore, isn't it?"

Hughes could barely nod.

Mr. Good, rising to his feet, brushed back Hughes' wet hair. The guard unstrapped him from the chair, helped him up, and walked him out of the auditorium, leaving behind a damp wheelchair and a small puddle of water.

"Ladies and gentlemen." Mr. Good continued. "I feel like a faith-healer mixed with the slimy showmanship of a circus carnie. But possession, is after all, possession. Mr. Hughes 'was under,' as we like to say, for only several hours before we discovered him, and saved him."

Mr. Good paused to sip from another plastic bottle of water he had hidden under his podium. Raising it for all to see, he said, "Water, by the way, is a very handy and useful thing, as you have witnessed."

No shit. I agreed too forcefully, for Mr. Good glanced at me with a raised eyebrow of disapproval.

Damn! He heard my thoughts.

"Ladies and gentlemen," the professor continued, "at no time, I repeat, at no time, are you ever to vocalize a demon's specific name. To do so is to summon it. And to summon a demon, unprepared, as in Mr. Hughes's case, is reckless, and constitutes grounds for expulsion from the spiritual community, subject to further review."

After this anonymous admonition, I cringed in my seat. After all, I had summoned, by accident, a very dark one during my undergrad days at the university.

*   *   *

After the class, Mr. Good signaled me to remain as the rest made their way to the exits.

"Mr. Stone, President Smithers wants us to meet in my office. Do you know where it is?"

"No, sir. But I'm sure you'll tell me."

"Even better, Mr. Stone, I'll show you."

Ten minutes later I stood before his office door on the second floor of the Meyers, or Medieval Building, a sturdily-built, peaked wooden affair with dark wrought iron hinges, beaten bolt heads, and a peep hole with iron grating. I sensed the vibe of monastic seclusion. In fact, the entire Romanesque style of Meyers in rough cream-colored limestone blocks reflected much the same feeling.

"Come into my lair … Mr. Stone … If you dare."

I entered his office, which was little more than a monastic cell. A narrow space defined by an arched wall portal, a leaded-in window, bare stone walls, one filing cabinet, a desk, and two chairs.

"Mr. Stone, President Smithers wishes me to bring you up to speed on your new position as Lictor of Magic. He directed me to provide you with some history and salient details that you might find … *helpful*," he said with raised eyebrows.

"First off," Mr. Good leaned forward with his hands clasped on his desk's top, "by design, each and every prior Lictor of Magic did not record anything about their tenure. It's a job perk, no paperwork. The reasoning behind that tradition is that each Lictor of Magic possesses good character, common sense, and restraint, not to mention other, more esoteric characteristics. In short, Mr. Stone, as the Lictor of Magic you are your own man, your actions are accountable to no one but your own conscience."

With my mental blocks in place, I understood from Mr. Good's words but one conclusion—total deniability. While the president of TIIIS or its Supreme Council may charge me to do something, I owned it, "come what may." I now appreciated much better President Smithers delicate situation, when he had been both president *and* the Lictor of Magic.

"Secondly, what is a *lictor*? Well, back in Roman times a lictor accompanied an elected Roman magistrate. His presence signified the magistrate's ability to meet out corporal punishment or even death. While a magistrate might adjudicate a trial and make a judgment, he did not carry out the actual execution of the punishment. That task fell to his lictor, whose very symbolic totem, called the *fasces*—was a bound bundle of wooden rods that contained an axe. Romans loved symbolism, Mr. Stone. The wooden rods, signified chastisement, while the axe signified a far more substantial, punishment.

"As this society's enforcer of civilized custom and codified law, your purview is the unauthorized or illegal use of black magic. Key here is your knowledge of what is, and is not, black magic."

"Sir, how can I tell the difference," I asked, "beyond reading an individual's mind or their aura?"

"If you can contain your lust for sheer, naked vengeance or retribution, follow your God-given sense for what is good. That, in addition to some legal training, will put you in good stead."

I felt like I hovered over a deep abyss.

"Be advised, TIIIS is not the only society that combats evil. The Vatican has been at it for quite some time, followed by the Eastern Orthodox Church based in Istanbul. The status of the Russian Orthodox Church, while in its early years quite robust, more recently has become far less so.

"The Judaic Great Sanhedrin has fallen on bad times, but there exists an unobtrusive group in Tiberias, Israel. Their advantage is their anonymity, and," Good punctuated with a finger in the air, "their close ties to the Israeli Mossad. I've had dealings with both of them, and in my book, they're top notch.

"As for Islam, it is dangerous to practice black magic within their sphere. The Saudis combat it through a religious police force called the Committee for the Promotion of Virtue and the Prevention of Vice. But their definition of what constitutes black magic is very different from that of Christianity. In short, they paint with a very broad brush.

"South Africa too has a special police force called the Occult Related Crimes Unit. They battle ritual murders on a daily basis.

"On the East Indian continent an anti-superstition bill still awaits ratification. And in Asia, specifically China, there are those who, *certa bonum certamen*, 'fight the good fight.' By the way, China and India are numbers one and two in reported cases of black magic."

"Mr. Stone, I am telling you this because the TIIIS Lictor of Magic wields a considerable amount of diplomatic clout. That must never be forgotten and always remembered.

"In closing, I would counsel the following: the active exercise of restraint. This is perhaps the most difficult part of being a lictor. As of late, dark activity is on an upswing. In military terms, we are waging a continuous, low-grade conflict. At all times remain mindful that you represent TIIIS and all that it stands for. As its Lictor of Magic you are judge, jury, and executioner. Wield that power with wisdom. And, Godspeed."

CHAPTER 9
Total Lethality

The day after what I called Hell Month ended, I received the following message:

> Mr. Stone:
>
> It has come to my attention that you require further self-defense training.
>
> Tomorrow we will begin, at 8 am sharp, in the athletic field south of Old Main. Wear the provided set of sweat pants and shirt.
>
> Until then, I remain,
>
> Ian Crowsby

I arrived at the athletic field ten minutes early so I could stretch out. All alone, I sat on the turf and began my warm-ups. The next thing I knew, I was being pinned to the ground, on my back. Above me stood three men in a triangle, all fit by the looks of their identical black, jogging suits. I had been ambushed again.

When am I going to learn?

"Good day, Lictor of Magic. I am Ian Crowsby, one of your trainers. Good of you to show up early for me and my mates here, Mr. Gregg and Mr. Jones."

Crowsby wore his brown hair high and tight. Gregg was the one with the longish curly black hair and Jones with a sun-bleached blond head.

An Aussi surfer perhaps?

"We're here to teach you what lethality means, and why you must employ it. Is that clear?"

Given my precarious situation, I reverted to military speak. "Sir! Yes, sir!"

"Ah, splendid, lictor. I'm glad that we understand one another from the get-go. Now get up off your arse, you disgust me. How in God's good name after a month's intensive training did you allow the three of us get the jump on you? Weren't those four sheilas bad enough?"

Damn, he knows about that!

So I did, and as I did, Gregg grabbed my shoulder from behind, and squeezed real hard pinching a nerve. My Marine training kicked in as I grabbed his wrist, gave it a twist, and flipped the guy over my shoulder. Except he never hit the ground as designed. Instead, he rolled in the air, reversed my wrist lock, and flipped me over *his* shoulder. And there I sat flat on my backside again, shaking my head and wondering what the hell had happened.

"And this is why you are here, lictor. You're too predictable, too soft-hearted, and above all, nowhere near lethal enough."

Okay ...

Then my mental blocks went up, my sixth sense bellowed, and I moved behind Crowsby. Whereupon I put the smug gentleman in a vicious headlock.

My instincts were correct, as Surfer Boy Jones had indeed attempted to do something, but couldn't, because I was no longer occupying the space that he was groping.

"Well done again, lictor," Crowsby gasped out, "but in a real fight a headlock is useless to you, because you would be already dead where you stand. Only a quick and clean kill will do."

I let go, my lips now forming a vicious sneer.

"You see what I mean, lictor?" Crowsby stated the obvious while rubbing his throat. "You're far too civilized to survive out the week. All the more since CMES will be sending only its very best to skin your hide as a trophy. You're a marked man, Lictor, get used to it."

*   *   *

Starting at that moment, the next five days were ones of black eyes, bloodied knuckles, strained muscles, and abused body parts. All of this physical and psychic exertion was performed without the benefit of any ley line as the athletic field had built into its foundation a vast grounding mat, a sort of Faraday Cage.

So what did I learn? How to fight, fight dirty, and without quarter. Yes, my Marine training, while good, was nowhere near good enough, nor was the past months. Along the way, while huffing and puffing for air, one notion was drilled into me: be always in energy conservation mode. By day four, I was getting used to the incessant three-on-one fights, was picking when and where to attack, defend, setup, and retreat, all within a twenty-foot circle of thugs.

By day five, I had evolved into an instinctive, aggressive beast, who was punching less and casting bolts of energy more, sometimes even two at once. Overall, I could tell that the grueling training had improved my reaction speed and thinking considerably.

Come that Saturday, covered with black and blue welts, two shiners, and cotton sticking out of my nostrils, I returned to the field, waited a good fifteen minutes for my "mates," before I heard a twittering emanating from the surrounding oak trees. Wandering over, but on guard for some sort of vicious surprise, there was Rasha, the Mistress of the *Argenti*, who stood along the bush line. As I approached, in a slight defensive crouch, she said, "Noble Lictor of Magic. You have nothing to fear from me. However, woe unto those who wish to harm you. I, Rasha, the Mistress of the *Argenti*, have never seen before a Lictor of Magic such as you. And, while you may not believe this, I am over five hundred years old. I have seen my fair share."

Then, she bowed toward me, turned, and disappeared back into the thick vegetation.

As I made my way back to my dorm room wondering what happened to my training "mates," I ran into, of all people, Mr. Dexter. He seemed to be waiting for me on a wooden bench and waved me over.

"*Monsieur* Stone! Come. Sit. Tell me of your many adventures."

Which I did, but not before shielding my thoughts to this canny operator.

Noting that, the foxy Frenchman just smiled.

"You know you look like *merde*. But your thoughts are secure as ever. For this, I am very pleased and not at all offended."

Then, the man stopped, looked down at his hands and confided, "I apologize for not having prepared you sufficiently. However, from what I have just heard from *Monsieur* Crowsby, you have become *très formidable*. He and his colleagues, are, right now, convalescing in the college's clinic from yesterday's final examination."

I must have had a shocked look on my face.

"Did you not know this?"

I numbly shook my head. "No, I didn't."

Wryly smiling and patting my forearm, "*Non*, I didn't think so. *Monsieur* Stone, you came within an eyelash of killing all three of them."

*   *   *

President Smithers' eyes were bloodshot from reading all the administrative missives that his assistant had culled out. The pile seemed never ending, but one brief report he stopped to read three times.

President Smithers:

You now have a lethal Lictor of Magic.

Mr. Stone underwent five days of lethality drills that would have claimed our best security personnel within the first hour of Day One.

The man is now, both physically and psychically, far tougher, quicker, and more lethal than anyone that I have ever trained.

Best regards, I remain,

Ian Crowsby

After the third reading, the president murmured, "My God. Forgive me for what I have done to this good man."

CHAPTER 10
Burned Sausage

That late afternoon smoke filled the rustic Italian kitchen with the smell of burned sausage, which had taken two solid days of labor to make. Normally, Valeria Costa would never have allowed such a thing to happen. But today she had received a portent that trumped her cooking agenda and stymied her near-legendary culinary talents.

Scowling at the wasted hand-prepared meats she said, "The pigs will relish these nonetheless."

As she scraped out the blackened pan, she continued, "Much like my beloved Gathering, they can eat their own as well."

Placing the pan in a sink of hot, soapy water, she wiped off her hands on her faded blue apron, poured herself a glass of red wine, sat down at the heavy oak table, and put her feet up—which were killing her.

Pen and paper before her, she began to recollect the vivid, dream-like vision that had stunned her unconscious, thereby causing the ruin of her sausages.

Fluffy high clouds, brilliant sunshine, and a well-tended grassy field surrounded by stately oaks.

A circle of twenty. Who were they? Hard to tell by their faceless appearance, clad so in dark, angular raiment. But men they were nonetheless.

In their center stood a solitary man, hard to see. Only his sun-cast shadow gave his presence away. Like the gnomon of a sundial.

Then, frenetic movement. The circle of those in

dark raiment broke into fragmentary clusters trying to defend themselves, standing back-to-back. But from what?

A blur attacked them, laying them low.

Then, that solitary sun-cast shadow stood once again before them, victorious.

Valeria shivered after she wrote those words. Their import was clear. This was the new TIIIS Lictor of Magic. Her greatest fear for the *famiglia* Presto and the Gathering had come to pass. Against twenty, he took mere moments to defeat them.

Against us, who knows?

Perhaps the best course is to make peace with this one, this *l'uomo potente*. Chairman Presto's ego would never allow him to do so, even if in secret. The Gathering, also would not. Instead, they would throw themselves like lemmings against his sword, in the vain hope that their sheer numbers would somehow, someway, ensure victory.

Cuanto stupido!

Chairman Presto does not deserve to know of this development. Besides, he wouldn't know what to do about it anyways. He'd only contract more assassins to the slaughter. No. I have warned him many times before. To inform him yet again would be a waste of breath. But what of the Gathering?

Then a thought intruded itself into the oracle's mind, more a racial memory than anything else. One of her ancient predecessors, a Vestal Virgin of Rome, had been approached once by a righteous man, who sought a solution to an abominable practice—infant sacrifice.

*   *   *

Within the darkened vestibule of the Temple of Vesta, where entreaties to the goddess were made, an impassioned conversation took place between the High Priestess Julia Aquilia Severa and a military officer named Marcus Aurelius Valerius Claudius.

"This practice must not be allowed to continue," the vexed centurion said. "It goes against all the gods! Priestess, what can be done? I beseech you for an answer."

"Centurion, you seek a magical solution to an immoral problem. As with many things in this world, a balance must be maintained. A *quid pro quo* must occur."

"Most Honorable Priestess, do you mean a sacrifice for a sacrifice?"

A nod.

"But there are so many of these blasphemous believers, and I am only one."

"It is said in Judaea that the righteous sacrifice of one can claim a multitude of sinners. Such a powerful spell is known to my Sisterhood. But to know of it is a great burden. Valerius Claudius, are you strong enough to bear it?"

"Yes, I am."

"Brave words, centurion. Fortunately, I have already foreseen this meeting, and its dubious outcome. I know also that you are a member of a secret faction—the CCI."

At this, the centurion paled.

"We, the Sisterhood, believe in your faction's righteous cause. And for that, we will assist you, train you in the use of this spell. After all, we too wish to safeguard the Eternal Flame of Rome and give honor to all its gods."

CHAPTER 11
Mr. Henry

After every day's physical training, lethal magic tutoring, and lectures at the Academy, the remainder of the day, which wasn't much, was mine. Dinner I spent with Mr. Henry to discuss the day's events and get an earful of his hard-earned wisdom.

As for Mr. Henry's antecedents, he was born in Louisiana and raised there on the lore of the bayou and its mysteries, which had awakened the man's natural paranormal gifts. Early on he joined the U.S. Marines, survived the Korean War, was honorably discharged and heavily decorated because of wounds sustained in battle. While in Korea, his Louisiana sixth sense saved him and his men many a time. TIIIS recruited Mr. Henry while he was recuperating in the VA hospital in Arlington, Virginia. One of its doctors, who chanced to see the man's aura, sponsored Mr. Henry, who, once made a member, developed into an adept of considerable talent. I first met the man while an undergraduate at the University of Pennsylvania, where we hit it off.

During my time at the Academy, I admit Mr. Henry became my paranormal Dutch Uncle in more ways than one. Next to him, this padawan listened while he, the wizened Jedi, pontificated on practically anything.

The Academy's dining hall was located in Old Main's basement. Pillared and trussed with massive oak beams, this low-ceilinged chamber had a ton of atmosphere. No surprise it became for Mr. Henry and me a surrogate for the Greasy Onion, that colorful university dive bar near the University of Pennsylvania.

Like the Greasy Onion, this crypt-like hollow had the crucial amenities—low light, great atmospherics, distressed wooden tabletops and chairs, and awesome food. Even the beer selection was first-rate. And in its many cubby-holes, a person could have a private conversation.

On this particular evening, Mr. Henry and I became part of the woodwork as we chatted about the important points of magic and the paranormal. During such sessions, I went into full recording mode with my lip zipped.

"So, Mr. Stone, you look all bright-eyed and bushy-tailed today," said the native of Shreveport, and later New Orleans.

"You're right, sir. Today, I'm indeed full of piss and vinegar. And do you know why?"

The octogenarian's shook his shock white mane as he attended to his pint.

"Because it's your turn to pay the check, *and* I found out what your full name is—Henry Horatius Johnson. What a great middle name, Horatius—that famous Roman patriot who single-handedly defended the Tiber Bridge. Can I now call you Mr. Horatius?"

To that I received a toxic, over-the-glass-rim stare.

"How?" He stopped himself. "Who told you?"

"Peter Glass, my university mentor back at the University of Pennsylvania. He also said his father and you were once tight. Is that true?"

A thoughtful nod.

"Hans was a good man, a fine father, and an excellent Egyptologist and archaeologist. I vowed if something ever happened to him, I would watch over his son Peter until he reached his formal adulthood within the TIIIS community."

Mr. Henry paused.

"That vow, I never regretted." He said with a slow, melancholy head shake. "Hans passed too early. Such a damn tragedy, both for his wife and Peter."

Mr. Henry, for his part, had delivered on his vow of Peter's protection. Then, he blind-sided me with a question.

"Mr. Stone, have you figured out what your soul's true purpose is on this God-given Earth?"

"Yes, I have. In fact, the First Soul and I are in total agreement—to conduct an all-out war on evil."

"You don't say. Do you think that you're prepared for such a task?"

"With all due respect, I have seen combat many times. In those situations, I have made choices, and I'm here to tell you I have lived with them."

"I respect your service in defense of this nation. I also realize the enemy today is not anywhere near as black and white as during my stint in Korea. But think on this. You have two jobs—as the carrier of the First Soul to maintain the equilibrium of the Cosmic Order, *and* as the Lictor of Magic to suppress evil in the mortal realm.

"My purpose is to prepare you as best I can psychologically for that first magical confrontation with evil. Prepare and work with your TIIIS trainers as hard as you can. Find new limits, explore them, surpass them. React according to your training, and don't think. Thinking on the paranormal battlefield is fatal. Having second thoughts, doubly fatal."

*   *   *

On another evening, Mr. Henry asked me, "What do you know about our paranormal opponents?"

"I can never know enough, sir."

Nodding his white-haired head, his icy blue eyes flashed, "CMES constitutes the most single-minded, disreputable, and hard-core bunch of power-hungry paranormals on the planet. Bar none.

"The purpose of, and motivation behind, this ancient consortium of sensitives and adepts centers upon the acquisition of material gain, influence, and dominion, both overtly and covertly. Their creed, *postestatem et dominium*—'power and dominion'—says it all, and demands results at any cost. Given that basic premise, is it any wonder they are in league with the demonic forces of the dark realm?"

"Mr. Henry, it looks like a match made in hell."

"Precisely, Marine. You get the picture.

"CMES, as an organization, is dominated by five powerful regional directors, called *praetors*. They run their territories like private fiefdoms. Infighting among them is the norm. Yet, perversely, all pay homage to their chairman, or *consul*, who resides in Rome, where he exercises his primacy."

"Sounds like some sort of king," I said between bites of my double-decker cheeseburger.

"For all practical purposes he is, because the CMES chairman heads up an extensive multi-national corporate network. The CMES membership accepts this fact without question, as the Gathering's origin extends back thousands of years. As for the term, 'the Gathering,' this is how they refer to themselves in polite company, never as CMES, or for that matter, as the *Consilium*."

Mr. Henry, a Class Four-rated Adept within the TIIIS paranormal hierarchy, where a Class Six was considered a near-Merlin like being, took a mammoth bite from his Reuben sandwich. When his beer tankard thudded to rest, he continued.

"As you might expect, the CMES chairman is expected to provide the agenda and delegate through his regional directors. But sometimes, he acts independently, and sometimes emotionally. What I'm trying to say is that the CMES leadership is hierarchical in the extreme and viciously competitive. Among their regional directors, all want to be chairman. As a consequence, the chairman has to be one vicious son-of-a-bitch just to survive."

Bite, chew, drink.

"Now get this, over the millennia, CMES' center of power has changed three times. The organization started in ancient Sumeria, at the city of Ur in southern Mesopotamia—today's Iraq."

"You're kidding!"

"Nope.

"They resided there for some fifteen hundred years until the Elamites sacked the city."

"Wait a minute." I said. "The famous *The Lament of Ur* recorded that event in gruesome detail. Where did CMES go after that?"

"Egyptian Memphis. For the next two thousand years CMES basked under the Egyptian sun. There, the organization garnered untold wealth and absorbed an incalculable amount of Egyptian magical expertise, not to mention their extensive magical corpus that was far superior to the Sumerian's. As a consequence, *mutatis mutandis*, CMES adopted hieroglyphic writing as its standard house script, which supplanted the cuneiform of Sumeria. This is why, even today, their charter, archives, protective spells, and official correspondence are all encoded in a dialect of that long-dead language."

I held my head in my hands trying to imagine spending two thousand years somewhere, close to one hundred generations of human experience.

Then I asked, "Then what?"

"With Egypt's fall to Augustus' army in 30 BC, CMES wisely read the tea leaves and bugged out to Rome, and has been there ever since. They even borrowed its bureaucratic framework. This is why they refer to that city endearingly as "Mother Rome." It's CMES' oldest continuously operational center."

"So, what about us? TIIIS? What's our history? Where do we fit into the picture?"

"TIIIS came late to the big dance. If anything, we are the interlopers, the johnny-come-latelies. Imagine this. Somewhere around 150 BC, a handful of Roman politicians decided to do something about the outbreak of Carthaginian human sacrifice in their fair city. Tradition says the Roman politician Cato the Elder acted as the ring leader of this political faction. Quite naturally, that led to an interest in any magical enchantments and enchanters who employed such rituals. Old Cato knew the score, because Carthage's infant sacrifices had become the scandal of the Mediterranean world.

"Our society's early membership focused upon civically-minded Romans reacting to the unsavory importation of a grisly North African religion. But as time passed, our organization realized that in order to battle the dark forces of evil, men and women, gifted in the sixth sense, the hidden sight, and the like, had to make up the society's membership, instead of the political elite of Rome.

"Our society's first name, the *Consilio ad Conservationem de Iure Naturali*, The Council for the Preservation of Natural Law, or CCIN, became abbreviated and camouflaged as CCI—the "two hundred and one.

"With the appearance of Christianity on the scene, our society, long associated with the preservation of conservative Roman mores, fell out with Christianity due to a misunderstanding about the early Christian mass. As a result, our society became reviled by the Christian Church. And so, in a curious twist, the CCI found itself outlawed by the First Council of Nicaea in 325 AD. Some historians, however, see other forces influencing the decisions of the early Church Fathers at that Nicaean assembly, which in essence, removed us from the scene.

"As a consequence, we went underground for the next three hundred and fifty years, only to reemerge during the Moslem expansion of the seventh century. Thereafter, the CCI flourished in the Islamic East until Europe was prepared to embrace it during the Enlightenment. At that time, its old Latin name was translated into French as the *Conseils pour la conservation de la loi naturelle,* where, in another twist, the society took a firm hold within the British Empire, instead of the French. Go figure." Mr. Henry shrugged.

"Thereafter, our society enlisted many influential British scientists, educators, humanists, and politicians. London became our society's official headquarters."

"Is that why President Smithers is located there?"

"Yes."

"When did America get involved?" I asked having finished my burger, and pushed aside my plate.

Mr. Henry continued, "During our Revolution, many members of our society immigrated to America. Philadelphia, our first regional headquarters, soon became supplanted by Washington. But following the War of 1812, the society shifted its American center of gravity inland. With great foresight, in 1813 President James Madison established the society's first North American Academy far away from the sea coast in southwestern Pennsylvania, here, at Old Oaks Academy.

"With the advent of the Industrial Revolution, our society again morphed with the times and became an international corporation with ties throughout the world. Backed by the wealth amassed over the centuries, our society again changed its name, this time to The International Society, or TIS.

"Then, with prescient wisdom, our society divested itself of central governance, choosing to allow regional and local chapters to form and govern themselves, in direct reflection of the British and American political temperament of the times. Consequently, wherever the sun set on the British Empire, one could say in every major city a TIS chapter existed.

"During the 1950s, our society decided to change its name again, this time to The International Integrated Interface Society, or TIIIS. This long overdue decision recognized that many, if not most, of our society possessed considerable paranormal abilities. In fact, TIIIS today is listed as a scientific research organization devoted to the investigation of the paranormal."

*   *   *

After a particularly grueling day, I again met Mr. Henry for dinner. I ordered soup that night because my jaw was sore from a telekinetic blow that I had gotten from Mr. Dexter. He had clocked me a good one.

Mr. Henry asked. "So what's your impression of the Academy?"

"Well, I have received a bunch of physical abuse and been exposed to a ton of information. While Professor Winter's lectures filled in a bunch of gaps, that Mr. Good topped them all."

At this, the Fourth Level Adept merely smiled.

"So all in all, I am learning a lot in a very short period of time."

"Well, had anyone told you what the word 'academy' means?"

"No."

"It's a Greek compound word that most believe signifies an institution of higher learning. They cite as proof Plato, who named his philosophical school in ancient Athens, "The Academy," after *Akadēmos,* a legendary Athenian hero of the Trojan War. Mr. Stone, I'm here to tell you that there is a far deeper meaning behind the word.

"The Greek word *akadēmos* is made up of two parts. Its second part, *dēmos,* means a division of society, or of land. But the first part of *akadēmos,* the *aka* part, means nothing in Greek, but plenty in ancient

Egyptian. For '*heka*' means 'magic' in that language."

"Really?"

"So, Marine, the word academy, when you put it all together means 'a separate people, or place, of magic.' And that's why our campus is called the Academy."

*   *   *

Two weeks later at dinner, Mr. Henry seemed agitated, hurried, and out-of-sorts. His voice had an uncommon urgency to it.

"Mr. Stone," he said tersely, "what do you know about CMES North America?"

Thinking back to Mr. Good's discussion I said. "Plenty. Their North American headquarters is in New York City."

"So what does that tell you?"

"I would think that if you gut their NYC headquarters CMES North America suffers big time."

"Certainly. But that would take some real doing."

"Why?" I asked.

"Marine, their New York headquarters building has forty-one floors, thirty-nine of which are above ground. Its exterior is clad in a dull gray colored, embossed sheet aluminum. Unknown to the public, each sheet is covered with Egyptian hieroglyphs on its unexposed, interior side. These texts contain powerful spells, defensive in nature. That place is a fortress."

Just like all the buildings of the Academy, I thought.

"Their actual purpose, composition, and triggering mechanisms remain a closely guarded secret. CMES owns the building outright through a dizzying array of corporations and blind trusts, as well as the entire block upon which it stands.

"And if that weren't not enough, the building has a subway entrance beneath it to the Fifth Avenue and 53rd Street Station. But under the station is a veritable labyrinth of secret tunnels and chambers. Access to these passageways, as one might expect, is restricted to the CMES membership, which in turn allows their comings and goings to be done in total secrecy.

"Now I ask you. How far away is Manhattan from the Academy?"

"A day's drive."

"Yes, it is."

CHAPTER 12
Open Season

The mortal world provides the battlefield upon which good and evil compete. Within its compass, souls have a choice—either to learn through mortal acts of charity, mercy, and love or permit themselves to wallow in hatred, prejudice, and acts of utter inhumanity.

Every soul deliberately makes this choice when it selects its mortal carrier, through which a soul experiences the trials and tribulations of mortal existence. Direct congress between a soul and its carrier, while rare, does occur.

Do not be deceived. While every mortal possesses its own personality and intellect, every mortal carries a soul with a plan that it wishes to follow—either to progress toward transcendence or degenerate into depravity.

The mortal world is an unforgiving place, often referred to as the crucible, the flame, or the balance.

The Knot of Eternity. (trans.) G.L. Love. 2nd edition with T. Good. (Old Oaks Academy Press, 1960), vol. I.1, 14-15.

The report steered me to a rural barn in Massachusetts, which stoically stood despite its decided list. With its weathered paint long since faded into silver, I thought it a lousy place for another murder.

It didn't take me long to peg it as a political hit camouflaged as a human sacrifice. At least that's what I told my boss, President Smithers, when he called me afterward for my fresh impressions.

The crime scene reeked of several choice bodily organics and the metallic stench of dried blood. This murder sent a message, which constituted hate mail on steroids. Someone wanted to prevent any further erosion of their political influence among the non-aligned paranormal communities. As to who bankrolled this assassination, I harbored little doubt. My money was on that hard-core bunch of maniacal and power-hungry paranormals—CMES.

The mutilated unfortunate, a reputable dream interpreter of a non-aligned paranormal organization, lay disassembled and largely missing in the barn's attic. His client apparently had not agreed with his take on their nocturnal imagery and, just for sick giggles, had decided to dismember him. Not a very civilized way of conducting business under any circumstances.

I arrived first on the scene to assess the threat, and act accordingly. Even though I am green as grass at this job, after my fourth such investigation this week, even thick-headed me could see a pattern. Someone didn't like diplomatic agents of non-aligned paranormal organizations freely circulating among those not treaty- or blood-bound. Whoever was doing this wished to encourage non-aligned entities to have second thoughts about their independent status and think long and hard about where to pledge their loyalties.

My organization, TIIIS, would never dream of enforcing such compliance on the non-aligned. Clearly, CMES felt otherwise. Such actions represented the exercise of their cornerstone policy of "power and dominion."

I stood over the victim. The report said that it was Paul Andersen, but I wondered where he began and ended, amid a horrid scene of overdone eggbeater-like splatter. Whatever nut case had done this, had reveled in the deed.

I focused on what remained of Paul, which was precious little—a dismembered hand here, his grotesquely distorted head there, blood everywhere. Not all of Paul was present. Someone or something had either removed the remainder, or had made a meal of him.

I looked past Paul to the litter of disinformation on the barn's rough-hewn plank flooring; the hurriedly chalked pentangle, the five burnt black candles, and the melted piles of incense. None of these Hollywood trappings possessed a hint of a paranormal aura, and thus not a dram's worth of evidence. Anyone can draw on a sidewalk with chalk, or light a birthday candle, or put a match to incense. Magic is not at all required. Spells do leave their telltale traces, but here, there was nothing.

No, this atrocity was all about Paul, a man whose talents went far beyond that of a *lector somniorum*. The report indicated Paul enjoyed respect within the paranormal community. As a neutral go-between, the community depended upon him to salve fragile egos, straighten out misunderstandings and interject common sense into an overheated negotiation. Someone wanted this effective ambassador with a fair reputation and unbiased sense of neutrality out of the way.

Then, I saw it—a broken claw, a raptor-like talon, right out of *Jurassic Park*. It had been torn whole from the attacker as sinew still clung to it. Somehow Paul had torn it free from his attacker, gripping it with all his strength, all while the claw was embedded in his hand.

What a superhuman effort that must have been ...

I squatted down for a better look at that hard-earned prize. I saw the claw's fast-receding aura, a pitch-black, slimy glow infused with orange and red flecks. This was the sure sign of a demon, but one that I was not familiar with.

I spat on it as a test—a rookie move. A viper-like hiss sizzled as my spittle sputtered and steamed across its hideously wicked shape.

Huh.

Well whadda ya' know.

My spit didn't leave any corrosive marks on it, whatsoever.

I'll have to discuss this with Mr. Good during my next debrief. Maybe he'll know.

Then I did something else I shouldn't have. Without thinking I stood up and began circling around the crime scene, trying not to step on anything too squishy. While looking for other clues, I spaced out the spit I had left.

The claw began to stir. It wriggled and squirmed this way and that. That ugly hook struggled to disengage itself from the fleshy muscle of Paul's palm, but once it was free, the claw flew at me!

And barely missed my face. Melaina's protective amulet that I wore around my neck had jerked me aside—hard. The claw continued on, ricocheting off a stout wood beam, leaving a nasty gouge in its wake. Its flight path curved like a heat-seeking missile coming back for a second pass. By this time, however, I was ready and caught it inside a Kevlar evidence bag. Now caught, the claw jumped and bounced about, displeased at being captured, while I zip-sealed the bag, holding it out at arm's length. After a few moments, the claw settled down as the bag's pure silver mesh lining took its toll. Demons, and even their flying demonic claws, don't play well with that element.

This was my first encounter with an *unguibus daemonis,* or demon's claw, a paranormal landmine sometimes left behind at a kill site meant to discourage those with a forensic bent. And since I had stupidly spat upon it, that gave the claw all the DNA it needed to pursue and attack the owner of said spit. Like I said, an extraordinarily stupid move on my part. Live and learn.

Yes, *even* after all of Mr. Good's lectures, and for that matter, all of Mr. Henry's practical field advice, I remained a green field operative, no doubt about it. But now I had evidence for the lab rats back at the Academy to analyze. With this precious item in hand, hopefully they will be able to identify the perpetrator of this heinous murder. How? *Because magic always leaves behind the unique signature of its practitioner.*

So went my first week on the job and my fourth murder investigation. As for the victims, too many would remain grim testaments of a hidden war, innocents in every right. I appreciated evermore why the mortal world has been described as "the crucible," "the flame," and "the balance," for it is here that the forces of good and evil do battle.

*   *   *

Professor Melaina Makris of the Department of Near Eastern Languages was startled by a flying blur and noisy crash in her office. A white cardboard jewelry box had just flown across the room, impacted against the opposite wall, and spilled out its contents—a handmade mummiform amulet with a leather neck thong. She looked down on the floor and noted that her amulet twitched twice more before it settled.

While the event caught the bright and protective Alexandrian white witch by surprise, she breathed a sigh of relief that this time the box had taken flight instead of her. Some months ago, Melaina had crafted two magically reciprocal amulets—one for herself and the other for her paranormal colleague, J.J. Stone.

Simply amazing, she thought. *Stone must be on the job again. Something must have happened to cause such a reaction from my talisman. I hope he's safe and sound. After all, that's why I gave it to him, all the more since he just started as the TIIIS Lictor of Magic.*

She smiled. *At least this time I didn't get a black eye!* Thinking back on her first brush with "sharing" the field experiences of that man named Stone.

That time, as I recall, Stone had taken on the evil Charles Smithers, an adept of considerable talents.

As the professor of Demotic and Coptic languages glided over to gather up the fallen box and its talisman, she could not help but notice the heat radiating from it—evidence of the amulet's ability to leach away excess paranormal energy.

Stone must have got himself into some mischief—again. She grimaced as she returned the errant talisman to its box and placed it back on the shelf.

Then she wondered, and not for the first time, whether her Egyptian parents had gone through similar vicarious trials and tribulations, as both of them had been gifted sensitives.

At that thought Melaina's mind wavered as to why she had even given Stone the totem. Her heart quickened. She chided herself, "Get back to work, Melaina."

CHAPTER 13
An Innocent's Possession

In a remote Tuscan village a frantic scene unfolded. Called Inno, on a prominent ridgeline in the hilly wine country, a young girl in 1991 became afflicted with a curious illness, which after much head-scratching on the part of the district's physician, led to an appeal to the local priest. From there, the case escalated to the Vatican, who deployed a young ordained Father Antonio Garibaldi to investigate.

*   *   *

The young priest looked down on the dozing face of a dehydrated and emaciated girl. Her long and glorious black hair snarled in a sweaty tangle of curls. Her furrowed brow showed much pain and suffering, and more, much more.

Without question, this demon I must classify as an "M" for "malum" or "evil," because of its jet black aura. Its additional flecking of color can perhaps help me narrow it down to a particular type. Still, there is no way of knowing whether this demon is an "SI" for sui iuris *or autonomous, or a P-Type, for* praeceptis— *making capable of answering specific commands. My guess that it's a M-SI that has a low C-Rating making it extremely unstable.*

"How long has your daughter been in such a state?" he asked her frantic parents.

"A week and a half, *Padre.*" Her overwrought father whispered in her presence, not wishing to waken her. The girl's tearful mother twisted her handkerchief into knots, this way and that.

"Ah." The priest nodded. "And her first name?"

"Claudia. Claudia Marie," the father added.

"Such a beautiful name. But she looks thirsty. Has she drank any water?"

"No, *Padre*." the father answered. "She only calls for wine. Much red wine. That's not at all like her."

The priest could see the girl's problem, if of course, you could *see*, as Garibaldi could, the muddy, black aura with swirling random flecks of red and purple. The priest knew a demon possessed her, which had to be exorcised and banished from the mortal world.

"*Signore*, do you have a bath tub?"

"No, *Padre*, just a shower."

Remembering the rural setting, the priest reframed his question. "Do you have a large water trough for the animals?"

"*Sì*. We have one for the cows and horses. It's right outside."

Nodding, the priest said, "We must move her to this basin. But first, we will need to fill it to the brim. We also will need four men, four strong men to hold each of her limbs, and for you to hold her head."

*　　　*　　　*

The father soon returned with four of his neighbors, all with serious looks on their faces.

"*Signori*," the priest instructed. "When we enter the child's bedroom you must not listen to what the girl says. Trust me. She may say the most scandalous things. Above all ignore any pleas for help. They are all lies. All you should think about is her salvation."

Five silent head nods.

"You will grab her wrists and ankles. Be prepared for a fierce fight."

Turning to her father, "As for you, you will hold and support her head from all injury.

"Are we prepared?" The priest asked one last time.

Another five nods.

When the six men entered the room, they surrounded the bed of a now very awake young girl, who smiled at each of them in a way that shocked them all. She even wagged her tongue at each.

Fixing on the priest, she said looking into his eyes, "Your name is Tony. Isn't it?"

That shocked Father Antony Garibaldi, as he had not told anyone his first name.

It's telepathic!

A lurid smile, "Do you like me, Tony?"

Then the men pounced, securing her limbs and lifting her away from the bed as one. So began the struggle, the screaming, the cursing, the accusations of rape, the entreaties for sex, and much, much more. While the priest had steeled himself for this verbal assault, it shocked the others.

"She is like an eel," one said as he struggled to hold onto her ankle.

"Careful!" the priest said, "Try not to break any bones."

But when the girl saw what the men had in store for her. As they neared the full water trough, the real fight began. Like an enraged animal she twisted and turned violently, clawed with her nails, and snapped at any reachable fingers or forearms, catching several, drawing gouts of blood.

"Down!" the priest ordered and into the trough she went, with sheets of water cascading over its sides into the surrounding black mud.

At first contact with the water, the girl's body seized as if electrocuted, then she began to shiver and quake uncontrollably, and her eyes went wide with raw fear. She spat out from her pain-clenched jaw.

"Priest, my priest.

"Be my first!

"Take me." She hissed through bloody teeth.

"Take me now, priest!

"Rumor has it, Tony—your name is Tony isn't it?—

"Rumor has it you're hung like a horse.

"So ride me, Tony.

"Ride me!" she breathlessly gasped.

Definitely a *succubus,* Garibaldi clinically noted.

The village men, amazed by the girl's taunting statement, horrified her father beyond words. The priest answered them with a fresh bucket of spring water dumped upon the girl's head. The water had effect. The girl's eyes rolled back and her tongue writhed like a snake as the men struggled to hold her in place.

Garibaldi, noting her reaction, dumped two more buckets on her head before he could detect any change in her aura. But to make sure, he doused her a fourth time, and only then, could he tell the demon had left her. Placing his hand on her forehead as if to test for a fever, the priest no longer sensed a demon within. It had been banished to whence it came.

Now wet and exhausted from their labors, the

priest told the four village men to let go of the girl. Her father, however, remained to support her drooping head above the waterline. Father Garibaldi blessed the girl, anointed her forehead with sacred oils, and said several prayers, in essence baptizing her once again.

"*Signore*, your daughter has been through a lot. But she is once again herself," Garibaldi said to the father.

"Take her inside and put her to bed. Tomorrow, she will begin her recovery."

"*Grazie*, *Padre*, for giving us back our daughter."

Then to the village men, "*Signori*. You just heard and saw a demon speaking through this poor young girl. She experienced supreme helplessness while under the power of the demon. This, I can guarantee. Everything the demon said, she heard. Her shame will be great. Forgive and forget. But before you go, I must thank all of you for your assistance. Sometimes God's work requires many to succeed. Today, we have succeeded."

Again thanking the young priest profusely, the father lifted out his soaked and exhausted daughter, and turned toward his house.

Then the priest asked, almost as an afterthought, "*Signore*, have any strangers passed through your village over the last couple of days?"

The father stopped in his tracks at this question and turned to address the priest.

"Only a handful of tourists have passed through our village. And of them, there is no one that sticks out in my mind. One did, however, express an interest in our local wines. He asked many knowledgeable questions. I mention him because he carried an umbrella in the sun. He said his family suffered from skin cancer. Why do you ask?"

"Curious. Just curious.

"Mi scusi, Signore, but did this man have light or fair skin?"

"Sì, Padre. His skin was like ivory."

CHAPTER 14
The Big Talk

For some crazy reason, this former Marine loves to go on long drives. Going from the Academy in western Pennsylvania all the way to Santa Fe suited me as just such a fine trek. The time alone calmed the mind; gave me the opportunity to think and reflect about recent events and weigh my options. During such long drives as this, the miles melt away like hoar frost caught in spring sunshine. On top of that, my old pickup, a red Colorado, always seemed to run better whenever it went in a westerly direction.

It seemed strange to stop in my hometown of Denton, Texas, and not visit mom and dad. That would have to wait until I reached Santa Fe, where TIIIS had relocated them after their attempted assassination. All I knew was when I got there, I looked forward to catching up, doing some chores, not to mention burying my face into some of mom's fine home cooking.

* * *

For old time's sake, I stopped in Denton anyway and paid a visit with my colleague, Professor Adam Gibson. Not only did this man help me find the right university, we co-authored my first professional article. Adam, a card-carrying member of TIIIS, stumbled across me that day in the Willis Library, while I was studying cuneiform on my own. That chance event changed my life in many ways.

As soon as Adam's office door closed, two frosty

long necks appeared from his secret stash. Once the necks clinked, and a long pull later, the good professor's grilling began.

"Well, J.J., congratulations on the Lictor of Magic position."

Then, the man paused. "Or perhaps better stated: good luck with the job. I hear it can be a real bitch."

"That's what President Smithers also said."

"So why are you in town?"

"I'm on my way to Santa Fe to visit mom and dad. See how they're doing."

"No doubt. By the way, the *Journal of Ancient Near Eastern Studies* asked me to review an article you submitted. The article, as it stands, is good, but there are some parts where I thought you were holding back on some information."

"Adam, I had to hold some stuff back because it was too dangerous to put into print."

"Oh, well, never mind about those comments.

"What are you doing for an MA thesis?"

"More demon-summoning tablets. Peter Glass and I are trying to construct a small catalogue of them. In fact, I want to test them in the Academy's demon lab Mr. Good told me about."

*   *   *

My folks several years back sold the family ranch outside of Denton, Texas, after I enlisted in the U.S. Marines. Because Dad said he couldn't manage all the chores on his own, they moved into Denton proper. There a hit squad armed with shotguns visited them intent on blowing them into tiny pieces. Fortunately, Dad had got this funny feeling while cleaning his guns in the garage, and turned the tables on them.

So I drove from the Academy to visit them in their new home in Santa Fe. It was weird, me with a strange address in my hand. Eventually, I found it. A modest single story with an attached garage and rocks and bushes instead of grass. TIIIS had bought it, moved them in, and provided them with new identities.

As I parked in front, a bunch of subliminal memories jarred loose of the ranch where I'd grown up. That triggered a mental cascade which included my Grace and the pickup crash that claimed her life. If that hadn't happened, I wouldn't have joined the Marines. Instead, we would have settled down. The ranch would still be in the family. If, if, if …

Intellectually, I knew that I would have discovered I carried the First Soul of Creation, God only knows how, and given the job description and all that it entailed, I still would have lost my beloved Grace, any kids that we might have had, and maybe even mom and dad. As hard as that was to swallow, the way things turned out seemed to be the best of a tough situation.

*   *   *

"So, J.J.," Mom began all excited, "tell Daddy and me all about what you're doing back East."

"Well, I've got a good job with this research outfit in western Pennsylvania. For helping them out, I get free room and board, and a fair wage. That means all the money I saved up while in the service hasn't been touched. In short, mom, I'm good and busy."

"What sort of work do you do for this 'research outfit?'" Dad asked, ever the practical one, and himself a former Marine.

"Well, that's why I'm here. As I said, I work for a research think-tank called the International Integrated Interface Society, or TIIIS for short. They were the kind folks who moved you and mom out here after the attack, bought this house, got you new IDs."

"Those TIIIS folks have been might nice to us, son," Dad interjected.

"But what about your studies, son?" Mom asked.

"I'm continuing with them, but on a part-time basis. My contacts at the university understand the situation."

"So, son, what do you do for TIIIS?" Dad prodded.

Sitting around the kitchen table, I reached out to my parents and held their hands. In their air conditioned, Santa Fe home, I found myself sweating as I decided to tell them the truth about my job.

"First off, I have a confession to make. I lied to you about what I really do; what TIIIS is really all about."

My dad brightened, hopefully. "They must be with law enforcement. They fixed everything right quick with the police back in Denton."

"Well, no."

"Didn't they move us out here to Santa Fe?"

"Well, yes, sir."

Confusion reigned supreme across their faces, so I raised my hands to stop anymore speculations.

"Just listen. Remember back to my eighteenth birthday when you told me about the reverend calling me a 'golden child'? Well, guess what? I am. What old Reverend Paul Roberts meant to say was that I had a golden aura, or a golden halo, all around me."

My dad's head jerked back at the memory. My mother gasped.

"That golden aura, or glow, or halo, is because I carry a very old soul, an ancient one. In fact, the soul that I carry is the First Soul of Creation."

"Son, I might have been a dirt-stupid rancher, but that sounds like outright blasphemy to me."

I sighed a deep sigh.

How do I explain it all?

"Dad, I know that it sounds crazy. But it's the truth. And because I carry the First Soul, I enjoy divine protection. Does that sound crazy? Think about all the stuff I got into as a kid. Did I ever get more than a bruise or scratch? Think about that truck crash that claimed my Grace. Was my survival just plain dumb luck? I don't think so. And there were all those times in Iraq, stuff I never told you guys about, because I knew that you it would make you worry. Yet, here I am, healthy and whole.

"But with that divine protection, I also have inherited some very heavy responsibilities, part of which have to do with my working for the International Integrated Interface Society.

"Let there be no mistake. There is pure evil out there in this world and TIIIS is the remedy for it. As a result, I am its enforcer. I am a force of good against evil."

At this point both mom and dad sat there staring back at me, with blank looks on their faces mouths agape. I didn't need to read their minds. Shock, tinged with some healthy fear, flooded them. I got an idea.

Mom, Dad, I thought, *listen to what your son has to say.*

Please. Both blinked at my entreaty.

Someone has to man the final line against evil, and

I'm it. Dad, it's not much different from being in the Marines. Instead of fighting the enemy, I'm fighting people who are evil, people who are possessed by evil, and sometimes, even demons.

TIIIS has trained me to deal with these challenges. The training's been hard, long, but effective.

I fight against evil, like those guys who sent to kill you, except Dad got the drop on them first. Didn't you, Dad?

A single, wide-eyed nod of understanding.

Dad, did you know that I inherited from you the ability to sense things before they happen?

A single shake of the head in negation.

Did you know that your ability to sense danger is so high that it ranks among the top two percent of the living human population?

His jaw sagged open.

When you were in the garage cleaning your guns before those guys showed up, why were you? What told you to do so? What did you initially intend to do?

At that point Mom spoke up. "J.J., he told me that he was going to fix that old lawnmower."

But you didn't, Dad, did you?

"No, son, I didn't.

Why?

"Because it just didn't feel right. I had this itch. Just like when I was in Vietnam. When I knew that somethin' just wasn't right."

And now I'm talking with you, like I am, without speaking, is called the silent tongue. It's telepathy. Mind communicating to mind. And once you get the hang of it, it's not hard to use.

Then I shifted back to vocalized speech. "So, do

you have any questions for me?"

"Oh, J.J.," Mom gushed, "I'm so proud of you, son, but I do worry so."

That earned a long hug.

Then dad piped up. "So, if I understand you, you're a soldier of God. Is that right?"

"Yes, sir. I do believe that about covers it."

That earned another big hug, but this one from dad.

*   *   *

"Officer Bergen is your private security force. It's her job and TIIIS' to protect you. If you need anything, call her. Here's her card, Dad. Trust her. She's a seasoned Iraq veteran and a crack shot.

"As for your old house in Denton, TIIIS has already sold it. If you check your new bank account in town, you will find all the proceeds have been deposited there. But here, in Santa Fe, this house TIIIS owns. Your new IDs protect you as well. Think of it like the Federal Witness Protection Program.

"Now that you're settled in, Dad and I will buy a new pickup. Mom, whatever kind of car you want, just let me know and I'll take care of it. Be aware, however, these vehicles will not be registered in your names. Instead, TIIIS will own them, insure them, and you will drive them, just as if you were TIIIS employees.

"One last thing. Mom, I want you to learn how to shoot and I don't want dad teaching you. I know this nice local lady who is itching to meet you both. She's wonderful. Her name is Betsy Silver Moon.

"As for you, Dad, I know this guy named John Running Deer. He owns a ranch and needs some help with it. Are you game?"

He agreed.

"So, son," Mom said. "How long will you be with us?"

"Couple of weeks, I figure. At least, until all the chores are done or the fridge goes bare."

*   *   *

One morning, with all the chores finished at my folk's place, I decide to run off to my favorite quiet place in the Santa Fe National Forest. I had paid close attention to the time when then-Governor Silver Moon had taken me into these wilds. I headed north on Highway 85 out of Santa Fe, exited at Highway 73, and drove into the pine shrouded foothills. I passed through Tesuque and ascended into the forest. Already by ten in the morning the pines smelled marvelous. Slowing down, I spotted a familiar rough-cut trail on the right. I followed it to a natural clearing, where I parked.

As before, I threw my head back, stretched out my arms, and breathed it all in. Luscious scents of pine, wild flowers, and earth filled my lungs. Looking around, I found the traces of a foot path, and followed them. Trying to be as quiet as I could, I walked for almost a half hour. Along the way, I managed to surprise several grouse and two frisky rabbits basking in the late spring sunshine. I arrived at a clearing dominated by two rocky mounds, each twenty to thirty feet high. A while back, Betsy Silver Moon had told me to climb and sit atop the one on the left. But at this time of the day, I didn't want any part of it, because I knew what lurked within it—snakes, the kind with rattles.

So I retreated back to the foot path through the tan clumps of grass and scrub, and found the perfect place to settle in and observe nature at its best.

Stepping off the trail, careful to leave no sign, I sat down cross-legged in a wind breaker and floppy hat and commenced to breath in the fragrant mountain air. The warming sun caused ripples of heat to run up and down my back. A gentle breeze tickled my nose. The pines swayed. Bees buzzed, insects flew, and a snake slithered by, crinkling the tall grass. I slitted my eyes and imagined myself as not invisible, but instead as part of the land. My mind wandered. I was content.

For reasons probably Freudian, that marvelous Alexandrian white witch Melaina came to mind and the protective amulet that she had given me. It had worked well during the rescue of the one hundred Pakistani boys and the encounter with the evil Charles Smithers. At the time, I didn't fully appreciate the amulet's reciprocal properties. The way it shares, and in the process halves, the impact of a magical conjuring. I know for a fact that Melaina hadn't expected to get a black eye like I had.

What an intellectually deep and exotic woman. But given my precarious occupation, I had to keep someone like that at a distance for their own protection, otherwise she'd only become a target. And that's a real pity, as Melaina has many things going for her—an accomplished scholar and a powerful witch, who just happens to be easy on the eyes.

Then, I got to thinking, a quiet relationship with such a person wouldn't be impossible. Yes, we'd have to be discrete. But, given Mel's obvious strengths and talents, why not? She knows what's at stake.

Yes, why not, soul carrier? Interjected the First Soul.

A strong companion fills out one's view of the world and how to deal with it. They provide support and a special kind of balance. Trust me when I say this, there are far more advantages to such an arrangement than not.

CHAPTER 15
Baiting a Lictor of Magic

William Alexander, the CMES regional director of North America, had asked for and received permission to kill a man who had managed to cheat death on multiple occasions. While his chairman did not realize it, his thoughts of convenient glee and derisive best wishes had been heard by the regional director. Besides, Alexander relished challenges.

Somehow, I must draw Stone out, the Dark One mused in deep thought. *Draw him out—like the slow extraction of a parasitic worm. But to do that, I require bait. Then I will crush him under my heel.*

The technical and human intelligence resources available to North American regional director rivaled those of many modern nations. Much like a spider's web, he ordered a sweep to find Stone, who had fallen off the grid since the ill-conceived bombing of his university dorm in Philadelphia. Much to his displeasure, that search came up empty.

Fine, the Dark One thought, *if a target refuses to surface, then close relatives and friends would just have to suffice. Eventually, even saints learn that they must enter the battlefield.*

* * *

Irene Willis was motivated, perhaps obsessed would be a better term, to be as good as her older brother. A member of CMES' Communications and Security Department on the technical side, Willis nevertheless wanted to prove that she had the right stuff for operations—again, just like her brother. When word came down from above requesting information on the whereabouts of the TIIIS Lictor of Magic, Willis jumped at the chance, and like the rest of her section, came up empty. But Willis had an idea.

What if I single-handedly took out Stone's parents? How would he react? As for my career, that would make some ripples. Maybe even get me a transfer to Ops. I'll take some vacation.

Going through Stone's online security file, her heart sank as the tall, thirtyish, brunette read about how five gangbangers armed with shotguns had somehow failed in taking out Stone's parents. Thereafter, Stone's parents disappeared.

No doubt TIIIS stepped in and moved them out. But where might they be right now?

After ten minutes typing into her laptop, Willis had an inkling. After another ten minutes and several dead ends, a thread began to develop legs. In the end, she printed off six possibilities that only shoe leather could confirm.

Willis theorized that since Stone had visited the Santa Fe area several times, that would be a natural place to start looking for his relocated parents. She now held in her hand six candidates who moved into the Santa Fe area right after the attempt on their lives.

Willis also managed to dig up several faded images of Andrew Richard and Constance Marie Stone. While dated, they portrayed a tall, lanky U.S. Marine and a petite wife; they would have to do. As for Andrew Richard's driver's license photo, it would come in handy for a close up identification.

Next thing, Willis, an avid participant in several Spartan Games, was the crack shot of her departmental section. Because of her larger than average grip, Willis favored the Glock .40mm.

From upstate Albany, New York, Willis decided that it would be wise to drive to Santa Fe, an odd place with one area code, but eleven zip codes. For her stalk, she bought a used car, something unremarkable, cheap, and, above all, disposable.

The biggest hurdle Willis faced was figuring out her cover for this in-your-face hit. Whatever it was, it had to be something friendly and recognizable. In the end, she decided upon posing as a neighborhood welcome committee member, complete with a jacket and wicker basket loaded down with a housewarming gift, useful coupons, and helpful brochures.

*   *   *

List in hand, Willis made her rounds. En route, she had been humbled by the beauty and wide open spaces of the American West. By visit number four, she had her practiced welcome smile on and shtick well-oiled.

Standing before a modest flat-topped one story with a pink pebbled xeriscape yard and single car garage, she confidently walked up to its front door, and jabbed the bell. Moments later there, on the other side of the screen door, stood Andrew Richard Stone, all six foot something of him.

"Welcome to our neighborhood! I'm Irene Willis from the neighborhood welcoming committee, and I have a housewarming gift for you. May I give it to you?"

A.R., taken aback, said, "Sure thing. Come right on

in. Honey Bee?" he called. "We have company from the neighborhood welcoming committee."

In short order, the old former Marine lead Willis into the kitchen. It smelled of fresh coffee, bacon, and biscuits. Candice appeared, a neatly dressed, white-haired lady with a ready smile.

"Hello, dear. My name is Candice." The elder said extending a gentle and age-freckled hand. "Welcome to our home. Could I get you a cup of coffee?"

Willis, overwhelmed by the hospitality and cordial nature of the couple, almost had to remind herself as to why she was even there.

"No thank you. May I sit down? This basket is heavy."

A.R. held the chair out for the visitor, as his antennae began twitching for some strange reason, causing him to almost frown.

"Mrs. Gundersen," Willis began, while noting the couple's wedding bands, used the family's new surname, "the neighborhood would like to present you and your husband with this bag of jalapeño bread mix. While basic, it typifies our regional flavor."

"Why thank you, Miss …"

"Irene Willis, Mrs. Gundersen. Irene Willis."

As Willis extended the weighty canvas bag to his wife, her jacket shifted, and A.R. noticed a subtle but distinctive bulge under the visitor's left armpit. He recognized the gun was in a perfect draw position.

"Excuse me, Miss Willis, but I've got to attend to something," A.R. invented, as he brusquely got up and headed for the garage.

"A.R.!" his wife chided. "Don't be rude to the dear thing. Come back here."

But A.R. ignored his wife's admonition as his mind made the connection between his funny feeling, what his son had told him, and when the five thugs had attacked him in his garage back in Denton, Texas.

Moments later, however, he did return to the kitchen table, but with a box under his arm. This he set before him with his left forearm casually resting across its lid. Inside rested his brand new Colt .45 1911 that his son had bought him. The weapon was loaded, chambered, and cocked. His right hand remained hidden under the table and at the ready, the box's panel facing A.R.'s stomach had been removed.

While his wife and Miss Willis chatted on, A.R. settled in, waiting for any hint as to what the visitor's real intent might be. The foxy Marine focused on her movements, her right hand and where it went.

Once both women were all talked out, Willis casually asked, "So where are you folks from? I'm originally from out East, Upper New York State."

Before A.R. could kick his wife, Candice blurted out, "North Texas."

Bingo! Willis thought.

A.R. read the visitor's recognition as plain as day.

A smart phone began to ring. Willis, in response, indeed a righty, reached into her jacket. A.R. sincerely hoped that their visitor was going for her phone. But instead a black-metal gun butt began to clear her jacket, while A.R. gripped his own within the box.

Time slowed.

A.R.'s weapon roared first with a 124 grain hollow point hitting Willis' upper chest. The sheer impact catapulted the CMES agent backward in her chair and onto the kitchen floor.

While falling backward, Willis managed to jerk off a round that trimmed a lock of Candice's hair, just missing her left ear.

Willis' second discharge, as she landed spread-eagled on her back, blew a hole in the kitchen wall the size of a fist.

Candice, wide-eyed and petrified, remained statue-still as the in-house discharges had thoroughly stunned her.

A.R. rose, walked around to his frozen wife, and stood over the injured visitor, who he now saw wore a bullet-proof vest. Willis soon stirred and looked up at him with pure hate and pain in her eyes. She tried to lift her weapon in his direction, but A.R. stopped that with his left foot, pinning Irene's hand to the floor, crushing her wrist in the process. Now training his Colt on Willis' face, A.R. calmly said, "Honey Bee, where's that emergency card that J.J. gave us?" His wife pointed to the drawer beneath the wall phone.

"Would you mind fetching it for me? My hands are kinda full at the moment. We're going to need some help right quick."

CHAPTER 16
Hard Realities

I was at the Academy when the IT and Security department called me up about my folks. The shock and rage hit me like an express train. To top it off, TIIIS had already evacuated them to an undisclosed location.

As for the assassin, dad had again miraculously acted upon his own God-given prescience. The woman named Irene Willis, was taken alive, but required hospitalization. Afterward, IT and Security confirmed that Willis was a bona fide CMES employee.

The bad news hit when John Running Deer called me up and told me that under no circumstances could I visit my folks again.

"Damn it, John! If I can't visit them, they might as well be dead!"

"Yeah, J.J., that's a fact. But at least you can still call them up anytime you like."

That reality sucked, but once I cooled down, I realized that I had been sloppy, had hung around their place doing chores, and had tipped off the bad guys.

Then and there I decided to get even, and to do that meant that I would have to get back on the grid, something that would go counter to my president's direct orders. My hope was to lure CMES into doing something that they would regret. But I first needed some advice from the IT and Security folks. What they had to say would be crucial.

On my way to visit them, I viciously crushed my phone under my heel and deposited it into a trash bin. Somehow that made me feel better.

* * *

The first person that I ran into at IT and Security was a young, fresh-faced fella named Josh Remington. Lean, red-haired, and with a face covered with freckles, he looked up at me from under his sun-faded St. Louis Cardinal's baseball cap and said, "What can I do for you, Mr. Stone?"

As I sat down in his guest chair I said, "How did you …"

"It's my job, Mr. Stone," he said leaning forward with a big toothy grin. "Now, what's up?"

"I've been off the grid for a while, Mr. Remington, as a precaution. Unfortunately, that did not work out as planned."

"Yeah, I heard. Sorry about your folks."

"Thanks. But what I need to know is if CMES has been looking for me lately?"

A quick chuckle. "'Lately'? Christ, CMES has been beating the bushes nonstop over the past three months."

"You don't say …"

"Yep. You're quite the celebrity."

"Huh. If that's so, how quick do you think CMES would detect me if I reemerged on the grid? Say, running a credit card transaction."

Remington thought for a moment, scratched his pug nose, and said, "Within twenty seconds."

"What?"

"Their network and search capacity is huge. Add to that, they have been looking for you for quite some time. All of their search criteria is established and 'out there' on the internet. You fart, and they'll smell it."

"So, Mr. Remington …"

"Call me, Josh."

"Okay, Josh, given that you're an IT and Security guy, how fast do you think that they might operationally respond to that info?"

"It all depends on how badly they want you dead."

I smiled. "That's just perfect, Josh."

CHAPTER 17
Billy Joe's

After informing President Smithers of my action plan, something that he didn't agree with but understood, I packed up Old Faithful and headed west. It was late afternoon as I neared mid-Indiana, when I got a surprise call from Governor Silver Moon.

"Where are you right now?"

"Just entering Indianapolis, governor. Why?" I said as I pulled over to the side of the Highway 70.

"The president told me what your plans were following the dust-up at your folk's house. Are you still dead set on this course of action?"

"Yes, ma'am."

"Well, in that case, I just wanted you to know that I have your back on this stunt. It's a gutsy move. One that might work."

"Thank you, ma'am. I appreciate the support."

"Where do you intend to ambush them?"

"Where else, but in the Santa Fe National Forest."

"Going elk hunting, eh?" she asked.

"No, ma'am. Fly fishing. Elk are out-of-season right now."

"I see. Well, be sure to get in touch with John Running Deer. He'll want to give you a hand as well."

"Thank you, governor. Will do."

"God-speed, Mr. Stone." And she hung up.

I pitched my smart phone out the window into a flooded ditch.

*   *   *

Two hours later I dug out a fresh cell phone and called up one of my old hunting buddies in Denton, Texas, Billy Joe, a dyed in the wool survivalist, you could count on with your life. He also had lots of stuff to share, swap, sell, and even more connections than God himself … well, sort of. I figured my laundry list wouldn't challenge him one bit. And the best part, I knew he had most of it already in inventory. One last thing—Billy Joe loved cash. After a folksy ten minutes of jawing with him, I threw the smart phone out the window. Watching it in my right side mirror, it bounced and shattered spectacularly. Eighty miles an hour can do that.

That night I crashed at a roadside hotel, spent the night, and paid cash. In the morning, I made another call, this one to John Running Deer in Santa Fe.

"John, how are you doing?"

"J.J.! Good to hear from you, bro. Where are you?"

"Heading your way, but after a stop or two. I need a favor. I need some detailed topo maps of the Santa Fe National Forest. Hiker maps. Do you think you can help me out?"

"Shouldn't be a problem. I have a source that will be happy to lend you whatever you need."

"That's great. Just bring a selection of up-country maps, that should do it."

"What do you have in mind?"

"Some fly fishing."

"Didn't know you were a fisherman."

"I'm not."

"Well, drive safe, bro."

"Thanks my friend. See you soon."

And out the window the smart phone flew, this time hitting a wooden fence post, shattering it.

Damn, I'm good!

*   *   *

Billy Joe's ranch can be found north of Denton off of Highway 77 toward Sanger. Pulling my truck onto his property, I unlatched the cattle gate, drove my truck in, and latched it back up again. It's the way we do things in Texas—leave the damn gate the way you found it.

After driving a good quarter of a mile, I reached his house all nestled in a pretty copse of cottonwood trees. I swear you couldn't see the place from the air, the trees are that dense when they are in leaf.

Billy Joe sat there, waiting for me on his porch. As I drove up, he smiled his big toothy grin.

"Well, J.J., it's been quite some time, boy. What brings you out here all the way from Denton and all?"

Smiling at this Texas cotton-picker turned near millionaire, I told him the truth.

"Billy Joe, I drove in all the way from the state of Pennsylvania to buy some hunting equipment. And this here gym bag is full of money. I took out a loan from my boss."

At that, Billy Joe's eyes widened with surprise. "All that way to spend your money with me?"

"Yep. Now instead of standing here jawing like two jay birds, what have ya got for me? I'm on a tight schedule."

"Well, I do have surprises in store. Follow me out to the barn. I have's it all laid out, just like those fancy restaurants do. All you have to do pick and choose."

Once in the barn—a heated, and air-conditioned steel-roofed structure with an immaculate concrete floor—I could see Billy Joe didn't lie. There must have been ten six-foot tables arranged at its center, with not an inch of surface space to spare. He even offered me a shopping cart for my convenience. What a guy.

"Nice touch, Billy Joe. Do you do this often?" as I gestured toward the barn's layout.

"More times than you might believe. Times, they are a changin'."

"No shit," I replied before I commenced to graze.

I filled my shopping cart with stuff like–dehydrated food; hunting clothing—tan camo; a light-weight sleeping bag; a Leupold range finder; a tan tarp; a backpack frame and rucksack, and a ghillie suit.

Things got interesting at the next couple of tables—mil-spec night vision goggles with spare batteries. A desert-camoed Remington 700 LTR .308 Winchester bolt action rifle with a fluted barrel, which came with a bipod, a mighty fine Nightforce Competition scope, and a nifty Gemtech suppressor. To my surprise, the Remington remained well-balanced even with the suppressor.

"Billy Joe. You have a fed stamp for this suppressor?"

"Sure do."

"Blank?"

"Yep."

"Damn. You think of everything."

I grabbed some ammo. For my 9mm, I took three boxes of Magtech 147 grain hollow points. I wasn't fooling around. For the Remington, I went with three boxes of Hornady 168 grain, boat-tailed, match rounds.

"So, Billy Joe," as I hefted the rifle, "what is this baby sighted in on?"

The big grin said, "Four hundred yards, big guy. Spittin' distance."

"Now, what am I missing?"

"Whadda' ya' mean?"

"What do you have under the counter?"

That caused Billy Joe to pause and frown.

"Now since when have you been shy to make a dollar?"

"Well, a man has to be real careful nowadays. Ya know what I mean?"

"Yes, I do. Now what else do you have that might be real useful to a hunter of big animals, like elk?"

"Follow me," the man said as he walked over to some storage cabinets along the barn's wall. Unlocking one, he said, "Now J.J., be aware none of this 'special stock' can I sell at a friendly discount."

As the metal doors rattled open, I could not believe my eyes at all the pyrotechnics. Pinching my lower lip in thought, I decided on six claymore anti-personnel mines. Seriously heavy mothers; I disliked the idea of lugging them around, but figured they would come in real handy.

Saying nothing as he closed and locked the doors, Billy Joe turned to me and said, "Those elk out west must be tough to drop."

Then he paused with a look of concern on his face. "J.J. You're not in some sort of trouble, are you, boy?"

"Not to worry. I'm not, but those elk sure are."

After I paid the man in wads of cash, Billy Joe, all smiles once again, asked if I needed any help loading up all the stuff in my truck. Instead, I said, "Do you mind if I pack up all this stuff right here?"

"Not at all. In fact, I'll grab you a fresh table to work on."

About a half hour later, I had packed the lot.

Then Billy Joe handed me a Boy Scout orienteering compass, the kind with a clear plastic base. "It's always good to be prepared. By the way, elk hunting season doesn't open in New Mexico until February."

"Yep, I know. What's your point?"

"Nothin', just sayin.'"

CHAPTER 18
Fly-Fishing

As I crossed into New Mexico, I pulled into one of those modern tribal gas stations with all the amenities. I topped off the tank and went inside and bought an out-of-state fly fishing license. I did this last part using my credit card—intentionally.

Ah, the game begins.

* * *

The CMES Security and Communications staff in Manhattan had the pressure turned on to the max by their regional director's assistant, an austere and dark woman named Rollins. Aggravated, with no results, Rollins suspected that there must be a mole within her own organization, and began to methodically flip over tables in search of something that didn't exist. Her regional director, in the meantime, basked in her frustration. As a result, a once very creative Security and Communications staff turned inward, daring not to attract any attention from this *enfant terrible*.

Then, a massive wave of relief flooded over the over-stressed department, when it detected Stone using his credit card in eastern New Mexico. He had purchased gas, and of all things, an out-of-state fly fishing license.

Now, having located her target, Rollins marshaled her thoughts, informed the Dark One of the news, and forthwith dispatched a portion of the North American security detail, which constituted a full company of six

six-man squads. Their marching orders: track down and kill Stone. To their credit, the CMES hit team took off on the CMES Airbus 330 sixty-three minutes after detecting Stone's credit card transaction. The unit's destination was Albuquerque, New Mexico, where an airport bus would meet them on the tarmac.

*   *   *

I went to the bus station first thing when I pulled into Santa Fe, and rented a storage locker. Into it I packed all my non-hunting stuff and again paid in cash. I satisfied the attendant's curiosity with a story of fly fishing for the next two weeks. Green with envy, he took my money and with a wishful shake of his head, said "Lucky dog," as handed me my locker chit.

*   *   *

Next, I contacted John Running Deer from a pay phone at the bus station. He told me to meet him at his favorite diner on Cerrillos Road.

To my surprise Governor Silver Moon showed up, bless her pea-picking heart, and she offered to be my scout on this rodeo. She handed over the topo maps I requested of the Santa Fe National Forest, in a big Ziploc baggie to contain them. We hovered over these for a good half hour, plotting and planning, while I buried my face in a cheeseburger.

Since I hadn't showered since I'd left Illinois, I must have smelled pretty bad as John Running Deer offered me his place to spiff up and crash. As no one argued with that assessment, I took him up on the offer.

* * *

The next day I left John Running Deer's place before dawn and took Hyde Park Road, Route 475, deep into the Santa Fe National Forest. I paralleled the Little Tusuque Creek within its canyon. A gorgeous drive in daylight, it's darn treacherous in the dark.

My basic plan called for me being "obvious man," no offense to the well-read cartoon and its creator. I portrayed myself as a law-abiding dude, who liked to fly fish, figuring that if they could track and react to my credit card, they had a description of my truck and its plates. That meant they would find a couple of local officers, who would assist them in finding me.

I decided I would help them out, and parked my red Colorado with white Texas tags out in the open in the Black Canyon State Park campground lot, unlocked. I figured they could find it, ransack it, and leave it without damaging it too much. I hoped they would think that I had forgotten to lock it up, thereby lowering their expectations of me, and make false assumptions. In the military, it's called psi-ops.

As dawn broke, I walked through the low scrub grass of an upland meadow, making sure to leave clear sign of my passage. I headed southeast on a gradual incline, following that grassy little valley deep into the forest. After about a mile and a half the landscape narrowed, pinched in by the surrounding terrain of stunted pine and pinyon. Once beyond that constriction, the terrain opened up into a second scrub grass upland valley that branched off in two directions—east and south toward two rocky narrows.

I continued on, heading east, and made my way

about half way into the eastern rocky defile, which was a slab-sided gorge of red sandstone. There, I set up three of my claymores up against the rock of the north side, spaced about ten feet apart, all facing south. Once satisfied with the setup of my monofilament trip line, I moved up the slot for about a hundred paces, turned right, and then scrambled up the sandstone scree of its southern slope.

The cover of the finger of land formed between these two erosion funnels was rough scrub and sparsely treed, as there had been a recent forest fire. Crossing it into the southern rocky narrows, I descended for about four or five minutes, found a good spot, and set up my second trap of three claymores. Afterward, I backtracked up the defile and ascended the finger.

Now relieved of the weight of the explosive mines, I practically floated as I moved upslope along the ridge of the finger, gaining altitude, until I found the perfect spot to dig in and wait. Prepared and in position, I knew I could last out here for at least five days.

Now imagine this: a broad and breath-taking vista of a fan-shaped upland valley. All around me grew tufted, wheat-colored scrub grasses and the mottled greens of a stunted upland pine forest. I busied myself with my ghillie suit until I disappeared into the landscape.

I enjoyed this entire panorama from beneath a fallen and charred pine trunk. I could even see the snaking trail that I left behind in the scrub grass of the valley. From here I dialed in my sightlines and ranges.

*   *   *

Almost eleven that morning, while resting comfortably and in a light doze, Governor Silver Moon called me.

"Hey, they just found your truck."

"Who?"

"A park forest ranger in a Chevy Yukon. He walked right up to your pickup, walked around it twice, got on his radio, and called in your plates. About ten minutes later a state patrol car showed up and he got on the horn. Right now the two of them are looking in your pickup."

"All the doors are open."

"Well, they haven't tried that yet."

Pause.

"Hang on. Oh, my, God, you won't believe this. A tour bus just pulled up."

"Where are you, governor?"

"In my truck. I'm parked at the far end of the lot."

"Can anyone see you?"

"Don't think so. Oh, about thirty to forty soldiers just got off the bus and they're armed to the teeth. That's the biggest, out-of-season, elk hunting party I have ever seen."

"What are they doing?"

Then I wondered, *Did that park ranger think to check them for their elk hunting licenses?*

"Two of the soldiers are talking to the ranger and the state patrol officer. They're looking over your truck again. One of the soldiers tried a door, and Shazam, it opened. They're looking inside now, rummaging around. They found nothing.

"Well, pardner, you better take care of yourself.

They're now heading your way. Looks like they have a local tracker with them acting as their point. These guys look real serious. They're all fully human, but have grayed out auras. Not a good sign."

"Got it. Thanks for the heads-up. Now get yourself out of there as soon as you can."

"Will do! And best of luck."

*　　*　　*

The soldiers made good time. About an hour after talking with Governor Silver Moon, using my rangefinder I saw the tracker enter the far edge of the grassy, upland meadow before me. Following my clumsy trail, the range finder showed more than two thousand yards. That's where it maxed out.

I started counting aloud and came up with thirty-seven guys. One tracker, and the rest organized into six groups, each with their own lead. That told me these guys were professionals, following U.S. Marine squad doctrine. But when I started checking out their arms, each team lead carried what looked like a small sub-machine gun, some version or another of an Israeli product, while the others carried AK-47s.

Then I noticed that not one of them wore a backpack. They assumed they could waltz in, do their job, and leave.

Well, we'll have to see about that.

*　　*　　*

As they entered the grassy, upland meadow, the six teams split up. The tracker stayed on point following my blundering tracks with four teams in tow, while one team each skirted the meadow's far perimeters toward the east and south. Their splitting up told me something important: they had tactical radios.

* * *

By the time the tracker reached the center of the grassy, upland meadow, I ranged him at eleven hundred yards. Remembering my training and that I had chosen an elevated position, I settled the crosshairs of my scope on him. He moved through the tall grass with a regular and predictable pace.

I wondered. *What will they do if I deny them their eyes?*

Quit?

I doubted it.

At this time of day, the wind barely whispered. I chanced a center mass shot, got lucky, and dropped the tracker square in the chest at a thousand yards.

Moments later they heard my muffled report, and everyone hit the deck. Since my boat-tailed bullet flew faster than the speed of sound, they couldn't duck the next round. Their second problem involved the report's suppression, meaning that they couldn't echo-locate its origin. They figured that I, the shooter, lay somewhere in front and above them. But that didn't help them one nit, given all terrain that stretched out before them.

Time to get moving.

Now began the fun stuff. I've always hated belly crawling, but right now I worked my way upslope and away from all my party favors.

But why move at all? Why not just sit and shoot fish in a barrel? Because any good sniper worth his salt has to be mobile.

About an hour later, I reached Position Two, which overlooked the eastern gorge where my blundering tracks led. Without their local guide, I figured at least a portion of their force would enter it. Actually, I counted on it. I also expected another portion would enter the southern narrows, hoping to outflank me.

Now within the tree line, I gazed down the slot of the rocky finger and erosion feature. I had just settled in when the claymores in the southern gorge exploded in rapid succession. The deafening concussions and follow-on echoes caused me to cringe and cover my ears.

*   *   *

The physical wreckage of two fire teams now sprawled dead and dying in the southern gorge. Two of the twelve remained "alive," screaming their heads off. Between the mines, the shattering rock, and the many shrapnel ricochets, all had been shredded. So much for their cleverly conceived flanking maneuver.

The explosions in the southern gorge caused the other two fire teams poised to enter the eastern narrows to have second thoughts. This I saw from my vantage point, as one of the team leads organized his troops. My rangefinder said 523 yards. I took another center mass shot, and missed high, and turned the man's head into an exploding tomato can of red mist.

Almost gagging at the sight through my scope, I shook my head to clear the image.

That's one fire team without a lead. That means one lead will have to take on those troops, which will lessen their tactical flexibility.

Time again to move.

*   *   *

At least this time I could creep toward Position Three located to the north, above, and to the right of the eastern gorge before me. It took me forty minutes. I found a spot about twenty yards within the pines that overlooked the two fire teams. In an aggressive move, I had flanked a portion of the CMES force that had stalled at the mouth of the eastern passage.

The soldiers by that time had deployed themselves in a defensive circle with their lead in the middle, who argued with somebody on his tactical radio.

Okay, I considered, *do I take out that guy right now or ...* Suddenly, I saw a swarming movement across the narrows, at my elevation, but on the central peninsula.

So, they sent two squads up the peninsula. Right at my Position One, and from the looks of it, two squads at the mouth of eastern gorge. That means two full squads went up the southern narrows, where they became woodland bacon.

It's a damn good thing I didn't pop that lead below me. The center two squads might have heard where the shot came from and spotted me.

Then I thought some more.

If those center squads continue for another hundred yards or so, they'll find my first hide, and discover my snail trail. That's not good. That means I'll have to keep circling them counter clock-wise, staying ahead of them, picking them off one by one, starting with their leads.

Time to get moving again, J.J.

*   *   *

Ten minutes later.

Okay, I'm now northeast of the two stalled eastern fire squads and the two center squads have found my first hide. Time to get to work.

I took another center mass shot from 257 yards out and dropped the argumentative lead of the eastern team right in the middle of his troops, who in a knee-jerk response all dived into the tall grass. Even the neighboring two squads on the central peninsula had hit the dirt.

Now what will they do? Down to two leads.

Time to book.

*   *   *

Around two o'clock in the afternoon, after I finished a trail bar, I descended from the tree line and placed myself on the eastern edge of the grassy, upland meadow, behind the stalled units. To my everlasting surprise, down the center of the peninsula the other two fire teams descended toward the leaderless troops at the entrance to the eastern narrows. The range finder declared 323 yards. I reached out, and scored a center mass hit on one of the descending team leads.

And then there was only one.

I don't know why, but this latest kill freaked out several of the troops who had been sitting on their duffs in front of the eastern narrows. Perhaps they felt exposed? But for whatever reason several of them jumped up and began running into the gorge, trying to escape. Initially four of them did so, but soon three more joined them. About half way in, their world

exploded in metal ball bearings and stone shrapnel.
Time to move again.

* * *

About thirty minutes later, I humped my butt again upslope and got near the constricted entrance of the grassy, upland meadow. The smoke from the latest series of explosions had cleared. But by my count, confirmed through the rangefinder, that left one lead and thirteen soldiers.

With the sun now over my right shoulder and the CMES soldiers to my east, I fired on a trooper, my first, and made a center mass hit. My quick second round nailed another.

Time to move again.

* * *

I had to fire twice for the first time, and the CMES troops now looked straight at me, but into the afternoon sun. I backtracked toward them, expecting them to belly crawl in my direction.

I needed two things: elevation and an opportunity to hit them again from their flank. Setting up a good ten yards within the tree line, I found that sweet spot. From this vantage point I could see eleven distinct trails in the scrub grass.

I waited to see if anyone would pop up his head to orient himself. And wouldn't you know it, one did. I fired a hair low and into the honey-wheat grass. I hit him, spooking the rest, who got up and starting running toward where I used to be, all the while firing their AK-47s in disciplined bursts into the tree line.

Methodically, I dropped eight of them in succession, but two of them got away clean. Where to, I hadn't a clue. I must have been busy.

That left the final lead, who I now suspected probably had a bead on me after that extended fusillade. In response, I began backing up deeper and upslope into the pine forest. I stopped, sat down behind a fallen trunk, narrowed my eyes, focused my senses, and took in my surroundings.

Suddenly the forest became far too quiet—no birds, squirrels, chipmunks, or insects. I heard a crunch; a sole on gravel. I concentrated some more, and this time I caught a brush of clothing against something.

Until that moment I had remained still, but I had to raise my rifle to get my scope on target. Moving like a sloth in the noon day sun, I spotted him about seventy yards to my right and down slope.

This guy moved well and stayed low, that is until I put a round into the side of his head. Being in the trees, my rifle's report disbursed further, but still I didn't move. Some instinct prevented me from doing so. Then I heard it, or rather, them, to my left. I couldn't believe it, but the lead had sacrificed himself so these two could get the drop on me. What balls!

What happened next wasn't pretty. The pine log in front of me exploded under a ferocious hail of close range AK-47 rounds. I ditched my rifle, drew my 9mm, rolled away from my position, and in the process double-tapped one of the charging soldiers in the face. His head exploded like a pumpkin; 147 grain hollow points do that. I couldn't see the last trooper, down slope to my right, but I could hear him moving toward me through the pine straw.

I scrambled, found a pine for cover, and held my breath.

Now where did he go?

Less than twenty feet away he rose up and opened fire, but he only had two rounds left in his magazine. The first tore up the tree that I was leaning against, while the second hit me in my right bicep. Fortunately, I'm a lefty and four nine mills fired to his chest dropped him like a stone.

Now bleeding like a stuck pig, I slumped against my tree trunk, tore at my sleeve, and doused both the entry and exit wounds with clotting powder. I made sure to wrap up everything nice and snug, and gulped down some Tylenol along with half my canteen.

The post-engagement shock hit me hard as I leaned there. The first thing that came to mind was my concern for Mel, who would be pissed off for sure. Then, I felt a heaviness fall over me, my eyes fluttered, and I passed out.

* * *

Professor Melaina Makris had finished her late morning lecture on ancient Egyptian magic when her right upper arm seemed to explode with blood. Staggering at the impact, several of her students screamed at the awful sight.

Gripping her arm with her left hand, she fought to stand and gritted out, "Damn it, J.J.! Look what you've done now!"

Then, surrounded by hovering and confused students, she barked, "Will you stop videoing me and just call a damn ambulance!"

*   *   *

About thirty minutes later I woke up stiffer than a Billy goat, but alive. The squawk of a field radio had woke me up. Now alert to a possible threat, I checked my handgun, saw that its slide had jammed open, empty of ammunition. As I reloaded, I heard the radio again.

The sound came from down slope, where I'd popped the CMES squad leader. I picked up my rifle and staggered down to the fallen lead and frisked him. He didn't carry anything of note, but I did find his noisy tactical radio. Again, I heard his dispatcher frantically calling for anyone to respond.

"This is Central. Respond, any group leaders."

So I did.

"Group Leader Six to Central. Over."

Pause.

"Who the fuck is this?"

"Your worst nightmare."

Some lines, from some movies, just have to be repeated.

CHAPTER 19
What to Do?

"Your worst nightmare."

With that reply, the CMES Security and Communications manager in Manhattan killed the transmission's feed, shook his head, and swore under his breath as his superior stood over him.

"Ms. Rollins, we have lost the entire security detachment sent into the New Mexican mountains."

"I find that rather hard to believe, Mr. Green."

"I am very sorry, ma'am, but we just did." Green replied.

"How do you know that for a fact?"

"On Paulson's radio, our last surviving lead, a new and unfamiliar voice answered my call. My money says that was Stone on the other end."

"Stone?"

"'Your worst nightmare,' ma'am. His words."

Rollins, while she didn't show it, felt her stomach clench at the thought of losing thirty-six good men. Reliable troops didn't grow on trees.

But as for Stone, Rollins now feared the man, and understood why her regional director had granted her such latitude. She now sensed a tightness in her chest, an elevation in heart rate. The Iraq War hadn't killed him, Chairman Presto's many hired henchmen hadn't either.

What or who could? She wondered.

*   *   *

While Stone extricated himself from the Santa Fe National Forest, TIIIS IT and Security went into overdrive. President Smithers had alerted them to the CMES presence in the National Forest and had told them what Stone suspected. TIIIS managed to isolate the CMES encrypted tactical signal. While they couldn't decipher it, they did locate its origin as somewhere in Manhattan. This information they sent to the president, who dispatched equipment to the area. Purpose: locate the CMES transmission source.

Disguised as a ubiquitous East Coast doughnut delivery truck, the TIIIS communications van began its meandering up and down the main streets of Midtown Manhattan. One long transmission got them to Fifth Avenue. The next, to one particular side of that thoroughfare, where they singled out a prominent building kitty-corner from St. Patrick's Cathedral—the CMES regional headquarters building.

*   *   *

"President Smithers, the source of the encrypted transmission came from the CMES North American headquarters in Manhattan."

Pleased it took his people less than four hours to locate the transmission's source, he said so.

"This is wonderful news. Great work, all of you. Congratulate everyone on the team," the president beamed into the receiver. "Now, get everyone on the ground out of there and back to safety."

"Yes, sir. Will do."

Hanging up his phone, the president now contemplated how best to deal with this development.

Stone no doubt will want be a part of it.

CHAPTER 20
Ramp Up

I hiked out of the Santa Fe National Forest and reached my truck by five that evening. A sleeping park forest ranger waited for me in his Yukon. Further down the lot sat an empty tourist bus with a sleeping driver, who no doubt waited for the return of his thirty-seven passengers. As for John Running Deer, I had called him up to let him know that I was on my way back. At my truck, I loaded up and drove away. Throughout, the forest ranger kept on snoring.

I met Running Deer at our favorite diner in town, the one on Cerrillos Road. I looked like any other beat hunter with sweat-streaked camo paint on his face and a packet of topo maps under one arm. I had re-bandaged the other in the parking lot and put on a fresh shirt. While it hurt like a bitch, I didn't wish to advertise that I had been wounded.

Both Running Deer and Governor Silver Moon greeted me like two excited kids at Christmas. Running Deer, however, noticed it immediately.

"J.J., you're wounded. Why didn't you tell us?"

"It's a simple flesh wound," I said. "Right now, I've other priorities. I'm starved."

We sat in a booth in an empty section and the governor somehow managed to beat her colleague to the punch. "So how'd it go?"

"I'm beat. Killing good men takes the stuffing out of you."

"Is there any evidence out there that needs cleaning up?" Running Deer wanted to know.

"Plenty. Thirty-seven bodies and their weapons. Some I suspect will not last the night due to predators. In a week, most of the organic evidence should be gone."

"Why do you say that?" the governor probed.

"Because when I left, murders of black crows and several wakes of turkey buzzards had already begun their grisly work. However, their weapons will have to be cleared, there's no question about that. You got folks who can do a quick sweep?"

"Yes, we do," said the governor, "just show us where on your map, and we'll do the rest."

I did my best indicating where all the carnage and mayhem had taken place.

"Damn," Running Deer commented, "you did get around, didn't you."

"Yeah. Like I said, 'I'm beat.'"

"Well, I have some good news for you." Governor Silver Moon smiled.

"What's that?"

"President Smithers dispatched the company jet to take you back to the Academy. It seems that our friends in Midtown Manhattan had a hand in all of this."

"Okay. When do I leave?"

"Ten tonight."

I groaned as I rubbed my face with both of my hands, now thoroughly smearing my face paint.

"Do I have time for a couple cheeseburgers and a chocolate shake?" I said from behind my hands.

"Just barely, and you can even grab a shower at my place if you wolf them down." Running Deer offered.

Showered, with a fresh bandage, and my hair still damp, I boarded the TIIIS company jet and crashed. I woke up when the cabin attendant shook my good shoulder. Glancing out the window, I saw that the beautiful flat black jet was already parked in its private hanger at the Pittsburg International Airport.

"Welcome to Pittsburg, Mr. Stone," the attendant said.

Sore and full of aches, I rolled and levered my frame up one-handed off of the reclined, wide leather passenger seat.

I need to work out more than just running three-milers.

I struggled down the narrow stairs of the plane with my gear and staggered over to the waiting black sedan. Getting in, I noted the darkness outside.

Disoriented, I asked the driver. "What time is it?"

"Four forty-six, Mr. Stone."

"How long will that take to get to the Academy?"

"Oh, about an hour and thirty minutes, sir."

"Wake me when we get there."

*   *   *

That day I attended several tactical operations meetings which theoretically discussed how to assault the CMES Manhattan headquarters building. During these sessions, the lead ops officer held an in-depth discussion of the structure's layout and construction, elevators, emergency stairwells, and potential magical defenses. His best guess estimated that the security staff of the CMES HQ numbered close to one hundred strong, maybe more. As to their composition, that remained a total unknown.

We expected to encounter layered, defensive countermeasures. What kind we didn't have a clue.

That meant that all forms of offensive spell casting had to be put on the shelf for two good reasons. Why magnify the effectiveness of a defensive spell and at the same time leave your paranormal signature? As a result, any assault had to be old school.

During the operations' discussion, I found out that I had been tasked in the assault plan to be the brute force tool, a battering ram in medieval terms, and all because of my perceived divine invincibility. Boy, did I like that idea.

But here's the best part. The head of TIIIS Operations characterized this all-out assault "as an extermination of an infestation." That is, until I opened my mouth.

"Ah, excuse me. I see no provision for the taking of prisoners, or for the care of wounded. Or, did I somehow miss that part?"

The head of TIIIS Operations, a burly man in a tight military haircut, named Johannsen, stared at me before he answered.

"Mr. Stone, you did not miss anything. There are no such provisions," he said with an odd accent.

"So, not only are we breaking a ton of state and federal laws if we assault that building, but also the Geneva Convention, the Ten Commandments, and our own God-given notions of right and wrong.

"Don't misunderstand me, sir, I just got back from my own personal massacre. But that action took place against a trained CMES security team. This action is against, for the most part, unarmed civilians. So, how do you sleep at night?"

An eat shit or die stare-off began and after several moments Johannsen broke it. "Does the vaunted Lictor of Magic wish to pull out from participating in this exercise?"

"No, 'the vaunted Lictor of Magic' does not wish to participate in the needless slaughter of innocents, even if they are card-carrying members of CMES.

"My suggestion would be that we gas the entire building, how, I don't know, incapacitate those still moving, capture the regional director, and ransack their HR files and computers. With the regional director in hand, we squeeze him like a prune, and when we are finished with him, we release him."

Johannsen's forced and sarcastic laughter lasted five seconds too long, and I decked him with one blow. I cold-cocked the blond-haired giant on his right temple and sent him crashing to the floor. Looking around the stunned briefing room, I asked them. "Since when do we operate like CMES? Can any of you tell me?"

As Johannsen regained his feet, muttering loudly about a sucker punch, I decked him again. This time he stayed down.

Pointing to the unconscious man on the floor, I stated for the record in my very best Marine command voice.

"Now listen up, and listen good. TIIIS always takes prisoners. Always cares for the wounded. And I don't give a shit whose side they're on. We don't indiscriminately harm civilians. We indiscriminately destroy demons. *Do I make myself clear?*"

I got five quick nods out of the ten in attendance.

"You five"—I pointed those who had not agreed— "you're outta here. *Move!*" And, to their credit, they did. "And while you're at it, take this godless piece of crap with you. He's stinking up my briefing room."

Now, with the room fifty percent roomier, I continued, "Gentlemen. We are not CMES. We would like to enjoy their freedom of action, but we're far better than that. We, as sapient beings, can do better.

"With that in mind, I want to buy us some time before CMES lashes back. So, whatever assault we come up with, we must do it stealthily, cleverly, with a minimum of magic, and a minimum of human loss. Now, that said, I am open to any and all ideas."

*   *   *

Johannsen, ever the good egg, along with his five cronies, Skyped President Smithers. Physically and psychologically bruised, the operations lead questioned Stone's commitment to TIIIS, and railed about his lack of courage and stomach for a fight. To all of this, the president listened.

Before Johannsen started in on his second wind, President Smithers asked a simple question, "Mr. Johannsen, are you aware Mr. Stone just got back from single-handedly killing, thirty-six crack CMES security soldiers who had been sent to assassinate him? Did you know that he is wounded?"

The pause on the line told the president of TIIIS all that he needed to know. Despite the trans-Atlantic distance, the president had been monitoring Johannsen's emotions and thought-processes. He was truly a bad egg.

"Mr. Johannsen. I want your resignation in my inbox within the hour. You are dismissed."

And the connection ended.

*   *   *

While Johannsen's conversation with President Smithers took place, Stone, along with the five motivated operations officers, had roughed out a feasible, and humane, assault plan. Was it perfect? Heck no. The plan resembled a roulette wheel with a series of probable scenarios, each with two or three countermeasures or options. After an hour of brainstorming, all agreed with it, which meant that half the battle had already been won. But would the president approve of such an audacious scheme?

CHAPTER 21
Insane Rage

The harsh news about the thirty-six CMES security agents lost in the Santa Fe mountains caused the Dark One to blink in disbelief. Thirty-six lost, and the lone survivor of that engagement, Stone, even heckled the panicked operations dispatcher.

Thirty-six!

He called his secretary. "Get Rollins in here," he choked out tersely, while he struggled to contain his building rage.

Moments later he heard from his secretary, "Rollins is en route, Mr. Alexander. Elevator One."

The Dark One surveyed his lavishly appointed office and noted that it would shortly be in need of renovation.

Rollins knocked and bravely entered the square, one thousand square-foot executive office. She saw the regional director, who stood with his back to her, looking out one of the massive windows that were the wall along one half of his office. An ornately carved desk separated them.

"Rollins," the Dark One began. "I can tolerate failure by my staff, to a point. But to send thirty-six of our best, and lose them all … well, that is unacceptable."

Then the man murmured into the glass before him, fogging it with his breath.

Before Rollins could blink, she was pinned on the luxuriant carpeting, held firmly in place by a horror. What she had mistaken for an ornately carved office desk, was in fact a huge Komodo dragon with brightly colored scales and disgusting breath. She knew this detail, because its long forked tongue licked at her face, its nostrils flaring, eyes wide with intent.

Turning around, the Dark One walked to his office door and announced, "As I said, I can tolerate failure, but more to the point, and as you might have guessed, you have exceeded it."

He closed the door behind him, muffling the screams of a human being slowly eaten alive.

*   *   *

"Franklin. You have just been promoted to replace Rollins," the Dark One said into the receiver of his personal secretary's phone. "I want a plan to find and kill Stone on my desk in four hours. Don't disappoint me."

*   *   *

"Mr. Alexander," Gene Franklin said, "I propose we make a statement and punish TIIIS on multiple fronts, on the same day, at the same time. That way, they can't react. When it is all over, we will inform our Gathering and allied members that this is what we do when we are attacked. TIIIS, on the other hand, will be forced into a corner, either to accept continued punishment or deploy its Lictor of Magic."

"Interesting approach, Franklin. Execute it." The Dark One smiled.

There is a ruthless edge to this one. He recognizes the equation of applied violence and how to use it for propaganda. He has promise.

*   *   *

The Dark One was not universally reviled nor feared. In fact, there was one who had nurtured this twisted soul for quite some time; metaphorically had whispered into his ear at salient moments, occasionally even warning him of things to come.

Ever since the Great Healing of the realms by the prescient actions of the First Soul, the Devourer of Souls, that thing, the demon that ruled the Dark Realm, had been marginalized. Its dreams of invading the Mortal Realm had been dashed to pieces.

Isolated the demon went back to the old ways, those tried and true, of communing with dark sensitives who were blind to its agenda, and doubly-blind to the inherent dangers of such congress. The honeyed lies were proverbial—the promise of great wealth, power, influence, and virility.

Without question, the Devourer of Souls hated the First Soul for denying its dreams; detested the First Soul for destroying many of its wayward children. But most of all, cringed as the First Soul initiated the slow process of bringing balance to the realms after the eight hundred years of evil's domination of the Mortal Realm.

The Devourer had used the Dark One before as a valuable tool. It would use him again to destroy Stone, and therefore the First Soul. Locked as it was within its realm, the Devourer needed such a valuable surrogate to do its bidding, to exact its ultimate revenge.

CHAPTER 22
William's Hall

It was a Wednesday. The time, 11 am, EDT.

Professor Peter Glass hovered over that semester's departmental budget spreadsheet, yet again. Departmental Heads have to do this on an all too regular basis. As usual, his office door was open, which was his style, as he preferred his departmental colleagues act accordingly. After all, enrollment in Near Eastern Languages could never compete with that of Computer Sciences, but by exhibiting an atmosphere of openness, Glass saw it as an attractive start. Today, for some reason, the department was as quiet as a tomb.

Nonetheless, CMES had plans for Glass, purely on the basis of his association with a former student, the man named Stone.

Ever since President Smithers had declared that a heightened state of war existed with CMES, TIIIS' IT and Security responsibilities had been stretched to the limit. Security personnel were shuffled around constantly to places perceived to be under threat. There were just not enough personnel to cover all the bases, and not all of TIIIS' security personnel were capable of perceiving auras. While some might be skilled in listening to their sixth sense, the ability to confirm that feeling by seeing an aura was crucial. Mr. Henry, a Fourth Level Adept, possessed this talent in spades.

To help alleviate this situation, Mr. Henry returned to Philadelphia and his janitorial position at the university. This ensured that Glass and his family had a 24/7 guard nearby.

The CMES raid on Williams' Hall, where Glass' department resided, was a simple blunt force strategy, designed to shock, cripple, and make headlines. The only tactical problem was that the professor's department was on the eighth floor. That meant the two goons who were suited up as suicide bombers had to make a choice: take the central bank of three elevators or the stairs? They chose the stairs.

* * *

That Wednesday morning, Mr. Henry was out-of-sorts. Not ill, just unusually cranky, and he couldn't put his finger on why.

What the hell is bugging me? The Fourth Level Adept pondered as he put an orange cone at the top of the fifth floor's stairwell which he just mopped. Then, the hair on the back of his neck tingled. He sensed it— no them!

They're coming up the stairs. I can hear their shuffling footsteps.

Without a thought, Mr. Henry retrieved his faithful .45 caliber 1911 automatic from his mobile work cart in the hallway. With speed born of long military experience, he slapped in a magazine of hollow points, and ratcheted the weapon's slide. Peeking around the corner into in the stairwell, he waited.

These guys even smell bad. Which can only mean one, damn, thing.

Final confirmation of Mr. Henry's worse possible fears clicked into place when the first goon made its slogging uphill turn into view. While appearing human, its aura was all wrong, pitch black. These unfortunates represented CMES' newest class of mercenary weapon—demon-possessed athletes called goons. Not zombies, but something else altogether, these were flesh and blood constructs that can pass on the street, but who are infected with a specific classification of violent and blood-thirsty demon. The logic behind them included manageability and absolute loyalty to their fully human commanders. Besides, why pay trained human mercenaries, when a disposable goon could provide the same result?

When it looked up, Mr. Henry double-tapped the goon square between the eyes and more than just organic matter sprayed out from the back of the possessed man's head, ugly black ectoplasm did as well, which began disintegrating as it flew in the air. Further confirmation that they weren't entirely human.

Seeing the mess, Mr. Henry cringed.

I just cleaned those walls.

The roar of the twin .45 caliber discharges filled the stairwell and caused the second bomber to stop, look down numbly, and detonate its bomb vest.

Fortunately for Mr. Henry and Peter Glass, the blast was contained within the emergency stairwell, which isolated damage to the structure and claimed no innocent lives.

Mr. Henry was rushed to the university hospital unconscious, battered, and bleeding from his nose and ears from the bomb's concussion. Peter Glass, unharmed, was whisked away by TIIIS' IT and Security Department, along with his family, to an undisclosed, secure location.

CHAPTER 23
Old Oaks Academy

That same Wednesday, at 11 am EDT, CMES struck again.

A yellow school bus pulled over and stopped with its emergency flashers on. The deserted, two-lane road cut through the middle of a grand oak forest. Thirty-six men filed out wearing camouflaged hunting gear and carrying heavy duffle bags. They grouped themselves into squads of six, looked, crossed the two-lane road, and disappeared into the adjacent tree line.

Once deep in the forest, the six squads emptied their duffle bags, revealing cut-down AR-15 assault rifles, ammunition, grenades, and webbed vests on which to carry them. Once settled in, the squads fanned out into a skirmish line and began their advance in a northerly direction.

Their goal, about a half mile away, was a small college campus called Old Oaks Academy. Their orders were straightforward: kill and destroy as much as they could. Only the fully human squad leaders concerned themselves with the exfiltration strategy, as their demon-possessed goons, euphemistically referred to as "mixed troops," were considered expendable. And did they ever stink.

The dense, old growth canopy made for easy progress through its sparse undergrowth. After about a quarter of a mile, the forest became unnaturally silent. Several heartbeats later, it came alive. The troops suddenly found themselves immobilized, bound with roots and prickly berry bush vines. Undisciplined rifle fire rang out—four goons and a squad leader succumbed to friendly fire. The other five squad leaders suffered severe, painful, and bloody scratches to their exposed skin.

The goons all died horribly; in some cases eviscerated by tiny chipmunk-like animals which burrowed into their bodies, killing them from within. After five minutes, all was still except for the whimpering of the bound humans.

The repeated fusillades had been heard from the campus, which dispatched their IT and Security team to find out what all the ruckus was about. What they found resembled a medieval battlefield of blood and gore. They released and cuffed the root-bound humans, who babbled on insanely about being attacked by killer chipmunks.

"What a fucking mess," one member of TIIIS Security said. "And the smell of these bodies is unbelievable."

"Okay everybody," said the TIIIS Security commander, "zip it, and bag what you can find. You know the drill. We have to clear this forest before any civvies show up. Parker, Smith, and Ruben, police the area for weapons. I want this forest pristine. Now get moving!"

An hour later, the forest had been largely returned to its former bucolic state.

"Now what do we do with these five?" the commander asked the Academy's Dean, Professor Humble.

"Clean them up, feed them, and put them in the brig. This is a real first for us. I'm going to have to call the mucky-mucks for further instructions.

"By the way, good job, Mr. Hicks. Be sure to tell your people that they did a fine job today."

"Thank you, professor, but it's the *Argenti* who saved the day. They savaged that force. Never seen anything like it before. By the time we showed up, it was a straightforward mop up job."

CHAPTER 24
Falls Church

Three weeks prior to all the Wednesday morning chaos and mayhem unleashed by CMES upon TIIIS' assets, while Rollins was still in charge of the Communications and Security Department of North America, an oddly timed interview took place.

Rollins had acquired some valuable intelligence because of an extraordinary windfall. A disgruntled employee named Gunter Johannsen, purportedly TIIIS' former operations commander, had walked into the front lobby of CMES' Manhattan HQ asking for her.

Twenty minutes later and after a thorough strip search which the subject cooperated with, Johannsen was seated opposite Rollins.

"What can I do for you Mr., ah, Johannsen?" The head of CMES North America's Communications and Security opened as she leaned forward in her office chair.

"Ma'am. I am the former operations commander of TIIIS out of Falls Church, Virginia and I am seeking employment within your organization."

Falls Church, Virginia. Interesting. Until this moment, that location was an unsubstantiated rumor.

"I have extensive experience and credentials in military operations and security. And, I have information that I suspect you and your organization would like to possess."

Direct and to the point. How refreshing.

"What will this cost me, Mr. Johannsen?"

Rollins saw the man double-clutch at the question.

His eyes wandered about. "Ms. Rollins, ma'am, I am only looking for employment. This discussion is not meant to be, nor should be seen as, a shake down."

Now it was Rollins' turn to metaphorically swallow hard and gasp as she found herself squinting at the South African in complete disbelief.

"Understood. You're *just* looking for employment within the CMES community. But, Mr. Johannsen, you must understand, I need to know why, or perhaps better stated, what caused your change of heart?"

"Ma'am, it's quite simple, this is one of those instances where I was employed far too long by one employer. Things, over the course of time, got stale. Now, I am seeking new challenges and opportunities to develop myself."

Now that was a well-rehearsed speech, the head of CMES' North American Communications and Security thought.

"Fair enough, I am willing to believe you. And on that basis I am even willing to take you on. However, you must understand that you will not begin in a position of authority. That, sir, you first must earn."

"I'm good with that, ma'am."

"Excellent, but before I whisk you off to Personnel for all the usual paperwork, I do have some questions."

Johannsen nodded for her to proceed.

Raising her arms wide, Rollins began. "What do you know about Jonathan Joseph Stone?"

The very mention of Stone elicited a pale stare.

"President Smithers appointed him as our a new Lictor of Magic. He's ex-military, a decorated veteran, and he's insane."

"Well, that's quite a statement."

Johannsen began to fidget with his bitten nails.

"Mr. Johannsen, I take it that you don't get along with Stone."

Stubborn silence.

"Mr. Johannsen, I expect an answer to my questions."

"Ma'am, to be frank, I don't know the man, except that Stone was unwilling to indiscriminately shoot first and ask questions later."

"So, am I to understand that you and Stone hold different philosophies regarding the execution of operational objectives?"

"Yes, ma'am."

"I see."

Pause.

"Thank you. You have been most helpful, and welcome to the team."

"Thank you, ma'am. You won't regret it."

Rollins didn't shake the man's hand. Instead, as her office door closed, another opened.

"Well, Mr. Franklin, what did you make of that?"

"Very interesting, ma'am."

"How so?"

"He has a formidable reputation as a field commander, which we can always use."

"What about his reliability?"

"That issue and, more importantly, his loyalty, can be solved by giving him what he wants, command of a team. Right now he's mad at TIIIS, and more specifically, Stone. I say, turn him loose on those he hates."

"Interesting analysis, Mr. Franklin. Johannsen is now your project. Watch him. One false move, eliminate him. Always remember, once someone betrays a master, the second time is far easier."

*   *   *

"Mr. Johannsen," said Gene Franklin, the newly promoted North American CMES Operations Director, "It's time to earn your spurs. I'm putting you in charge of an assault detachment of twenty-four mixed-troops."

At the announcement, Franklin, a well-built man with a no nonsense demeanor, and under the gun to produce, could see that the former commander of TIIIS U.S. Regional Operations, Gunter Johannsen, stood a bit straighter, taller.

"Thank you, sir. Thank you very much for the opportunity. What, sir, do you have in mind?"

"The total destruction of the TIIIS Falls Church facility. Now don't disappoint me." Franklin said with steel in his voice.

Once Johannsen was out of earshot, Franklin turned to his second in command, "Peters. Keep an eye on him. If you suspect anything fishy, odd, or suspicious, you are weapons free. Got that, mister?"

"Yes, sir. Absolutely, sir."

"I despise traitors." Franklin said with a wrinkled lip.

*   *   *

The City of Falls Church, of Fairfax County, Virginia, resides near enough to the Federal capital to be considered part of its embracing sphere. Within this quaint town first settled by the Algonquin Nation, TIIIS owns, on West Broad Street, an unremarkable poured concrete and aluminum stilt structure of seven-stories. Its conglomerate central paneled façade is reminiscent of any insurance company's building from the 1960s.

Within this ho-hum looking building resided the main IT and Security Department of TIIIS' U.S. Region along with a robust technical development laboratory, which required its own security detachment. Similar regional facilities existed at the Old Oaks Academy in Pennsylvania, the Chicago suburbs, and in Livermore, California. The reason that CMES targeted this one was simple: its proximity to the U.S. Capital.

The building's non-script appearance aided its security profile, reducing it to practically zero. Although, if one was observant, an angled peek through any of its windows revealed a laminated sandwich of three layers. Everything else was hidden, just like the structure's three subbasements, a feature that only four on-site personnel had access to.

*   *   *

It was Wednesday, and the time, 11 am EDT.

"Men," Johannsen began with a shiver of revulsion about his mixed-troops, "we have been tasked to lead an assault on TIIIS' Falls Church facility. We are to, in the words of the Director of Communications and Security, Mr. Franklin, 'destroy it and its inhabitants.' This we will do."

Drooling grunts of approval and dilated eyes filled with the anticipation of wholesale destruction stared back at him. Just being in close quarters with these, *smelly things*, made the turn-coat TIIIS ops commander want to gag.

"We will arrive in four paneled vans, one for each squad—red, blue, green, and yellow, just like the colored insignia on your left shoulders." Sure enough, all rechecked their left shoulders.

"We will start our assault at eleven this morning. With luck, we will annihilate this nest while it's still full of targets."

Now the grunts of anticipation became outright frightening.

"That is all. Now, clean and inspect your weapons, rest, hydrate, and prepare yourself for victory."

The sounds now were, well, inhuman.

*　　*　　*

The next day Johannsen drove the lead van with the windows wide open in an attempt to clear the air. With him were seven mixed troops, all wearing black-hoods and black one-piece uniforms. Two were burdened with a .50 caliber air-cooled machine gun, its tripod, and ammunition. Two carried RPG rocket launcher tubes. The rest were armed with grenades and AR-15 assault rifles.

Johannsen's infiltration plan was sheer brute force. Given their target's spacious parking, his troopers were to dismount, set up the .50 cals, and launch all the RPGs. Thereafter, they would wade in to clean up whatever might remain. On the other hand, the South African's exfiltration plan was far sketchier. Whatever troopers could walk, he would drive back to their rally point. Any wounded, he would cancel on the spot.

The drive from the rally point to the target was a three-minute drive with no traffic lights or stop signs, but several turns. As best as Johannsen could see from his mirrors, his line of chicks managed this hurdle. The four vans stopped on the street, one behind the other, in front of their target. They dismounted and eagerly got into position. While this was happening, several bystanders gaped in total disbelief at what they saw.

Johannsen waited several heartbeats while everyone settled into position behind their weapons. He fired his AR-15, which was the signal for the four .50 cals and RPGs to let loose.

The deafening din that erupted in this tiny town of thirteen thousand souls eclipsed imagination. Johannsen didn't have to direct any fire. The four machine guns raked the seven floors of glass, but oddly with little affect. The hot, spent brass grew into small mounds. The rockets, however, caused telling damage as one corner of the structure threatened to collapse.

After two minutes, the actual assault began with Johannsen running into the ruined entranceway with his mixed troops howling in inhuman glee at what they had just done. The South African knew where he was going. Nonetheless, he couldn't help but marvel at all the punishment that the laminated glass had withstood.

Since Johannsen judged the ground floor wasted, he split his troopers into two teams: red and green up one set of emergency exit stairs, yellow and blue up the other. The latter he followed. Johannsen was unaware of the existence of the facility's subbasements.

Savage fire fights broke out on the upper floors. Johannsen could tell, by the sound of their AR-15 reports alone, that his mixed troops were advancing.

Johannsen, however, broke off from the carnage to pay a visit to the IT Design Studio. Knowing where he was going was his distinct advantage, but not for his former co-workers which he mowed down with an efficiency that surprised even him.

"Just what the fuck are you doing, Johannsen?" one had screamed from the top of her lungs before a quick three-round burst silenced her.

Advancing over the fallen form, Johannsen began rummaging through the design studio, examining this and that on the lab benches, all the while trying to find items worthy of plunder.

Meanwhile, in the back of the CMES commander's mind a little voice was screaming at him.

Johannsen!

Listen!

It's all gone quiet.

And that was the last thing that Johannsen's traitorous brain processed as he felt the thud of his body crashing to the floor, destroying his nose.

"You fucking, arrogant, South African bastard!" an emotional voice screamed, before its owner threw up all over the corpse.

"Not bad shooting, Andy!" another said. "We got 'em all."

As Andy Remington of the IT and Security Department wiped off his chin, "Thanks, Danny," the newly minted member of "the-god-I-didn't-sign-up-for-this-experience-team" said.

"Here I just get promoted and my facility gets wasted," while he gestured at the body before him.

"This mother fucker ratted on us. I remember the day he got shit-canned by President Smithers. It happened right here in this very building.

"Well, at least we now know how hard those goons are to put down," Danny said.

CHAPTER 25
London & After

It was 4:30 pm GMT, a Thursday.

President Smithers sat stunned at his London desk with a mixture of helplessness and rage coursing through his blood. He had intellectually known that this time would come, but he had emotionally dreaded its arrival. But the reality of the multiple attacks, their lawless ferocity and scale, had claimed six and wounded fourteen. The pulsing vein on his forehead told it all. Words like "heedless," "indiscriminate loss of life," and "brazenness," framed his thoughts.

Geoffrey, the man's personal assistant asked, "A penny for your thoughts, sir?"

A grimace, "Geoffrey, we have been a fine team for a long time. Am I getting too old for this chair?"

The question startled Geoffrey. "Sir?"

"Whenever we have dealt with CMES, the loss of life has been always kept at a minimum. Yet, these attacks by possessed mercenaries have all the earmarks of sheer, wonton mayhem. I do not know how to respond to such willfully inflicted carnage."

"If I might, sir. That is no longer your job." The assistant said in reference to Stone's current job as TIIIS' Lictor of Magic.

"No, that is not what I mean. We—TIIIS—have never done such a thing. It's not in our DNA."

"Well, sir, there was that one instance at the Council of Nicaea." Geoffrey reminded.

Sourly, "Yes, you're correct, but even that attempt at mass destruction was thwarted."

Silence. "But, sir, we are nonetheless at war. As sad as it may seem."

The phone rang.

"I'll take this, Geoffrey." The president said.

"Smithers here."

After several minutes of listening.

"Are there any casualties?

"God be blessed!

"Yes, thank you again for calling."

A breathless Geoffrey sat expectantly and wide-eyed.

"That was the Academy. CMES attempted to raid the campus, but the *Argenti* got in their way. They captured five fully human squad leaders. The question now is, what to do with them?

He paused thoughtfully, "It seems, Geoffrey, that CMES is pissed."

"Sir, if I might, it seems that all of these targets have something to do with Stone. What about him?"

Silence.

"Sir, we must prepare for the next attack."

"I know, Geoffrey. But the question is where?"

*   *   *

That very afternoon two bomb-vested goons entered and blew up a modest fourth floor London office at 17 Sussex. Thus ended the long life of Peter Ignatius Edward Smithers, the President of TIIIS, and his life-long friend and assistant, Geoffrey Allen Bloom. Their sudden extinction caused all of TIIIS to take a deep breath.

CHAPTER 26
Insane Plans

The Dark One luxuriated in his freshly reappointed penthouse office that overlooked the panoramic view of his obsession: St. Patrick's Cathedral, a scant block away. So near, yet so far.

On his wall a new ornament hung, the crucified and eviscerated corpse of Franklin, his former head of Communications and Security. It was getting a bit ripe.

Oh well, probably should have it removed.

While the man had indeed made things interesting for a time, his Pyrrhic bravado failed to make Stone appear, much less die.

The Dark One's eyes returned to the cathedral.

I must possess it, he thought. *Every last block of stone.*

I must devise a plan to discredit the papists and bring them low with scandal and innuendo. I will put into motion a series of atrocities against those papists that will ruin that scum forever.

A hopeful thought emerged.

Maybe that coward Stone will finally show himself. Wouldn't that be grand.

That will be my plan, but I require some assistance.

Yes, yes, I see it all now. The result will be so delicious.

*   *   *

His chosen assistant in this venture was a familiar colleague, if you could call a voracious succubus such a thing. Conjured often from his compendium, *The Book of Spells*, the Dark One called out a favorite thumb-worn spell, precisely outlined its terms, and pronounced its words with care. Not to do so could prove calamitous.

The strengths and needs of this particular she-demon the Dark One knew well, as also the rules by which it could be controlled. Just by the formulation and vocabulary of the spell, the Dark One identified the origin of this one as ancient Egyptian, a probable creation of the Sekhmet cult—the once would be destroyer of mankind. But before he did so, he needed to find a host, young, attractive, and with long dark hair—a preference of this nasty narcissistic entity.

He went for a ride in his black stretch limo, a Mercedes-Benz 600 Maybach, fitted out with blackened wire wheels. As the Dark One cruised a shady part of Manhattan, he took on the airs of a john on the make. The finding of an appropriate host didn't take long. After stunning the young woman with a crude immobility spell, he mouthed the conjuring and She-Who-Devours-Men's-Souls took possession of her. After several bodily jerks, once innocent brown eyes took on a dangerous, snake-like quality.

"Greetings, my dark one. Welcome to the twenty-first century. I hope that you find your mortal carrier to your liking."

After the she-demon took an inventory, it just hissed through a jagged smile.

"I'll take that as a 'yes.'"

"As to why I summoned you, there is a *priest* that I want you to *bedevil*. I will *instruct* you as to your *tasks*. But what you will *enjoy* is that you know of him, for this priest painfully *exorcised* you from a young Italian woman some years back."

The she-demon's eyes narrowed, and widened in positive recognition. It hoarsely said, "Tony."

"Yes, my dark one, that is indeed the one."

*   *   *

The she-demon's patent leather boots echoed *click-clack* in a crisp staccato across the sacrosanct limestone paving of the cathedral's central aisle. The one-piece, black patent leather body suit accentuated a taut and gyrating hour-glass body set on stun. In its swinging right hand, it grasped a mewing black cat by the scruff of its neck. In its left the she-demon brandished a grotesquely large, flat black knife. A drunken Roman centurion could have easily mistaken it for a *gladius*.

*   *   *

Cardinal Anthony Giuseppe Garibaldi of the Archdiocese of New York knew he wore the target of a marked man. After all, in a city where everything could be negotiated, he refused to be influenced. The cardinal, who led an exemplary religious life, liked to haunt the cathedral's soup kitchen as a common server, listening, welcoming, blessing, but mostly listening to keep in tune with the streets.

A measured and contemplative man, he knew what pure evil looked like when he saw it. And the thing before him, a young woman, possessed an aura like a wriggling mass of slippery black snakes. Its disrespectful presence, brazenly displayed in his cathedral, made the cardinal's blood boil.

Right in the middle of the Tuesday night Novena, dedicated to the loss of several much-loved parishioners, in walked this *thing*. Decked out head to toe in tight and shiny patent leather, this Catwoman wannabe with long black hair theatrically slit open the helpless cat's throat before his gasping congregation. It rubbed the screaming, struggling, and bleeding feline all over itself in an exaggerated, lascivious fashion. When the poor creature expired, the she-demon threw its carcass into his sanctuary, where it dramatically slid to a stop against the first step of the high altar. The ultimate non-verbal, anti-institutional challenge—a veritable casting forth of a gauntlet.

"This pussy is for you, cardinal!"

The she-demon bellowed.

"Take it.

"And when you're finished with *it*,

"You can have mine, too—again!"

The she-demon screamed at the top of its throaty lungs, timing its raucous rant in such a way that its echoes, bouncing off of the four-story gothic ceiling, wouldn't step on one another. The parishioners present gaped in utter disbelief.

"You know, Tony,

"You're hung like a horse.

"Wanna ride me—again?

"Next time I stop by, Tony,

"I'll bring in our baby boy for you to bless."

The parishioners gasped at the shocking revelation.

Now grinning at its stunning performance, the she-demon turned, a perfect runway pivot, and strutted in its high-heeled boots toward the nave's main exit, all the while flaunting every alluring advantage.

*　　　*　　　*

The cathedral's security personnel apprehended the young woman before she made it to the cathedral's massive bronze doors. Thereafter, her escort, a pair of New York's finest, took her to the nearby 17th Precinct station. There the intake officer booked her on criminal trespass, drunk and disorderly, and for good measure, the torture of an animal. The officer, when he heard the full story what the young woman had done and where, wished he that had more statutes at his disposal with more teeth. Three hours later, she was sprung from lockup, courtesy of a lawyer from a prominent local firm with a wad of crisp new bills. A good thing, too, because the three women in the holding cell with the suspect had all been beaten unconscious.

*　　　*　　　*

The Dark One deemed the opening move of the grand plan a total success. The she-demon's well-choreographed performance had been captured by a paid media plant, who had been sitting among the parishioners. The video's superb quality had captured the entire scene, even down to the spurting cat's blood.

The next day, the tabloids splashed the cathedral incident above the fold, and the salacious rumor mill began its slow churn. One cable commentator, hungry for ratings because of sweep's week, decided to run with it, hard. She saw the story as a calculated risk-reward situation. Staid, traditional institution assaulted by edgy sex kitten with a kinky twist and the hint of illicit paternity.

"Be sure to tune in at seven for the latest update!" she purred into the camera's red eye.

So goes today's news cycle.

* * *

For Cardinal Garibaldi, this shocking incident reminded him of a certain village girl he had exorcised some twenty-four years earlier in provincial Tuscany. At the time he had been a new member of the Society of Saint Paul, devoted to special Vatican cases involving the rite of exorcism. There, he trained hard and studied harder under his mentor, the greatest exorcist of the time, Father Gabriele Amorth. At that time, Garibaldi studied from cover to cover a book, *De Exorcismis et Supplicationibus Quibusdam—Of Exorcisms and Certain Supplications,* the seventeenth century version.

CHAPTER 27
A New President

The two bomb-vested goons had been close to a half hour late in completing their dastardly deed all because of heavy London traffic. Nonetheless, the lives of two men, President Smithers and his assistant Bloom, had been snuffed out.

The sudden demise of these men paralyzed TIIIS. Betsy Silver Moon, the Regional Southwestern Governor of the U.S., understood the challenge that the event implied, when she composed her encrypted email.

Dear Colleagues:

The U.S. Region and our society's leadership have suffered multiple attacks.

Just thirteen minutes ago, President Smithers, his assistant Geoffrey Bloom, and several TIIIS security personnel, were assassinated in the London office by multiple bomb blasts.

That event followed the near simultaneous assaults and bomb detonations that took place at our Falls Church facility, the University of Philadelphia, and the Old Oaks Academy.

At this time a count of the fatalities and wounded is unavailable.

Be advised that I will not let this stand.

Expect another email within the hour announcing an emergency meeting of the Supreme Council. This will held via encrypted video teleconferencing for your convenience.

This meeting's agenda has only one item—the election of our next president. Come prepared.

*   *   *

Three hours later, Governor Silver Moon, via the aforementioned encrypted medium, called the Supreme Council to order. All thirty-one invitees were on the line—a rock solid quorum from which to proceed.

"Thank you for attending on such short notice. I am Betsy Silver Moon, the Regional Southwestern Governor of the U.S. Region. I am now accepting nominations for the president of our organization."

After a brief passage of time, a voice was heard.

"This is Governor Kemal Kartal of Turkey. I wish to nominate myself."

"Do I hear a second?"

"Yes. I wish to second Governor Kartal's nomination. This is Param Singh, Sub-Governor of Northern India."

"Thank you, Sub-Governor Singh. Are there any other nominations?"

"Yes, Regional Governor Silver Moon. This is Sir James McElhinney. I wish to nominate, you, madam."

"Oh, I see. Do I hear a second?"

Silence.

"I second Sir James McElhinney's motion. This is the Governor of Mumbai, Jazim Patel."

"Thank you, Governor Patel. Are there any other nominations?"

After thirty seconds of silence, Silver Moon formerly closed the nomination process.

"Governor Kartal, do you wish to share with us why you seek the position of the President of TIIIS?"

What followed could only be described as a twenty minute justification for an immediate return to the traditional external policy of *status quo* regarding CMES, the outright condemnation of former President Smithers' policy that Kartal characterized as addled, aggressive adventurism, and an immediate recall and stand down of the current Lictor of Magic, in order to prevent any further and unnecessary loss of life.

Try as she might, Kartal's rant turned Silver Moon's stomach into acidic knots that grated on her ingrained sense of liberty and autonomy. She bridled at the condemnation of her old colleague and dear friend, President Smithers. Furthermore, she saw no reason to give CMES any quarter whatsoever. By the time the governor of Turkey concluded his points, for the second time, Silver Moon blood was on high boil.

"Thank you, Governor Kartal, for that clear enunciation of your position. I know that everyone on this telecast is most grateful.

"However, if I am elected by this council as the next president of this society, during this precarious moment in our history, I can promise each and every one of you that I will *not* follow, mirror, or entertain any of Governor Kartal's positions. In fact, I will proceed to do exactly the opposite, as I believe any show of weakness on our part would be tantamount to our society's dismemberment. And that, my dear colleagues, is where I stand.

"I thank you for the opportunity to express my position."

The governor paused to gather herself.

"Now, for the next few minutes, we must elect a new president for our society. I will mute our conference during this period. Select your choice at the bottom of your screens, or choose to abstain."

Six minutes later the final tally was complete. Of the thirty-one voters, three abstained. Silver Moon garnered twenty-six votes, Kartal the paltry remainder.

When the newly elected president of TIIIS reported the results, Kartal exploded and demanded a voice-vote. The Governor of Mumbai, Jazim Patel, intervened. "Kemal, you lost. Now is not the time for childish tantrums."

While Kartal simmered and sputtered, Silver Moon smoothly moved on.

"Dear colleagues, thank you for your vote of confidence. My first act as president is to appoint my successor, John Running Deer, as the new governor of the Southwestern Region of the U.S. He has my utmost confidence and will be a fine governor. My second act, will be to continue in the footsteps of Peter E. I. Smithers, a man whose shoes will be very hard to fill.

"For now, that is all that I have to say, because I need to appoint an assistant, post haste."

CHAPTER 28
Outside Muscle

Sex Kitten Begs NYC Cardinal
To Bless Their Child

(NYC) A skin-tight, patent-leather clad seductress interrupted an evening service at our city's cathedral to beg Cardinal Anthony Garibaldi to bless their love child.

Sacrificing a black cat before the congregation was not enough for this sashaying hottie, while she yelled out taunts of, "Wanna ride me—again?" while referring to Cardinal Garibaldi as, "Tony."

The best part—the entire proceeding was captured start to finish on video by a quick-thinking parishioner, which has since gone viral on the Internet.

(*The New York Daily Inquirer*, 1A)

Cardinal Garibaldi didn't believe in coincidences. Far too many details had been replicated—the words of sexual enticement, the demon's jet black aura with the swirling purple and red elements, the choice of mortal flesh, young, beautiful, and black haired. Garibaldi concluded someone had summoned the same demon from the dark pit, and that it walked again among mortal kind. But for what purpose? That he wanted to know. His religious flock depended upon him for their protection. Fortunately, he knew who to call and dialed the number from memory.

On the fourth ring, a deep male voice answered. "Good day. How may I be of service?"

"This is Number 1703. I wish to speak with 0606."

"Number 0606, sir, is no longer available. To whom do you wish to speak?"

"Your president," the confused cleric stated.

"One moment, please.

"Connecting."

By the sounds on the line, the cardinal suspected he had been routed to another line. Finally, he heard a domestic telephone ring on the other end.

"President Silver Moon," a female, all-business voice announced.

"This is Cardinal Anthony Garibaldi of the Archdiocese of New York City."

"Good day, Your Eminence, I must say I am not at all surprised that you called. What recently happened at your cathedral is quite unsettling."

After the briefest of pauses. "By the way, how are your parents?"

"My mother passed away three years ago. My father lives on, playing bridge and eating too many sausages."

"Your Eminence, I am sorry about your loss. But you didn't mention your brother. How is he?"

Smiling, Garibaldi marveled at how this new president of TIIIS commanded his personal verification codes.

"Madam President, I am sorry, but I do not have a natural brother, but rather many brothers in Christ."

Verification complete, President Silver Moon asked, "So, Your Eminence, what can I do for you?"

"I am in need of your organization's services. I

require your Lictor of Magic, to catch and exorcise a she-demon that is bedeviling my cathedral and causing a media storm around the Holy Mother Church, and me, in particular."

"Your Eminence, what sort of time table did you have in mind?"

"Like yesterday."

"I see. Our society will not be able to respond to your request within a New York minute. I, however, will immediately look into it."

"Thank you, Madam President."

* * *

Silver Moon set down the phone in its cradle and gazed up into a cloudless and peaceful New Mexican sky.

This cardinal is quite upset about the desecration to his cathedral, his faith, and his reputation. Given everything that I have heard about him, this must be serious.

Silver Moon again reached for her office phone.

CHAPTER 29
Directing a She-Demon

The Dark One sat in the evening gloom with the heavy curtains drawn back. Before him sat his ornately carved desk of considerable proportions—a thing strangely alive, but not quite at the moment. With two full walls of glass overlooking the glittering lights of Manhattan, his penthouse lair on the forty-first floor possessed an eagle's eye view of the intersection of Fifth Avenue and 51st Street—the block where the St. Patrick's Cathedral stood. He stared contemptuously down at the peak of the papist's offending roofline, an illuminated Christian cross. The symbol mocked him.

At ten twenty-five in the evening, his late appointment irritated him. Then the intercom on his desk com announced: "Mr. Alexander. Your appointment has arrived. Should I send her in?"

Finally.

"Do so."

As he spun his chair around to face his overdue nocturnal visitor, he thought, *This had better be good,* as he turned up his office lights to the dusk setting.

Before him stood a horrific sight. A blood-caked patent leather jumpsuit seldom makes a good first impression. Nor did the young woman's bruised and bloodied knuckles or dark hair carelessly gathered in a lop-sided pony tail.

"Your late." Alexander stated without emotion.

"Your lawyer was late." replied the shapely young woman with an unnaturally husky voice. It dripped with concealed insolence.

Alexander made a brief mental note, and invited with a directing hand gesture. "*Sit.*"

The she-demon let out a sigh as it did so.

"Tired?"

"Yes. This body is weak. I barely survived a mugging in lockup."

"So tell me about the presentation of the gift. How did it go?"

The woman's eyes, two dark pits, now sprang to life. Her gestures exaggerated. Her speech accelerated.

"I was magnificent. His flock of sheep gasped in rapture at my performance. I could tell the priest recognized me. I used the same words as I had before. I sensed his arousal at my very presence."

"Excellent, excellent," the Dark One said clapping his hands together. "You have done well. *Very* well, in fact. So much so, I have another opportunity for you to flaunt yourself before this ... priest. But your present attire must be cleaned or discarded. You will need to purchase something more festive. Something for a high class wedding. Something stunning. It must be whiter than white."

He reached forward with a thick roll of bound currency.

"Here, my dear. This should cover your *expenses*. Now, *go* back to your apartment, *feed*, *sleep*, and *take care* of your mortal's body. In two days' time, I will give you further *instructions*. You may *go*." He commanded with coded hand gestures.

The demon-possessed woman smiled her sensuous lips, snatched away the bank roll from the edge of the desk, and left with purpose.

Once again alone with his office's lights dimmed dark, the Dark One murmured, "Someday, I will have you priest. I will slowly turn you on a spit until your roasted flesh falls off your bones. Now wouldn't that send a message back to those damn papists. It would be delicious."

*   *   *

Deep within the recesses of the Dark Realm, its resident master, the Devourer of Souls, approved of its marionette's plans.

"He is so pliable and accepting of my every suggestion."

CHAPTER 30
Free Agent

I got a phone call from President Silver Moon's assistant, Robert, who told me I had an appointment with the cardinal of New York City, and to get myself back East pronto. The president thought I was ready to deploy. I had to agree as I did have an inside advantage, the First Soul. I was again part of a team and that meant a lot.

Unbidden, Mr. Henry's past intensity and his offhand comment came to mind.

"Now I ask you, Mr. Stone. How far away is Manhattan from the Academy?"

"A day's drive, max."

"Yep."

Then I wondered.

Is he a latent seer too?

* * *

Once I got into Philly, I parked the truck and grabbed a train to New York. A quick taxi ride and I arrived at the cathedral on Fifth Avenue in Midtown Manhattan. I made for its rectory, a separate side structure on the neo-gothic property.

Under renovation, the finished sections of the cathedral's white limestone exterior glowed in the sunlight, to the point I put on my sunglasses. Its twin spires facing Fifth reached toward heaven, while its tall stain glass windows, like giant spear points, afforded a welcome relief amid all that blinding limestone.

I entered the rectory on the Madison Avenue side and told the security guard that I had an appointment with the cardinal. He buzzed me in.

The young priest behind the reception desk asked for my ID and scanned it. His name plate said—*Fr. Flanagan.*

"It'll be just a few minutes, Mr. Stone. The cardinal is on the phone. Please take a seat."

I had barely sat down, when the phone on the receptionist's desk rang.

"Mr. Stone. The cardinal is ready to see you."

*   *   *

The modest office of the shepherd of over two hundred and fifty congregations was floor-to-ceiling shelves filled with books or else standing filing cabinets. A wooden desk and two visitor's chairs fit itself into this cramped clutter.

The cardinal's desk proved to be a war zone of paperwork. The man himself displayed a bright blue aura with textured hues that betrayed his exhaustion. With the black sleeves of his common cassock rolled up to his elbows, he greeted me with a smile.

"Thank you for coming, Mr. Stone, and on such short notice," said the stocky, fiftyish man with a wealth of graying curly hair.

Then his eyes widened. "Oh my, Mr. Stone, President Silver Moon failed to tell me about your glorious aura."

"Thank you, Your Eminence. May I sit down?"

"By all means."

I got down to business. "Your Eminence, what can TIIIS do for you that the Vatican cannot?"

"Direct and to the point. I like that," said the high cleric. "Especially with all the nonsense that has been going on around here. Mr. Stone, my cathedral is being bedeviled by a demon, one I encountered before, as a young priest many years ago. One I banished back to the Underworld. Someone, however, has chosen to summon it back. Have you been reading the newspapers?"

I nodded.

"Well, it's all portrayed quite luridly. But what the newspapers don't know is this: What the demon declared for all to hear matched what it said to me all those years ago."

That must have creeped him out.

The high cleric paused for a moment, gathered his thoughts, and continued. "It's clear to me someone is trying to smear my reputation, and secondarily, my cathedral. Why? I have no idea. But I will not allow either to happen. Hence my call to your society's president, and the true reason for why you are here. I want that demon stopped. I don't care how. The best scenario, of course, would be to find and exorcise the woman involved.

"I am certain the Holy Father has been apprised of this circus, but action by the Vatican will take time, time that I believe I don't have. This is why I called TIIIS first and my colleagues at the Vatican second. I expect a delegation from the Society of Saint Paul to arrive soon and assess the situation. But in the interim, I see you, Mr. Stone, as a free agent. Someone who can get things done—today—and quickly.

"Am I right?" He asked for confirmation.

I shrugged my shoulders. "I suppose so. After all, I

did participate in saving those boys in Syria."

"That was you?"

"Not single-handedly; I had lots of help. The same demon possessed every last one of them. Those who recovered underwent a bee sting inoculation, and thereafter went back to their families in Pakistan."

"President Silver Moon did not tell me this."

Another shoulder shrug. "Your Eminence, I'm an ex-Marine noncom. I have seen my fair share of blood and guts. Now, what kind of demon are we talking about here? You said that you've dealt with it before. Is it susceptible to water, fire, wind, light?"

"Definitely water. But it will have to be a full submersion to do the job. A sprinkling of Holy Water won't do it. My first encounter with this demon required its dunking in a filled animal trough and four buckets of water dumped on its head before its dark aura receded."

To this valuable information, I said. "Basically, if I understand you, you first grounded it, and then smothered it."

"Yes, yes indeed. That is how I remember it," the cardinal agreed.

"It sounds like an M-SI type.

"That makes this a powerful demon, self-directed, and potentially of ancient Near Eastern origin. I will have to double-check my notes to see if I can find a match for it."

"What are you talking about? Near Eastern origin, your notes, I don't understand."

"Your Eminence, I am a graduate student at the University of Pennsylvania. My research, underwritten by TIIIS, deals with ancient cuneiform tablets, magical tomes that summon demons, invoke curses, and the like. If I can find one that is a potential match, that gives me a significant edge when I confront this demon.

"But even if I find and convert this poor woman, there remains the ultimate issue of the demon's conjurer to contend with. In short, he or she who directs this hellion. What are your thoughts on that?"

The question put the cardinal's mind into motion, and he sat back into his leather office chair, thinking. Usually, I can peek in on such ruminating, but not with the cardinal, as he had his mental blocks up and running. That fact alone troubled me.

Are we going to have trust issues? I played along, and waited, as if fishing for a grand-daddy of a catfish.

"I have some ideas." He finally added, "Some suspicions."

"Your Eminence, your suspicions are only of value if you share them."

"Most perceptive. What do you know about the history of this plot of land?"

"Zero, zip, nada." I replied.

That earned a quick amused grunt and a wry half smile for my candor. "Most people don't know this, but the building of this cathedral almost didn't happen. A competing business concern almost bought this land during the first third of the twentieth century. In fact, only through the prescience and dogged efforts of an Irish priest did this hallowed ground remain in the hands of the Roman Church. That competing business concern still exists and remains a dominant force in Midtown Manhattan. I know this to be a fact because of several run-ins the archdiocese has had with this business firm, or its subsidiaries, over the years. As a result, my predecessors, and the Vatican, have remained watchful for any further business or legal incursions into our affairs."

At this point I had to ask, "Can you identify this competing business concern. It might be helpful to know if I run into it."

"I'm talking about CMES, Mr. Stone. I'm quite sure you know who they are. Their North American headquarters is located across Fifth Avenue and down the street, one block to the north."

Of course!

Now I frowned in thought. The cardinal had it pegged. Why it hadn't occurred to me sooner, even with Mr. Henry's emphasis, I don't know. But it made a lot of sense.

"So what do you believe are their intentions?"

Still sitting deep in his chair, the cardinal, with hooded eyes stated for the record, "First, the ruination of my reputation. Imagine for one moment, given the current media environment and its built-in liberal and secular biases, what a sensational paternity suit about a high church official would do? Circus, total media circus, Mr. Stone, resulting in an instantaneous judgment by sheer innuendo. And what could the Roman Church do in response? Hold its ground and fight back? Or become a box turtle and cave in to the pressure? In both of those scenarios, the Roman Church loses as you can't defend something as delicate as your reputation during the 24/7 news cycle.

"CMES' second goal is to smear the Roman Church's reputation. If you thought the many sexual scandals by the lower clergy, and the Church's many attempts to sweep them under the rug did damage, now ratchet it up several notches to include a cardinal—a church official one step away from the papacy. I can see the media throwing away the red paint brush of scandal and reaching for an industrial-grade spray gun.

"Their third goal is to acquire this property. If that occurs, an army of zoning lawyers will ferret out a way to condemn all of this property's structures, followed by their swift demolition. Given the extraordinary market value of this city block, I would expect the erection of one, if not several, secular structures upon it, in essence, wiping away all memory of what stood here.

"*Damnatio memoriae*, Mr. Stone, that is the ultimate goal of CMES regarding the Roman Church."

"Excuse me, but how could CMES first acquire and demolish a national historic landmark like St. Patrick's Cathedral? Only a madman would attempt such a thing."

To that the cardinal said, "Precisely, Mr. Stone. That's what we're up against—a madman. The regional director of CMES North America has just such a reputation. Rumor has it that he threw one of his security supervisors who dared to challenge him off the roof of his headquarters building. I believe him capable of anything."

The cardinal's take on the cathedral incident, and what it represented, caused me to see it all as a slowly developing chess game with pieces still in motion. Even I could see the cat incident represented nothing more than the opening salvo, a mere preliminary to the potential knockout punch.

"So what have you done to protect the cathedral from any more sensationalistic incidents?" I queried.

He spread his hands, "Mr. Stone, what can I do?

We already have our own round-the-clock security, our own video surveillance inside and out, and the good graces of our friends at the NYPD, and several other city service departments. I can't build a moat filled with Holy Water around my church, although I have thought about it."

I smiled at that fantastical idea.

"Our hands are tied. Remember, this is a house of God, open to the public to serve the public. This is why *you* are here. We will continue on with business as usual. But what's new to the landscape is *you*. You're the wildcard now on the table."

Now that description fit me to a tee.

"Do you have any information regarding the young woman in question?"

"No, I don't. Even the NYPD is scratching their collective heads over that one. Her lawyer posted her bail rather quickly."

"Can your sources in the NYPD tell you which legal firm represented her?"

"I like you. You're quick. Here's all I have."

A sheet of paper appeared with a name and a nearby Madison Avenue address. It would have to do.

*   *   *

With the lawyer's name and his legal firm's address now in hand, I had my opportunity for some good old fashion recon. I would be looking for auras, those sketchy ones with muddied and dark hues that were a giveaway. They would indicate things of questionable legality or nastiness. And given the place I just left, the cathedral's rectory, I figured, based on healthy paranoia, anyone who left it would either be under technical observation or physically tailed.

If they used tech, an anonymous fact of modern day urban life, I couldn't do a thing about it. With security cameras everywhere, access to their data feeds should be secure. But in my business, I chose to be paranoid. The bad guys probably had their own arrangements.

But if they put an actual tail in place, that's old school. Then we're talking about a living and breathing thing that possessed an aura, which to me, looked like waving a flag or flashing beacon on their head.

So when I left the rectory, I made a production of opening a city map and gaping around with my eyes focused on aura-detection. What I saw was a field of gentle pastel and brilliant hues, in short, normal folks. But I wasn't looking for normal.

While in the Marines, I was trained to master the battlefield through exhaustive physical training, superior weapons, and mental toughness. When I was first deployed in 1993 as part of Task Force Somalia, we ran into their informal militias, who we called "Skinnies" and "Sammies." Why? Because we were trained to denigrate the enemy—it dehumanized them, making them easier to deal with. This mental tactic isn't something new. Consider, the "Krauts" and "Japs" in World War II, the "gooks" in Korea, "Charlie" in Vietnam, and "towel-heads" in Iraq. In order to preserve our humanity, we couldn't think of the enemy as human, but instead as something else, by giving them nicknames.

As I continued to survey the block, I saw three very muddy auras out there. The first was a drugged out dude standing in a doorway looking hungry and strung out. The second guy stood about with a newspaper. He blended in well because of his general demeanor, reasonable grooming, and for a lack of a better term, his plainness. The last muddy one, a young woman, I spotted because crack heads have a very distinct aura. So, I filed away all three auras, folded up my map, and started south on Madison Avenue toward the law firm's address.

*   *   *

It didn't take me long to reach the northern corner of Madison Avenue and 49th Street. I stopped again pulled out my map, and looked around to orient myself. And there they were, all three of my new found friends, tailing me in a classic triangular, double-point configuration. Druggy on my side of the street, Crack Head on the opposite sidewalk, and the Newspaper Boy brought up the rear, backing up Druggy.

Interesting, I thought. I promoted Newspaper Boy on the spot to General Newspaper Boy. With my rear quarter now understood, I, just for grins, scanned Madison Avenue to my south and guess what? Two more muddy hued individuals blocked my advance. One looked like a gang banger in his cock-eyed ball cap covered with stickers. On my side of the street stood a purple-haired creature in black leather, smoking a vape and texting with a lost look on her face. Their presence, and in this configuration, I could not accept as a coincidence. They must all be in league with General Newspaper Boy. Tactically that made him my target for a gentle conversation, because the others didn't matter.

In the back of my mind I didn't need to be an ex-Marine to recognize that if I continued on toward the law firm, I'd be walking into an ambush of some kind. I turned right on 49th, and bee-lined for the door of a sushi joint. I needed some ammunition.

* * *

"What's he doing now?" the earpiece asked.

"Seems he's lost, sir. After leaving the rectory, he started south on Madison—Wait. Now, he's backtracking north. No, he's turning west on 49th. I've lost contact."

"Then *get* in contact with him, you imbecilic moron!"

"Yes, sir. I'm closing," General Newspaper Boy said as he broke into a slow jog. Reaching the corner, he peeked around and said, "Got him. He's going into a sushi restaurant."

"Excellent. It's noontime; he's getting some lunch. Settle your people into position and wait for him to reappear," said the ear piece. "Keep in contact at all costs, but do not, I repeat, *do not* confront him."

"Yes, sir," General Newspaper Boy responded to the already dead connection.

"Okay people. Get into position and chill. He's in the sushi restaurant on 49th. Whatever you do, don't move on him until told to do so."

* * *

It's amazing what you can conceal in the pockets of a windbreaker. But in my particular case, two plastic bottles full of pure drinking water nestled nicely into each pocket, at a cost of four bucks each. A ridiculous price for drinking water, I know, but necessary nonetheless. Something about "any port in a storm" struck a chord in the back of my mind.

I decided to take the offensive. It's my favorite tactic, because nobody expects it. Since it was lunch time, the sushi joint had filled up all its seats. My tails would recognize that, be off guard, and settle in for a long wait. After fiddling a bit with my water bottles, I went out the door to hunt for General Newspaper Boy.

I caught him flatfooted while he scanned his newspaper on the corner of Madison Avenue and 49th. When I appeared, his face and gaping mouth indicated his surprise. With a plastic water bottle in each hand, their plastic tops already popped and primed, one quick squeeze of my powerful hands drenched General Newspaper Boy's face.

He went down to his knees in agony while gripping his face. His reaction to the sudden drenching was a classic Near Eastern demonic response. On top of that, he had breathed some of the water into his nose and mouth, which silenced him. Emptying the rest of the bottles over his head, I got down on one knee as if to help him, which of course, I intended to do.

With both of my hands on his shoulders, I could feel the demon struggling within as his eyes rolled back leaving white orbs. For the next thirty seconds I prayed, hard, while my thumbs touched his neck. As quickly as the fight began, the man cleared, and his natural aura of a crystalline pastel green mixed with a brilliant yellow showed through.

Now gasping, General Newspaper Boy looked up into my eyes filled with heart-felt gratitude.

"Thank you."

Pant.

"Thank you so much."

Pant.

"What a nightmare it's been. You saved me. You're glowing …"

Ignoring for the moment the man's comment, I said. "I'm here to help you. You had a seizure. I dumped my water bottles to shock you out of it. Can you stand?"

"I think so," he said in a wobbly voice.

I helped him to his feet, still holding his shoulders, but now in physical support instead of in an act of prayerful intervention.

During this, at least twenty people had passed us by as we occupied the middle of the sidewalk. Not one pedestrian stopped to offer any assistance.

Ah, New York!

"What's your name?" I asked.

"Peter, Peter Simon."

"What do you do for a living, Peter?"

"I'm in publishing. I work in Jersey." He looked around and took in his surroundings, "But what am I doing in Manhattan?" Peter said with confusion and growing alarm in his voice.

"You were following me, Peter. Why?"

"Yes. Yes! A man wanted you followed."

"Do you know why?" I prodded.

"No. Just that he was a bad, bad man."

Peter's words overflowed with mental images of things far worse than just "bad." Pure fear was more like it. I prodded again, employing my mental listening talents, ready to catch any nuances.

"So, Peter. Where did you meet this bad, bad man?"

"In his penthouse apartment. Real swanky place, but dark. I didn't see any sunlight way up there. I thought that odd, it being noon."

"This swanky penthouse apartment, do you remember which building it was in?"

Peter looked around and said, "I can't see it from here, but it's on Fifth Ave. That way, north a couple of blocks, right down the street from the cathedral."

CMES' North American headquarters.

"Can you describe him for me?"

"Yeah. Middle-aged, I think, with smooth, ivory-white skin. Spoke with an accent that could have been either Italian or French. Light brown or sandy-colored hair. Not a big guy, kinda average build."

"Did you meet anyone else in the penthouse, other than the bad, bad man?"

"Yeah, this young woman … with a creepy vibe I can't quite put my finger on. I didn't get a good look at her. The middle-aged guy, I remember now, his name's Alexander, William Alexander, got through talking to me about publishing this manuscript he had. Then, he signaled this chick with a wave of his hand."

He shivered, "I lost all control, until now."

So the creepy she-demon of cathedral fame must have possessed him on the spot, I concluded.

"Did the creepy chick touch you, Peter?"

"Yeah. I remember her grabbing the back of my neck. She surprised me with her strength, and that's when stuff got strange."

Yep. Direct contact.

"What day did you visit this, William Alexander?"

"Monday at noon, that's the only time I could fit the interview into my schedule."

Well, today's Thursday. Peter's been "under" for three and a half days. Jeez.

"Are you hungry Peter?"

"Starved!" He said with big eyes for emphasis.

"Then, let's go grab some lunch. It's on me."

As a result of our lunch together, I figured out the bad man named William Alexander used people, at random, to do his bidding. He would pollute them with a demon, through skin to skin contact, and run them into the ground through dehydration, hunger, withdrawal, whatever. Used up, he abandoned them to the streets. A pretty cold way to treating people.

Then I got an idea.

"Peter. Would you be willing to go with me to the precinct and look at some head shots? Maybe we could identify this creepy young woman you mentioned. Do you think that you're up for it?"

Gulping down his Diet Coke, Peter nodded, "You bet, J.J. I want some payback."

*   *   *

The take down of the tails' lead impressed the Dark One. The man who had visited the rectory had made his tails, and taken action, and at high noon no less. He took the lead tail to lunch and thereafter the pair paid a visit to the local police station. The Dark One, however, got what he wanted—over fifteen digital images of this white knight.

So that's how a TIIIS Lictor of Magic operates when caught out in the open. He mused.

It also means that our dear cardinal has TIIIS connections, which, given his background within the Society of St. Paul, makes sense. While the Vatican figures out how to react, our flustered cardinal deployed the TIIIS Lictor Stateside.

Interesting ...

It seems that my long-time nemesis Smithers has found his replacement—this impressive young buck—and had he all trained up before I had him done away with. How delicious.

*　　*　　*

The Dark One donned a pair of surgical gloves to protect himself, snapping their tops around the cufflinks of his dress shirt just to make sure. He went to his office credenza, opened the lower left-hand door, and pulled out a heavy and awkwardly sized book with wooden covers engraved with Egyptian hieroglyphs: *The Book of Spells.* This he placed upon his desk upon a fresh terry cloth towel since the codex's wooden covers and pages were impregnated with a one-of-a-kind lethal poison devised by himself.

"What should I send to greet Mr. Stone? To welcome him to the City That Never Sleeps," the Dark One said aloud. "So many choices ... so many ways to die."

The heavy vellum pages of the great book had to be carefully turned, one by one, by grasping the page's thumb-worn corners. After several minutes of hemming and hawing, the Dark One smiled.

"Ah, here is a splendid selection. Now, all I have to do is address the issue of its timing."

CHAPTER 31
Second Atrocity

Wedding Ruined by Paternity Appeal

(NYC) Executed with theatrics that would have made a Broadway director proud, another histrionic scene took place within St. Patrick's Cathedral. An uninvited, prancing, young woman in full wedding white and train interrupted the wedding of a New York socialite's daughter.

The woman shrieked that the cardinal perform a blessing for their alleged love child. The cardinal ignored the request and called security, while the interloper threw an epic tantrum. Then she and mother-of-the-bride collided.

While bested by the raving woman, the mother did exact her due as blood flowed from the woman's scratched face. In retaliation, the gatecrasher went on a rampage causing flower stands to fly and altar candles to fall. The cathedral's own security guards quelled the disturbance.

The perpetrator, arrested on the spot by the NYPD, was escorted to a nearby precinct and booked.

(*The New York Daily Inquirer*, A1)

"This is outrageous," Cardinal Garibaldi railed to his captive office manager.

"What do we have to do to keep this she-demon out of my cathedral? And the absolute gall to again accuse me of siring a child with that … *thing*!

"I'm sorry, Father Flanagan, for venting at you. It's not personal. It just vexes me that in this day and age such things can happen, and appear as gospel on the five o'clock news."

To this, Father Flanagan wisely chose to exercise the vow of silence.

*   *   *

The media, of course, ran with this latest "cathedral incident," as it once again resurrected the hot and juicy subject of an alleged paternity case. Predictably, the incident turned into a media circus fomented by elements rubbing their hands together in absolute glee. Calls for DNA testing abounded. Probes into the cardinal's background were called for. Interviews of his friends, family, and colleagues threatened to disrupt the everyday business of running a house of God. You could almost hear them off-camera. "The white starched linen of the Church is getting soiled. How grand!"

Local news outlets posed damning questions like: "Given the current allegations, can this cardinal effectively administer his flock?" "Is he up to the challenge?" "Has he broken his vow of celibacy?" "How can the cardinal guarantee the efficient functioning of the cathedral?" "What steps should the cathedral take to ensure its sanctity and peace?" Throughout all of this, like drooling harpies hovering over a maimed carcass, the talking heads had a field day.

*   *   *

The demonic visitor stood before the Dark One's desk once again. But this time it raged with anger.

"I'm ruined! I'm no longer pretty, because of that bitch!" The she-demon ranted as it flashed the ruined sides of its face before its master.

"She clawed me to death! Disfigured, how can I now serve you?" it pleaded.

Sitting within the leather embrace of his chair, the Dark One commiserated.

"My little demon, this afternoon you did quite well, *quite* well indeed." The Dark One said with several innocuous hand gestures that insured calm and appeasement.

"No, I would say your *masterful* performance had its *desired* effect. So, take heart. Job *well* done!"

This high praise did not remove the frown from the she-demon's face. But for what he had in mind, the Dark One believed that was sufficient to bring it around.

Instead, the she-demon brazenly spoke its mind. "I want my hands on the cardinal. I want to rape him on his high altar. Only this will appease me."

"What a *fine* idea, my little demon," the man cooed, "but perhaps we should save that *luscious*, *delicious* moment for another time. For now, I counsel *patience* regarding the cardinal. I have far *grander* plans for you."

*   *   *

The new Lictor of Magic captivated The Dark One. The digital photographs taken by his street urchins depicted a tall, light-haired, almost angelic, figure.

Now that he has appeared on the street, how can I get under this man's skin? He wondered.

I have read cover to cover his thick dossier. What can I use to destroy him?

Wait.

I know.

The media loves red meat. I will provide it, because I have just the thing on hand.

And I'll even have my little demon deliver it.

CHAPTER 32
Third Atrocity

Grotesque Murder Grips NYC Cathedral

Last night a grisly special delivery was made to the city's cathedral during a localized power outage.

"It was a human sacrifice," said one source on the basis of anonymity within the NYPD, "pure and simple."

Another source, who also wished to remain anonymous, said, "A male infant was clinically eviscerated and dumped like so much garbage on the church's main altar." "Never, in all my years on the force, have I ever seen anything like this," said a third.

To date, this is the third incident involving the cathedral.

(*The New York Daily Inquirer*, A1)

The first responders had to control their gag reflexes while they worked the crime scene. A quick inspection of the cathedral's interior security video showed that an unidentified, heavily clothed figure had deposited the tiny bag on the high altar. Once there, the figure cut away the bag as if to proudly display its contents. No fingerprints could be found.

The authorities found nearby some documents in a sealed Ziploc baggie.

Because of the nature of the crime, the on-scene investigator sequestered all the forensics' photos and evidence. Nonetheless, human nature held sway in this city where everything could be had for a price, and the media, somehow, managed to get their hands on some grisly images.

*   *   *

The coroner looked at the ragged remains, shook his head, adjusted his overhead microphone, and whispered under his breath, "I'm getting too old for this.

"General overview," the coroner announced into the microphone.

"The supplied birth certificate indicates that the subject is Anthony Garibaldi, Jr., a male infant about two months old, Caucasian, with black curly hair and olive complexion"—bending over to raise an eyelid— "with brown eyes.

"Length: twenty-four point seven inches. Weight: undetermined, but perhaps fourteen pounds *in vivo*.

"Cause of death: unknown.

"Overall assessment: a textbook evisceration of the body cavity.

"Evidence of massive blood loss, as the body cavity is almost dry. The torso and abdomen have been opened and all principal organs are missing.

"Perpetrator's use of precise incisions suggest medical or veterinarian training.

"Samples have been taken and sent to the lab to assess DNA and blood group type."

The autopsy went on for another sixteen minutes documenting the minutiae of what true horror looked like.

Stripping off his latex gloves, the coroner reached up and turned off his overhead microphone. Pitching his soiled gloves into the HAZMAT container along with his gown, booties, mask, and sweat-soaked head wrap, he went into his office and closed the door.

Sitting at his desk, he opened its deep lower left-hand drawer and removed a half empty bottle of scotch. Next came out a dusty tumbler covered with fingerprints. Filling it with three fingers worth, he drained it. Without another thought, he filled it again.

"I'm getting too old for this."

*　　*　　*

The cardinal sat at his desk in the rectory, head in his hands, with the typed letter and birth certificate laying before him in their plastic evidence bags. He couldn't believe his eyes as his gaze went from one document to the other.

Dearest Tony,

I know I have been a bad girl, but I still want you, want you bad, so bad I can taste it.

You never blessed our little Anthony, Tony. He never was baptized. I played with him until his little heart gave out.

But even worse, Tony, you have been playing hard to get. Worse, you have sicced your dog Stone on my trail, and that's not fair.

I want you, priest. I will have you. You cannot deny me. And Tony, I'm very good. How can you resist me?

Love,

Candi

*   *   *

I had driven back to the Academy, where I buried myself in the editorial insanity that is the creation of multiple indices for my MA thesis.

I was sitting in the womb-like semi-darkness of the main library within the Peterson Building, a structure that looked like an Egyptian temple. I felt like I was the sole person in the lotus-pillared reference gallery that morning. I heard, in the back of my mind, the tread of quick steps approaching from across the limestone flooring.

"Mr. Stone?" the tentative voice said.

"Josh. What's up, man?"

"Ah, I have some bad news, sir."

Then I saw it in Josh's aura. He was agitated about something.

"Spit it out, Josh."

Then the nervous IT and Security staffer told me about the cathedral murder—no, the human sacrifice. Check that—the *infant* human sacrifice, the precise thing that my job title was first created to eradicate from the mortal realm.

Then my internal teammate, the First Soul, piped up.

Soul carrier. A truly evil one did this. Listen, my soul carrier. This is the time to act, but do so with care and prudence.

I, however, felt a deep emptiness at the loss of the child and sensed the outrage within me building. It was a terrible thing, like a tsunami wave, growing, and ever expanding.

This is a test, soul carrier. I have gone through this before. We will act, but, again, with care and prudence.

With those thoughts the wave passed through and under me as if I rode a bobbing boat, and found not peace, but a firm conviction.

Yes, I answered, *we are indeed a team. And I thank you for your counsel.*

Only then did I realize that I had my eyes were clenched. My hands gripped the sides of the library desk. When I opened them I saw Josh Remington looking at me with deep concern on his face.

"Are you okay, Mr. Stone?"

"Yes, I am, Josh. But this inhuman act will be dealt with. Someone's gonna' pay, big time."

*　　*　　*

The following weekend, a small, private funeral took place. New York's finest managed to keep the media at a distance, but could not prevent the prying of their telephoto lenses.

In attendance at the babe's graveside stood a somber Cardinal Garibaldi, his assistant Father Flanagan, twenty of the cardinal's own security force, and me in a black suit and matching London Fog.

"Your Eminence, I heard that the infant's DNA didn't match yours even remotely. Nor did his blood grouping. As for the birth certificate, that was a forgery, nothing more."

The cardinal grunted. "Try selling that to the media. I'm already being turned over their spit."

The muted ceremony, the heart-felt grief for the anonymous infant, became surreal as there was an energy in the air, a thrum detectable by all. The cardinal's security force felt it as an itchy, "what is about to happen?" kind of tenseness. They couldn't shake the depressing overpressure, and it was reflected in their nervous, herky-jerky movements. But the cardinal and I knew from where the stifling feeling came. Us. For it was a primal, psychic call for vengeance.

Focused on the grave, none of us noticed the dark speck in the sky high above.

*　　*　　*

"How quaint," the crazed Dark One giggled from the rooftop his forty-one-story headquarters.

"Stone is attending the sacrificed infant's burial. Out in the open air. Ripe for plucking! Well, it's high time that someone put Stone in the ground as well."

Standing before a collection of oddly shaped bones on the roof, The Dark One chanted from his *Book of Spells* the memorized, triggering stanza—

Go forth, Draco!

Find he of the golden aura,

Greedily feast upon him!

Then return forthwith in glory, oh mighty and great one, to your Master.

In broad daylight, the Dark One conjured without care a long-necked, mottled dragon with the coloration of a rainbow boa. Along its spine, a dense crest of maroon feathers extended with pride as it luxuriated and stretched in the bright sunshine. Its heavy bone talons scratched against the hot noontime tar paper. A single, throaty bark from its cavernous maw announced that it was ready.

"Go, oh mighty one! I bid thee take flight!"

Leaping off the roof at the command, the flying reptile at first disappeared, only to reappear after several powerful beats of its sixty foot wingspan. The beast, now free, blatantly cast its signature shadow across the NYC skyline. With a loud flapping of leathery wings, the modern world was introduced to a mythological horror of the European Dark Ages.

As for its conjurer, the Dark One, protected under a floppy oversized sun hat, SPF 80, sunglasses, and gloves, giggled, clapped, and marveled at what he had done.

"I haven't had this much fun since my days in Alexandria!"

*   *   *

Minutes later, the dragon perceived its golden prey from high above. So small, so insignificant. It would hardly make a meal. It dived nonetheless, true to its master's wishes.

*   *   *

With the infant's grave being filled in by the cemetery's grounds crew, nothing further was required. The cardinal's downcast head, heavy sigh, and blood-shot eyes said it all.

Then, the First Soul jarred me back to the here and now.

Soul carrier! Look up!

I did, and couldn't believe what I saw. A dragon, in full dive, was dropping like a stone. Head on, all I could see was its gaping mouth of curved teeth. But from below its outstretched wings were poised, raptor-like talons, grasping at the air, coming for me.

"Scatter!" I yelled, "Dragon!" as I shoved the cardinal out of harm's way and into the soft soil of the half-filled grave. My Bone Sword appeared as if by magic from the folds of my black London Fog.

I took a deep breath, let it slowly out, and whispered in my mind *coil, slide, and strike,* while I focused, and forced time to slow.

Having descended to about a hundred feet above the ground, the reptile performed a magnificent flare with its colorful outstretched wings in preparation to snatch me off the ground. Astonished at the raw beauty of that maneuver, I noted the network of veins and muscles in the bright sunshine that had accomplished that feat. I also took note of its slithering dark aura that marked it as demon kind. Meanwhile, the cardinal's security team began firing their weapons to no telling effect.

As I continued to watch the beast's descent, chunks of hide, skin, and scale were blasted off, which disintegrated in the air as blackish wisps of evaporating ectoplasm.

Interesting, I thought. *It leaves behind no evidence of its passing, whatsoever. How convenient.*

With a mighty down beat from its wings, it swooped in on a graceful, but predictable, glide path. I didn't move, but instead braced myself.

Then I saw it. A flicking white motion across the beast's eyes. It possessed a nictitating membrane. It, like a great white shark, attacked blind.

I just stood there, waiting, waiting, and thinking … *coil, slide, and strike!* As I sidestepped out of the creature's path, I sundered its log-like left leg at the joint, splattering blood everywhere, which formed a grayish fog of evaporating ectoplasm.

The severed member fell to the ground in a tumble, and took out several bushes, and broke up into another gray fog bank that began to dissipate.

The injured dragon now wobbled off balance as it flew. At first appearing confused. It looked down at its loss, and became enraged. Its angry scream shook the ground and reverberated off my chest.

I just stood there, waiting … watching it turn majestically in the air with its brush-like, maroon plumage erect and bristling in anger. Its leg trailed blood what looked like smoke in the sky.

The dragon, however, never took its eyes off of me while it looped overhead and executed a perfect Immelmann turn. It dived again, motivated, screaming in rage and pain at the same time.

But I just stood there, waiting …

The cardinal's security team again unloaded with a barrage, and again to little effect.

This second pass came in much slower, as the dragon tried to grasp me with its canoe-sized mouth festooned with multiple rows of curved teeth. It's purple forked tongue wagged obscenely, tasting the air, seeking out my scent. But as before, just before it struck, the dragon's nictitating lids blinded it.

Again I jumped aside spoiling a grasping lunge. In the process, I broke every rule that Mr. Loomis had taught me about proper sword craft. I did, however, manage to place myself in position for a vertical cut through the dragon's outstretched neck, severing it, and splashing me with another gout of blood.

Now without its head, the beast's remains tumbled and crashed. Its flailing wings and body gouged the cemetery's manicured lawn and rolled into a small copse of trees, where it thrashed about. Once still, the dragon's corpse broke down into a vast cloud of evaporating ectoplasm. The same happened to its decapitated neck and head.

So much for a trophy.

The unexpected attack caused me to search the skies for another, but none there were to be seen.

* * *

Atop his headquarters' roof, the awaiting Dark One slid to his knees in utter exhaustion. Today there would be no retrieval; no return of a demon to its master. Instead, with the destruction of the Dark One's dragon, all of the energy expended in its conjuring had been lost.

Panting heavily from the exertion of the conjuring, the Dark One grunted out. "Damn you, Stone. You bastard! You have so ruined my day!"

* * *

Meanwhile, within the Dark Realm, the Devourer of Souls sympathized with his minion's plight, while it greeted yet another shattered victim of the First Soul's handiwork.

Grimacing, "Oh, how I despise thee, First Soul. But with luck, your time too will soon come to pass."

*   *   *

That evening I drove back to the Academy, my clothing stiff with dried sweat from the aerial attack. As for the cardinal, he had his hands full with the cemetery's grounds crew and management over the devastation—not to mention explaining away what had caused it all.

About half way into my drive, I remembered to call the cardinal about the she-demon. This I had to do, before I began the "stalk" of it, and its conjurer. I also wanted to run the plan that I had in mind by my friends John Running Deer and President Silver Moon.

CHAPTER 33
Mixed Results

The Dark One had always believed that good things happened in threes. First, the black cat sacrifice, then the ruined June wedding, and now, this ruse—nothing more than a convenient disposal of a male infant, whose liver had already served its purpose. But the swift loss of his favorite dragon-demon unsettled him.

Fascinating. The cardinal and his cathedral, both under siege, have not lifted a finger in their own defense. Only the NYPD, the coroner, and TIIIS have come to their aid. But the media, like piranha, drone on and on with their imaginative speculations and lurid innuendos. It's amazing at what a few well-placed bank notes can do.

As for Stone, he took down my favorite dragon. I can now better understand why the chairman was gleeful at my offer to remove him. Perhaps there is more calculation to that narcissistic moron than his racing team after all.

Now what should I have my little demon do next? Ah, yes, I know. Let's complete the ruination of the cardinal's reputation and finish off Stone. That would be most delicious—a twofer.

* * *

While the Dark One schemed, I called President Silver Moon and laid out what I wanted to do in retaliation for the cathedral's attacks and the infant's sacrifice.

"Well, I must say that your plan, as you outlined it,

is ambitious. That said, I authorize you to go ahead with it. But be sure to discuss it with Henry Johnson. His input will be crucial. I also encourage you to include Cardinal Garibaldi in it as well.

"In many respects, we are faced with a human sacrifice that forces our hand, as a society, to act. As our Lictor of Magic, you will know what to do."

"Thank you, Madam President, but I need your thoughts as well on this. While I have been in on the planning and execution of many military operations, this one will be taking place within a civilian environment, and that's very different. I also have a theory about when the next attack on the cathedral will take place."

"You do?" the president said with some surprise. "When?"

"Next Friday night."

"How did you settle upon that date?"

"Our quarry likes regularity. In fact, I remember Mr. Good lecturing on the proclivity of demonic spells that specify how often a demon must act within certain specified time limits. For example, in this instance, let's say, every thirteen days."

"Good catch." The president observed.

"So I plan to be waiting for the she-demon in the cathedral with some bait, and a whole bunch of Holy Water. Once the possessed woman is successfully exorcised, we go after its conjurer. And that's where the cardinal's and your help will be needed."

A day later I got Cardinal Garibaldi's buy in. That left Mr. Henry to be briefed on what had become, "The Plan."

"Well, Marine, I must say this is an interesting

operations plan that you have cooked up. Ambushing a demon and then turning around to take down the CMES headquarters building. Like all half-baked plans, it's too tricky. But I love it! It's unlike anything CMES would ever expect us to do. It's flat out outrageous! Let's make it happen," Mr. Henry said as he rubbed his hands together.

"Okay, Mr. Henry, I'm glad you're on board. Let's start at the beginning and hash it all out."

"With pleasure," the man said with a bright sparkle in his eyes. "But you must expect that the CMES building can defend itself."

"You mean like all the buildings at the Academy?"

"Exactly. I expect it's magically hardwired to repel all external magical threats," my mentor declared with absolute conviction.

"Well, sir, I'm counting on that, and that its owners will overly depend on it. By the way, I did a cursory recon on the CMES building's security setup the last time I visited New York. I sauntered around some of the stores on its ground floor. Even there I detected a subtle magical component. Psychically, it felt like wearing a heavy, wet blanket, and the air seemed to get thicker the deeper you went. This sensation is the same kind I got when I reconstructed those magical tablets back at the university—a thick, oppressiveness to the environment. On top of that, I noted some of their security personnel had special auras too, as in muddy, dark ones."

So we began, cutting and pasting our way through every angle and contingency we could think of. The biggest issue pertained to the CMES building's roof. Was it defended, and if so, how?

*   *   *

As plans went, this one had two interdependent phases, at least from my point of view. While complex to execute, I had a high level of confidence both phases would succeed. Now I had to run it by Cardinal Garibaldi, because he had huge role to play.

So I called his office with my operational wish list.

"So, Mr. Stone, what news do you have for me?"

"Your Eminence." I said. "First off, I know when the she-demon will strike again. It'll be on next Friday night. That's the good news. The better news is that while I'm waiting to ambush it, I want you to act as bait."

"I'll act as *what*?" the incredulous high cleric exclaimed.

"Bait. I need you to attract and distract the she-demon before I can lay my hands on it."

Now intrigued, the he asked, "What do you have in mind?"

"Your Eminence, several things, along with several big favors to ask."

*   *   *

Early afternoon on Friday became a blur as I juggled operational details with Mr. Henry and Cardinal Garibaldi. So much to do, so many involved, and so little time. Bitch, bitch, bitch. Each team—the NYPD, FDNY, city services, and the TIIIS techies—had their roles to do on time and without individualistic embroidery. I put the scheme into motion in a mere four days, a short enough time span in hopes it would prevent a leak to the street.

Sunset on Friday occurred in Manhattan at 8:25 pm. While everything and everyone was hustling to get into position, my stomach filled with fluttering butterflies.

CHAPTER 34
Nocturnal Message

Valeria sat bolt upright awake in her bed. Looking over at the clock on her bed stand. It said: 2:45 am. This was not a vivid dream. No, something awful was about to happen, but what? Frustrated, the oracle threw on her bathrobe and made for the *famiglia* chapel, the bottoms of her hurried slippers scraping on the limestone floors like sandpaper.

The chapel, an ancient annex to the rambling house, was more a man-made grotto made of rough-hewn stone. Within, to the left of its single entrance, stood a crude stone pedestal that supported a polished silver basin filled with clear, mountain water. In the back, smoldered a small fire within a battered bronze brazier—the original Eternal Flame of Rome. Placing a small log within it, the oracle returned to the silver basin.

Valeria gripped its sides and prayed.

I, Valeria, call upon Thou, oh ancient one.

I, Valeria, devoted high priestess of Vesta, seek a vision.

I, Valeria, spiritual daughter of Coelia Concordia, *Vergio Vestalis Maxima*, command you to do so.

I, Valeria, keeper of the most sacred flame of Rome, command you to do so *now*!

With those words the basin's waters began to roil. A clear image appeared—that of a modern city with tall buildings. Bright flashing lights sparkled from vehicles that surrounded one of these man-made giants.

Is a building afire? Valeria asked herself.

Many more vehicles appeared, as if from nowhere, as well as police and firemen, who forced their way into the stricken building.

Then, nothing. Nothing more seemed to happen. After an exhausting hour and a half of patient observation, a green light—no, a flare—fell from above to the ground below. More nothing.

Now suffering with cold knees and feet, the oracle witnessed two firemen carrying one of their own, who, after loading up the stricken one, drove off into the night.

What happened? Valeria asked herself.

She returned to her bedroom and called a special emergency number to the CMES campus in Rome.

"Communications and Security."

"This is *Signora* Costa. I need to speak to the head of security, *pronto.*"

"*Sí, Signora* Costa. *Un momento.*"

A brief delay occurred as lines were connected.

"*Signore* Justinio. May I help you?"

"This is *Signora* Valeria Costa. What just happened in New York City?

"I don't know what you mean."

"Can you make contact with New York City?"

"*Un momento.*"

Moments later.

"*Signora* Costa! I cannot! What has happened?"

"I do not know, but if I were you, I would put the Gathering on high alert. I think the New York City headquarters has just been attacked!"

CHAPTER 35
Game Time

The she-demon had been lurking about New York City for over a month, running loose among its mortal inhabitants. While sympathetic to the cardinal and his predicament, the NYPD didn't have the manpower to track such a hit-or-miss assignment. If the hooded figure that deposited the murdered infant in the cathedral could be tied to the other two incidents, that would have been another story. NYPD did, however, offer access to the street-level cameras of the city and their facial recognition software. Also, plain clothes police began attending masses, their presence providing an additional level of security. While this was a good start, even that could only do so much.

Stone, however, knew when the she-demon would come. He sat in the cathedral's last pew on the far left, next to the alcove that contained the baptismal font. Pretending to be in his favorite spot in the Santa Fe National Forest, Stone, decked out in his UCS, sat motionless, and became part shadow, part wooden pew.

Between the security cameras on the cathedral's exterior and interior, and his wireless ear bud, Stone knew he would be alerted the moment the she-demon arrived. By agreement, the cathedral's security personnel cleared the nave of its parishioners and took up positions out of sight. Stone and Cardinal Garibaldi would handle the she-demon themselves.

At 8:27 pm the sun had set. To the second, Stone's ear bud chirped the news. "Mr. Stone. She's here."

*   *   *

It arrived eager, feeling invincible, and without a care in the world. In one hand the she-demon carried a bottle of cheap bourbon, in the other, a couple of paper cups. She-Who-Devours-Men's-Souls wanted to party. She wore the same outfit as the night of the black cat sacrifice—the one-piece black patent leather body suit with thigh-high heeled boots. Strutting its stuff, the she-demon intended to find the cardinal, make him chug, and rape him in his fancy house of God.

As the *succubus*' heels again *clicked* and *clacked* their way up the central aisle toward the semi-darkened high altar, it saw a lone figure kneeling before it with his back turned. The she-demon's pulse spiked when it recognized the cardinal. Unconsciously, it sped up with a broad grin spreading across its ruined face.

It's my priest!
And he's waiting for me!
Oooo, this is going to be sooo much fun.

*   *   *

Cardinal Garibaldi prayed for the strength of his youth as he waited in the sanctuary. Kneeling before the high altar with his back to the main, central aisle, he felt exposed and defenseless. Well, sort of. Between his prayerful hands the cardinal held a black plastic water pistol, which contained several ounces of Holy Water. The only question in his mind remained—would this stunt work?

*   *   *

Stone, who remained as still as a midnight shadow, tracked the she-demon with his eyes as it walked briskly down the central aisle, ludicrously carrying a half empty gallon of booze and some paper cups. About midway, the she-demon's back stiffened in recognition. As its pace quickened, it reached into the top of one of leather boots, and cast before its path a handful of small noisy objects that skittered across the limestone pavement.

*   *   *

Beads of nervous sweat popped out on Garibaldi's forehead as soon as he heard one of the cathedral's massive bronze doors close behind him.

Maybe it's Stone or one of my security men moving into position, he tried to convince himself.

But when the distinctive sound of approaching high heels reached his ears, his heart sank.

Time to man up, Anthony!

He closed his eyes, sighed, and pretended not to hear the succubus' advance. But the hairs on the back of his neck stood up and told his brain to go into full flight mode. Then he heard numerous chitinous skittering sounds, which seemed to be moving of their own accord.

*   *   *

Stopping about twenty-five feet from the cardinal's back, She-Who-Devours-Men's-Souls put down its booze bottle with a noisy clink. With arms outstretched and back arched grotesquely, it announced its echoing declaration of love against the distant vaulted ceiling.

"Tony!

"My love!

"I'm here to ravish you!

"Like totally!"

"And, please accept my gifts! They all want a piece of you as well!"

*　　*　　*

Stone shifted from his position toward the central aisle as the she-demon neared the cardinal. His shadow flitted across the cathedral's pavement. He didn't intend to use any of his weapons, just his training, wits, hardened Marine/TIIIS hand-to-hand combat skills, and maybe a few other surprises.

But Stone's biggest advantage was fifty pressurized fire extinguishers filled with Holy Water. All located within the pews and distributed throughout the nave within easy reach, just in case.

Stone, moving like a ghost, advanced up the central aisle in a low crouch on the unsuspecting she-demon's left rear quarter. A mere ten rows of pews separated them. Then, Stone saw them, all making their way toward the cardinal.

*　　*　　*

Garibaldi's back stiffened at the she-demon's echoing love call.

Game time, Anthony.

He breathed another prayer—*Mother Mary, Queen of Victory, pray for us.*

*   *   *

Stone saw the cardinal's neck jerk upright at the she-demon's love paean.

Now don't overplay it, Your Eminence.

The man stood, squared his shoulders, and turned to face his opponent with a mixed look of pure hate and absolute horror as a semi-circle of seven black scorpions arrayed themselves about ten feet away from him.

*   *   *

"Ohhhh, Tony." The she-demon moaned as it seductively slinked ever closer to the cardinal, crisscrossing its stride luridly.

"Boy am I going to fu—"

It never finished the sentence as a stream of Holy Water hit it squarely between the eyes. The scream that followed erupted forth full of pain and pure fury.

"Not in my cathedral, demon!" Garibaldi vented with a snarl as he thoughtlessly advanced to the bottom step of the altar. The she-demon, now down on one knee, had covered its face.

Another stream hit it, staggering it again. "Be gone demon!" the cardinal bellowed over its screams. "Be gone back to your vile, maggot-ridden realm!"

The scorpions advanced as one, in defense of their kind.

The she-demon looked up and grinned, "Oh Tony! You want to play! I love to play—"

The cardinal's ears did not record this entreaty, as his attention fell to the advancing scorpions. The first he drenched with Holy Water and it exploded into a black ectoplasmic cloud. Encouraged, he began on another.

The she-demon lunged at him with its fingers extended, claw-like.

That's when I closed the gap.

As it coiled to spring at the cardinal, I gripped its waist and muscled the emaciated she-demon high up into the air above my head. While the lift itself represented little effort, a squirming, shrieking, fighting, one hundred pounds of pissed off she-demon turned out to be something else again.

Turning, I retraced my steps in a fast walk back toward the cathedral's baptistery. Disoriented, but still full of fight, I couldn't get there fast enough and almost lost my grip on it several times. I squeezed harder, feeling a rib snap, which causing an even greater, harsher scream from overhead.

Still, the she-demon kicked. It wriggled like a snake. It tried to claw its way free. Executing a practiced gymnastic move, it doubled over and broke my grip, falling to the nave's floor with a thud, followed by a grunt as it favored its left side. Recovering, the succubus attacked me with a perfect vaudeville high kick. Caught flat-footed, I instinctively arched back and away from it. The spike high heel of its right boot missed my face by mere millimeters. While its right boot still pointed toward the ceiling, I closed on it, and my left fist smashed into its right temple. The frail form crumpled into an unconscious pile.

Meanwhile, Cardinal Garibaldi had dispatched only two of the demonic scorpions before his squirt gun ran dry. He sprinted left to the nearest pew, lifted a fire canister, and made short work of the remaining scorpions. And it was well he did, for one had lodged its stinger into the heel of his right shoe.

*   *   *

Then came the tricky part and, fortunately, I had the cardinal for assistance. The cathedral's baptismal font, an ornately carved six-sided stone monument about three feet high, had a great basin hollowed out at its top filled to the brim with Holy Water. I lowered the she-demon's head into it, face first, with a great overflowing splash.

The she-demon revived.

I cannot describe the challenge of pinning down this kicking, flailing, fighting bundle of energy. Perhaps wrestling an alligator, but I've never done that to know for sure.

Raising its head for a quick breath, I drove it back down. "Your Eminence! Pop open an extinguisher. I need more water!"

Hearing the hissing depressurization, the cardinal rushed up and stood beside me at the ready with the canister poised.

"Okay, Your Eminence, I'm goin' to let her breathe again. Get ready to dump it on its head. Now!" And the move worked to perfection, just the way we had practiced it. The woman got her gasping breath and the cardinal doused the she-demon's head. In the process, he had refilled the basin, and down its head went again, while the cardinal ran off to retrieve and prep another canister.

This dunking process taxed us and we had only done it twice. But the she-demon began to peter out, too. The kicks lessened and the flailing became more disoriented. While its aura remained as black as ever, now came the difficult part—rolling it over.

"Okay, Phase Two. Are you ready?"

"Yes, Mr. Stone."

I flipped the she-demon over like a beached catfish, its back now arched against the side of the basin.

"Careful of her back!" the cardinal warned.

"Understood!"

Holding it by the neck over the surface of the water, I snatched a small shiny object from a small slit pocket at my waist, thrust it between the she-demon's teeth, and clamped its jaw closed with my two hands.

"Now!" I signaled.

The cardinal gripped its ankles and raised them high while I again submerged the she-demon's head for the third time. The squirming struggle had now become epic. Its claw-like hands raked at anything and everything within reach. I could feel the welts forming. The cardinal, however, had a fight on his hands as its legs kicked.

After about fifteen Mississippi's I allowed the demon to breathe through her nostrils, snorting water and snot everywhere, but its aura had grayed out some. Down it went again for the fourth time using our crude form of water boarding. After another fifteen Mississippi's, and another breath, the aura had become a muddied brown, and another submersion followed, the fifth. Glancing at the cardinal, he now held aloft two limp legs; the guy was hanging in there. Another breath for the woman that I was trying to save and I could see the fight neared its end, as vague pastels began to show through the light muddy brown.

"One more time!" I called out. "We're almost

there!"

When I raised her head the sixth time, I saw only a bright green aura. Clear, if a bit broken, the young woman lolled in my arms, bruised, battered, and soaked to the skin.

Lowering her down and sitting her on the baptistery's soaked floor, I leaned her up against the stone pedestal and examined the lolling head. I could sense no evil within her whatsoever. Next, I opened her mouth and retrieved a slimy, blackened object, and dropped it into a small pool of Holy Water.

"Dear Lord! Look!" the cardinal exclaimed while pointing toward the coin.

The consecrated, mint condition, 1923 Liberty silver dollar I had forced into her mouth, appeared to be cleaning itself off in the sacramental fluid. Better, it sloughed off the blackened coating, which bubbled and broke up right before our very eyes, an evaporating black mist.

"The disintegrating ectoplasm of a demon. I have never before seen the like, but I have read about it," the cardinal remarked as if commenting on a known and expected chemical reaction.

After a few more moments, he continued. "I think you can pick it up now. It has cleansed itself."

Right then the young woman came to, and her first words had a distinctive southern quality to them.

"Oh, oh, my."

Pant.

"Thank you … So much."

Pant.

"All of those horrible dreams."

Then, with some alarm, "Where am I?"

I looked down at my watch: 9:19 pm.
Time for me to roll.

*   *   *

The Devourer of Souls screamed and mourned the silver-tainted remains of what once had been an ancient, rare, and powerful demon, She-Who-Devours-Men's-Souls. Meanwhile, its colleague, the Ledger Keeper, calmly recorded the demon's passing.

*   *   *

It turned out Candi Abbott, a high school computer whiz and runaway, turned hooker by the she-demon, came from North Carolina. Sitting with the cardinal by her side in the 17th Precinct, Candi was ashamed and horrified with what her mortal body had done over the past fifty-three days. Not to mention the terrors she tried to describe to the watch-captain about her soul's sojourn into the dark realm. During that time, her hands had been bruised, two fingers broken, along with two cracked ribs. Her once beautiful face had been turned into a series of long, brutal vertical wounds made by the claws of an outraged Manhattan socialite.

So much for her living the dream in the Big Apple. However, Cardinal Garibaldi had his own ideas about "living the dream." He had contacts, and he made arrangements for all of her ailments be taken care of at Bellevue Hospital, even down to one good cosmetic surgeon. His feeling was that Candi had been cruelly used. Now she had to be restored as best as the Church could provide.

Before Candi left in an ambulance, the NYPD

asked what had happened to her. Candi, as it turned out, knew her cars. She recalled being picked up by a nice man in a black stretch limo, a brand new Mercedes-Benz 600 Maybach with wire wheels. She described a well-dressed, middle-aged, Caucasian man with light brown to sandy colored hair, and perfect ivory white skin, but snake-like eyes. Well, Candi had not liked what she saw and tried to exit the vehicle, but the john prevented her, after which he made several hand gestures. Thereafter her nightmare existence began.

Candi's testimony provided enough information, and the NYPD found only one black Maybach limo registered in the entire state of New York—a lease to a corporation headquartered on Fifth Avenue.

CHAPTER 36
First Assault

An examination of the street-level NYPD security tapes revealed that over the last thirty-odd days the she-demon identified as Candi Abbott had repeatedly visited the CMES headquarters building, always after hours and always after 10 pm. This pattern held true for all the evenings of the cathedral incidents as well. This suggested to me that tonight would be no different, as the she-demon reported in to its conjurer. On the basis of Peter Simon's description, I had a pretty good idea who that might be—William Alexander, aka, The Dark One. That would place the CMES regional director in his office on this night.

*   *   *

Two days prior to the Friday evening assault on the CMES building, five TIIIS technical personnel had temporarily moved into the cathedral's rectory to use as a staging location. They had to penetrate and render useless the electronic security suite of the CMES building. While this effort could not open mechanically engaged locks that required a key, all the building's electronic intruder defenses—motion detectors, infrared heat detectors, and the like, went offline at 9:45 pm.

*   *   *

At 9:40 pm, a nearly empty NYPD Bell 412 helicopter took off from Floyd Bennett Memorial Airport, twelve and a half miles from the CMES headquarters building.

It was a mere eight minutes away. En route, the pilot turned off its running lights.

Their lone passenger, a trained soldier and fast-line specialist, had dressed in FDNY fire gear while in the hanger. This dignitary carried a small black duffle bag. Vatican Guard Chaplain Gerhard Manfred Schmidt had repelled countless times onto rooftops, but never a forty-one-story building in the middle of Manhattan. The chaplain concerned himself most with the many fickle updrafts and winds that high-rises and their neighboring artificial canyons produced.

With his legs dangling over the edge of the starboard door opening, Schmidt couldn't believe the view of the fast approaching city. For this native of Basel, Switzerland, the moment would never be forgotten. His helmet radio chirped him back to reality.

"Target in one minute."

"Roger," Schmidt replied as he tried to pick out his target building.

Es gibt so viele.

"Target in thirty."

"Roger," Schmidt said as he felt his toes tingle with anticipation.

"Over target."

At that, Schmidt reached into a full plastic crate and began dropping water balloons onto the roof. Nervous, Schmidt broke two in the cabin. With each impact the water stain grew until they drenched a circle twenty foot wide. Satisfied, Schmidt barked into his headset, "Belaying line," as he dropped the weighted coil of one-inch nylon rope and saw its final length bounce in the middle of the small pool on the flat section of the roof.

"Roger."

"Deploying. *Und vielen Dank!*" Once Schmidt disconnected his helmet from the helicopter's communications tether, the Swiss Guard Chaplain disappeared over the edge and into the darkness.

*   *   *

"I have a visual," the New Jersey co-pilot said to the helicopter pilot.

"He's down and clear. Just got a thumbs up. Those Holy Water balloons seemed to have done the trick.

"Get us out of here, Joey, before someone sees us."

"Roger that."

*   *   *

Conditions atop the roof became calm once the helicopter's downdraft was removed. Orienting himself to what he had memorized from the building's aerial photo, Schmidt looked around and tested the air. Just to make sure, Schmidt reached into his duffle, removed a two-liter water container, holding a very special liquid-water blessed by the Holy Father himself, and sprinkled its contents experimentally on a dry section of the roof. Squatting down close, he neither saw nor smelled any reaction. He then removed a pair of laser glasses from his duffle. Again looking around, he saw not one photon from a laser light detection system.

"Unbelievable," he whispered. Pleased, he continued with his mission. He located the exterior paneling of the building's massive fire systems reservoir. Chuckling to himself, Schmidt thought it rather difficult to hide a one million gallon water tank.

What the chaplain could not test for was his weight, which had been noted by the sensor scales embedded in the roof's surface.

* * *

Far below, within the building's security suite, a silent red light blinked on an unmanned computer console. The perimeter alert from the roof's scale sensors went unnoticed because the security staff had bigger fish to fry—they had just lost all computer connectivity with the outside world as well as external power.

* * *

Standing at the southern corner of the roof's water tank, Schmidt removed the now half full two-liter water bottle from his black duffle. Schmidt traced out with his fingers, about two ounces in the form of a crude cross, blessed the site, hugged it with the open palms of his hands, and prayed.

> O water, creature of God, I exorcise you in the name of God the Father the almighty, and in the name of Jesus Christ His Son, our Lord, and in the power of the Holy Spirit. I exorcise you so that you may put to flight all the power of the Enemy, and be able to root out and supplant that Enemy with his apostate angels; through the power of our Lord Jesus Christ, Who will come to judge the living and the dead and the world to come. Amen.

This Schmidt did to all four corners of the water tank, and to make sure, he revisited each corner and anointed each with holy oils.

In the Name of God, I exorcise all influences of evil, that they may be cast out from this oil and balsam which we are about to dedicate to His service, in the power of the (sign of the cross) Father, and of the (sign of the cross) Son, and of the Holy (sign of the cross) Spirit.

Finished, Schmidt let out a deep sigh. He had traveled over 4,200 miles to complete this blessing.

I pray it works.

Glancing at his watch, it read 9:57 pm.

Ah, I still have a few minutes to pray.

At 10:00 pm, Schmidt heard the distinctive rumble of pumps coming to life.

Es geht los.

The audacious plan called for the nullification of the building's built-in magical protections and defenses from the inside out, using its own fire system, a thing never envisioned by its owners; the saturation of the building's core with Holy Water.

Soon I must begin my long decent to the ground level.

Now where is the roof's service door?

*   *   *

Mr. Henry, a bundle of nervous energy, coordinated the security cordon in the subway station below the CMES building. The former Marine sergeant had borrowed his battle gear from a New York Emergency Service Unit, or Special Weapon and Tactics Team (SWAT). He stood in the center of the train platform, in command and prepared to fight the good fight. But against who? Even with this well-armed security force, Mr. Henry realized that he didn't know who or what his enemy might be or how many. That, he didn't like one bit.

But what he disliked even more was what that young brute Stone was up against—the ascent of forty-one stories in fireman's gear. That duty didn't appeal to Mr. Henry.

He and his security team had arrived on the E Train at the Fifth Avenue and 53rd Street Station below the CMES building. The plan called for half of them to proceed up to the fare and turn-style level of the station, while the remainder scattered out to cover all the entrances on the lower level. It being 9:30 pm, their collective nerves twitched, so Mr. Henry did what came naturally.

"Men, gather around. I know what I'm about to say will sound hokey, but believe it or not, tonight we're fighting evil, pure evil. Anyone who comes down those stairwells from the building above must be detained and brought to me. Forget your typical profiles. What we're trying to find is an arsonist. Your business is to make sure not one individual slips by. Not one! You got that?" he said as he looked around into everyone's eyes. "Okay, now spread out to your stations, keep your eyes peeled, and turn your helmet radios on."

* * *

At 9:30 pm. four bright white telecom trucks, following each other, turned on to Fifth Avenue southbound from 54th Street. Reaching 53rd, the first three turned right and began to spread out with one truck each pulling up onto the sidewalks on 53rd, the Avenue of the Americas, and 52nd Street. The fourth remained on Fifth and it, too, pulled up on the sidewalk in front of a casual clothing store. Parked, all the drivers deployed four orange safety cones at the corners of their vehicle. With that task completed, they all returned to their cabs and waited for further instructions from their radios.

These trucks had an odd-looking vertical boom with several long and slab-sided antennae mounted on each side. Inside each sat two TIIIS technical staffers. By 9:45 pm, all four trucks had succeeded in isolating the entire city block with their Wi-Fi jamming equipment. Nothing got in, nothing got out.

*   *   *

At about the same time, 9:45 pm, locally sourced communications technicians cut all the land lines leading to that same city block. While the fiber optic bundle had only been about four inches in diameter, it would take over a week of splicing to repair it. The foreman in charge of this purposeful vandalism, the cardinal counted as a devout Catholic and personal friend.

*   *   *

In the conference room of St. Thomas' Church, located across the street from the CMES headquarters building on Fifth Avenue, another team of TIIIS technical personnel busied themselves with perhaps the most daunting part of the assault: the hack of the building's fire alarm and control systems. At 10 pm, a building wide fire alarm sounded with its ear-splitting, cacophonous blaring. The fire system then sent a full four-alarm signal to the surrounding FDNY departments. Simultaneously, the building's internal sprinklers turned on full blast, trying in vain to put out a fire that did not exist. Locked in "open mode," the sprinkler system could not be overridden from within the building. Instead, the water pumps would continue to run until the storage tank on the roof went dry. The pumps' motors, water cooled, would continue to turn until they burned themselves out with heat-seized armatures.

*   *   *

In conjunction with all the other activity along Fifth Avenue, the DSNY, or Department of Sanitation of New York, went into action. Five trucks and five teams tackled five manholes that serviced the electrical power to the CMES building. At 9:45 pm, the DSNY cut all power to that city block, which included the train station beneath it as well, stranding one train in station and removing from service the E and M lines. The foreman of these trucks, also a Roman Catholic, happened to be the uncle of a certain socialite's daughter whose June wedding had been ruined.

*   *   *

At 9:55 pm, the fire alarm in the E and M Train Station went off, followed by the loss of electrical power. While the darkness lasted mere moments before the battery-powered emergency lights kicked in, Mr. Henry wished for a pair of night vision goggles. *You never know,* he berated himself.

How could you forget something as simple as that? Must be getting old.

"Sit rep!" Mr. Henry barked into his helmet's

microphone. All twenty-five of his crew reported in. Pleased beyond words, the octogenarian smiled.

Now we wait for the rats fleeing the sinking ship.

Four minutes after the alarm began sounding, their first fleeing building personnel began to appear. Most wore very damp business attire, clear evidence of the sprinkler systems effectiveness. Of those herded over to Mr. Henry, three of the sixteen late night staffers displayed muddy auraic hues. The ex-Marine grilled each for several minutes. One he asked to step aside for a more extensive discussion. Down deep he couldn't resist hassling this twerp. At the very least, Mr. Henry felt that he could provide him with a firm dose of reality.

*   *   *

At 10:04 pm, the FDNY from three fire stations arrived and set up around the CMES building on three of its sides—on 52nd Street, 53rd Street, and Fifth Avenue.

By 10:07 pm, the first fire teams broke through the building's main entrance and began their ascents of the interior's fire escape stairwells. Among them were three imposters dressed as firemen. Once inside the building, these three broke away from the main fire teams.

The cardinal had been adamant Stone should not ascend to the penthouse alone, so two men joined him in his marathon stairwell assault of forty-one stories.

"Friends," the cardinal called them. "You can trust these men, Mr. Stone. I can guarantee you'll need them."

*   *   *

By 10:10 pm, the NYPD had cordoned off the entire block at street level in response to the four-alarm fire. With traffic on 52nd and 53rd Streets blocked, the Avenue of the Americas narrowed to two lanes as did Fifth Avenue. While the NYPD managed crowd control, they also had been alerted to apprehend anyone fleeing the building at ground level on suspicion of arson.

*　　*　　*

At the stroke of 10 pm, the building-wide fire alarm went off without warning. The sprinklers gushed. Water collected and pooled everywhere, cascading down the internal fire escape stairwells and elevator shafts, forming small streams and waterfalls. By the fifteenth floor, the stairwells had taken on the appearance of mountain streams.

With the power cut, all the elevators frozen, only localized, battery-driven emergency lighting soldiered on. To this internal deluge, the CMES North American headquarters building meekly surrendered to its fate.

With the emergency stairwells commandeered by the firemen ascending the structure, few above the second floor got out unnoticed.

For some reason, the building's head security officers suffered the most from the event, caught in the manmade rain, they fell down to their knees in excruciating seizures, which seemed to pass after a few minutes. Thereafter, they appeared disoriented and asked their colleagues questions that revealed their complete confusion. Only then did they evacuate.

*   *   *

I led the charge up through the rush of water descending from one particular emergency stairwell. The building's plans indicated it serviced the penthouse, and it alone.

It was an excruciating, ball-busting climb. Forty-one floors are eighty-two flights of twelve steps. Think about that. Loaded up we looked like FDNY's finest, which meant close to fifty pounds of gear. But when you include the antiquated fire canisters across our backs, figure another forty pounds. I also had to contend with the sheer heat buildup from my UCS under the fire suit, which, as one veteran called it, felt like a "slow cook on low." Even the resistance from the bibs slowed our progress. But after a heart-exploding fifty-five minute ascent, we reached the penthouse level. With its crash door sealed, we took turns bashing it with our fire axes.

When we broke through, the glare of our LED headlamps revealed a blacked out, lavishly appointed, but soaking mess of a penthouse apartment.

Move with care, soul carrier. This portal cannot be touched. Once through, examine it, the First Soul whispered in my mind.

CHAPTER 37
The Dark One's Lair

I entered first, turning sideways. Water squished out of the thick carpeting under my fire boots, leaving tracks behind. I turned around to my colleagues and gasped, "Look out!" pointing to the rippling doorjambs of the ruined fire door which were now covered in glowing red hieroglyphs.

"The jambs are booby-trapped. Don't brush up against them!" I bellowed. Without question the inscriptions were wards against unwanted intruders like us. But now, with rivulets of Holy Water flowing across them, they glowed on defiantly, while their spell's workings had been grounded.

After entering, we continued to recon the penthouse. In places, the wallboard ceiling bowed down and looked like it would fall in at any moment. Water rained from above and streamed down the walls everywhere.

"There must be at least three centimeters of water on this floor," one of my colleague's quipped.

In all, we cleared twelve rooms, taking care when passing through each doorway. Finally, we found a secretarial niche with a desk and credenza. Beyond it stood a closed door.

I almost touched its latch-style handle, but stopped. Even though I wore heavy leather fireman's gloves over my UCS' gauntlets, something just didn't seem right. My teammate, the First Soul, remained strangely silent. I looked around the secretarial area, found a coffee cup on the credenza, and scraped up some water from the drenched carpeting. I dribbled the liquid over the latch handle and was rewarded with a hiss and snap as it cooked off the brass. I did this several more times until the latch handle hissed no more. Only then did I pull open the door.

The door's threshold granted entrance to an immense darkened room located at the penthouse's southern corner. Windows stretched from floor to ceiling on two sides, affording magnificent views of the city and its brightly lit up neighbor, the cathedral. Backlit by these lights was the silhouette of a man holding an open umbrella sitting behind the shadow of a massive desk—or was it?

From where I stood I saw two dreadful auras—one associated with the seated man and the other of his desk, which clearly was a living thing, writhing in silent agony. My flashlight revealed that its claws grasped the soaked carpeting in mindless pain, its many coils sizzling in the Holy Water. Scales curled and many open sores oozed a wretched smelling black ectoplasm. I was witnessing the slow death of the dragon-like form.

Soul carrier. Your plan has trapped this most evil one. But take care as you near it, the First Soul counseled.

*   *   *

I side-stepped into the room and took care not to brush against its jambs. I tried to advance, but ran into a wall of thick, heavy, cold air that slowed my progress. The conjurer behind the living desk had sucked the energy from the room, lowering the temperature to form this magical barrier. Once stabilized, I knew that the will to sustain it would have to come from the conjurer himself. I shuffle-sloshed forward inch by inch. My feet created wavelets that broke against the front façade of the massive living desk. These ripples caused intense shudders of pain as they splashed against the recumbent form, which I could see because the pain looked like lightning flashes in the demon's aura.

Regarding the silhouetted man as I neared, I could make out that his dark-socked feet had been tucked beneath him up, legs folded cross-legged in his chair. The umbrella kept the man completely dry.

I continued my slow slog forward and said, "It seems for all of your protections, Mr. Alexander, you hadn't planned on a flood—a flood of consecrated Holy Water. The flood has also crippled your dragon-demon-desk. It's trapped, suffering in hideous agony. Seems that you have a thing for reptiles."

At that point, the two other firemen, also struggled forward, with one flanking me on each side, causing ever more wave action. At this, the desk actually groaned and shuddered.

"Fuck you, Stone," the Dark One rasped; a whip-crack fueled by pure frustration.

"Oh, you know who I am?"

"Of course I do. The entire Gathering does. We have known of you since birth. We even arranged for a certain pickup truck accident."

The reference to the crash that took my Grace's life and two innocent others caught me up short, and for a moment I allowed my mind's blocks to slip.

"Yes, you do remember, don't you?" the Dark One crooned. "Poor little Grace, so horribly mangled. All the while she shielded you, tried to protect you."

"You know," I whispered.

"Of course, you fool! We all know. We keep extensive records in our Gathering. But you survived that crash, didn't have the guts to kill yourself.

"You're a coward!" the Dark One raged, spittle flying.

"You went out and joined the Marines out of pure, self-pity, didn't you? You ran away. You yearned for your own heroic demise on some god-forsaken battlefield. Didn't you?" As the Dark One shook his head in sad disapproval while wagging his finger at me. "All so you could forget about your poor little Grace."

At that point, I slipped my hand around to my back, grabbed my canister's hose control, and tested a theory. I arched a clear stream of the cardinal's best Holy Water across the desk, under the umbrella, and into the creep's lap.

Alexander reacted as if a bucket of hot coals had been dumped on him. His crossed legs started jumping this way and that, his overstrained immobilization spell broke like a dry twig, and we were no longer seeing fog for breath.

I wanted to reach out and wring his scrawny little pencil neck. Yes, I admit it, I barely had control, but managed, somehow, to stop myself. My mind blocks returned, stronger than before. Now the three of us stood before him like a high tribunal, while his living desk wheezed and heaved.

"If you know so much about me, then you can see my aura. What does it tell you?"

The Dark One just stared back at me in total defiance with the edge of his mouth twitching.

"You ... your aura ... No one has one like that ...

except *you*." My anger had manifested itself, causing my aura's color to bleed from metallic gold into a blinding electrum glare.

"Yes, that's true. And hello, I'm the new TIIIS Lictor of Magic as well."

While the Dark One now had positive confirmation of something that he had long suspected, his maddened mind had difficulty grasping the magnitude of his precarious situation. This I could see in his twisted mind and from his aura. He thought he was still in total control.

So I again triggered my hose nozzle, but this time I hit him point blank in his face. His ear-splitting shriek echoed through the apartment as the skin of his face and hands reddened from the brief squirt. In the process, the Dark One dropped his umbrella, which landed beyond his grasp, and floated away on the flooded carpeting.

Whimpering in pain, "Now you have gone too far, Lictor of Magic! This is private property! This is breaking and entering! This is trespassing! And I see two witnesses to your gross mistreatment of me. My lawyers will have your head on a stake!"

At his mention of my two colleagues, I glance at each and said, "Gentlemen, why don't you join in? Briefly."

Two more quick pressurized streams doused the man's head and upper torso. The screams began anew, again filling the room. After several moments, choking gasps emanated from the man's now blistered face and hands.

"Stop. Please," came the weak plea.

"You know, Mr. Alexander, you really should cooperate. These fine men are not from the FDNY, but the Vatican. In fact, they are Cardinal Garibaldi's colleagues, members of the Society of Saint Paul."

Horrified eyes stared back in realization of what that meant, and he began trembling uncontrollably.

"Yes, Mr. Alexander—or should I say, the Dark One—they're trained and experienced exorcists."

Spasmodic jerking of the head to the left commenced as the Dark One realized his trapped situation. He couldn't even make for the shatterproof windows.

"I find it pathetic," I continued, "that you're threatening me with legal action and all because of a couple of squirts of Holy Water. After all, we're just here to save you during a fire alarm. To assist in your safe evacuation."

The Dark One bowed his head in silence.

"Did you know your conjured she-demon sacrificed an innocent male infant?"

"Yessss. I did, Lictor of Magic." Again with a left twitch of his head. "It was a mere discard. Nothing really. A convenient way to dispose of something that I had processed."

By the look on the Dark One's face, I could see the manifest madness of the man. Someone who had lived for control, and now, did not possess a shred of it.

The Dark One could not hold my gaze. He just bowed his head, which again twitched spasmodically to the left.

"Do you not realize that TIIIS' very purpose is the eradication of human sacrifice and dark magic?"

Complete silence from the occupant of the office chair.

"Still have nothing to say?"

Total, stubborn silence.

"You're not cooperating, Mr. Alexander. Once again, gentlemen, briefly, if you please."

Three pressurized streams struck the man and somehow, someway, he kept his mouth shut. His body jerked violently about in a most grotesque fashion, and all within the confines of his padded desk chair.

The streams stopped.

Labored gasps emanated from the man. His now ruddy and ruined skin looked more like sagging plastic.

"One last question, Mr. Alexander. What source did you use for the she-demon's conjuring?"

Again that defiant silence.

"Where is THE BOOK!" I bellowed in my very best Marine command speak, which filled the office.

Fractionally, at the verbal assault, the Dark One's mind glanced in the general direction of the credenza.

Recovering himself, he screamed, *"Fuck you!"* full knowing I had caught his careless thought.

On and on, he raged madly for several minutes, furious at himself that he had fallen for such an amateurish parlor trick. Worse, that a Lictor of Magic had managed it.

"I thought so," I said with considerable sadness.

As I beheld this miserable, mad creature, its aura a mass of writhing jet black and slippery tentacles, I found myself pitying him.

"Dark One. You must know you are beyond any hope of rescue, at least save yourself. Save your soul. Do you wish to repent?"

The man remained silent.

"Do you beg forgiveness for all your evil deeds before the loving, all merciful, and almighty God?"

Again, only dripping water could be heard.

"We forgive you, nonetheless," I said with a softness that betrayed my great disappointment.

With those words, the wretch cringed in silent agony, twisting this way and that like a trapped eel.

Then, with a heavy sigh of resignation, I said. "Gentlemen. Empty your tanks."

"Niiiiiieeeeeeeeeeeeeeee!"

In the end the Dark One's remains looked like an indistinct, sagging, gelatinous mass supported by a bent and ruined skeleton. No aura remained.

The Dark One had passed.

Since I had some Holy Water left, I emptied mine on the desk itself, which shuddered, blurring the definition of its surface. The whole thing sagged, imploded, and broke down into a mass of blackened ectoplasm, which evaporated right before our eyes. All that remained was a quickly filling oval impression in the carpet.

Before we exited the room, we did several things. One of the false firemen punched a hole through a glass pane with the pick end of his ax. He lit a green flare and pushed it through, where it fell forty-one stories to the 52nd Street pavement below.

Meanwhile, I removed from a pocket a sterile vial and took a sample from the remains of the Dark One. Not my idea, the eggheads back at the Academy wanted it.

That grisly task complete, we swept the office. And there we found it, in his credenza, *The Book of Spells*. Its cover decorated in golden Egyptian hieroglyphs. Huge in size, measuring maybe one by two feet, and looking to be about fifteen to twenty pounds.

Careful, soul carrier, the First Soul whispered.

One exorcist reached into the credenza to lift it out.

"Stop! Don't touch it without gloves."

"Stone, you've got to be kidding," said the one named Richardo.

"The evil one is dead, that makes it powerless," as he recklessly reached inside and pulled out the heavy book with his bare hands.

"See, Stone? Just one very heavy book," were his last words.

Several things happened and none of them good. First, Richardo dropped the book, which I caught midair before it hit the flooded carpet. Second, his colleague, Gaetano, caught his impetuous friend under his arms as his knees buckled. Blood began to leak from his eyes, nose, and ears as the stricken man started coughing up even more. His breath became labored. With eyes rolling around in bloody sockets, he gagged on his own bodily fluids. Suffocating, his fingers clawed for his own throat seeking to create an air passage. It was all over in twenty awful seconds. Richardo's hands, where he had touched the book, now were a heavily blistered and a bleeding mess. I avoided them as I slipped on his fireman's gloves.

Gaetano, white with shock, continued to hold Richardo upright.

"I will carry him down," Gaetano said. "You just take care of that cursed book."

"No. We'll do it together. I'll grab some pillow cases to carry the book in and tie it to my canister's harness. But first, let me check on something.

I used my flashlight to illuminate the credenza's shelf and there they were. Discolorations and lines, marks where the book once sat, there, there and there. And each time, the book left behind oily-looking smudges.

Poor Richardo.

*　　*　　*

At the arrival of the Dark One's ruined soul within its dark realm, the Devourer of Souls first played with it and thereafter tore it apart, all while it screamed in abject terror. Three days later, an eternity within that dank realm, the Devourer destroyed it because of its nagging hunger. This passing, too, the Ledger Keeper noted as it dutifully made its calculations.

*　　*　　*

That night—or early morning—I didn't know which, I collapsed into a post-op mess and went over the deep end. Exhausted and stressed out, I couldn't sleep. My nerves were fried from adrenalin levels that had peaked and crashed. I couldn't think straight. Still rolling in sweat after two cold showers, I was shot. I couldn't stop twitching. I did what countless warriors have done before me. I found a dark hole, curled up into a ball, and broke down. It was Iraq all over again.

That morning they found me in the corner of my hotel room, balled up like an infant, clutching a tear-soaked pillow. They later told me they found me rocking back and forth, whispering something over and over again into it. They didn't dare approach me. They knew better. They let me be for the next couple of hours until I came out of it.

CHAPTER 38
Aftermath

Failed Alarm System Costs Landlord Half a Billion Dollars

(NYC) An estimated one million gallons of water from a failed fire alarm system flooded the interior of an office building on Fifth Avenue last night.

One FDNY fireman on the scene said that as they climbed the stairwells, they had to make their way against torrents of descending water.

The building manager said, "Somehow our building-wide fire alarm system was tripped. Then we lost all power. That isn't supposed to happen, but it did. It was a perfect storm."

A contractor on the scene estimated that the renovation of the forty-one-story building's interior would cost nearly a half a billion dollars.

(*The New York News*, A2)

The swamping of the CMES building turned out to be a TIIIS intelligence windfall. With the building's interior compromised, its electrical wiring shot, the structure had to be gutted as mildew had already taken hold within its sealed environment. In the process, TIIIS agents, planted within the many tradesmen, recorded the backsides of the building's many exterior panels and door jams, and managed to gain a view into CMES' magical defenses. Meanwhile, other TIIIS agents raided the Communications and Security department, seizing hard drives and removing computers, while others did the same to the Human Resources Department. Add to that, several secret passageways were discovered in the building's subbasement.

The ruin of the CMES North American headquarters reverberated throughout the paranormal community. But that paled in comparison to the reaction when word got out that the Dark One's much-rumored *Book of Spells* had been stolen. It was well recognized that whomever possessed it, if willing to use it, would wield unlimited power.

*   *   *

The lab rats at the TIIIS Academy confirmed the lethal nature of *The Book of Spells'* cover, as they flat-out could not identify the toxic agent, which meant there was no known antidote. Thoroughly frightened by the book, the lab sealed it a vacuum bag, placed it in a locked Halliburton storage box, and deposited it somewhere on campus, where it would be forgotten, forever.

I also heard the same bunch of squeamish lab rats had digitally recorded the entire book, cover to cover, in visible, infrared, and ultra-violet light prior to locking it away. With this copy at his fingertips, Mr. Good had been tasked to decipher it.

This news I didn't welcome. If the possession of *The Book of Spells* didn't represent a sufficient liability, why the hell make a digital copy of it, and then task one of your scholars to translate it? That meant, at least in my mind, TIIIS intended to use it. For me, this equated to letting the nuclear genii out of the bottle, or, publicizing on the internet, the words for invoking a

279

death wish spell. Eventually, someone would hack TIIIS' database or steal Mr. Good's laptop, and end up with a working copy for themselves.

I asked myself, *What the hell is going on?*

I soon found out.

*   *   *

Two weeks after the raid, TIIIS flew Cardinal Garibaldi and me in their flat-black commuter jet to Rome. The cardinal went as our unofficial representative to the Vatican. I got to courier, guess what: a digital copy of *The Book of Spells,* which I carried in a special locked container. If tampered with, its contents—in this case a thumb drive—would magnetize said drive, destroying all of its data. I carried this "gift" as a peace offering from TIIIS to the Vatican. "Gift" in the German language, by the by, means "poison."

This sharing of the Dark One's compilation, I thought unwise. But ever the good soldier, I handed it over. The priest who received it, an older gentleman who reminded me of Mr. Henry, assured me the copy would be well cared for. Fine. *Trust, but verify.*

Cardinal Garibaldi showed me around, and insisted at every door to introduce me to yet another bunch of his friends. While grateful for the public relations opportunity that this represented for TIIIS, the ritual became old, grating, and the fawning ever more effusive. What bugged me the most was that I lost my once anonymous face.

While at a reception, I met a chaplain of the Swiss Guard, the only one present, which I thought odd, it being the Vatican and all.

So I introduced myself and said. "I couldn't help

but notice that you're the only Swiss Guard at this party. Why's that?"

At my question, a dashing smile radiated from this guard with brilliantly bright auraic hues. A big guy, he looked me right in the eye said. "I know who you are, Mr. Stone. After all, it was I who made your little operation possible."

Big, young, bold, and confident, I amended.

"How so?"

"I was the one the NYPD helicopter dropped off on the roof. I blessed the water tank. If anything, Mr. Stone," he said with a finger in my chest, "you owe me big time."

With wonder and awe on my face, I asked, "Is your real name Clark Kent?"

After a quick laugh at my lame attempt at praise, the Swiss Guard said seriously, "*Nein*, Mr. Stone. My name is Father Gerhard Schmidt. I'm a simple, run-of-the-mill, Swiss Guard Chaplain."

"Bullshit!" I coughed into my closed fist. So it began, a torrent of stories, exaggerations, and being ordinary soldiers.

In the end I invited him to visit the U.S. sometime. He in turn invited me to his hometown of Basel.

*   *   *

It had been a busy summer and I looked forward to returning to my graduate work at the Academy. I won't sugar coat it. After two days of soul searching, I figured it out in my own terms. While my natural inclination said protect the innocent, I also could not, in good conscience, place in danger another human being. That meant I could not expect to have, much less maintain, a normal family life. Though that still left open the possibility of someone who knew, up front, what they were getting into. And that could only mean one person on my current dance card: Melaina. When that epiphany sank in through my thick skull, I realized a kind of liberation, the sense of something having been decided.

CHAPTER 39
Early Assessment of the Damage

Two weeks after CMES' North American headquarters fell, a conference took place at a posh Italian casino nestled in the hills north of Rome. Representatives from all the CMES regions attended, in addition to many treaty-bound enclaves. An intense nervousness radiated among the attendees. The CMES leadership needed to reassure its membership. Its chairman and keynote speaker, Giovanni Presto, intended to provide it.

"Ladies and gentlemen. The savage attack on the North American regional headquarters will be avenged."

The man stopped amid a torrent of hisses, whistles, and shouted expletives in a variety of languages. When the clamor died down, he continued.

"Based upon the evidence, a group of agents, acting in concert, did this to our Gathering."

Presto stopped theatrically to sip from his favorite red wine, a Malbec, 1993, from Mendoza, Argentina. It also gave those who wished to verbally vent another opportunity.

"My sources indicate that Regional Director Alexander may have overstepped his mandate and underestimated the local reaction to his well-known proclivities and excesses. I say this because it is far too simple to assign this brazen attack solely to that papist state. From all accounts, local, grass root entities within New York City proper, had a role in this as well.

"Why do I emphasize, and in such detail, this local insurgence against the North American regional headquarters? Because it reveals our failure as a Gathering to successfully recruit, nurture, and promote our goals and ideals."

Another sip of wine as the audience rumbled.

"Due to the extensive damage done to the North American regional headquarters, it has been decided to sell the property."

Another interruption of whistles, hisses, and cat-calls. While this extended demonstration dragged on, Presto began memorizing the principal faces of dissent.

When the din receded, the Roman aristocrat continued. "Dear colleagues. The last time our Gathering lost a regional headquarters was almost four millennia ago, when barbarian desert tribes sacked our founding city, Mother Ur."

Again Presto paused, while his audience voiced their displeasure.

"Then, a proud remnant of our Gathering resettled at Beloved Memphis, where we thrived. Thereafter, we moved again to the Eternal Rome, where we remain to this very day.

"But dear Gathering, in New York, the barbarians pillaged our data, stole our treasure, and our brethren have scattered in fear for their very lives. These barbarians even brutally murdered the regional director in his own office." Presto emphasized by pounding the podium with his clenched fist.

Silence.

"Make no mistake, brethren. Barbarians sacked our regional headquarters in New York City."

Now the remarks shouted forth demanded retribution, a counter-strike, something, anything, to address their lust for swift action and revenge.

How easily they are swayed.

"Before we retire to our break-out sessions, keep this one thing in mind"—he wagged his finger—"those responsible *will* pay."

With his clenched fist held high in the air, he concluded, "Long live the *Consilium magorum et sagarum!*"

Absolute pandemonium broke out.

Fifteen minutes later a much smaller gathering of power convened in a sumptuous, gilded baroque suite. Six chairs had been arranged around the circular marble table. Present were the regional directors of Baghdad, Mombasa, St. Petersburg, and Hong Kong. The chairman of Rome joined them. A lone empty chair remained as a poignant reminder of their absent North American colleague.

"Gentlemen, I have some news that you are not to share," Presto stated. "It has come to my attention that Regional Director Alexander was 'liquidated' by his attackers; as in reduced to a large gelatinous mass. The corrosive agent, consecrated water, did this. Thus I must conclude that the Roman cardinal of New York, perhaps even the Vatican itself, played a role in the fall of the New York headquarters, and the assassination of Regional Director Alexander.

"This concerns me. Potentially, all of us are at risk. As for Regional Director Alexander, I am sure that many of you would have liked to remove him yourself. As they say, 'he was not greatly loved.'

"Also of concern is the plundering of the North American region's database and files, both financial and human resources, and the loss of a rather valuable ... *book*."

At the mention of "the book," Presto knew he had their attention, as they—Presto included—coveted it.

"Dear colleagues. Can you imagine what would happen if the Vatican got its hands on that invaluable compilation? A loss of face, not to mention the erosion of our supremacy among the paranormal community."

The regional director of Mombasa, Zakia Owusu, asked, "Mr. Chairman. Do we have, at this time, any hard evidence of who perpetrated this raid?"

"None, Mr. Owusu. We have preliminary interviews of those members who were on the scene that night. What they describe was executed with military precision. Catastrophic loss of power, loss of communications, and the complete takeover of the building's fire system, flooding the entire structure.

"As a consequence, while we should think of the Vatican as our first suspect, we should also ask ourselves, who else could they have done this?"

"Gentlemen, I would not be surprised to find during our investigations that another, minor group, wishing to establish its credentials, was responsible for the Manhattan debacle.

"And one other thing. Imagine, gentlemen, if Alexander's book has indeed fallen into the hands of one of the non-aligned. While I would expect a certain amount of restraint in its use from the Vatican, I would not from an organization wishing to make its mark upon the paranormal community."

"So, Mr. Chairman, what is to be done?" Victor Alexandrevich Volkov of the Russian region wanted to know, while quoting the words of Vladimir Lenin.

"That, Mr. Volkov, is a very good question," the chairman replied. "Given our current ignorance, we do not have a hard target. Rash action will not be useful. What I counsel is that we cast our nets widely, gather evidence, and consider all options.

"One more item. Mark my words," Presto emphasized with his raised manicured finger, "this could be the beginning of a war."

CHAPTER 40
Early Assessment of the Advantage

While CMES gathered evidence for its campaign of revenge, beneath Old Main on the Old Oaks Academy campus existed a large cavernous space excavated out of the region's native limestone. Old Main's architect deemed the chamber needful. He never said for what, but the usual theories abounded—a secret powder magazine or treasury.

Regardless, the Vault, as it came to be known, was so seldom used that its very existence became largely a matter of conjecture. The difficulty to access the Vault may have had something to do with this. Only those who sought adventure dared to tread on its several rickety wooden staircases built during America's Colonial Period. Once within its confines, all agreed, the artificial cave's natural coolness, silence, high ceiling, and spaciousness produced a calming atmosphere.

TIIIS finally found a purpose for the Vault. President Silver Moon had it cleaned, its stairs refurbished, its interior appointed, and the necessary amenities installed. Arranged in its very center stood a handsome, cherry wood conference table sixteen feet in diameter, open in the center, and surrounded by thirty-three black leather chairs. The indirect overhead lighting warmed the space. Individual LED light stalks had been installed before every chair, along with a pad of paper and pen. A thick carpeting muffled all sound.

All of this was done because President Silver Moon had done something quite extraordinary—she'd called a face-to-face meeting of all TIIIS principals worldwide. These included the regional governors of Chicago, London, Nicosia, Ankara, Mumbai, Singapore, Damascus, and Mecca. The remaining attendees constituted sub-regional governors from the U.S., Canada, England, Scotland, Ireland, India, Israel, Jordan, and Turkey. In all, thirty-one attended with two absent due to either illness or the requirements of duty. The last time such a meeting took place, in 1998, the crisis *du jour* involved the CMES inspired, but Chinese led, invasion of Mongolia to acquire certain holy relics of power and the mummified corpse of a Yeti.

* * *

President Silver Moon began: "Thank you for coming today, and for some of you, from very far away indeed. Usually, it has been our custom to use the encrypted teleconferencing systems, but not today. You can see your cell phones have no signal. That is by design, as the Vault's very nature blocks all such signals, which also means that no one can listen in on our deliberations.

"So why all the security, if not paranoia? Because from this day forward, I am placing TIIIS on our highest alert status."

Exclamations in a variety of languages raced around the Vault.

Silver Moon continued once the furor died down.

"Ever since our successful raid on the CMES North American headquarters in New York City, their encrypted global transmissions have gone through the roof. While we cannot decipher them, an educated guess would be they're angry, vengeful, and are looking for a culprit to wreak vengeance upon. Their problem, however, is who to target.

"CMES is also reeling financially from our sacking of their headquarters, as we have begun siphoning off their hoard of U.S. currency. The last time I checked, over $1.45 billion."

Gasps again rippled throughout the attendees.

"We have broken up those spoils and banked it in several, rather reliable, and disparate locations. I wish to emphasize that that figure totalled only their North American liquid assets. As for their hard assets in real estate, land, industry, and the like, we left them alone, but have marked them in such a way so we can now track their transfer. With such knowledge, we can better understand their global financial network and how it works.

"As for the human resources data we seized, we now know who makes up their North American membership, along with their vital information. In short, we have their numbers, and believe it or not, they are not the staggering hordes we had once thought.

"In Manhattan, for example, there are seventy-three CMES members, most in decision-making positions of considerable financial power. In New York state, excluding Manhattan, there are 430 members.

"What is interesting about their membership data is this that as you leave New York state, their membership declines precipitously. For example, in Boston, there are four members, but all well-placed lawyers. In Philadelphia, eleven, again, all well-placed lawyers. On the West Coast, Los Angeles has 303 members of various political and financial persuasions. As you might expect, half that number are involved in media.

In San Francisco, forty-three, in key business and technology sectors.

"Most telling, however, involves our nation's capital. 156 members are CMES, and among them, twenty-two are members of the U.S. Congress. Several of these chair influential congressional committees.

"In the heartland of the United States, CMES is non-existent, while, as we all know, those regions are our strength.

"So, in review, CMES, at least in the U.S., is predominately an urban East Coast, West Coast phenomenon. This is the first time we have such hard data on their demographics. Useful parallels might be extrapolated for regions outside of U.S.

"Now, why the raised threat alert? Because sooner or later CMES will figure out that it was us. We must prepare for that day, so that we, as a united front, can repel them. And repel them we shall, for we have an advantage CMES perhaps does not know about, or, might not yet appreciate.

"That advantage is our new Lictor of Magic, Mr. J.J. Stone, who masterminded the fall of the CMES North American headquarters, and who interviewed its regional director prior to his passing. Our Mr. Stone also found the regional director's near-apocryphal work, *The Book of Spells*."

Stunned silence.

"Yes, dear colleagues, *The Book of Spells* is not a myth, but a frightening reality.

"And in case you have forgotten, this is the same Mr. Stone, who relieved us all of that oppressive psychic burden known as 'the curse.'

"In short, we have in our Lictor of Magic, to

paraphrase Mr. Henry Horatio Johnson, 'a *bona fide* first-round draft pick,' a decorated Marine officer and veteran who carries the First Soul of Creation."

The president heard another audible intake of air and it distressed her.

They do have a short memory.

"As a consequence, no longer will TIIIS passively endure the privations of CMES. Instead, henceforth, we will react in kind, and if at all possible, in a way that is crippling. No longer are we to react like a defensive box turtle. Instead, we are going to be the mongoose."

As one might imagine, this harsh reiteration of the former president's external policy caused discussion among the thirty-one, both positive and negative. Several understood it given the presence of Stone. Others remained skeptical, citing it depended all too precariously upon one individual. When President Silver Moon outlined the significance of the First Soul in terms of sheer survivability, two naysayers moved to a more neutral position.

Still and all, President Silver Moon did not like the atmosphere of the meeting. She came to realize, as much as she disliked acknowledging the fact, that TIIIS' leadership had grown old, soft, resistant to change, and yes, even far too accepting of the *status quo*. The president recognized she needed an angle, a way to prove that being active, instead of passive, while unfamiliar territory for this group, had its distinct advantages.

With that in mind, the she again called the meeting to order.

"Dear colleagues. I believe if we voted today, right this minute, on the ratification of my predecessor's external policy, that we would be deadlocked. So, may I offer this amendment—that the U.S. Region based in Chicago, alone adopts this 'eye for an eye' policy on a provisional basis, while the remaining regions continue to follow the *status quo*. Do I have a second?"

The representative from the populous city of Mumbai raised his hand.

"I see a second. Is there any discussion?"

"The regional governor from Ankara wishes to ask why the U.S. Region is willing to take this risk? To take on the enemy in such an aggressive manner."

"A fine question, Governor Kartal. Because a famous and sacred Christian house of worship, and its clergy, had been placed under assault. They came to us for assistance, and we did so. Further, a human sacrifice took place. On the basis of our historic origins, I am willing to take such action again, *if* necessary.

"Note that my argument is not a clarion call for open attacks on CMES, or any other organization for that matter. Rather, it is an institutional commitment to draw a line in the sand, and act if necessary. Nothing more."

"And," Governor Kartal continued, "what of the spoils taken from the CMES headquarters? How are they to be divided?" The director voiced a question that several others, no doubt, didn't have the fortitude to ask.

"Governor Kartal," President Silver Moon said with cold eyes, "the ruination of the CMES North American headquarters, the U.S. Region undertook alone. Furthermore, our society's charter has no provision for such a division based on the industry or initiative of a particular region."

Now ruddy-faced, Kartal demanded, "This is outrageous, Madam President! There should be a sharing of the spoils among all of the society's regions."

To this display, the president said nothing. Instead, she waited, with her hands folded. She had stated her position and would not budge from it.

Sub-Governor Sir James McElhinney of Central Canada chose next to speak. "Well, isn't this ducky. Here we sit, in this damp and dreary cellar of all things, quibbling over a few million of this or that, when none of us had to lift a finger, nor had to bear any of the risk. Shameful, I say. Simply shameful." As he wagged his balding head in Kartal's direction.

But the Canadian sub-governor had only just begun. "Few of you have grasped the real crux of what our president has put before us. She has already proven the effectiveness of our new Lictor of Magic. CMES North America is reeling as a result, because someone dared to slap them around when they deserved it. That risk the U. S. Region accepted, and taking a risk like any other gambler, managed to win."

Bless you, Sir James, Silver Moon thought to herself.

But Kartel, like a wounded steer, blundered on nonetheless, "It is not our tradition to seek spoils."

McElhinney ruddy-faced and tight lipped, just sat there, and shook his head in resignation.

Before the emotional level of the meeting reached critical mass, the Governor of Mumbai, Mr. Jazim Patel, broke in.

"Excuse me, ladies and gentlemen. I wish to take this opportunity to thank the U.S. Region for its part in the successful retrieval of the Pakistani students. Which, I might add, their administration executed at no cost whatsoever to any other of this society's regions. In fact, I know the U.S. Region paid the entire bill for that humanitarian act. And, I also note, no one at this table offered to help defray or share in that expense. Instead, all of us stood idly by. At the very same time, what occurred in Manhattan, I see as a U.S. regional affair, handled most ably by the U.S. Region."

So ended the morning's session, in spite of the best efforts by the Governor of Mumbai to ameliorate the situation, the Governor of Turkey and Sub-Governor of Central Canada, remained at each other's throats over a successful operation run by a third party that neither had been privy to nor involved in.

CHAPTER 41
The Journalist

Need ASAP, information about who was involved in the raid on the North American HQ in NYC.

Leave no stone unturned.

Two weeks maximum.

Payment will be made in the usual way and potentially with something special.

Meneer: the situation is gravely serious.

(Encrypted email from: Giovanni Presto, CMES Chairman, to: Gordon Meneer.)

Giovanni Presto could be an epic control freak when it came to the details. As evidenced in the way he ruled his private Formula One racing team with a Microsoft Project spreadsheet which continuously threatened to crash because it had so many tasks and dependencies.

So it was no surprise that Presto wanted to know who took down the North American headquarters. He had to, otherwise, it might happen again. And if it did, Presto calculated his chairmanship would come to a crashing end. He tasked a U.S. contact to look into the matter.

Gordon Meneer haled from wind-swept South Dakota. Educated at the Ernie Pyle School of Journalism at Indiana University, Meneer, while a little guy, had a big brain and knew how to use it. Some thought him a savant, but really, Meneer just used his smarts and had a knack for pulling things apart and rearranging them into a coherent picture. Which was why he followed in the footsteps of the long-time crossword editor and puzzle king, Will Shortz, of *The New York Times*, and minored in Enigmatology.

Meneer also had another advantage, he didn't stick out in a crowd. Mousy-haired, slight, and bookish, the journalist blended into an urban landscape. While Meneer had earned his place on the freelance staffs of several news services, his real job involved ferreting out information for Presto, who usually employed him to scout out his racing competitors. Two additional things—Meneer, a card-carrying CMES member and amateur racing driver, lived for the rush of speed and reveled in the head games racers like to play. If Meneer had a weakness, a vice, auto racing was it, and Presto knew it.

* * *

Meneer sat reading his morning newspapers while drinking his coffee when Presto's encrypted email arrived. Such research requests caused Meneer to speculate how his payment would be realized. In the past, the toys had been a Miata, a Lotus Elan, and even M-3 BMW for some damning evidence on an opposing racing team. But Meneer's bespectacled eyes widened at the closing statement: "the situation is gravely serious." Racing is racing, but racing is never "gravely serious," unless of course, you're the one in the ambulance, or worse. Glancing back at the email's content, noting the qualifiers "ASAP" and "Two weeks maximum," the research journalist surmised, "Jesus, this must be hot."

And any pay off will be big as well.

*   *   *

While Meneer had read about the fiasco that had occurred at CMES' North American headquarters in Manhattan, he now appreciated Presto's intense interest in it, especially given the internal scuttlebutt about Presto's undying hatred for the North American regional director, Alexander. Without question, the Roman wanted to know who did what.

Okay, Gordi, who could have pulled it off?

Thorough and painstaking as an archaeologist, the journalist immediately scoured the internet for all the stories and imagery he could find. He noted who in his profession covered what and made some assessments.

Then Meneer glanced at his smart phone.

I know, I'll call Marie. She's—was—Alexander's personal secretary.

After six rings, a familiar female voice answered.

"Hello, Marie. It's Gordon.

"Is this a good time?"

"Well, I suppose so. Like a lot of people, I'm out of a job. I've got tons of time on my hands. But make it quick. I've got a pressing nail appointment" came Marie's sarcastic reply.

"I have been *ordered* to find out who pulled off the raid on our place. I'm on a tight deadline. Can we meet for lunch? On me of course, to discuss this?"

"Is this an official investigation?" a now far less cocky voice asked.

"No. It's unofficial, but some big muckety-muck requested it. No names. Just facts. What happened. That sort of stuff."

"Well, if that's the case—no sources—then we're

good. But if you want my take on who was involved, it'll cost you more than a lunch."

"Marie, I don't have a budget for that, but what would make you happy?"

"10K."

"Christ, Marie, where am I going to come up with that kinda dough?"

"Not my problem. Call me back when you have the cash," and the connection ended.

Huh.

Now that's interesting.

Seems like Marie has something. I'll wait a couple of hours before I call her back and make her an offer.

Next, Meneer interviewed as many CMES employees who had been on the scene as possible. After much phone tag, he talked with three of them, and of those, only one would agree to discuss it. But that one guy *wanted* to talk, badly. He said of the sixteen to eighteen people interrogated by the NYPD, only he had been cuffed and detained.

This guy, Andrew Green, had been the IT manager of CMES North America's Communications and Security. He described the total take down of the building's communications and Wi-Fi at 9:45 the night of the attack, a mere fifteen minutes before the false fire alarm sounded. This guy had gone ape over the complete loss of his communications suite.

Now, how is that even possible?

When the fake fire alarm sounded, he, like any other sane human, fled, and out of habit, toward the subway station instead of exiting at the surface. At the subway station, he and the others encountered a full SWAT team. Some got a brief interview, but for some reason Green had been singled out by a short, no nonsense, commander in full SWAT gear.

A full SWAT team in position in the train station?

How'd they get there so fast?

But more importantly, why were they even there?

Green said this SWAT commander looked at everyone who left the building in an odd fashion, as if looking for something in particular. Green commented on his piercing blue eyes that seemed to scan his very soul. He described how he had been cuffed and verbally whiplashed by this blue-eyed SOB, reducing him to tears. At this point, Meneer suspected this SWAT commander had more than just police training.

A Vatican interrogator, most likely a Jesuit.

I've heard tales they can be savage.

So, at the end of day one, and after only two interviews, Meneer realized he had been handed one hell of a mess to figure out.

* * *

After four intense days of nosing around, Meneer sat down, adrenaline pumping, and roughed out his report to Presto. Rewriting it four times, the journalist decided on a global assessment followed by bullet points and a recap of his on-site observations.

That night Meneer slept like a baby. The next morning, on the fifth day, he went to his office, ate breakfast, polished his assessment, added some final thoughts, and sent it off to Rome by ten am. Then the journalist sat back and stared at the ceiling waiting for the phone call that he knew would come.

"Mr. Meneer?"

"This is he."

"This call is to confirm that we have received your email. Please check your inbox for a reply and follow its instructions to the letter." The distant voice of William DeSalvo, Presto's personal assistant, hung up.

When Meneer checked his inbox, there indeed was an encrypted email waiting from a familiar source. Biting down on his lower lip, the journalist opened it. It was a form letter informing him to be patient and watch for a follow up email.

Three weeks later, while reading the morning paper at his office, the promised email arrived. It contained a Plainview, New York, address, and the directive, "Pick something out." Meneer Googled the address—a Ferrari dealership on Long Island.

CHAPTER 42
Rumblings

"Survival of the fittest." With those words the naturalist and geologist Charles Robert Darwin postulated how the evolution of species occurred and the mechanistic role natural selection provided. The very same could be said about survival among paranormals.

In an aggressive environment, "fence sitters" supported the *status quo*, while the principal contenders balanced each other out. This reality never became more apparent than at the CMES conference outside Rome, where the representatives from several non-aligned paranormal organizations attended.

As followers of Otto von Bismarck's policy of *Realpolitik*, these non-aligned entities made pragmatic allegiances with CMES based upon practical, material factors, and current conditions. Few of them lent any credence to CMES' explicit ideology and ignored its lack of ethical underpinnings. Put another way, fear drove them to CMES.

However, post-Manhattan collapse, the non-aligned found themselves in a bind. The unexpected fall of CMES' North American headquarters sent shock waves of apprehension, if not outright fear, throughout their leadership. Informal alliances with CMES, almost always bargained from a position of weakness, now required reassessment, given the perceived shift in the balance of power. The question was "but to whom?"

The dearth of information about the fall of the CMES North American headquarters exacerbated the uncertainty. No one knew who did what. No one took credit for the daring exploit. Given the well-known and signature tendencies of the principals, the Vatican and CMES, no one believed for an instant that the Roman Pontiff had turned bellicose. Much went unsaid, as no one dared to speculate that Manhattan had been an internal power struggle within CMES itself.

All this uncertainty led to high-flying speculation as to whether a third-party interloper had been the culprit. Perhaps, the learned rumors went, this represented a one-time, hit-and-run sort of operation by someone more bent on destabilizing CMES than anything else. On the other hand, some counseled patience, to take a wait-and-see approach, to see whether the other principal, the Vatican, might be targeted next.

Regardless of which camp one adhered to, two things did occur. First, the non-aligned sensed their empowerment. No longer did they see themselves as the pawns. This heady feeling had to be controlled. Second, those already aligned with CMES began hedging their bets with an unlikely ally—TIIIS. Private third-party overtures were initiated, followed by more substantive discussions. The aligned gaped in wonder at TIIIS' straightforward civility. Regardless, all parties knew the fragility of such provisional "agreements" or "accords," no matter how cordial.

ACME typified such an aligned organization caught in the middle. While the size of its membership remained secret, their unique skills, as recognized among paranormals, rated among the highest in quality and reliability.

Such became the case for a certain ACME spell whisperer, who could coax from the merest shred of evidence the identity of a spell caster. This specialist had been requested by the CMES' chairman himself to go to New York City and examine the roof top water tank of the Manhattan property. In the past, such a request would have been considered an honor to accept, and at a reduced fee, all in the hopes of currying favor with the powerful Roman paranormal.

But as it was, this request arrived after the raid, and the spell whisperer in question had already been deployed, on contract, to a location in Australia. For the first time in its existence, the corporate leadership of ACME found itself in a very delicate situation, because everyone in the paranormal world, even Presto, understood one immutable thing—a contract was a contract.

Presto, however, understood the economics of the situation as well as any businessman, and for the first time, he offered ACME a sizable monetary incentive that even its president could not ignore. In two days' time, said spell whisperer shuttled from Perth, Australia, to New York City. After an hour and a half cab ride from Newark International, another two hours trek up to the Manhattan rooftop, the spell whisperer began gathering data from the four corners of the bone-dry water tank.

Three days after that, the results arrived in Presto's encrypted email box.

Dear Sir:

The results, gathered from the fire suppression system's reservoir atop the specified Manhattan address, are as follows:

Chaplain Gerhard Manfred Schmidt, Vatican Swiss

Army Guard, of Basel, Switzerland.

Thank you for considering ACME.

Jocelyn Gleason
President & CEO

*   *   *

As Presto saw it, this report provided him with all the evidence he needed. Far more vexing, his attacker resided just on the other side of town. But even more than that, the cardinal of New York City, too, must be implicated. After all, Meneer's report suggested the cardinal's personal influence played a significant role in the fall of the Manhattan facility.

The chairman, now with a confirmed target, acted. After all, the Vatican and its cardinal had murdered one of their very own, a regional director no less. Presto now had his just cause, but chose to transform it into a very ancient one, *Wehrgeld*, "man-money." In fact, Presto preferred it that way, expressed as a calculated, fixed value, which took out of the equation *most* of the emotion, and replaced it with the cool mathematics of an accounting ledger.

But he had a problem with the equation as it stood. How could a mere Chaplain of the Swiss Army Guard be compensation for the loss of a regional director? Answer: he couldn't. Presto decided that his satisfaction required a two-for-one scenario. After all, he reasoned, didn't that high cleric have a hand in the murder of his much beloved regional director?

Then there remained the outstanding issue of Stone. Presto's current evidence could not link him to the Manhattan raid, even though some circumstantial evidence pointed to the possibility. But deep down, what stayed Presto's hand was that he just could not accept the notion of TIIIS participating in such a daring act of aggression.

CHAPTER 43
Collection of Wehrgeld

Virtually no place on the planet was beyond the reach of CMES if it wanted in. Their network of human operatives, familiars, and demon-possessed were that extensive. Their legendary manipulation of human greed, ego, misguided politics, stupidity, and outright gullibility were too practiced. In many ways, much like outmoded land sieges, treachery always had a price. Vatican City was in no way impervious to greed, CMES had many agents within. Presto chose at that moment to awaken a mole that had long lay dormant within the Holy City.

* * *

The Vatican buzzed with rumors about the acquisition of a document that "could turn the tables on the conflict with evil." The CMES source who heard this worked within the special collections of the Vatican Library. While he had not seen the document in question, he had overheard a senior staff member discussing it with a cardinal from New York City during a private reception. As for the soirée itself, the mole noted it as low-key and of uncertain purpose, with a bland mixture of laity and religious in attendance.

As far as Presto was concerned, this confirmed that the Vatican now had Alexander's book in its possession. It was high time that the *Consilium magorum et sagarum* flexed its muscles.

One month to the day after the fall of the CMES

North American headquarters, Chaplain Gerhard Schmidt failed to report to his mess. His whereabouts unknown, his colleagues feared the worst and alerted the Vatican intelligence network. Later that day, a baker came across the man's body hanging above his alley trash bin. The man had bled out, after being gagged, slashed, and crucified upside down. The Vatican chose to smother all news of the matter.

That same Sunday morning enjoyed a bright and cloudless blue sky. Ten o'clock mass had packed the cathedral. Cardinal Garibaldi, per his habit, tended to his flock on the broad Fifth Avenue steps afterward, listening to heart-felt wishes as well as petitions.

His homily had been an inspired one of hope and love that had come from the heart. He sensed his congregation had received the message loud and clear—good does triumph over evil. With the physically damaged and psychically overwrought images of Candi still fresh in his mind, the homily had not been hard to deliver.

Garibaldi, among his flock on such a fine day, thoroughly enjoyed himself. Smiling, joking, laughing, and thanking those for attending.

Suddenly, the cardinal felt winded, his chest heavy and weak. Looking down he saw the bright red of his chasuble had become too red, too bright. The man of God collapsed dead in a heap.

Two buildings over and forty stories up, the sniper had already begun breaking down his weapon.

Easy job.

Piece of cake, the sniper thought. He had already decided on what he would do with his hefty fee.

CHAPTER 44
Phone Call

I was back at the Academy when I first heard the news of the cardinal's assassination. I swear I felt the psychic shit hitting the fan. I wanted to do something, but it being Sunday and all, I waited for instructions.

That afternoon, the dreaded call arrived.

"Mr. Stone," the tense voice of President Silver Moon said, "where are you?"

"At the Academy, Madam President."

"Are you aware of what happened in New York City today?"

"Yes, ma'am, I am. I'm awaiting your orders."

"It seems our dear friends have made a decision. In Rome today a chaplain of the Swiss Army Guard passed away as well. This is no time for hasty reactions, but since you're at the Academy, be prepared to deploy at a moment's notice."

Pause.

"But Mr. Stone, for the moment at least, be a ghost and disappear. Understood?"

"Yes, ma'am. Loud and clear."

* * *

I would be lying if I said the cardinal's assassination surprised me. Such a beloved public figure stood exposed in bold relief as a natural, in-your-face, target for CMES. But Schmidt? How the hell did they sleuth that one out? It hit me like a head slap.

Magic, stupid; they used a spell whisperer.

Because prayer, like a magical spell, leaves a trail to its owner...

That's how CMES fingered him. Nonetheless, Gerhard's loss hit me hard.

CHAPTER 45
Realignment

Giovanni Presto noted with pleasure that the public execution of the papist minion in New York City had the desired effect. The voracious media didn't even need to be prompted into action. Like a pack of savage dogs, they descended upon the Roman temple and fallen high priest screaming their vile questions and spreading their innuendos.

Perfect.

Since yesterday, over eight non-aligns had come forth to offer their renewal of allegiance. As for the Vatican, a neat and quiet crucifixion of one of their own seemed to have been taken in stride. They might stand as CMES' most bitter of enemies, but they understood the longer view, their high clergy grasped the mathematics of an equal for an equal, even if they chaffed at the sacrifice of two for one.

The one problem that could not be dispatched easily remained the issue of the ruined North American headquarters building. Its defenses betrayed, its secrets laid bare, the enormous estimate for its refurbishment, Presto judged it at this point to be nearly worthless. At the moment, its footprint had a price tag worth more than the structure.

What remained? Only the administration of the North American membership and the tatters left behind of its once considerable financial portfolio. The wretched condition of the latter Presto held secret, since he did not wish it circulated out of concern of the non-aligns bolting again. So, as a smoke screen, Presto astonished all of CMES when he decreed he would, for the moment, take over the burden of the leaderless and rudderless North American region. Such a blatant power grab did not go unnoticed by the regional directors. Their whispers began, some even leavened with dark wit. "The Roman chairman, does he wish to be *consul* or *imperator*? So little time, so many choices."

In reaction to the Roman's grand designs, the regional directors began pairing off and forming their own informal agreements. After all, it could be argued, "Today is today, and tomorrow has yet to be conquered."

* * *

In near-perfect symmetry, TIIIS held another executive meeting about the changing landscape of their paranormal universe. The initial assessment pointed to little direct damage, while the Vatican's collateral losses had been substantial. Via diplomatic channels, the council sent appropriate declarations of official regret, soon followed by acknowledgments and heartfelt wishes for future cooperation.

Meanwhile, TIIIS had not expected the flood of both aligned and non-aligned paranormal groups. They, as one, decried CMES' brute application of thuggish violence. Seeking protection, many small associations, insignificant beyond their own national boundaries, sat in wide-eyed astonishment as TIIIS representatives listened to their entreaties, and thereafter crafted preliminary documents of recognition. Another thing these groups noted with TIIIS—the lack of any coercive "leverage" in these semi-legal agreements.

Throughout, at least in the eyes of TIIIS, these associations had begun to make their choice. The next question became how might TIIIS assist in the acceleration of that process?

*   *   *

"Council members," President Silver Moon asked the full complement of thirty-three on the encrypted video conference feed, "How shall we proceed? Should we continue our former policy of rolling over? Hiding? Ducking for cover? Or, should we now take the initiative, and put CMES permanently on the ropes, off balance, and in disarray?"

One member raised her hand and asked, "Why is not the Lictor of Magic privy to our discussions? Why is this superhuman not present?"

Superhuman? The president found that amusing, and yet troubling in its ignorance, and almost said so.

"Madam, the Lictor of Magic is not privy to this council's discussions because that post is not a deliberative one. Instead, the Lictor of Magic executes the will of this assembly. Therefore, it cannot decide what it will do, *unless*, of course, I or the council abdicates its executive role to his whim.

"As to the current disposition of the Lictor of Magic, I have ordered him to stand down, as he represents our greatest strategic and tactical advantage. One which I will not frivolously endanger."

"Madam President," the Canadian sub-governor McElhinney began, "I am very interested in placing CMES in as much discomfort as possible. Are you suggesting another operation similar to the one executed in New York City?"

"That would mean I have a hard target in mind, Sir James. I do not, but I am willing to entertain any reasonable suggestion."

"How about an operation against the CMES' center in Rome?" the Canadian pressed. "It would be ambitious to be sure, but the loss of prestige alone, being besieged, might be worth the losses."

"I do believe, Sir James, I prefaced my remark with the word 'reasonable.' Attacking the CMES Rome complex would be near suicidal. Unless, of course, you yourself would be willing to lead such a charge." That shut up the saber-rattling Canadian.

A fourth hand rose, seeking recognition by the president. Being granted, the middle-aged governor of the Southwestern Region of the U.S. began: "The best campaign against CMES is the kind that deploys no soldiers of light, no Lictors of Magic, but rather uses the internet to ruin its reputation as Stone ruined their Manhattan headquarters. I refer to a public relations smear campaign funded by the monies confiscated during the Manhattan raid, using the data we acquired. Madam President, here is what I have in mind…"

CHAPTER 46
French Press

While at the Academy, I received a call from my thesis director, Professor Peter Glass at the University of Pennsylvania.

"It's good to hear you, Peter."

"You as well. I understand that you have been busy."

"Ah, yes sir."

"Well, I'm calling to find out when are you going to finish that MA thesis you owe me?" Peter said with a smile that I could hear across the ether.

"I'm working on it as we speak."

"Wonderful news. Keep at it and send me your updates.

*   *   *

I made a point to add to my Academy dorm room a very high-tech accessory—a hot plate. During my brief visit to Rome, my late buddy Chaplain Gerhard Schmidt had taken me to a local bakery and coffee shop. His personal favorite, he had said that its pastries had reminded him of home. Of Austrian inspiration, the sweets created from a light and fluffy dough included sliced almonds, cinnamon, marvelous fruit glazes, and poppy seed. Yum.

Now, keep in mind this hyper-tiny shop consisted of no more than a roofed over gangway between two ancient buildings. Space inside the shop was at such a premium, after waiting in the long queue, it was standing room only. The pastry that Schmidt had ordered for me tasted like sweet air, but the coffee knocked me off my feet, because *un caffè* amounted to a coffee cup half filled with milk accompanied by a full French press. No espressos here.

Seeing my surprise at the press, Schmidt had remarked, "I can tell you have never seen one of these before. J.J., it is the most civilized way to make a cup of coffee. All you have to do is boil water. The magic you provide. Which kind of coffee? What kind of grind? How much? Will I put anything in it? Ah, it's an endless journey that you and you alone control. Now, my good friend, enjoy! And, welcome to my addiction."

This is why I bought the hot plate, out of remembrance of that fine man and his passion for coffee.

CHAPTER 47
Snitch Hunt

While remaining faithful to President Silver Moon's admonition to lay low, and having received several more throw away phones from the IT and Security Department, in the back of my mind I knew that I had to do something. I contacted the rectory at St. Patrick's Cathedral, got the former cardinal's assistant on the line, Father Flanagan, and made a very specific request. After some discussion, I agreed I would make an unofficial visit. Two days later I drove to New Brunswick, New Jersey, spent the night in a hotel, and took the Amtrak into Penn Station the following day.

* * *

I stood before twelve of the Cardinal Garibaldi's parishioners. We assembled in the back room of a discrete restaurant in Little Italy. Among them was Father Flanagan. All still wore the grief of his loss, but all carried that look, a hardness in their eyes, that screamed for vengeance. Standing before them, I felt humbled.

"What I am about to discuss and propose is not to leave this room. Is it agreed?"

All but one nodded. Noting him, I plowed on anyway.

"My name is J.J. Stone and I once worked with Cardinal Garibaldi. He called my organization after the first cathedral incident took place; the one with the black cat sacrifice. Think of me as a hired gun, an enforcer, a detective, and a man of God.

"I put together the plan that flooded out that building on Fifth Avenue, which some of you may have participated in."

Half nodded acknowledging their contribution.

"I participated in that event, which couldn't have happened if Cardinal Garibaldi hadn't bought into it, along with the aid, assistance, and cooperation of his parishioners and friends.

"As a direct result of that building's ruination, someone ordered the cardinal's murder as someone, somehow, connected him to that operation. As it turns out, his passing didn't end the carnage. Far from it; a Vatican Swiss Guard chaplain also died on that same day, horribly, by crucifixion."

Several gasps and several firmed-up faces.

"The people who own that Fifth Avenue property ordered these two assassinations, these brutal murders. The reason why I asked Father Flanagan to bring you all together is this: I want to know who ratted out the cardinal. I want to know who nosed around after that Friday night event. Because, if I can find that individual, I will be a whole lot closer to finding out who ordered these murders. Folks, I'm a hunter looking for a scent to follow. I need your help."

I sat down. I prayed that someone from this group could give me a lead of some kind, any kind.

Everyone in the room clearly knew one another as they all began looking around, exchanging looks. I, a stranger, had asked them to give someone up. Would anyone? Or would I be stonewalled? To my relief, it didn't take long before the waterfall began.

"Mr. Stone. What's your angle on all of this?"

"Sir, I lost two friends. Father Gerhard Schmidt, the Swiss Guard chaplain, ended up crucified upside down over a dumpster in Rome. And, of course, the cardinal himself, a very gutsy and brave man."

"Mr. Stone, my name is Joey, and I apologize for that stupid question, but I had to ask. Please accept my sincerest condolences. I work for the NYPD and I think I can help you out.

"About two or three weeks ago, me and my assistant at the precinct got a visit twice from this journalist, named Gordon Meneer. He's a stringer for a couple of newspapers in town. He's all over the event, wanted to see the city's street-level security video, and had a whole bunch of questions. We gave it to him. Good relations with the media is a big thing around here. You just gotta do it." He said with open hands. "I even have his contact information back at the precinct. Gimme your email and I'll send it to you." He finished with sincerity.

My jaw dropped. But before I could thank the man, another chimed in.

"Yeah, Joey, I know that guy, too.

"Ah, Mr. Stone, my name's Pauly. I work for the FDNY. Meneer visited us, curious about a whole bunch of things. And like Joey, we showed him the paperwork." Now shaking his head, "I'm sorry, Mr. Stone, but you'll have to get his contact info from Joey, here, as I don't have it."

"That's great information, but what does this Meneer fellow look like?" I prompted.

"He's a little guy," Joey said. "Caucasian. Light brown hair, maybe five-five, lean build, about a hundred and thirty pounds max. Looks like he's in his mid-thirties. He's a guy you can easily miss in a crowd."

While Joey gave me his description, I peeked into his head and marveled at what I saw. He had described Meneer to a T.

Our discussion ended there as no one else had anything further to add. The information they had shared provided me with a sufficient start on this Meneer guy. I stood up, thanked everyone for coming, and said my goodbyes, but before I could leave the room, an elegant, patrician middle-aged woman blocked my exit.

"Mr. Stone," she said, "I know you are a good man. Would let Father Flanagan know when the job is done? We'd all appreciate that, both for the cardinal, and your friend." I said I would.

True to his word, my throw away smart phone chimed with an email from Commander Joseph M. Lageri of the 17th Precinct of the NYPD, while I sat on the train back to New Brunswick. Remembering Mr. Good's instruction to make friends wherever and whenever you can, I thanked the man profusely.

Once I got back to the Academy, and now with a name and contact information, I made a visit to the IT and Security Department. I asked for Andrew Remington, and as luck would have it, he was on duty.

"Mr. Stone, what a surprise! How can I help you today?"

"Andy, I need a very big favor."

"Not a problem. What do you need?"

"I have a name with contact information. I need you to cross-reference that with the HR data acquired during the CMES Manhattan raid. I need to know like if this guy is CMES. Can you do that for me?"

Remington paused while he digested my request.

"Let me think about that one," as he scratched his head. "Yeah, that's doable. Give me the particulars."

Fifty-four minutes later my smart phone chimed. The text said:

> Gordon E. Meneer. Member in good standing since 1996. Home address: 43 West 9th Street, NY, NY. Good luck, Mr. Stone. A. Remington.

I had my lead. As for my smart phone, I had used it four times. Per Andy Remington's instructions, I took out its battery, snapped its SIM-card in half, and discarded the gutted shell.

Next, I called up my good buddy, Mr. Henry, on a new smart phone and outlined the situation.

"So, what do you think, Mr. Henry? Do you think we can turn this guy?"

"J.J. my boy, there's no telling what the guy will do. But I think it's worth a try. Besides, it's been some time since I took a day off. You never know, it could all work out."

So we agreed. Mr. Henry would pay Meneer a visit, armed with the physical description I lifted off Commander Lageri, and several other items. After all, I was the one who had to lie low.

CHAPTER 48
The Pressure Cooker

Back to the grind. I had bottomed out on my thesis' appendices. It was time to visit the Academy's demonic testing lab. I was eager to see the facility because I had a mind toward testing some spells from my thesis within its controlled environment.

I made an appointment with Mr. Good, the very person who had been my instructor for Demonology, and who also acted as my second thesis director. Approaching him seemed appropriate. I walked off toward the fortress-like Meyers Hall.

Bounding up its narrow stone staircase to the second floor, I reached Mr. Good's office door, which I found wide open. And there the man sat, within his monk-like cell, engrossed at his desk.

I knocked on his door frame. He didn't look up, but said, "Come in, Mr. Stone. I have been expecting you. Take a seat. I'm a bit engrossed at the moment."

I sat there for the next three minutes, while Mr. Good teased at something before him.

Then, he looked up and announced with a broad smile, "So, you would like to see it?"

Once again, the wily Mr. Good had caught me off guard. *How does he do it?* I wondered with my mind shielded. During this entire time, the instructor sat there, hands folded before him, beatifically glowing back at me.

"Mr. Stone. First off, I have been at this for quite some time. While you watched me fuss about with this item here, I *watched* you.

"Now, about that testing lab you have been pining about, let's go. Besides, I need your help with something."

*   *   *

We walked across campus to an old and narrow crowned macadam road that led deep into the woods surrounding the Academy. Counting my footsteps, I estimated that we went a good three quarters of a mile.

"How long has this road been here, Mr. Good?"

"Since the construction of the lab. Now-a-days it has become a service road. Why do you ask?"

"It looks old, unused and abandoned, that's all."

"That 'look' is by design. Ah, here we are."

My first thought "here we are ... where?? We stood in the middle of an old road deep in a dense oak forest. But what of it, I thought, as the road led off even deeper into the curtains of verdant green until lost around a right-hand bend.

"First off, try never to leave this road when you return to the lab, as this forest can be quite a handful. For—"

Interrupting, I asked, "What do you mean 'a handful?'"

"In the military you used claymore mines, am I right?"

"Yes. They're a mainstay."

"Well, imagine a magical claymore mine."

"Magical mines?"

"In a sense. They react to anything that wanders off this road."

"How?" I pressed.

"Well, that depends. If you are a dark demon, there

are several frightful deterrents. If you're a mortal, a silent alarm is sent to come fetch you, while roots and vines secure you in place."

"Oh."

Then Mr. Good stopped speaking, deep in thought. "I have an idea," he said as he sat down on the left-hand side of the pavement cross-legged. "Come join me, Mr. Stone."

As the sunlight fought its way through the viridian canopy, it framed a scene quite beautiful, idyllic, and peaceful.

"Now, I want you to relax and take in what's before you. Don't close your eyes. Slit them, relax, and above all, observe."

After several minutes of this, I began to see what Mr. Good had been getting at. Indeed, I began to detect shadowy movements in the undergrowth and on the tree trunks. Who or whatever they were, they were masters of camouflage, innocuous until discovered, like an ant trail revealed beneath the leaf of a large hosta plant.

Mr. Good narrated in a low voice. "What you are seeing is the industry of an interesting life form. We don't know where they come from or what *phylum* they should even be assigned to, but they call themselves the *Argenti*, which in Latin means, 'the silver ones.'

"For habitat, they prefer oak forests, like this. In fact, TIIIS had to negotiate a lengthy contract with them before we could construct our lab, called the Pressure Cooker. Once they understood why we wanted to build it, they assisted us in finding an appropriate location and in the construction of its security entrances.

"I would say by the look of things, they are curious about you, Mr. Stone. They perceive auras quite well, which is why they are so useful as a barrier against dark demons and those unfortunates possessed by them."

I finally got a word in edge-wise: "Mr. Good, why 'silver' for a name?"

"When they first meet you, be sure to use '*Argenti.*' What is critical, Mr. Stone, is the name that you first use, you always use thereafter. Think of it like a computer password."

"No, Mr. Good, why '*silver*,' for a name? Why not gold for instance?"

"Oh. Well, I think you are about to find out."

And, I did, for out of the heavy grasses, flowers, and ferns that flanked the roadside, appeared a silver-striped chipmunk that stood about six inches tall. Perfect in all respects and proportions, the tiny creature walked right up to me, bowed its head, spread wide its forelegs, and announced in proclamation.

"Behold the new Lictor of Magic! He who protects all from the darkness! We, the *Argenti*, welcome you to our home! And, if We might add, your beautiful radiance is like that of a bright summer's day!

"Welcome!

"And be at peace!"

Finished, the beautiful creature bowed, turned, and disappeared into the undergrowth.

"Well, there you have it. A formal welcome from their Brood Mistress. It doesn't get much better than that."

"Once again: why 'silver'?"

"Well, Mr. Stone, as you already well know, silver is like Kryptonite to demons and demon-kind. These creatures mine it, eat it, and as a result their scratches and bites can do quite a bit of harm to a demon.

"Now, aren't you going to say something back to them?"

Me? Oh yes, I remembered. *The Lictor of Magic is a diplomat as well.*

I got up, brushed off my backside, and assumed my very best U.S. Marine formal posture as if attending a Class-A uniform inspection. I bowed from the waist toward the vast expanse of thicket, rose back to my original rigidness, and boomed out.

"Oh, most noble *Argenti*, I, J.J. Stone, Lictor of Magic, of the Brood TIIIS, salute you as the most worthy guardians of this oak forest! May you live long and thrive in peace, forever!"

After the half-stolen Vulcan wish and greeting, I remained standing at attention before the thicket, when from both sides of the road, the vegetation began to tremble, a deafening wave of whistles and chirping commenced that lasted for at least a half minute. When it ended, I again bowed from the waist. Only then did Mr. Good and I move off down the road.

*   *   *

We didn't go very far before Mr. Good turned and again faced the left side edge of the road. Before us, a few paces away, stood, a thick-trunked old growth oak of tremendous age. From his tweed jacket pocket, the man pulled out and pointed at the tree what looked to be a small garage door opener. To my utter amazement, a double door showed itself, splitting the tree, opening to us, and extending forth a ramp to the road's surface.

"Okay, how did you do that?" I demanded.

"Holographic camouflage."

The tree trunk turned out to be a narrow elevator,

like one found in an old European hotel, complete with an accordion grated gate and herky-jerky motion as it descended.

"So how far down are we going?"

"Questions, questions. Always with the questions. About three stories, Mr. Stone."

*   *   *

I thought I had fallen down the proverbial rabbit hole in *Alice in Wonderland*. That is until the elevator stopped and Mr. Good triggered the light switch. That's when I realized the elevator had deposited us at the edge of a large, natural cavern, complete with stalactites and stalagmites.

Chilly and moist, I found myself rubbing my bare forearms. In the center of this underground grotto sat a rectangular cube about ten by ten feet, braced with steel flying buttresses on all of its sides.

"Here we are. This is our demonology lab, the Pressure Cooker." As we walked around it, I could not find an entrance.

"Another question, Mr. Good. How do you get in?"

"Ah, yes. The entrance is right here," he pointed at a hinged oval outline with a central locking wheel. How I had missed it, I don't know.

"Note the hinges to this submarine-like hatch are on the outside while the hatch itself opens inward."

Reaching the cube's fourth side, I saw several parallel lengths of piping of various gauges that led up to and disappeared over the cube's roofline.

"Let me guess. Those pipes carry water. Am I right?"

"In part. One controls air pressure, the center one is

gasoline, the large one is an exhaust, and the fourth, spring water. The only thing better is consecrated water. But given your recent exploits, you know all about that."

"Can we go in?" I asked.

"I'm afraid not. The chamber is occupied."

"What?"

With embarrassment, Mr. Good admitted. "I conjured a demon from the CMES *Book of Spells*, which refuses to be banished back from whence it came. Water doesn't faze it. Pure vacuum doesn't either. I hoped you might be of some assistance."

"What about wind or fire?"

"We cannot generate any wind. As for fire, well, it danced in a petroleum-induced blaze."

Stone nodded.

"Does it speak? Does it have intelligence?"

"Oh, dear my, yes it does. In fact, it's quite a philosopher."

"You said you conjured it from *The Book of Spells*. Did that work offer any hint as to how to control it, or banish it?"

"Oh yes, it did indeed. Only a drugged mortal sacrifice, with pure opium, will send it back."

"So, why this particular demon? Why would you conjure up such a nightmare?"

"That, I cannot rightly answer. I did so on impulse. I cannot explain it better. However, it seems this demon once possessed Josef Mengele, the Nazi physician, or at least, that's its claim. It even bragged about it.

"What amazes me, is whoever first conjured up this hellion must have realized what a double-jeopardy situation they faced, because it turned the conjurer into a murderer. I am not quite ready for that step."

"So who conjured it during the Second World War?"

"No doubt a terrible one, for he, or she, may still walk the earth."

I paused for a moment, and asked again, "Why, Mr. Good, of all the spells in that book, did you choose to focus on this one? And one with such a damning penalty?"

Good hung his head. "I don't know, but I suspect that the book itself has an influence that I have yet to figure out. Fortunately, I cast the spell while in the tank."

I couldn't accept that answer for an explanation and said so. "I'm sorry, Mr. Good, but you're too intelligent a fellow to screw up that bad. What were you doing to make such a harebrained mistake?"

Good looked up, scratched the top of his head, and said, "I sat in the tank, while working out a translation for this particular spell. In fact, whenever I work on *The Book of Spells*, I do from within the Pressure Cooker. That's my fallback security position.

"Well, this particular passage, I struggled with. Then, I made a brilliant breakthrough. I realized the Dark One had altered the usual CMES-accepted syntax. I began by reading things backward and forward, trying to make sense of the spell's meaning—"

I interrupted. "Mr. Good, please don't tell me you vocalized any part of that spell backward or forward."

The man caught himself, and put his hand over his mouth like a school boy talking out of turn. He blanched and whispered, "My God in heaven, I must have."

"You triggered a hidden, secondary spell, Mr. Good. Do you see it?"

A wide-eyed and panicked look nodded back at me.

"That means this demon can be broken."

"How?" he begged.

"Think back on your Demonology seminar. Think back to the *Law of Opposites*, how that which is environmentally opposite harms a demon—water, light, heat, etc., etc. Are you with me?"

He nodded vigorously.

"So here you are dealing with a difficult passage. You play with it and inadvertently trigger a hidden spell that clouds your judgment. Whoever last released this demon was hoodwinked the same way, only they didn't have benefit of the Pressure Cooker. You did, and its containment freaked out the demon. Professor, you've both been tricked."

"Yes! Very much so, I'm afraid."

"Now, what did the demon look like when it first manifested itself?"

"A black goat. Not huge, not small, just a normal looking, black goat."

"Okay, what that suggests to me is, in the culture of this demon's origin, a black goat was a fearful or scary thing. But as you yourself said, it didn't work on you. To you, this image was not threatening in any way. The demon had to find something that would scare the crap out of you, and Mengele fit the bill. Why do you think the demon fastened on to that particular Nazi?"

Furrowed brows, "Because I lost my parents to that monster."

"So, that tells me that this dark demon is most

likely telepathic; that it might even feed on a mortal's stress. And what is more stressful to a righteous mortal than to first drug, and then sacrifice a fellow mortal, all to banish the guilt of an evil mistake?"

"But the spell said that would trigger its banishment."

"Really? Or did the hidden confusion spell make you think that is what the hieroglyphs said?"

"Oh, my, God. You could be right!"

"No, Mr. Good, I am right. What do you suppose, now given this new perspective, will banish this demon back to the Underworld? What potential solution can the *Law of Opposites* offer us?"

The man sat down on the cavern's floor and held his head in his hands and began to rock. He did this for almost a full minute before he came back enthused.

"I know. It must be the truth! Its entire construct is based on deception. The hidden spell to release it. The demon's need to feed off of human stress and anguish. That's it, Mr. Stone. The truth."

"And, Mr. Good, which ancient culture made an art form of pursuing truth?"

After a moment of thought, the scholar said, "The ancient Greeks! And the Greeks had significant goat-imagery in their mythology!"

"Yes! Yes, there is! With their satyrs, and God knows what else."

"So, there you have it. Truth will stop it cold."

*   *   *

In my closet in my dorm room at the Academy, I stored the UCS that Mr. Loomis constructed for me. That very evening, after a quick reexamination of the pertinent passage from *The Book of Spells* and a light dinner, Mr. Good and I returned to the Pressure Cooker, but this time with a plan. Mr. Good thought my solution to his errant conjuring insane. I thought we had a serious mess to clean up and an opportunity for me to gain valuable experience.

"Mental shields on full, Mr. Good," I warned.

Looking at the interior of the chamber through the fiber optic cameras revealed a plain-looking black goat sitting at its center.

"This must be its natural state," I said, "but for you, it telepathically clued into your thoughts on Mengele. How did it do that? Did you ever get into direct contact with it?"

"No. But I did talk to it through the intercom after I made my escape from the chamber."

"Okay, now, let's get it focused on me. I'll kill the demon of all lies with truth. What could be better?"

*　　*　　*

Mr. Good, shaking his head in disapproval, monitored the video feed as I entered the chamber. To my surprise, the goat-demon remained in the chamber's center and made no attempt to escape. It just sat there on its folded legs like goats do all around the world, looking indifferent. Then I realized, its next victim had come to it, much like a funnel spider awaits its prey.

Closing the chamber's hatch with a clang behind me, Mr. Good locked it down on the outside.

Then I turned and said, "Hello, Mr. Goat. What do they have you in here for? Murder? Arson? Or just plain old mayhem?"

At this the goat pivoted its head to the side, as if

listening. I had thoroughly thought that statement out, word for word. I waited for a response, acting impatient with my hands on my hips.

"For a Lictor of Magic, you are a brazen one," the goat-demon said.

"Yeah, and I can be a real son-of-a-bitch, too."

At that, I swear to God the goat morphed a smile. "You don't say …"

So I challenged it again.

"Funny, you don't impress me as a demon capable of motivating a Mengele. You're just some barnyard goat ready for slaughter," I said dismissively.

The goat-demon's eyes narrowed as it digested that comment, but it remained silent, no doubt assessing what to do to me, which edge to manipulate. I remained good and cocky as I walked around it, all the while its head tracking me the entire three hundred and sixty degrees, something no normal goat could do. That trick, while creepy, gave me an idea.

"Nice trick, Mr. Goat, but Hollywood has already done it. Haven't you seen *The Exorcist*? Which reminds me, when do you start vomiting chunky green pea soup?"

When I teased it with those words, I intentionally made a sloppy mental slip of Grace's memory, who had seen the movie with me, and how she had had been frightened by that scene. I angled, chummed, and trolled with that mental bait, hoping for the goat-demon to latch on and attempt its usual trickery, mimicry, nonsense, and mischief.

Then, it bit. The goat got up on all fours and transformed itself into an accurate facsimile of Grace in her favorite polka-dot dress, in fact, the very one she had worn to the movie. There she stood, all smiles, her hair a halo of orchestrated wisps.

"Do you recognize me?" The former goat-demon asked.

"Indeed, I do," I said.

"You know, J.J., it was you who killed me. I gave up my life to save you in that truck crash."

"Yes, you did, and I will never forget it," I said as I made my move. I grabbed the pseudo-Grace's jaw, popped in my palmed silver 1923 Liberty dollar—which Cardinal Garibaldi had himself blessed, and slammed its jaw closed around it.

Now, with both of my outstretched hands on each side of its face, I secured its jaw. The telepathic goat-demon, now trapped in this false construct, could not escape either the corrosive silver within its being, nor the sheer love that I directed at this pseudo-mortal form. The demon's panicked reaction became predictable. Squirming, scratching, wriggling, fighting, all the while I continued my assault of true love and gratitude to the memory of my beloved Grace.

I did not know how much time elapsed, I just kept on pouring my love like buckets of imaginary water into what my hands held. What I held collapsed like sand, but blackened sand, a granular substance that disintegrated before my very eyes as it reached the floor of the chamber. Next, I heard the bouncing clink of the silver dollar, blackened beyond all recognition.

"Mr. Good," I called to the overhead microphone. "Turn on the overhead shower."

A few moments later, cool water fell across my sweat-soaked head and suit. It felt glorious. As for my silver Liberty, it too cleansed itself as the last ruined ectoplasm of the destroyed demon washed away and evaporated.

When I emerged from the Pressure Cooker, I staggered, soaked to the skin and spent.

As for Mr. Good, his face betrayed pure wonder.

"Mr. Stone," he stuttered out, "you destroyed it."

"Yes, and boy, I'm beat. Could eat a couple of cheeseburgers right now. How long did that take?"

"About a minute."

Then I caught the look. "What's wrong?"

"You, Mr. Stone. You killed it with your aura. A brilliant beam of your aura beamed out of your eyes. It collapsed the demon you held in your bare hands. My eyes are still recording the after-image of that titanic blast of pure energy. What did you invoke?"

"Love, Mr. Good. The purest, truest, love."

*   *   *

Deep within the bowels of the dark realm a shrieking bellow reverberated throughout that domain. The Devourer of Souls, the realm's master and apex predator, lamented the loss of yet another demon branded by the taint of purest silver and the imprint of the First Soul. Meanwhile, the accountant of souls, of all the realms, the Ledger Keeper, made a note in its accounts of another dark demon's destruction.

*   *   *

After Saturday evening's adventure in the Pressure Cooker, I could still feel the effects of that foolhardy experiment the following day. Achy joints, general fatigue, in short, the general malaise common to coming down with a cold. The best antidote I found was stretching out in the sun and chowing down on a chocolate milk shake. They seemed to invigorate me.

*   *   *

When President Silver Moon heard about the incident in the Pressure Cooker, she could feel her anger rising. Being analytical, she realized that only part of her ire was directed at Stone for being impetuous. But found that her hackles rose when Good had called her Lictor of Magic foolhardy for doing so.

Examining her reaction to the call, Silver Moon asked herself a fundamental question: *What was a demon of that classification doing in the Pressure Cooker in the first place?*

CHAPTER 49
Mr. Henry's Stake Out

While Stone was busy at the Academy, Mr. Henry tailed Meneer on his Friday commute. Not familiar with the journalist's neighborhood, Mr. Henry packed a light backpack accordingly, with various articles of clothing that he thought would help a geriatric to better blend in.

Meneer lived in an upscale four flat, on a tree-lined street in eastern Greenwich Village, north of Washington Square Park. This handsomely built structure of faded red brick had full stone casement windows and potted flowers surrounding its street side ash tree. Someone took pride in this property, because they made every effort to green it up and make it look inviting.

By the overall look of things, the building's tenants paid dearly for the privilege. This property meant only one thing to the old Marine, big bucks. How could Meneer afford this as a mere newspaper stringer? Mr. Henry asked himself, *Who pays his bills?*

But more importantly, Mr. Henry needed to find himself a spot to wait for this guy to emerge on this early Friday morning. Given such a pristine neighborhood, no street person in their right mind would hazard their presence. He simply stood at the curb, reached into his pocket with his pack over one shoulder, looked disinterested, and pretended to wait for a cabbie to appear.

To his surprise, Meneer wearing a golf shirt, cotton slacks, and a similar backpack appeared two minutes later and began walking west toward the 9th Street Path

Station on 6th. Mr. Henry waited, granting the youngster a good lead, painfully pulled a hair from his right ear, and with a puff of breath, blew it at Meneer's backpack. There it settled in a convenient crease.

"You're now tagged." The Fourth Class adept whispered.

Thereafter, Mr. Henry followed the journalist from afar. Even though he managed to grab the same train car toward Uptown and was the last to get off at the Rockefeller Center stop.

As Meneer made his way toward that warren of passageways which is the Center, Mr. Henry didn't bite and held himself back. And it was good that he did, because Meneer headed for a bakery on the corner. Judging from the size of his purchase, Mr. Henry judged he bought his breakfast and maybe even lunch. Leaving those delicious smells in his wake, which made the old Marine's stomach growl with evil intent, Meneer now headed down 6th and entered the Rockefeller Plaza. At this point, Mr. Henry just thanked his lucky stars for having placed his magical tracking device.

Once Meneer entered Rockefeller Plaza, Mr. Henry put on his ear buds and fiddled with the volume on his smart phone. Much like any tourist, the white-haired man leaned back against the outside of the building and listened.

He heard first the distinct "ding" of an elevator, the shuffling of feet, random conversations, another "ding," no conversations, the opening of a door, a brief "good morning" greeting from a feminine voice, another opening of a door, and then the crunching cloth sound of the backpack being set down.

Lots of crinkling of paper told Mr. Henry that the kid had started in on his breakfast.

Minutes passed.

Paper rustling announced the end of breakfast. More paper noise, but this time it sounded different; Meneer reading the newspaper.

Then, lots and lots of typing, punctuated by the distinct stab of a key.

Twenty-one minutes later the journalist's smart phone chirped with an email.

Again, with the rapid typing of key strokes. Mr. Henry heard Meneer mutter under his breath. "Check an address in Plainview, New York? Pick out something?"

More rapid key strokes.

"Holy shit! It's the Ferrari dealership on Long Island! What a payoff for five days' research!"

Did I just hear that?

Payoff "for five days' research"?

* * *

"J.J., we've hit the jackpot. I have Meneer on tape chortling over his payoff 'for five days' research.'" Mr. Henry glowed.

"So, what's his payoff?" I countered.

"Someone told him to 'pick out something' at a Ferrari dealership on Long Island.

"Huh. That's bad news." I deadpanned.

"How so, J.J.?"

"It means this Meneer guy won't come cheap."

CHAPTER 50
Bad Press

Ever since the last video conference, TIIIS had been hard at work. Their task suited them. It required thought, timing, and careful misdirection. Best of all, once started, the smear campaign should evolve and take on a life of its own, all without resorting to violence and the shedding of blood. Their premise— expose a hidden organization and it will wither.

The opening salvo began with a well-positioned piece in a noted financial newspaper, religiously read on a daily basis by the entire financial world. A brief article appeared on Monday about a shadowy international organization that had ties with every market segment and government on the planet. The author swooned over the possibilities of its rumored, upcoming IPO, suggesting that ownership of its stock would replace his own considerable positions in several diversified money markets. Why? Because of the diversity of the organization's internal positions. Berkshire-Hathaway move over. The organization cited in such laudatory financial terms was CMES.

The article's author, a senior editor named William Danridge, had been fêted four days prior at a private lunch by an articulate and mesmerizing personage named Betsy Silver Moon, who systematically laid out CMES' roll in the recent New York cathedral incidents. Danridge, Silver Moon knew, had been the husband of *that* well-known New York socialite and father of *that* daughter whose June cathedral wedding had been turned upside down.

At hearing the entire story, Danridge jumped at the opportunity to expose the organization. Silver Moon shared, in good faith, copies of specific documents, retrieved from the CMES North American headquarters building. These papers described, in outline, the extent of the CMES North American financial and governmental empire. Specifics, Silver Moon withheld. That way Danridge would appear to uncover CMES, and its multi-faceted influence, in an ever more damning series of installments.

To all of this, Danridge agreed, as he had two clear motivations: revenge for his wife and daughter's experiences and the possibility for a Pulitzer. After the sumptuous lunch with President Silver Moon, Danridge wondered, in a moment of historical reflection, whether Bob Woodward and Carl Bernstein of *The Washington Post* felt this way, when Deep Throat had first approached them.

*   *   *

Minutes after the article went public, online and in print, a mad scramble began by every investigative financial reporter, and what they would uncover, they would not like. CMES, for the first time in its long history, no longer remained in the shadows. Instead, it occupied the bright lights of center stage. CMES, like a vampire caught in the noonday sun, withered, and Danridge vowed to turn up the heat.

*   *   *

A heavy manila envelope arrived at his editorial desk marked special delivery. Seeing it, Danridge smiled.

Betsy kept her word.

The envelope contained page upon page of dense financial and real estate data, the kind that would put lesser mortals to sleep, but stuff Danridge lived for—entangling financial puzzles. After about two hours of solid reading, scanning, and reading some more, the senior editor had completed his first pass. Sitting back in his desk chair, his back cracked. His lips formed, "Holy shit."

Now Danridge began reorganizing the fifty pieces of what he now thought of as evidence.

So, it's CMES North America who owns that ruined building on Fifth Avenue, but not directly, Danridge realized.

Rummaging through some pages, he located an innocuous Corporation A's name. Suspecting a loose thread, he teased it by cross-referencing Corporation A to another page where it appeared as the controlling entity of Corporation B. Now he stopped, grabbed his legal pad, and began taking notes of who owned whom. By Corporation F, Danridge had completed the trail to CMES.

Damnation!

With this revelation, the senior editor moved on to the real estate notice announcing that the Fifth Avenue property had been put up for sale. Knowing how tight the real estate market was in Manhattan, he nonetheless checked online for the real estate valuations for that particular block in Midtown Manhattan. He whistled in disbelief at the figure—*over $1,360 per square foot.* Glancing back at the declared square footage of the building from the real estate ad, Danridge rapped out a quick and dirty calculation and whistled again—*$2.04* *billion! But CMES is asking for $1.89 billion for the building.*

Why is that?

What gives?

This got the senior editor to thinking, until a light bulb came on, which set him to rummaging again in his pile of papers until he found the photocopy of a brief newspaper clipping. In it, a contractor had said it would take almost a half billion dollars to restore the building to code.

Whoever put a price on this building doesn't know the extent of the building's damage. Or do they?

That thought propelled Danridge into a full court press on Corporation E, a foreign entity, located in Rome, Italy. He asked himself, *How does an import/export textile business based in Rome become the seller of this Manhattan property? What's the connection?*

Sighing at the insanity of his own question, he glanced up at the clock and realized that if he wanted to make his deadline, he'd better get writing. Danridge wrote a pithy, concise, and a tad wistful ditty about a Manhattan landmark building that had fallen on bad times. Three paragraphs in length, the last Danridge crafted turned out to be the longest as he meticulously traced the ownership of the property back to CMES, the outlandish seller's price given the building's current condition, and a hinted question about the ethics of the seller.

* * *

As before, as soon as Danridge's piece became available, a gasoline reaction broke out. Several prospective buyers of the building backed out, not wishing their colleagues to think of them as being that dim as to buy an overpriced and distressed asset. By week's end, the asking price had been lowered to the bargain basement price of $998 million. The price drop smacked of a seller's desperation. The sharks smelled blood in the water. But even at that price, a sour taste had been planted in many mouths, not with the property, but with the seller itself—CMES. The property became toxic as more and more information became public.

*　　*　　*

The following day another fat mailer reached the senior editor's desk. Expecting more financial information about CMES, Danridge instead received an inundation of what looked like political memorabilia. In all, the résumés of twenty-two members of the U.S. Congress lay before him. Most of them he knew. Of them, thirteen occupied congressional committee chairs of the present administration. To each résumé had been attached copies of CMES paperwork indicating their last four years of paid membership, down to check numbers, dates received, when cashed; in short, the entire paper trail.

These documents stopped Danridge cold—himself a Democrat—and they got him thinking. While he knew it wasn't illegal for someone to be a member of an organization per se, he ruminated on the potential for heavy-handed influence.

Why would a public figure want to be a member of CMES? What would that buy you?

Could, for instance, any of the decisions of the

thirteen committee chairs represent a conflict of interest?

Another thought struck him. *What did CMES believe in? What is their mission statement?*

He didn't know. The financial editor began digging, making assumptions, and following his well-tuned investigative gut.

After intense research, Danridge found CMES had an international reach. It's organization, on the basis of its officer titles alone, tended toward centralization, with all of its regional directors answering to a central chairman. Within the United States there was only one regional headquarters, wedded to a corporation of doubtful purpose, which was owned by an entity of dubious purpose in Rome.

Among the twenty-two congressional members, all sat in or chaired several Senate and House committees—both Armed Services, Finance, both Intelligence, Energy and Commerce, Foreign Affairs, Homeland Security, Natural Resources, and Ways and Means.

Danridge returned to the question of CMES' interests. His gut told him that he had been on this road before, one that led to dark things like scandal, malfeasance, and fraud. But with only his informed intuition, the senior editor didn't have a leg to stand on. He had nothing to hang his hat on. Then something caught his eye on one of the congressional résumés—the Foundation for the Preservation of the Seas.

An avid ecologist himself, Danridge mused, *Now that's a new one. And, why not the more inclusive "oceans," instead of "seas?"* Then Danridge got a real shock, the FPS appeared on all twenty-two résumés—

all declared members. The senior editor went online to find out what the FPS stood for and flat out couldn't. That shook him.

How could five percent of Congress be members of something that doesn't exist?

While not a political watchdog, Danridge began writing his next installment on CMES nonetheless. Try as he might, his choice of words and tone described an ever-darkening landscape. He couldn't help it, because he felt like Paul Revere on his horse, alerting his countrymen about the arrival of the British army. In all, his shortest contribution to date on CMES, its title said it all—"Does CMES Run the Federal Government?"

*   *   *

While Danridge's article did indeed run as written in the morning edition, so did another, which appeared below it: "William F. Danridge, Senior Financial Editor, Murdered in Manhattan Garage."

Signore Presto, who had heard enough, had ordered Danridge's murder a day late. With such huge implications, even the morning news show anchors had figured out that something sinister was afoot.

*   *   *

CMES Rome reeled like a suntanned vampire at all the media exposure. First, they had to contend with the flap over the extraordinary devaluation of the Manhattan property. Somehow, someone had found out about the organization's gerrymandering within the United States government. And now, CMES had to face the all-too-convenient murder of the senior journalist who had blown the story wide open. But more revealing, many of the aligned and non-aligned stood aside or outright fled like cockroaches into the woodwork in the wake of these revelations.

In response to the media clamor in print, on television, and on the internet, Presto did something surprising. He fled to his estate near Tivoli. The many pressures had blown the control freak's mind. His old tried and true method of shutting up and shutting down any opposition through assassination had not only failed to work, but had made the situation worse.

As for the rest of the CMES hierarchy, and, in particular, its regional directors, Presto's ineptness had cost them all dearly. His retreat to his estate smacked of weakness. Someone had to do something about this embarrassment before the heat became unbearable.

CHAPTER 51
Traffic Stop

Following the assassinations of the cardinal and chaplain, and another meeting with his oracle, Presto resurrected in earnest his manhunt for the *l'uomo potente*, Stone. Before he launched the search, Presto wanted specifics. He again contacted his mole within the Vatican and a certain New York City journalist.

* * *

Father Francisco Arroyo had returned a fragile folio back to its dedicated place within the Vatican's special collections. Looking down at his hands, Arroyo cringed at the powdered leather dust, the color of rust, that soiled his white cotton gloves.

"Age requires extreme care," he murmured to himself. "I am going to place this on the conservation list."

Walking back to his office to fill out the required paperwork, his smart phone chimed. A quick look at the email sender's address caused the priest's heart to skip a beat. He got up and closed his office door, only then did Arroyo sit down, and read the brief message.

High priority.

Gather ASAP all information on any Americans recently in the company of the late Cardinal Antonio Garibaldi.

High priority.

Mio Dio! Arroyo thought. The last time he saw the deceased New York cardinal was at the Vatican, when he attended that odd assembly of characters before he … died. He couldn't bring himself to say the word "assassinated."

But he did seem to remember a tall, well-built, almost military type. The cardinal seemed to be very pleased with him for some reason, because he introduced him around to almost everyone.

Let's see now, Arroyo thought as he took pen to paper and began to compose every detail his declining memory could recall of the man.

*　　*　　*

Gordon Meneer found himself running late for a presser in Princeton and gunned his new, bright yellow, Ferrari 458 Italia Spider. Less than a week old, the sounds that came out of the exhaust pipes made him quiver with ecstasy. Top down, the entire experience of shifting gears with paddles, Meneer enjoyed. On top of that, the traffic on the New Jersey Turnpike at this hour in the early afternoon remained light. The stringer began thinking he might make Princeton on time after all.

The journalist's phone chirped with an email. Seeing the encrypted address he put his life temporarily on hold. Turning on his blinkers, he pulled over to the side of the highway to see what the email contained.

High priority.

Gather ASAP all information on the three mystery firemen seen at the raid on Manhattan.

High priority.

Why?

Meneer furiously thought as he pounded the steering wheel with the palm of his free hand.

I have already given Rome everything I had.

*   *   *

"Good afternoon, sir. Am I disturbing you?" the New Jersey State Patrolman said to the bowed head engrossed in reading what appeared on his smart phone.

"What?" Meneer said looking up at the big patrolman in total surprise.

"Sir, may I see your license and registration?"

Blinking in disbelief and confusion, a silent Meneer squirmed in his tight racing seat, extracted his wallet, and numbly handed over the documents.

The patrolman, after looking over the car, returned to his loaned patrol car courtesy of a favor owed to the New York Archdiocese, and proceeded to pretend to check the driver's license and registration.

Surprised by the sudden appearance of the patrolman, Meneer realized that he had done nothing wrong, and so re-focused and reread the Roman's email.

*   *   *

"Mr. Henry," Stone said into his phone, "I've got Meneer parked on the side of the road. Near mile marker sixty-seven southbound, just before Exit 8. Time to make your grand entrance, Smokey Bear."

Thirty seconds later a similar late-model patrol car pulled up and parked, but this time in front of the yellow Ferrari, boxing it in. A short, white-haired man exited the vehicle, walked briskly past the embargoed vehicle, up to where Stone had parked.

He said through the open window, "Okay J.J., let's do this."

*   *   *

Meneer looked up from his pad and began to react when the second patrol car arrived. *What the hell is this all about?* He wondered.

As the second patrolman walked by, ignoring him, irrational alarm bells began going off.

Then he heard the approach of noisy scuffling footsteps on his side of the car. By that time, however, Stone had silently approached the Ferrari from the passenger's side, reached in, and grabbed the vehicle's key fob from the center console, while Meneer's head was turned.

Mr. Henry, meanwhile, placed his both his hands on the driver's window sill, and announced, "Hello, young fella. You're in a heap of trouble."

Meneer, shocked, recognized Mr. Henry as the old fart that he had seen in front of his flat. "It's you— What's this all about! Officer?"

Mr. Henry smiled from beneath his Smokey the Bear hat and said, "Like I said, young fella, you're in a heap of trouble. Did you know your so-called 'research' got a New York cardinal and a Vatican Swiss Guard Chaplain killed?"

At this, Meneer's self-preservation button was pushed hard. He stabbed at the car's starter button to no avail. Now looking to his right, he saw me with the partial fob swinging between my thumb and forefinger, in my other hand, its battery. Looking back at Mr.

Henry, Meneer saw his blue eyes and made an intuitive connection.

"You must be that the SWAT commander, too!"

"Well, sonny, you're pretty smart for figuring that out. Congratulations."

Then I reached in and snatched the journalist's smart phone as well.

Reading the text still displayed, I asked. "So, Mr. Meneer, I see here your handler wants you to do some more research. Is that correct, sir?"

Meneer, with nowhere to run, crumpled in on himself and mumbled he wanted a lawyer. But, feeling sorry for the man, Stone offered him the following.

"Mr. Meneer. It says here you need to find out all that you can 'on the three mystery firemen.'"

Taking off my Smokey Bear hat, I grinned, and said, "Well, sir. You're in luck, because I'm one of them. In fact, I suspect I'm the guy you need to talk to."

Meneer, looking up into Stone's smiling, cherubic face, shook his head twice, and groaned.

* * *

Two highway patrolmen and a driver had a friendly roadside talk where reality was lucidly outlined. Stone shared with Meneer some choice mental images and recollections. Told him what Alexander had tried to do. Reminded him of what Presto had done to two of his friends. Then the TIIIS Lictor of Magic suggested to Meneer his options in the silent tongue.

So, Mr. Meneer, Stone said looking into his eyes, *I can see you have a strong sense of self-preservation. I like that. I'm even willing to preserve that.*

But now, I want you to work for me. While I do not

have the endless resources and deep bank accounts that CMES possesses, I do have something that is almost as valuable. Do you know what that is?

Meneer, wide-eyed and shell-shocked, shook his head in disbelief and silent negation.

You have my friendship, Mr. Meneer. It's the very last thing you don't want to lose.

Are we clear, Mr. Meneer?

A positive head bob.

No, Mr. Meneer, I want you to say it, aloud.

"Yes, Mr. Stone. I wish to have your friendship."

Good, Mr. Meneer. And most important of all, I wish to be your friend as well. Stone thought to the hypnotized journalist.

"Jeez, J.J. Where'd you learn that trick?" Mr. Henry whispered.

"John Running Deer."

* * *

Presto shook his head in amazement. His journalist in New York City had beaten his cross town mole by twenty-five minutes. Holding their printed emails side-by-side, the Roman now had all of the firemen's descriptions. His Vatican mole had provided an almost identical physical description of an American who accompanied Cardinal Garibaldi at a Vatican function, but importantly, had provided a last name—Stone.

Smiling to himself, Presto thought, *Now I have absolute proof that you and your organization participated in the sacking of my North American headquarters.*

CHAPTER 52
Field Promotion

William DeSalvo attended university in Rome. His subjects covered the gamut from classical Roman architecture to international accounting and banking. A detail man through and through, these traits Chairman Presto coveted and so hired DeSalvo. That, and the fact DeSalvo had an unbridled lust for fast and expensive cars. He himself owned, after some fifteen years of service to his master, two Maserati's and a late-model Lamborghini. All had been gifts. None would ever be sold off, for that would have been an affront to, and betrayal of, one's patron.

DeSalvo liked to consider things, and the Gathering's recent entanglements with its enemies were instructive. In his mind, the entire situation had gotten way out-of-hand. It all began with the loss of an entire assault team in the New Mexican mountains. Point TIIIS. In a mad flurry, CMES North America bombed out of existence the TIIIS president and destroyed his London office, destroyed their Falls Church facility, but lost another assault team in the process. Then there was the failed bombing of a university building and the loss of yet another assault team in the Pennsylvania woods. In an historic and improbable assault, TIIIS managed to ruin the Manhattan headquarters and kill its regional director. During the fallout from that event, the Gathering added in reprisal a Vatican cardinal, a Vatican chaplain, and a financial journalist to the charnel pile. But the ruination of CMES' public reputation world-wide could not be calculated.

By anyone's standards, DeSalvo thought, *recent events have been a Pyrrhic Victory, at best. At worse, we look like incompetent fools.*

So armed, DeSalvo, unafraid, knocked on his chairman's door.

"Entrare."

"Mr. Chairman. I have the preliminary results of our campaign against TIIIS and the Vatican."

"Excellent. Tell me."

DeSalvo did. To his surprise, the chairman took it well. He only threw one wine glass against the wall. Never once did his poison pen twitch.

"And what of Stone?"

"At the moment, Mr. Chairman, we do not know where he is."

"Then find him. And when you do. Kill the bastard!"

"Yes, sir."

At that moment, DeSalvo's position of personal assistant got upgraded to field general.

*   *   *

DeSalvo asked himself several questions. The first was where are Stone's parents? Answer—unknown, since the recently botched amateur assassination attempt. TIIIS, obviously, had snatched them up again and provided them with new identities. Result—dead end.

Next question—where might Stone be? At the University of Pennsylvania? After the failed bombing there, most likely not. Result—dead end.

Next question—might Stone be at their Academy? After the ruined assault on it, perhaps, but most likely not. Result—dead end, again.

Finally, DeSalvo recognized that this was why the chairman had delegated Stone's hunt to him. It would require patience and the will to act decisively. Right there and then, the assistant placed a fully-human assassination squad on stand-by, complete with a dedicated plane, and full logistical support once on the ground. With that in place, DeSalvo had to wait before he could pounce.

Then, he got an idea, but first asked for permission.

*   *   *

"*Signore* DeSalvo, what a pleasure it is to meet the man behind our beloved chairman," Valeria Costa said from across a table landscaped in fine linen, sparkling stem ware, porcelain, and silver.

"I found your suggestion the other day ... interesting. It displayed thought and cunning. I like that in a man," she purred.

DeSalvo, listening, now wondered what his chairman had told his *famiglia's* oracle.

"*Signora* Costa, you are most kind, but a heavy task has been delegated to me. Nonetheless, I will solve it. But first, I thought that you might grant me some insights into my prey."

Polite. Diplomatic. Prey. I like this one. I just wonder ...

"*Signore* DeSalvo, this American, Stone, I have been observing since his birth some thirty-odd years ago; this *l'uomo potente*. Of course, I reported to your chairman, who to date has ... *never* ... been able to ... deal with him." The oracle stated with cold and emotionless eyes.

"Now, it is your task, *Signore*, and I pity you." She

took a languid sip of red wine.

"However, *Signore* DeSalvo, you did come to me seeking assistance, and assistance I will give you. Stone will eventually head toward the American West, toward a region where the Silver Nile resides. I suspect that he doesn't even realize why that region attracts him so. It is *because* of the Silver Nile."

DeSalvo, confused, asked, "I am very sorry, *Signora* Costa, but what is this 'Silver Nile' that you refer to?"

Again, pleased with the man's deference, and even willingness to admit his ignorance of such well-known paranormal matters, Valeria decided to educate him.

"*Signore* DeSalvo. The Silver Nile is one of the principal ley lines that reside within the United States. Its power is legendary. Native American Indian religious beliefs are founded upon it. And, mark my words," Valeria emphasized with a raised finger, "*if* Stone ever merges with this powerful, paranormal source, *Signore*, our Gathering will be in serious trouble."

At these words, DeSalvo's brow furrowed deep in thought.

"*Signora*, does the chairman know of this?"

He received an indifferent shrug.

"Just so I understand, *Signora*, Stone is moving West toward this powerful source. If you were me, what would you do?"

Oh, I do so love this man. He listens. Seeks advice.

With a sly smile over the rim of her wine glass, "*Signore* DeSalvo, I would send fully human troops led by your very best. I would pray to whatever deity you prefer for their success."

Sip.

"Which I sincerely doubt will occur."

"What?"

"Yes, *Signore* DeSalvo. I have told you what I believe. And once Stone merges with the Silver Nile he cannot be stopped. *Signore*, he is a rational man who knows God is on his side. And that *Signore* DeSalvo," again with an upraised finger, "makes him invincible."

CHAPTER 53
Politics Unusual

With the murder of Bill Danridge, CMES showed once again its total disregard for American sovereignty. With the damage done, and the media in full frenzy, Congress scheduled a special closed-door session. Some political pundits described it as being "an outright inquisition" of "the twenty-two."

The U.S. President, wishing to distance himself from his tainted congressional colleagues, ordered all of their assets frozen, passports revoked, family members removed to an undisclosed location for their protection, and the individuals in question delivered forthwith to the special congressional session.

This extraordinary U.S. Congressional hearing was a first, for never before in that young nation's history had the loyalty of such a large portion of its ruling aristocracy been placed in question.

Eclipsing all of the previous congressional scandals with such comparatively mundane charges as bribery (Credit Mobilier, Teapot Dome), political maneuvering (Army-McCarthy), executive overreach (Watergate), and international intrigue (Iran-Contra), the FPS/CMES Special Investigative Hearing stood apart and remained unprecedented in several ways.

First, the hearings met in closed session, without exception. The media expressed its displeasure, but their demands fell on deaf ears. Only a manual stenographic recording of the proceeding had been authorized.

Second, the hearings took place within the House

of Representatives, since this space alone could accommodate all the members of both parties. To miss the first session meant exclusion from the rest, if there might be any. Again, no exceptions. As a result, the initial hearing had almost full attendance.

Lastly, the twenty-two members of Congress under investigation had all been sequestered without access to counsel, as this hearing did not constitute a judicial proceeding, but rather a simple inquiry.

The Speaker of the House gaveled the chamber to order and instructed the sergeant-at-arms to lead the twenty-two into the main chamber. Following single file, their seats had been arranged before the rostrum, two each sharing one temporary six-foot table with their own water decanter, drinking glasses, and microphone. Behind each stood a member of the Secret Service, to make sure that they stayed put. One senator remarked, as the twenty-two entered the chamber, "All that's missing are their shackles and orange jumpsuits."

Once all had been seated, the speaker yielded the floor to a young firebrand lawyer from the South. He had been designated, by an overwhelming vote, as the principal investigator. Well-known for his rapier interrogation style, common sense logic, and devastating acumen, all in the chamber knew that the griddle had plenty of heat.

At 9:15 am, the Representative from South Carolina, Richard Meacham, began. He had before him a seating chart of the twenty-two and his opening remarks.

"Gentlemen. This is a special investigative hearing into your association with, and membership in, two curious organizations. We, the United States Congress, believe, because of your association with and membership in these organizations, you have broken your oath or affirmation of office to this sovereign nation. In case any of you have forgotten those sacred words, allow us to remind you of them.

> I do solemnly swear, or affirm, that I will support and defend the Constitution of the United States against all enemies, foreign and domestic; that I will bear true faith and allegiance to the same; that I take this obligation freely, without any mental reservation or purpose of evasion; and that I will well and faithfully discharge the duties of the office on which I am about to enter: So help me God.

"Gentlemen. Be advised, this is not a court of law. As this is an inquiry, all rights to counsel have been waived. And since this is a simple inquiry, our mandate is to discover as much as possible, as soon as possible. Gentlemen, I can assure you, we intend to do just that.

"Gentlemen, we encouraged you prior to the start of this inquiry to visit the men's room. If you followed that suggestion, good for you. If you didn't, tough luck. Cross your legs."

This instruction generated some chuckles from the assembled.

"Gentlemen, you appear before us as innocent men, but men of considerable influence. Sitting among you are chairmen, current or past, of the following Senate and House committees: both Armed Services, Finance, both Intelligence, Energy and Commerce, Foreign Affairs, Homeland Security, Natural Resources, and Ways and Means.

"Let it be noted in the record that no one is wearing any sort of physical restraint. That is a collegial courtesy which has been extended to each of you. Be advised, however, that I did not favor this courtesy. I would have preferred leg-irons for all of you.

"Gentlemen, you are here today because of a recent article in a world-renowned financial newspaper. In that article, each of you appeared as dues-paying members of an organization called "The Foundation for the Preservation of the Seas." Would one of you please tell us what this foundation is about and its purpose?"

Silence stonewalled the representative from South Carolina with either blank faces or bowed heads from the twenty-two.

"Gentlemen, also in that recent article, each of you were described as being dues-paying members of another organization, called CMES. Would one of you please tell us what this organization is about and its purpose?"

Again, silence from the twenty-two, but the special prosecutor did note several nervous glances from his charges toward the right side of the assembled individuals. The southern prosecutor made a note of that observation by circling the five on his seating chart starting with the middle right.

Well, that's a start. Now for some heat.

"Further, gentlemen, the information revealed in that article someone judged to be of such sensitivity, that the author and senior editor of that article, Mr. William P. Danridge, died from gunshot wounds on the very day this article appeared. That places all of you under suspicion of murder."

To this reaching allegation, several more of the

twenty-two shifted in their seats. Meacham made another note on his seating chart.

"Gentlemen, before we pursue further the allegation of murder, I wish to share with you that "The Foundation for the Preservation of the Seas" appears nowhere on the internet, nowhere in print. I've checked, as have my staff. It appears nowhere in the Library of Congress.

"*Nowhere,* gentlemen does the FPS appear. Gentlemen, whenever I run across such a black hole of information in my profession, I get curious. Again, I ask you, what is this organization and its purpose?"

More silence, but this time, the three Meacham had caught squirming in their seats furtively glanced again to those seated to his right. Seeing this, the prosecutor crossed off the three on his seating chart.

Those three are not principals.

"Gentlemen, you are indeed uncooperative. How about CMES? Again, I ask you, what is this organization about and its purpose?"

Silence again, and no twitches either this time.

Time for some more heat.

"Gentlemen, from everything that I have been able to amass about CMES, from its broad international scope to its many financial holdings, precious little can one find about its mission statement. But I have run across one very interesting tidbit, that I know the rest of Congress, here assembled, does not know."

Now taking in the twenty-two, Meacham theatrically drew out the moment—the reveal. Meanwhile, the rest of Congress leaned forward in their seats to hear it.

"Members of Congress, what these twenty-two

gentlemen do not want you to know is that CMES is an anagram, an abbreviation for a classical Latin phrase—*Consilium magorum et sagarum*. This Latin phrase can be reasonably translated as the 'Council of Wise Men and Women.' But to do so would be a grave mistranslation, for what CMES really stands for is the 'Council of Magicians and Witches.'"

With those words, the chamber exploded into total mayhem. As for the twenty-two, Meacham saw five wince, three smile, and one who looked completely at ease—the chairman of the Ways and Means Committee.

Now that's my man!

So cool, calm, and self-possessed. Meacham's mind screamed.

He's got to be the leader of this filthy cabal.

* * *

It took the sergeant-at-arms a good fifteen minutes before he could restore order to the chamber, and still, there remained a background buzz that Meacham had to speak over.

"Order! I say. Order!"

Throughout the entire outburst, three of the twenty-two had tried to make their escape, but their Secret Service minders had removed all hope of that silly thought. Meanwhile, the prosecutor had kept an eye on the cool one, the one who didn't seem fazed in the least by the proceedings. What no one knew was that this representative had almost gotten away. The Secret Service apprehended him by blocking him off in his driveway while attempting to make his escape.

Time for my second surprise, Meacham thought.

"Sergeant-at-arms," he bellowed over the still buzzing background, "Summon, the special examiner to the chamber."

Nodding, the man disappeared, and shortly returned with a towering and fit-looking man dressed in a blue pin-striped Brooks Brothers suit. Pure military, that's what his carriage said in capital letters. His demeanor said no nonsense. Meacham's kind of guy—a real hard-ass and all business.

The prosecutor had targeted Representative Paul Lavender from Virginia in his notes as the chief culprit. As the special examiner came down the central aisle, Meacham noted that his head turned on a swivel, and without any direction whatsoever, made his way to Lavender, approaching the man from behind.

Now how did he know which one to go for? Maybe there is something to this Stone fella after all.

* * *

Per President Silver Moon's orders, I appeared at the House of Representatives. My role, be Representative Meacham's ace-in-the-hole—a special examiner. As I waited for my grand entrance, and given Congress' reputation, I thought that while I cooled my heels I would relax, take a nap or something. But then I heard an incredible roar from within the House chamber that sounded like AT&T Stadium after a Cowboy's touchdown.

Understanding that as my cue, I stood up and straightened my tie. The house sergeant-at-arms appeared, beckoned to me to follow him, and I did so. As I entered the chamber I scanned auras left and right and saw nothing out of the unusual. I caught sight of the twenty-two from behind. Over half of them had various grades of cloudy to muddy hues, but one in particular, on the left, displayed a seething, roiling, pitch black aura, which indicated a demon-possessed mortal. As for the rest, their hues told a story common to any crook.

I tapped on the shoulder of that individual's Secret Service man, who stepped aside. I, looking down on the demon-possessed one, placed both of my hands on his shoulders with my thumbs touching his neck. I began to silently pray for the return of this poor mortal's soul. The intensity to banish this possession I took on much like what I had done in the Pressure Cooker, except that I now held a mortal in my grasp. While I lacked a silver coin to place in the man's mouth, I did have something almost as good. On each of my thumbs I wore a thimble made of pure silver, which had been blessed by a Baptist minister. The thimbles had not been my idea, but my mom's.

To my best knowledge, few civilians had ever witnessed me perform an exorcism. Now, all of Congress sat front and center to witness first-hand what evil looked like. I didn't care, as this possessed man's soul needed serious saving.

*   *   *

As Mr. Stone stalked Representative Lavender, the sergeant-at-arms bellowed, "Order! Order!" more to distract Lavender's attention than anything else, and to keep him focused on the rostrum.

Then, when Mr. Stone placed his hands on Representative Lavender the most God-awful piercing shriek came out of the ambushed senator's mouth. He ranted, raved, swore, struggled, twisted, and fought, but

Stone kept the man pinned down in his chair. Throughout this laying-on-of-hands, something Meacham had only heard about, but thought he would never witness, the rest of the chamber stood as one and stared dumbfounded. Representative Lavender's colleagues to his left vacated their chairs in fright.

Meacham stared in disbelief at what he saw not forty feet away. A man pinned in his chair, screaming, struggling, and in distress. But what kind? Then, this intense golden light beamed from Mr. Stone's face onto the back of Representative Lavender's head. Its intensity filled the chamber and the senator began to gag and snort out this black, foul-looking liquid from his mouth, nose, and ears. The whites of the man's eyes rolled into view. After about twenty seconds of this dramatic performance, the flowing of the black liquid ceased, and that still in evidence, evaporated in a cloud of black mist, which disappeared before my very eyes.

As for Representative Lavender, he sat quite unconscious, slumped over on the table before him. Mr. Stone, in what looked like considerable fatigue, leaned heavily on the back of the representative's chair. He looked up at me and signaled a thumbs-up.

You could have heard a pin drop in the chamber.

"Members of Congress," Meacham said solemnly, "you have just witnessed the exorcism of a demon. This is what we are up against. This is the face of CMES."

Now looking at each and every one of the remaining twenty-one, who had been reseated, the lawyer began again. "Again, I ask you gentlemen, what is this FPS organization about and its purpose?"

This time, several hands rose in order to be recognized.

* * *

Deep below, in the depths of the dark realm, the Devourer of Souls again received the shattered remains of one of its own. This time it did not howl, scream, or moan. It did, however, note the wounds made by silver and the telltales of who had done this—The First Soul. It also saw that another potential meal had been taken from it, as the original soul of the once-possessed mortal began its rise toward the boundary with the light realm.

"This First Soul vexes me," the Devourer growled out.

Meanwhile, the primordial Ledger Keeper kept note of this transaction, this coming and going of destroyed demon and returning soul.

* * *

The Special Investigative Hearing on FPS/CMES concluded its deliberations that very day, which lasted from nine that morning until four o'clock that afternoon. Given Congress' usual penchant for time management, several knowledgeable outsiders quipped it must have been some sort of a record.

Much had been accomplished. One demonic exorcism, the detailed testimonies of twenty-one individuals, and, when he came to, that of the twenty-second. Having listened to all of them, Meacham accepted their testimony as the truth. A very tired special examiner, now seated next to him, confirmed the judgments as he read each of their individual auras.

The testimonies of the twenty-two revealed a laundry list of under the table deals, favors, policy considerations, and several legislative acts in force, which benefited either FPS, CMES, or both. In short, there was much to be undone.

Without question, and on the basis of their own words, the twenty-two broke, multiple times, their oath or affirmation of office. The body resolved that all would be removed from office in the next formal session of Congress. All would rejoin their relocated families or significant others. All had been offered menial, dead end, Federal positions in their home states. All, chastened, took them.

However, the testimony of Representative Paul Lavender of Virginia remained the most gripping of the twenty-two. Addressing the entire chamber, Lavender described in tearful and lurid detail his demonic possession. The agony of having one's soul tortured in what he called, "The Pit." The total helplessness of seeing his body doing that which he would never do. Lavender expressed his eternal joy at being released from the demon by a golden angel, who he tearfully thanked no less than seven times.

For Meacham, this powerful testimony supported his religious background, but at the same time scared the living hell out of him; the revelation that the afterlife existed, that souls exist, that reincarnation is their natural course for development, that there are forces of good and evil, that angels and demons exist, and that there are serious consequences attached to one's actions. Lavender's heartfelt testimony made all present think hard and reconsider many of their positions on many issues.

Then something odd occurred, five members of Congress, not of the twenty-two, stepped forward to volunteer that CMES had approached them as well. When asked by Meacham as to why they didn't join, they all said as one they had had a creepy feeling about joining. As to who did the recruiting, none could remember the individual, only that it had happened during a Washington, DC social gathering.

*　　*　　*

The only casualty of this hearing, excepting the demon, turned out to be the lone video camera that Meacham had secreted in the chamber. Apparently, the sheer energy of the special examiner's golden radiance had fried its internal circuitry and memory. As a result, the only transcript of the proceedings had been the manual record of the stenographer, who had tried his absolute best to capture the historic moment in mere words.

*　　*　　*

After that grueling special investigative hearing, Congressman Meacham invited me over to his office in the Longworth House Office Building on Independence Avenue, Southeast.

Once settled in—he with a scotch and me with a beer—the representative from South Carolina said, "Mr. Stone, you did a fine job today. That exorcism thing you did went quite well. What did I witness?"

"I freed a mortal's soul and destroyed a demon."

"That's amazing."

"Congressman, how long do you think the impression of this event, of what CMES is, will last?"

Meacham, now waving his hands in an expansive manner replied. "Oh, maybe if we're lucky, about a month. Maybe less."

I sat there dumbfounded.

"Yeah. It's pitiful. Politicians are without question the most godless and two-faced professionals on the earth. For them, it's all about the pursuit of power and influence."

"And what about you, congressman?"

"Oh, me? I contacted your society's president on the recommendation of a Baptist minister friend of mine. All in all, President Silver Moon and you turned out to be the right thing at the right time."

"That's all?"

"Yep."

At that I put down my half-finished beer, got up, buttoned my suit coat, excused myself, and walked out on the man. I had hit the ceiling and needed some air. Here I had put myself on the line, all to provide a side show for a bunch of jaded political hacks.

I am supposed to be a diplomat for TIIIS, but my first line training is anything but diplomacy. I'm a soldier, a demon slayer, an enforcer, a Lictor of Magic, the operational arm behind TIIIS' policy deliberations.

CHAPTER 54
The Directive

I cooled off during the drive from the Capital back to the Academy. Yes, my exorcism had been reduced to a carnie sideshow, but I did kill off a well-placed demon and freed a soul. While I declared that a righteous and good thing, the enormous political ramifications reached way beyond my pay grade.

As I cruised across the border into Pennsylvania I began examining my situation. I acknowledged my usefulness to TIIIS, but I wished to be a scholar as well. I was eager to get back to my Sumerian tablets and finish my thesis. I realized that while one might support the other, I first and foremost carried the First Soul. That brought a smile to my face. I had responsibilities that went far beyond the pursuit of another academic degree and a membership in some paranormal organization.

When I arrived late at the Academy, I crashed in my dorm room. It felt good to be back in my intellectual cocoon, my Fortress of Solitude.

My wristwatch said 9:37 pm, but I didn't care. I brewed up some decaf in my French press, whispered a prayer for Gerhard, and burrowed into Peter's latest edits of my thesis.

The coffee tasted great, and I went into cruise-mode, making headway, and got some great writing done, until I felt a presence. Looking up, my desk clock said 11:50 pm. The remaining coffee in my carafe had turned cold, down to the dregs, and still my antennae kept picking something up.

So, I sat back in my chair, looked around, and scanned my office for an aura and saw zip, zero, nada. Still, I didn't sense a threat, but, oddly, was not alone either.

What the heck? Am I going nuts?

No, you're not going nuts, J.J. You're just hard to corner. That's all.

And there appeared the diaphanous image of my good friend and colleague Professor Melaina Makris.

"Is that an astral projection?" I asked in childlike wonder.

"Yes, do you like it?" the Alexandrian white witch said.

"It sure beats the hell out of Skype. Is this something new that you've been working on?"

"Yes, but it takes a lot of concentration and energy. J.J., you did a great job today. Hopefully, you made an impression that will last. But more to the point, don't be down on yourself. Sometimes it takes years for institutions to change. You have just begun. Be patient. And while you're at it, get some rest. Your aura has the look of camel dung."

At that observation, I had to laugh.

"Okay, Mel. I get the message. And thanks for the kind words. Coming from you, they're special."

Well, Mel had been right. Come to think of it, Mel is right most of the time. I had indeed been overextended. I slept till noon the next day.

* * *

Now primed and rested, I roared through Peter Glass' latest edits. Late summer in these parts are hot, so I had left my door wide open to encourage a breeze. Shortly thereafter, I heard a knock on my door frame.

"Come on it," I remembered saying without looking up.

Silence.

When I did look up, I saw my boss, President Betsy Silver Moon, in the flesh, standing at my door's threshold.

"May I come in?" she said.

I blurted out, "Absolutely!"

Rounding my desk, I offered a chair, seated the president, and closed my door.

Returning to my own chair, I said, "Wow! What a surprise. What's up?"

The president said, "I come with a request for the Lictor of Magic."

"I am yours to command."

Leaning back in the black folding plastic chair, the president said, "The high council has received a very interesting informal communiqué, and I would like your opinion about it."

President Silver Moon cleared her throat.

"In a nutshell, a request has been made to remove the chairman of CMES. How that is accomplished is unimportant. What is important, however, is that the chairman's demise is to be done in a discrete manner that leaves no trace."

"That's all?"

"That's sufficient, don't you think? And by the way, this outside request has been discussed by our Supreme Council, who is still smarting about the London bombing of our own President Smithers."

"Ma'am, do you believe the veracity of this informal communication?"

"Yes, I do. And while I do not usually cave to the blinding illogic of emotional revenge, this does seem to be an extraordinary opportunity."

"Why?"

She paused, her thoughts shielded from me. Not a good sign.

"Mr. Stone, you are a man who respects balance. Because of the various ongoing scandals, CMES finds itself in need of an effective leader to weather the storm. Its current leader has shown himself to be anything but. If anything, he is a crude thug. Can you imagine what would happen if any of their regional directors acted independently to remedy the situation? Would his colleagues read that remedy as a destabilizing provocation or a simple power grab?"

"I would have thought such a situation would be welcomed, if not encouraged."

"Oh, we have, Mr. Stone, but I am afraid the situation has escalated far beyond even our wildest dreams. Imagine for one minute if CMES went to war on itself? What then? What would the world look like?

"Mr. Stone, CMES' interests throughout the globe are so integrated into the world economy that any hiccup on their part would likely upset it. Any warfare between CMES' interests could escalate into regional conflicts. Have I been sufficiently clear, Mr. Stone?"

"So, are you ordering, or directing me, to take out this slug?"

"What I would like you to do is to approach this task the same way you did for the CMES North American headquarters assault—with pure, out-of-the-box thinking and creativity. Put another way, this man had Cardinal Garibaldi gunned down on his cathedral's steps right before his parishioners. This man had Chaplain Schmidt crucified. This man had a New York City journalist murdered. This man tried to kill your parents. And this same man arranged for your assassination, twice. Now, sir, what are you going to do about it?"

The president has such a way with words.

As soon as she left, I called up Mr. Henry to tell him that I had another mission to plan, and I needed his input.

"Sir, I need to see you."

"What about?"

"You know better than that, Mr. Henry. It's company business."

"Ya' don't say. Italian, perhaps?"

"Could be."

"Okay, but I'll have to drag Peter Glass along."

"Why?"

"You'll see."

*   *   *

The next day, Mr. Henry appeared at lunch with Peter Glass in tow. But before I could say hello, Peter stood before me with a look on his face.

"What's up?" I asked.

Sitting down with a thump, my thesis director said, "Have you heard from Dr. Melaina Makris?"

"No. Why?"

"Because she wants you to give a paper on a panel that she's chairing. Interested?"

"Well, I suppose. But why are you asking me, instead of her?"

"Because, J.J., she is going through channels.

You're my graduate student, remember?"

"Where's it taking place?"

"University of Chicago."

"When?"

"In about four months."

"What's the panel?"

"'Ancient Magic in the Near East.' Think that you can come up with something? Perhaps pirate something out of your MA thesis?"

"So, what she wants is an abstract and a catchy title. Right?"

"Yep."

"Will do, boss. Anything else on your mind?"

"Yes, there is. We had a talk with our dear president. It seems you had one, too. Am I right?"

"Yep. She wants me to plan and execute another operation. This time in Italy."

"Yeah, we kinda gathered that as well," Peter said as he glanced over at Mr. Henry. "So, what are you going to do?"

"Not sure. That's why I invited you and Mr. Henry here to the Academy. To sit around, do some brain-storming, and come up with something."

"Hmph," Mr. Henry grunted. "What, and spoil another all-Marine planning session?"

"I would love to," retorted Glass. "I might even have some worthwhile ideas."

Curious, I asked. "How so?"

"I've been to the chairman's estate."

CHAPTER 55
Pre-op Planning

We Three Musketeers sat together around a table in the basement of Old Main with a skyline of empty beer bottles before us.

"When I visited it last," Peter began cryptically, "Presto's estate looked like a well-established two-story house made of limestone blocks with a tan tile roof. In all, maybe 20,000 square feet. A big, rambling place. Surrounding the main house, stand four guest houses, each a two-story built of limestone with tile roofs. Maybe 4,500 square feet each. The compound has a two-story, limestone and tile roofed twelve-car garage, complete with an above ground gas pump and tank. A limestone block wall surrounds its four-acre, rectangular footprint."

Peter sketched out the compound on his legal pad as he recited the information.

"The place is situated above and northeast of Tivoli proper, below a ridgeline. The view toward the estate from the town is obscured by its surrounding wall.

"As for the terrain itself, it's an eroded, stony soil covered with coarse grasses, scrub, and a few stunted trees. There is little top soil, and what there is, is wind-blown sand."

"So," Mr. Henry summarized, "little cover. What about roads?"

"One semi-paved road winds up to the estate from the town below. That's all." Peter said as he sketched it in.

"Wide open, windswept terrain near a ridgeline.

Almost sounds like prime glider country. What do you think, Mr. Henry?" I said.

"More like a parasail or glider suit assault. Where's that ridgeline, Peter, in relation to the estate?"

More sketching provided a northeast to southwest line east and above the estate.

"You know," Mr. Henry warmed, "what we need is a topo map, but it looks like you could land behind the ridge," he indicated with his finger, "and hike down from above with the estate before you, using Tivoli as a backdrop."

I countered, "Yeah, like no one's ever going to expect that maneuver. You'd be silhouetted against the sky. No way. Any ground assault will have to come up from the direction of the town."

Mr. Henry grunted at my critique. "Damnation, you're right."

Peter added. "Why a ground assault at all? Why limit your thinking to just that?"

"What are you getting at?" I said.

"The compound is large, has lots of security. I'll bet they eat a lot. We could tamper with their food."

"Or, we screw with them." Mr. Henry added, "We parachute in J.J. here, and he lets loose inside the main house that favorite scorpion demon of his, the one that he accidently conjured at the university. It runs around turning everyone into intellectual slugs. Then we arrive and take care of business."

That silenced the table. I had a dryness in my mouth that wouldn't go away, because I could see the potential of Mr. Henry's off-the-cuff suggestion. After all, why risk an assault team, when just one might be enough to do the job?

I asked Peter about the interior layout of the main estate building. Before he started, he placed his elbows on the rough wooden table, held his head in his hands, and closed his eyes.

"The floors are limestone, some covered with Persian carpets. The furniture is wooden, beautiful stuff, built in a rustic manner. The rooms have stucco walls with ten-foot ceilings. High clerestory windows vent hot air and allow in the cool evening breezes. They crank open with long poles."

At this point, Peter, with his eyes still shut, seemed to be visualizing himself within the main house, and indicated directions with hand gestures.

"On the ground floor, there is the foyer that opens in three directions. To the right, you'll find a large reception room with book shelves. To the left a large sitting room with a huge flat screen where everyone gathers to watch soccer games. In front is a short hall that leads to the back set of rooms. On the right, the dining room. On the left, a common bathroom. Straight ahead, are the kitchen and pantries.

"The second floor is reached by a broad set of stairs from the foyer, where there are"—he counted on his fingers, still with his eyes closed—"eight separate bedrooms, each with their own bathroom as there is no common one on that floor."

"What about the bedroom furniture itself. How tall are the bed frames?" I prodded.

Peter paused with his hands on the sides of his head, and he appeared to be looking around him.

"The bed frames are about six to nine inches high. The top of the bed with the mattress and bed cloths is about … two feet. Why do you ask?" Peter asked.

"How high can scorpions climb?" I answered.

"Oh, yes. That. I would suppose it depends on the surface itself. If its polished, I wouldn't think so. But if the bed linens reach the floor, I would think with little effort."

"Wait a minute," I interjected, "Peter, when did you last visit the Roman's estate?"

Peter opened his eyes, looked surprised, and more than a little sheepish.

"You were just there, weren't you, Peter?" I said with a broad grin.

Now a bright blush appeared across my thesis director's face. "Yes, in so many words."

"So, sitting right here, right now, you projected yourself into the estate. Am I right?"

"Yes, J.J."

"Astral projection. Damn. How long have you been perfecting that skill?"

"Most of my life. In fact, that's how TIIIS found me. One of their 'projectionists' and I crossed paths, you might say. At the time, the experience scared the living crap out of me. But like all things, I got over it."

I looked at Mr. Henry. "Real time intel. That's outstanding!" I stopped, reconsidered, and looked Mr. Henry in the eye, "And you knew about this the whole time, didn't you? It was the reason you dragged Peter here in the first place, wasn't it."

"Yep. And it sure as hell didn't take you long to figure it out either," the sour-puss Marine stated.

"This changes everything." I said.

Then I said, "Peter, check two things. First, are there any magical inscriptions on the door or window frames of the main house?"

"Good catch, J.J.," Mr. Henry said with some admiration.

"Yyyess. Yes, there are," Peter said squinting. "The characters—no hieroglyphs—are subtle. They're not carved. They're impressed into the door frame. I even see the slight evidence of a square edge. Yes! That's it. Someone hammered these glyphs into the wood using a die."

"That makes sense." I pondered. "Peter, would you do a quick check of Presto's bedroom? Check his door and window frames as well."

Moments passed. "Yes, they're there, too, on both the outer and inner bedroom door frame and on the interior casings of the clerestory windows."

"Peter, are the inscriptions the same, or different?"

Some more time passed. "No, J.J., they're not. While I cannot read them, they are different."

"Crap. Peter, are they very long?"

"The ones on the window casings are much shorter."

"Do you think you could transcribe one of those shorter ones from a window casing?"

"J.J., I've never done that before, but I'll try."

Peter positioned his note pad before him with his pen at the ready, closed his eyes, and began to write out what he saw. His hand shook from the strain, but what Peter transcribed was recognizable. After about sixteen glyphs, Peter opened his eyes, blushed at his amateurish first attempt, and began cleaning it up.

"Okay, J.J., there you go. Now what?"

"Mr. Good needs to see this. My guess is he can sight-read it. Only then will we know what we're up against."

"Agreed," Mr. Henry confirmed.

"What's your second item for me to check, J.J.?" Peter interjected.

"Oh, yeah, thanks. Can you move anything, Peter? Anything at all?"

"I can try. There is a pantry at the estate, right next to the kitchen. I'll try and move a can of soup or something."

He settled in again with his eyes closed. Peter reached out into the air with his hand with great concentration. He gripped something, moved his wrist, and let go with an explosive exhale.

"That was a bitch," the linguist of ancient languages said, sweat beading on his forehead.

"Did you move something?" I asked.

"Yes, a half-liter can of crushed tomatoes. I think I moved it about an inch."

"That's fantastic!"

And we were off and running.

*   *   *

After our meeting, I called up the president to let her know I had an operational plan that I wished to share. She was intrigued and I began counting off my needs on my fingers.

To all of my odd requests, she listened. "So, Lictor of Magic, you wish to use technology instead of magic. Is that correct?"

"Yes ma'am. I expect the premises has magical defenses. Why alert them to a magical assault? I also don't want to endanger a single soul on a suicidal assault of Presto's estate. In my eyes, this is a political hit on a very evil man. Any clues I leave behind must be those that point in another direction, and not ours."

"I believe you have become something of a chess player."

"Thank you. But ma'am, we have to hurry as the next new moon is twelve days away."

* * *

I felt like a kid going to the North Pole on Christmas Eve, because two hours later the president called me up. She had an address and a time for me to make a visit to a certain location in Virginia. There I would assess whether or not certain technologies would satisfy my operation's needs.

The next day I drove to the appointment that was located in an industrial park. At first glance, it screamed vanilla as to its importance, but the many neat loops of razor wire atop its perimeter fencing told their own story.

Upon entering, I went through two ID checkpoints, a full body scan, and found myself left all alone in an isolated waiting room. Three minutes later, an Asian man in a white lab coat appeared and escorted me into a hyper-clean laboratory area. There, several more white lab coats stood around, busy at a stainless steel table. Oblivious to my arrival, I stood there, waiting for an appropriate moment to introduce myself.

Suddenly, I heard a buzz, saw a blur out of the corner of my eye, and felt something wet splatter against the side of my face. Jerking away, I wiped my cheek and it smelled of alcohol, rubbing alcohol.

Then I heard from behind me more buzzing and I saw it, barely. A small dragonfly-sized drone that expertly dodged and darted about my head. Marveling at how tiny it was, I received another dousing, this time to the top of my head. Still amused, I stood there grinning ear-to-ear. Boy, did this fit the bill.

"You must be, Mr. Stone," another lab-coated man stated for the record. "I am Dr. Hu Gee. Welcome to our testing playground, and I might add, thank you for being such a good sport."

"Not a problem. Is the drone squirting rubbing alcohol?"

"Yes, indeed it is. What do you think of it?"

"Based on my first impressions, it's perfect. But what's the drone's operational range?"

"Ah. Yes. Operational range. That depends on conditions. Wind is the great variable, but within a building, quite long, perhaps as far as six hundred feet."

"Do they carry cameras to direct them?"

"Yes. Tiny Wi-Fi optical lenses direct them."

"And how much liquid can they carry four hundred feet?"

"Again, depends upon conditions, but usually a two-milliliter payload maximum. About one half a teaspoon."

"Excellent! Now, how hard are they to fly?"

"Mr. Stone, as with anything, flying them takes practice. Would you like to try?"

"You bet!"

*   *   *

That same day Peter received an answer from Mr. Good about the hieroglyphs he had copied from Presto's the window casing. From what Mr. Good could tell, the inscription had several parallels with the protective markings that had been uncovered at the CMES headquarters building after its sack. In short, the inscription said:

> May he (who) is alive or dead pass through this portal, (may he) suffer Apophis' burning spit and venom!

Yep, your basic ancient Egyptian portal curse against the living and the dead, perfect for a narrow window eight feet above the ground. It made me shudder to think what had been inscribed on the chairman's door jams. My mechanical drones, neither alive nor dead, shouldn't bother them. And best of all, they didn't have a byte of magic in them.

*   *   *

Meanwhile, at the Academy, four chemists labored over the poisonous oil that they had scraped from the impregnated covers of the Dark One's *Book of Spells*. The chemists worked with care not to break down the poison into it constituent parts, but rather to convert it into an evaporative alcohol distillate. As a consequence, the chemists garbed themselves in full HAZMAT gear with respirators. Since a minute amount of the distillate had been requested, the nervous lab techs prepared only four, two-milliliter, doses.

Their preparation of the mini-pipettes included an alcohol wash that both cleansed and lubricated them. Unfortunately, the lethal doses appeared as clear as the alcohol.

*   *   *

I used Google Earth to scout out the CMES chairman's estate and searched for a good drone launch point outside the surrounding limestone wall relative to the main house. As best as I could tell, that distance amounted to about three hundred thirty feet.

Virtually walking around its perimeter wall, I identified three spots where I could setup. Rotating around its four-acre expanse, I familiarized myself with the details of its central main house, four guest houses, huge garage, and its gas tank. Nowhere could I see any indication of security personnel or measures. My bets put them there anyway, along with plenty of heavy-duty magic. In fact, I figured on a mixture of pressure plates along the wall's outer foundation and skulking demon-dogs roaming the interior's grounds. At least that's what I would have done.

I arrived in Tivoli two days before my midnight caper. Posing as a tourist, I found the flower shop President Silver Moon suggested I contact. That chore done, I wandered the streets in order to get a better feel for this ancient place, scanned auras, and found that no one paid much attention to me.

I wandered the Roman ruins, the medieval castle, and even spent some time thinking at the many waterfalls. I must say all the spray-painted graffiti on the ancient monuments irritated me. It just didn't seem right.

I discovered, however, several "to die for" little mom-and-pop *ristorantes*. I found myself in hog heaven and on an expense account. But as it turned out, I didn't need it.

CHAPTER 56
Lunch with an Oracle

By two-thirty in the afternoon, with my tourist sight-seeing over, I needed to find a place to eat. However, most of the mom-and-pop places that I had scoped out before, now had closed their shutters for the mid-day, only to reopen sometime after seven or eight in the evening. That is the way it works around here.

Suddenly, I had a hunch and turned onto this side road from the main drag. It was called the *Via Scuole Rurali*. My handy Italian dictionary translated that as "Rural School Road." After about a hundred feet I found the restaurant on the left, its open door inviting me in from the street. Within I could see a lone woman sitting at a linen covered table sipping a glass of red wine.

I stopped, worried that it might be a bit too pricey, but my stomach growled when I caught a whiff of cooked onions and garlic.

I ducked through the doorway and gingerly entered into the dim light, allowing my eyes to adjust. I beheld a single room filled with eight tables, all set with fresh linens and silverware, each with their own bottle of wine, glasses, and wild flowers arranged in pretty blue glass vases.

Standing there at the threshold, we locked eyes, and she gestured to me with her glass to join her. Nothing ventured, nothing gained, so I did. I put down my light pack on the floor next to me.

"You are a tourist? Perhaps American? Yes?" she asked with a halting British accent. "Perhaps even a hungry one?" She was a stunning dark-haired woman, who took me by surprise for some reason. She appeared ageless, even though I saw a few gray strands at each of her temples.

I smiled and took a seat, "Yes, yes, and yes. Is the kitchen still open?"

"Indeed it is. What would you like?"

"Something local. The house specialty would be fine."

"For an American, you are adventurous, and open minded. I think we can help you, Mister …"

"Stone. J.J. Stone. And you are?"

"*Signora* Valeria Costa," she said while extending her hand. "Welcome to my brother's restaurant. The wine on these tables is from our *famiglia*'s villa." Now twisting and viewing the tilted bowl of her glass, she added, "It is quite good. Would you like to try some?"

Drinking wine, me a total beer hound, represented a true adventure. But what the heck; when in Rome …

"Sure. I would be happy to try some."

As she poured me about two finger's worth into my large and rounded glass, I appreciated the delicate gracefulness of the act, down to the slight twist of her narrow wrist at the end, all performed to prevent the very last drop from spilling.

"Enjoy, *Signore* Stone," she said with a tip of her glass in my direction and true amusement in her dark brown eyes.

Then I felt it. That tickling at the back of my skull.

Soul carrier! Beware. She's a powerful strega—*a witch. And a seer of an ancient cult,* my old soul and teammate advised.

What about the wine? Is it poisoned? I asked.

Doubtful. Just be on the alert.

So I took a small sip, closed my eyes, and shut down her attempted telepathic mischief. Meanwhile, the flavors of the red wine exploded across my pallet, passed over the back of my tongue, and down my throat. The experience was breathtaking.

"Wow," I heard myself say with widened eyes.

However, *Signora* Costa's eyes had markedly changed. No longer amused, they had become hard, almost flinty. Proof positive that I had foiled her mind-reading attempt.

The waiter arrived with a pitcher of water and some warm bread. He poured out some olive oil from the table's cruet onto a flat dish.

"Do you like linguine and shellfish in a garlic wine sauce, *Signore* Stone?"

"Sounds delicious."

"It is, *Signore* Stone. It is my brother's specialty and happens to my favorite as well. He makes it fresh every day."

"May I order for you, *Signore* Stone?"

"That would be great."

A quick exchange took place that ended with, *"Subito Signora."*

Signora Costa paused while she examined her wine glass.

"*Signore* Stone. You are not the foolish and bumbling child that you pretend to be," she said, assessing me with those penetrating, soft brown eyes.

Interesting characterization.

"Allow me to be direct. I received a portent thirty-three years ago that announced your birth. One day ago, I received another that we would meet today for a late lunch. And by the way, *Signore* Stone, I know why you are here, in Tivoli."

Holy shit! I thought as I sat back against my wicker-backed chair with a squeak.

"Your family's wine is excellent," I deadpanned, while stalling for time to think.

She blinked at that oblique statement.

"Why, thank you, *Signore* Stone."

"So, if I understand you, you lured me here off the street, perhaps with the benefit of your many charms, for a delicious lunch, and perhaps some pleasant conversation. I am correct?"

"*Sì, Signore* Stone." She said with a slight tilt of her head and crease of a smile.

"So, what can *I* do for you?"

Again, she blinked, I suppose now at my directness.

"*Signore* Stone, I am blood-bound to watch over the future of the *famigila* Presto and treaty-bound to the Gathering. I have great concerns for both. Our present chairman has outlived his usefulness. Chairmen come and go, just like your presidents. However, the Gathering must endure, remain strong and vital." This last she expressed with a tight fist.

"This is why I have not told anyone of my portent, your presence in Tivoli, and the reason for why you are here. You see, *Signore* Stone, I wish you to succeed."

Wow. Presto is that bad.

"In fact, your success is key to the freedom of my *famiglia*. To improve your chances, be aware that *Signore* Presto's estate uses not one, but three security dogs, which are … quite special. Take the utmost care if you encounter them."

The waiter returned at that moment with two steaming plates of food, asked *Signora* Costa something, and left.

"*Signore* Stone. Please eat." She gestured. "I know that you are hungry. I heard your stomach growl from the street."

* * *

After a dynamite lunch, we talked shop, of all things. By the time we finished, the sun had almost set. Our main topic centered on CMES politics and how the current chairman had made such a hash of things, repeatedly. She told me of her many responsibilities and her family's long heritage back to ancient Rome. I found it all fascinating. Here I sat talking and drinking wine with a for real witch, vestal virgin, and seer from the other team.

When my turn came around to reveal all, I did, unblushingly. After all, she had "witnessed" my birth, knew about the many attempts on my life and my parents, from half a world away. I did manage to surprise her with my part in the rescue of the Pakistani children.

She also revealed to me that she knew the details about the fragile alliance between TIIIS and her religious cult regarding the creation of the death wish spell, and she believed the prophecy from her ancestor that TIIIS represented an organization for good, still held true.

"Valeria, I have enjoyed our lunch. Superb food, divine wine, and a most enlightening conversation. I do, however, have one last question for you. You should know that you do not have to answer it."

"Yes, J.J." She languidly smiled with her chin resting in her open palm. "What is your last question?"

"When Presto is no longer around, what happens to you and your *famiglia*?"

"We survive. It is our way."

With the words of Mr. Good in my head about the diplomatic side of my position, I dared, "Then, Valeria, I insist that we keep in touch."

"I would be most honored, J.J. Here is my card."

*   *   *

"Valeria! Are you out of your mind?" Vincent asked his sister.

"No, or, at least I don't think so."

"If *Signore* Presto catches a whiff of any of this, our *famiglia* is doomed."

"Vincent, are you going to inform on your older sister?"

"Never!" the younger brother vehemently stated as he threw his wine towel down.

"Good. Now if you can hide your concern for the next several days, you will see that our *famiglia* will remain safe and sound."

"Fine. But what of the Gathering?"

"We will survive, Vincent. As we always have. Let's take this one step at a time."

CHAPTER 57
Counter Hit

The next day, I scouted the road that led to the Presto estate, situated northeast of the town and above it, about two miles away, on foot. Camouflaging my interest in the place, I pretended to visit the municipal waterfalls beneath it.

The upslope view of the estate made it invisible as its surrounding walls hid all of its details, just like Peter said they would. But I did find its access road, a graded surface of crushed rock. Walking it in the dark wouldn't have been difficult, but I avoided it altogether because I knew the road had to have its fair share of pressure plates embedded into it, and who knows how many other kinds of sensors as well. Besides, I didn't want to risk being caught on the road at night. Since I had a pair of night vision goggles, I planned to go overland. It would be challenging, but a far better choice.

*   *   *

The night of my operation turned out to be a cool one with a light breeze. In short, reasonable drone flying conditions. The new moon left the terrain a black and shadowy landscape, but with my night vision goggles, it was an eerie, sparkly green place. I wore a No-See-Em Kevlar backpack that blended in with my UCS, and carried my favorite 9mm, a bush knife, and Bone Sword.

Around midnight, I seamlessly merged into the black night. I stalked a megalomaniac who had tried to kill me and my parents, had succeeded with two of my friends, and God knows how many others.

The trek up to the estate from below took me an hour of careful steps. I paused often to listen in the still night, and exercised a ton of good old fashioned caution.

I stopped a hundred feet from the southwestern-facing wall, which stood about ten feet high. I began a circling movement to the left, to my first observation point. Reaching it, I discovered a small tree interfered with my direct line-of-sight. I continued on, to my second option. It didn't work out, either. I continued on to my third option. This one was opposite the first, and I found my clear shot, having worked my way around half the property's perimeter. With all of my senses turned up, I thought it far too quiet.

As it turned out, I was right. A moment later, I heard the distinct sound of crunching gravel off to my right, from the direction I had just come, maybe twenty to thirty yards off. Crouching down, I scanned the area with my night vision goggles and couldn't pick up anything. I heard the crunching again, this time much closer. I drew the Bone Sword. In a thinning of the dried tall grass, I saw it, and froze.

There it stood, a massively muscled dog sniffing the ground, following my scent. When it raised its head and looked in my general direction, I knew I had been spotted. Shining red eyes locked on me, and a drooling muzzle forested with huge teeth grinned.

Okay, Presto has demon-dogs. So where the hell are the other two Valeria mentioned?

As if on cue, I heard more crunching gravel from my rear and left side.

They have me surrounded.

What to do? With my sword drawn, I crouched, slowly pivoted, and in the process, managed to spot the other two … *dogs.*

It didn't take long before Mr. Ugly Number One let out a low growl and charged me on silent feet. Let me tell you, there's nothing worse than being blind-sided by a nearly silent, big ass, demon-dog the size of a small pony, and weighing close to two hundred pounds.

Time slows in times of crisis and this instance fit that description to a T. As Mr. Ugly Number One lunged at me, the other two charged as well, just starting from farther away.

I coiled to greet Mr. Ugly Number One and, as he leaped to engage me, I slid my right foot into the lunging animal, side-stepping it in the process. The Bone Sword sliced cleanly through the beast, cleaving it from its open jaws through the back of its head, covering me in a flood of blood and brains.

Pivoting on my left foot, I allowed my momentum to bring me around to meet Mr. Ugly Number Two, who, conveniently, was now in range of my blade. Already coiled, I again stepped forward, side-stepped, and removed half of its head in another wet gush.

Then, something big hit me from behind, staggering me, then shook me this way and that, as if I was a rag doll. Mr. Ugly Number Three's massive jaws had locked onto my backpack. Without thinking, I twisted the Bone Sword's grip, felt a distinctive release, and drove the pommel's end through the hound's throat and brain stem. Now released from its jaws, I finished it off with one downward cut, decapitating it.

In all, the encounter lasted about ten seconds.

While I was intact and functional, I was also slick with demon-canine blood, which began its evaporation process. I waited and listened within its fog as it dissipated.

Sheathing my sword, I squatted down and inspected my backpack's delicate contents. One of my two drone controllers was broken, and the four drones were now misshapen, in spite of their protective carrying case. Two drones were set up to get us into Presto's room, and two were loaded with the poison.

Sitting down in the dirt with my one functioning drone controller, I selected a drone, saw that it was in the green, triggered it off, and sent the mini-mite on its way over the wall, toward the main house.

While those tasks seemed simple, if not ordinary, try them sometime when your body is flooded with adrenaline and you're listening for any threats that might be sneaking up on your six. Under these conditions, my focus on the delicate control sticks became challenged and my concentration on the controller's screen was not my best.

*   *   *

An ocean away at the Academy, Peter Glass strained his abilities to their limits. We needed to gain access to Presto's bedroom through one of its clerestory windows. Peter examined them one by one, and located the one which had been used the most by the shiny patina on its crank mechanism. The windows opened and closed from the interior using a long pole with a metal hook at its end. This hook, when slipped over the articulated loop of the window frame's crank, opened and closed the window. But Peter now had to grasp the loop itself with his astral hand and twist it counter-clockwise, not an easy thing to do, even in the flesh. The challenge is all about torque.

Perspiration popped out on Peter's forehead as he gripped and twisted the chosen window frame's loop with his astral hand. In a sense, Peter could feel the loop bite into his palm as he twisted harder and harder, but the loop only moved half a turn. Then another half turn. Glancing at the window's frame, he saw it had indeed moved, but the gap was not wide enough to admit a drone. Peter strained harder and earned another half turn. Now the gap was an inch wide. Encouraged, he focused again and twisted, this time another half turn. The window that overlooked Chairman Presto's sleeping form now gaped open a full two inches, more than enough for J.J.'s mini-mercenaries. For his troubles, Peter's physical right hand had been bruised by the window crank's looped end.

*　　*　　*

The mini-drone's camera image glowed light green on my controller's screen. With the lens on wide angle, I could see the main house as the drone approached it from above.

Presto's open bedroom window had been painted white on the interior side of the window frame. Flying the mini-mite up to it, I landed it on a vertical surface, using the drone's many grasping claws, turned off its fluttering wings, which folded back neatly.

Now for the fun part. Switching the lens to close-range, I began to walk the drone through the gap of the window. There, I found a corroded metal screen.

Time to go to work.

This particular drone, and its two clones—one which had been damaged, had been preloaded with two milliliters of corrosive hydrochloric acid in their glass pipette tubes. Sighting on a section of screen nearest to the framing, I triggered a brief ejection of acid onto the screening and waited for the chemical reaction to take effect. To my surprise, that one brief blast of acid ate away a dime-sized hole in the screen!

I repositioned the drone over another section of screen and repeated the process two more times. The result produced a hole the size of three overlapping dimes. With this mini-mite's miniature squirt gun empty, I flew it back.

So much for the window casement's curse.

Acid drone number two soon went airborne, and made a crude triangular hole in the screen's corner, more than enough for my drone to crawl through.

While walking it out and flying back for recovery, something unexpected happened.

* * *

Peter remained viewing the entire scene from within Presto's bedroom, with a mixture of amusement and breathless anxiety. The Roman, sound asleep, did his part, snoring loudly and rhythmically. Stone, in the meantime, had handled his drones well and now had an ample hole in the screen's corner.

* * *

There one moment, gone the next. Somehow, I lost the second returning drone. I knew that a sudden wind could knock a mini-drone off course, but as I fiddled with the controller I got this flash image on the screen of a mouth full of teeth.

Something's eaten it?

So I sat there for a moment and thought about what I had witnessed. Then came to me: bats, had to be. It couldn't be anything else.

Or could it?

No, I decided. It had to be a plain old bat, just like on the ranch.

I opened up my second set of drones. These killer drones had their pipettes loaded up with the alcohol-based distillate of the Dark One's own poison. Checking that they still functioned, I sent off killer mini-mite number one into the night.

*   *   *

Peter, sitting in the semi-darkness of his room at the Academy, remained on post hovering above the sleeping CMES chairman. The man lay on his stomach with his head facing right toward the open window casement. The upper half of his torso remained exposed. Perfect.

In drifted Stone's first killer drone. In practice, it had been agreed to not land and deliver the killing blow. Instead, the plan required him to hover the drone several feet above, out of ear-range, and discharge its deadly concoction from that vantage point. That took some practice as the targeting point-of-view turned out to be quite a challenge.

Stone's first droplet hit Presto on the ridge of the Roman's upper spine, numbing the immediate area. As an alcohol distillate, the poison would be absorbed faster than the origin oil-based solution. Holding its position, Stone ordered the drone to discharge the remaining three droplets. All fell across the man's upper spine. In the laboratory, four trials proved that such a dose was lethal when applied to any skin surface of the upper torso. But the sleeping man rolled over onto his left side and continued to snore on peacefully.

Peter couldn't believe it.

Is this guy somehow immune? Or, has Stone's ampoules been sabotaged?

* * *

It was hungry. The last tidbit had not satisfied its cravings in the least. And it tasted funny.

Now it hunted for something better. Its sonar detected another juicy morsel and the bat's instinct took over, enveloped it in its wings, and devoured it. Somewhere in its brain, it registered confusion. As the bat swallowed it, ingesting the torn parts of metal and circuitry, the delicate glass pipette broke into several fragments, releasing the last remnants of its liquid into this tiny mammal's gut.

Still hungry, the bat flew on, making its nocturnal rounds, now in search of something more substantial, like a big, juicy moth.

* * *

I had watched as, once again, the drone's image disappeared from the controller's screen. Listening at the still night, I heard nothing. If the poison had been in the drone, I reasoned the tiny bat should have died. But nothing of the sort took place. Now, my combat sweat had been replaced with the stink of pure dread and fear.

Here I sat deep in enemy territory. I had dumped my load and had seen no effect. Why was I shooting blanks?

But to make sure, I extracted killer drone number two—my last, checked out its systems, and launched it with a silent prayer for its success. As before, I got the drone on site, crawled through the screen, and launched it into the darkened bedroom. Noting the figure below had not moved from its left side, I hovered the mini-mite again, aimed, and discharged its entire payload. This time it landed across the side of the prone figure's neck, and coursed down the sides in two streams, forming a necklace of death.

I hovered the drone. Thirty seconds later I could see the evidence of blood streaming from the man's nose, eyes, and ears.

Bingo!

Retreating from the bedroom, crawling through the screen, and flying out the window, this drone, too, became intercepted by the hungry bat. Except this time the result proved catastrophic. The bat, lethally stricken, plummeted to the ground. The drone disappeared from my monitor, and this time I heard the bat's impact close by. It landed with a noisy thud.

Must have been a bad batch, or someone mislabeled one of the vials. That was my sincere hope.

As I packed up the delicate gear and began to police the immediate area, my ears again picked up the sounds of something scraping about in the night. I slipped on my night vision goggles, listened, and discovered the cause of all the racket—a field mouse.

CHAPTER 58
The Bat

Any other day the ever-frenetic Presto habitually rose early. After a quick shower, he limited himself to one cup of cappuccino and toast with jam. When the weather turned cold, he preferred some hot muesli with fresh fruit.

But not this morning, and his assistant, DeSalvo, noted this deviation from the usual routine. He had been up an hour prior, preparing the Roman's schedule and organizing the news into a digestible summary.

Before DeSalvo had a chance to check on his master, the estate's head of security, a South African named DeGroot, appeared at his office door with a concerned look on his face.

"*Scusami, Signore* DeSalvo," the agitated man began, "Bruno, Tito, and Marcellus did not return from last night's rounds. Will you authorize a search party?"

"*Assolutamente, Signore* DeGroot. And inform me of anything you find out of the ordinary."

"*Sì, Signore* DeSalvo."

DeSalvo went to his chairman's door. It was seven in the morning, long since the man should have been up and about. The assistant knocked on the bedroom door. Hearing no movement from within, he knocked again, this time calling out, "*Signore* Presto. *Signore* Presto, are you awake?"

Again, hearing nothing from within the bedroom, his senses now attuned for the unexpected, he stopped at the threshold, shoved opened the door, allowing it to swing wide open. The door frame's glowing protective symbols, which were intact and clearly activated, prevented DeSalvo from advancing any farther.

Dio mio! DeSalvo's brain screamed. Presto's pallor was ashen, bloodless. His pillow and sheets were dyed a rusty red by a broad pool of coagulated blood. The man looked to have bled out.

Then DeSalvo's nose picked up something, a faint smell ... of ... chemicals in the air as well.

This is a crime scene.

The chairman's assistant went into crisis command mode. Briskly returning to his office, he rung up the head of CMES' forensics team in Rome. Curtly outlining his wishes and punctuating his desire for complete secrecy. He received the promise that the team would arrive within the hour in full HAZMAT suits. DeSalvo, under no circumstances, wanted to endanger one of his own nor contaminate the scene.

The CMES team arrived in fifty minutes, something that DeSalvo noted with a mixture of relief and pleasure. Led by its departmental head, they shut down the bedroom's wards, took air samples, photographed everything, and only then did they approach the still figure.

As for DeSalvo, he had dispatched the estate's security team to reconnoiter the grounds within the wall. The search had turned up nothing.

Then, a delivery truck arrived at the property's gate. Its driver wanted to deliver some flowers from a well-known Tivoli flower shop.

Flustered by the intrusion, DeSalvo refused to let it on the grounds. He went out and confronted the driver.

"Signore," the upset driver retorted, "I'm just a delivery man from the florist."

"All right, let's see what you have for us."

Exiting his truck, the driver opened the back doors to reveal a massive funerary floral arrangement of white lilies in a crafted vase.

Astonished at the sight, DeSalvo whirled on the driver and said, "Who sent these!"

"I don't know, *Signore*, but there is a card attached to the arrangement."

"Get it for me!" DeSalvo pointed.

The driver located within the floral arrangement the funeral card and handed it to the chairman's assistant. Savagely tearing it open, DeSalvo read:

My deepest condolences for your loss.

May these flowers' scent help sweeten your day.

—William Alexander

As the chairman's assistant frowned over the card, his mind churned while his lips tightened across his teeth.

This is not possible. Alexander, the Dark One, is dead. Therefore, this delivery must be some sort of a ruse or cruel joke. And these flowers, with their overpowering scent and plentiful pollen, are another barb as well. As it is, my security men cannot approach this truck. Luckily, it's still outside the gate.

Turning to the driver, DeSalvo told him that there must have been some sort of mistake and ordered him to take the flowers back to the shop. That task done, he generously tipped the man, and shooed him away.

I need to think.

Too much is happening too quickly.

But DeSalvo didn't have the luxury of taking any time to think it over, because as the delivery truck pulled away, DeGroot came running up to him.

"*Signore* DeSalvo! We have found something you must see!"

*   *   *

The head of security escorted the chairman's assistant to what DeSalvo hoped would be the proverbial "smoking gun." About fifty feet outside the perimeter wall lay the bloated, decomposing, ragged remains of three dogs—Bruno, Tito, and Marcellus. In addition, there was a nearby patch of crushed down vegetation with several sets of distinct boot prints, and what appeared to be an impression of someone's backside in the dirt.

Then DeGroot said that the same boot prints had been tracked half way around the perimeter to this spot. Three other security men were continuing to track them down the slope toward the town itself.

"So," DeSalvo said to no one in particular, "someone did visit us last night.

"*Sì, Signore* DeSalvo," DeGroot confirmed.

"But how come we did not get an alert?" he now asked the head security man.

"Because he didn't walk on or near any of the pressure plates near the wall itself. In fact, his trail, both coming and leaving this spot, went nowhere near any of the plates. It is almost as if he knew where they were."

The instinct of a professional.

"As for my dogs, he slayed them right here."

"How is that possible, *Signore* DeGroot?"

"I do not know, but they all died horribly from a

sharp implement," the saddened man indicated, but dared not touch.

"By the look of these still festering wounds, the blade had poison on it. My dogs didn't stand a chance.

"As for our infrared video cameras, they are of no value because they are only trained on the grounds within the estate's perimeter. All they recorded last night were the usual flying bugs and bats."

Interesting, DeSalvo thought.

Again, all indications of a professional. One who knew how to dispatch three demon-dogs—quietly.

Remarkable.

That narrows down the possibilities.

But if he didn't leave this spot outside the walls, how did he kill Presto?

This line of thinking caused DeSalvo to look up and walk toward the perimeter wall, while he scanned the ground for any indication of disturbance or strange telltale signs. The chairman's assistant saw none, but did find something odd. A dead bat. Squatting down to examine the creature, he noted the foam at its mouth, and asked his head security man for a plastic bag.

I wonder?

CHAPTER 59
Disinformation

In all, it took the CMES forensics team thirty-two hours before they provided their preliminary analysis of the crime scene. Their departmental head, Angelo Corvi, understood the gravity of the situation and the importance of his team's extraordinary findings.

"*Signore* DeSalvo," Corvi began, "Chairman Presto died of a toxic and fast-acting substance. This substance Chairman Presto's exposed skin absorbed through the skin of his neck, ensuring a quiet death. Evidence of its application was marked by two raised lesions.

"We believe the toxic material was diluted in common rubbing alcohol. This is what you smelled when you first opened the chairman's bedroom door that morning.

"As remarkable as this toxic substance is, the delivery of it is the stuff of science fiction. Our first clue came with the discovery of a partially opened window in the chairman's bedroom. A corner section of its screen had been dissolved with hydrochloric acid, a sharp stench you might have also detected.

"The key to the delivery system of that poison you found yourself, *Signore* DeSalvo. Remember the bat you found? Well, when we tested its blood chemistry, we found it had died from the very same poison that claimed *Signore* Presto's life. But more importantly, when we dissected the bat, we found in its stomach, these."

Corvi revealed a small plastic zip-lock bag filled with several small fragments.

"These fragments, *Signore* DeSalvo, are the remains of three tiny flying drones."

DeSalvo took the bag and could barely make out its contents, and said so. "Are you sure about this?"

"*Assolutamente, Signore* DeSalvo. Here, take a look for yourself with this magnifying glass."

After a few moments of observation, the chairman's assistant whispered, "*Merda.*"

"*Sì, Signore* DeSalvo. That's what we thought as well. When we looked very closely, we discovered that one of the drones contained traces of hydrochloric acid, another rubbing alcohol, and the third the poison. That means, whoever operated these drones, used one to dissolve the window's screen, while the last delivered the death blow. *Signore*, I do not understand the purpose of the one with rubbing alcohol."

"Okay, who builds such devices?" DeSalvo now asked with authority.

"I have been thinking about that myself, *Signore*, but my first inclination is either Japan, China, or Korea. They are the current leaders in drone miniaturization.

So, is Feng Bai behind all of this?

"As for the fragments you hold, none of them are traceable, yet all of them are identifiable. What is unique about these tiny drones is their cleverly conceived configuration."

"What do you mean, *Signore* Corvi?"

"These tiny drones are compact, efficient robots built for a specific purpose. Considerable thought went into their construction. They are masterpieces of technology."

DeSalvo paused to absorb that information. While *Signore* Corvi was quite enamored with the delivery system he and his team had found in the bat's gut, what DeSalvo wanted to know was *who* did this? *Who* killed *Signore* Presto!

"And what about this special, unknown poison, *Signore* Corvi. Who formulated that?"

"*Signore* DeSalvo, you will not like my answer."

"*Signore* Corvi, I am not the late chairman. I do not punish the messenger. Tell me what I will not like."

"There is one match in my database for that poison—only one. It is an exclusive agent that *Signore* William Alexander, the former regional director of North America, used, repeatedly. There is no known antidote for it."

Alexander! Again! First the flowers, and now this!

DeSalvo tried to hide his shock with another quick question.

"And what about the boot prints found outside the estate. What of those?"

"The prints match any number of treads that are available. Special forces organizations throughout the world use such soft rubber soled boots. The trail itself began and ended on the outskirts of Tivoli. After that, there are no traces to follow."

"What sort of 'special forces organizations'?"

"The French BFST, the German KSK, the Australian SOC, the American SOF, the list goes on and on."

"What about the Vatican's Swiss Guards?"

"That, *Signore* DeSalvo, I will have to look into."

"And what of Bruno, Tito, and Marcellus? What killed them? More of Alexander's poison?"

"No. They died of massive, almost surgical trauma, and, secondarily, of silver poisoning," the head of forensics added with a whisper.

"The trauma appears to have been accomplished with a sword blade of exceptional sharpness. The cuts, *Signore* DeSalvo, were all cauterized due to the silver content of the implement."

Now that is a professional's eccentric choice! But one very knowledgeable professional.

"One more question, *Signore* Corvi. Who opened the chairman's window?"

"*Signore* DeSalvo," Corvi said shaking his head, "That I have no answer for. Perhaps the chairman had himself opened the window."

"Check the finger prints on the window pole. See who used it last."

Embarrassed at missing such an obvious potential source of information, Corvi answered, "*Assolutamente, Signore* DeSalvo. *Subito.*"

"And, *Signore* Corvi," DeSalvo said while extending his hand, "Thank you for your speed and efficiency in putting together your analysis. Your extreme professionalism and continued discretion regarding this matter are much appreciated."

Bowing his head, Corvi replied, "Thank you *Signore* DeSalvo. You can always depend on me and my team."

*   *   *

DeSalvo sat in his office on the estate, and for the first time in a long time, felt the walls closing in on him. Two issues troubled the man—the first, the murder of Presto. While only a small number of individuals knew of it, as every second ticked away, that number would rise. Regardless, he had to inform the Rome Gathering and the international CMES community of the passing of its chairman. Such an announcement would no doubt trigger a mad scramble for succession, and that DeSalvo wanted no part of.

The second issue—*who* did this. The entire makeup of the operation smacked too much of an internally orchestrated CMES coup. The telltales of the high technology employed pointed to Feng Bai, the poison to a dead man, Bruno's, Tito's, and Marcellus' quick and efficient elimination pointed to a professional, and the many well-known enemies that the late chairman had muddied the waters and made the confusion worse. DeSalvo also noted the absence of magic in this event, which removed the usual track and trace countermeasures.

But the funeral flowers troubled DeSalvo the most, to the point that the man's ulcer began acting up. Could William Alexander still be alive? If so, then the North American regional director had every right to lash back against Presto for all of his ham-fisted mishandling of the North American region.

Alexander ... still alive!

Now that is a frightening prospect indeed.

Then DeSalvo had another thought. What if all of this was pure disinformation? Who would benefit from such a ruse and why?

More to the point, who would benefit the most from the chairman's passing? Any one of CMES' regional directors for sure. The Vatican, less so, as they rarely assassinated a rival's leader. But would TIIIS? That submissive, quiet, and Luddite-like group of white wizards and witches? If history were any indicator, TIIIS had never undertaken such a daring move; they didn't seem to have the stomach for it. And yet their new Lictor of Magic purportedly ruined the headquarters of the North American region and slayed Alexander in his den.

TIIIS? Would they dare?
We did kill their president.
I need more data.

CHAPTER 60
Postmortem

"President Silver Moon," a British-accented, feminine voice said with undisguised joy. "Thank you for handling our chairman so deftly. You are to be commended."

Silver Moon stiffened at the compliment. "You're welcome ... Oracle."

Before she ended her call, *Signora* Valeria Costa quipped, "Ah, Madam President, your Mr. Stone is such a magnificent showman, and, I might add, quite a specimen."

At that, Silver Moon blinked hard.

* * *

Meanwhile CMES' paranormal leadership, as viewed from provincial Mombasa, Kenya, remained serene following the brief funerary announcement from Rome. Its regional director, Zakia Owusu, smiled and said to himself, "It's about time."

As perhaps one might expect, Feng Bai saw the current internal political uncertainty as a distinct opportunity for advancement. He did not care one wit about the botched situation in North America, but if he became chairman, he knew how to address it.

The regional director of Baghdad, Mukhtar El-Najjar, while young, had begun to lobby for the vacated North American regional directorship. He wanted CMES' presence to remain in Manhattan, the heart of the Wall Street financial district.

As for the regional director in St. Petersburg, Victor Alexandrevich Volkov, he slammed his encrypted phone back into its cradle at the news.

"This is not good. I am not ready.

"I must prepare," he gasped out, as his blood pressure rose to a dangerous level.

In all, each of these men had a good idea of what motivated their peers. The selection of the next CMES chairman would present few issues or obstacles. All concluded that Feng Bai would succeed.

But as with so many things, the devil lurked in the details. Would Feng Bai administer the far-flung CMES organization from Rome or Hong Kong? Who, for instance, would rise to fill in the vacated regional directorships of North America and China? Would the non-aligned organizations renew their allegiances, or instead choose to remain on the sidelines, or worse, defect?

CHAPTER 61
The New Chairman

In spite of Victor Alexandrevich Volkov's greatest fears for CMES' future, a seamless transition of administration took place when Feng Bai assumed the chairmanship. Five minutes later, William DeSalvo, the personal assistant of the former chairman, received an invitation to visit Feng Bai in Rome. Two hours later, Mukhtar El-Najjar became Feng's first choice for the North American regional directorship. By tradition a new chairman's first administrative choice rarely encountered any opposition. The next day the trio met to discuss many things.

"I wish North America to be up on its feet within one month's time." Feng Bai stated. "The property itself I have taken off the market. Instead, it is your task to renovate it. In the interim, you will arrange for temporary headquarters. Are my wishes understood?"

"Absolutely, Mr. Chairman," El-Najjar said submissively, not realizing how daunting those tasks were. No doubt he soon would.

Feng Bai turned to the third person sitting in his new palatial office, and as he did, he seamlessly shifted from Arabic to Italian.

"*Signore* DeSalvo, the previous chairman preferred to kill first, instead of interrogating first. However, you strike me as a far more cerebral individual. Your immediate handling of the chairman's murder investigation, the orchestration of his tasteful funeral, and my orderly transition from Hong Kong to Rome, I found to be both competent and efficient. But regarding the murder of my predecessor, perhaps you can shed some light on this matter?"

For the first time DeSalvo saw a glimmer of hope for an extended future with CMES, if not his very life.

"*Sí, Signore. Grazie, Signore.* I think I can. It is my considered opinion that TIIIS, and TIIIS alone, murdered your predecessor."

Then, without batting an eye, the chairman asked.

"So, who do *you* think accomplished the swift fall of our North American headquarters?"

"TIIIS, Mr. Chairman."

"TIIIS? What nonsense," blurted out El-Najjar in Italian. "Those hacks can't fight themselves out of a wet paper bag," he emphasized with a dismissive wave of his hand.

Unfazed by El-Najjar's uninvited outburst, Feng Bai found himself intrigued by DeSalvo's assertions.

"Why, *Signore* DeSalvo, do you believe this to be so?"

"Because, Mr. Chairman, they have a new Lictor of Magic, and because they have motive."

To this, El-Najjar again waved his hand in dismissal.

"*Signore* DeSalvo, why should we take note of him?" Feng Bai softly beckoned with open hands.

DeSalvo, looking down at his quaking hands, thought, *This is the interview of my very life.*

The Roman looked straight into Feng Bai eyes with conviction, and said, "Mr. Chairman. The TIIIS' Lictor of Magic represents an amalgam of many things, which, when put together, makes him virtually invincible."

El-Najjar's ill-advised snicker was quelled with one quick glance from the chairman.

"Consider, Mr. Chairman, Stone is a highly decorated and battle-hardened field commander, a U.S. Marine, who has led men and killed his enemies. After his service, Stone graduated *cum laude* from a prestigious university, where his studies focused on ancient Near Eastern demonology, which required him to master ancient languages."

To this detail, Feng Bai nodded in deep appreciation, as the mastery of languages was one of his fondest hobbies.

"Critical to this analysis, Mr. Chairman, there is strong and compelling evidence that it was he who acquired *The Book of Spells* from Director Alexander, and most likely killed him in the process. But our greatest concern is that this man carries the First Soul of Creation."

El-Najjar, not impressed with the recounted resume, remained silent this time.

While Feng Bai's attention peaked at the mention of *The Book of Spells*, his eyes noticeably widened when that most ancient designation, the First Soul of Creation, was spoken aloud; they took on an almost dreamy aspect and his head tilted in thought.

Then, "Are you sure of this information, *Signore* DeSalvo?"

"*Sí, Signore.* Chairman Presto's oracle had informed him of this, more than once. The former chairman ordered the assassination of Stone twice, and each attempt failed."

"Most interesting." Feng Bai responded as the former chairman had not failed often, *much less twice*.

"*Signore* DeSalvo, do you speak English? Perhaps better than my humble grasp of Italian?"

"Sí, Signore."

"Have you ever been to New York City?"

"No, Signore."

Feng Bai smiled and opened his arms expansively. "Well, you will now, for I am appointing you Mr. El-Najjar's second in command. Henceforth, you will be the Assistant Regional Director of North America."

At this unexpected news, El-Najjar didn't dare move a muscle.

"Signore DeSalvo, I know that this represents a step down from being the chairman's own personal assistant, but I think right now you belong in New York City. I will be looking forward to your monthly progress reports," the chairman said as he settled back into his chair, most pleased with his decision.

"You may leave now, *Signore* El-Najjar and I have some sensitive matters to discuss."

*   *   *

Before DeSalvo had the chance to close the chairman's office door behind him, El-Najjar's eyes bugged out of his head.

"El-Najjar," the chairman inquired in Arabic, "is there something that you wish to say?"

"I thought I could appoint my own executive staff."

"Under normal conditions I would say that would be a most logical assumption. But these are anything *but* normal conditions. If anything, I have removed from your plate one very politically sensitive matter.

"May I suggest that you focus upon the tasks that I have given you? Do not disappoint me. As for the operational and investigative issues surrounding my predecessor's murder, those are for DeSalvo.

"Absolutely, Mr. Chairman," El-Najjar said while bowing toward his new boss. "May I assume DeSalvo will have access to everything he may deem needful for his investigations in terms of manpower and technical resources?"

A simple nod answered the question.

Feng Bai, not wishing to see his first appointee fail, basically granted the native of Baghdad *carte blanche* with one proviso—"Be thorough in your tasks, El-Najjar. As for DeSalvo, he will report directly to me."

CHAPTER 62
Chicago

I had two weeks to prepare a paper to deliver on an academic panel devoted to the magic of the ancient Near East. Given my full plate, I wished I hadn't made that commitment. My complicated life as Guardian of the Cosmic Order, TIIIS Lictor of Magic, and budding academic had finally collided. Something had to give. I decided to make this presentation my last—an academic swan song. Peter and Mel might not like that decision, but one's desires often have nothing to do with the cards reality deals you.

*   *   *

When I landed in Chicago, Mel had talked her way past the security screen to meet me at the gate. While her aura gave away her excitement, her smile exploded when she saw me exiting the gangway—something that surprised and warmed me all at the same time. Her hug crushed me, but her brown eyes transmitted something that made me wonder. She just buzzed.

"Welcome to Chicago."

"Thanks. Mel, what's up?"

"You have been missed. And, I see"—as she insinuated two fingers into my shirt—"you are still wearing my protective amulet," she said, her dimples showing.

"In the field, yes. While training, not."

"Of that I am well aware, handsome."

Handsome?

"Because of that amulet, I have suffered two black eyes and suffered a mysterious gunshot wound to my right arm, and still I'm here to pick you up from the airport. What does that tell you?"

I didn't know what to say. I blurted out, "We're good friends?"

"I suppose," she said with a pout.

"Mel, I'm dangerous. Remember?" I said as we began to make our way toward baggage.

"Indeed, J.J., I well know," she said while taking my arm. "But I have decided I can live with that. The question is, can you?"

I hadn't expected this feminine assault, this personal commitment cross-examination. My life had become complicated enough. Now this.

Soul carrier. Do not turn away this white witch's advances, the First Soul recommended with a chuckle.

My shock at the sudden intrusion caused me to miss a step, and in the process, I lost track of my conversation with Mel.

Her patience at an end, Melaina poked, "Well?"

"Why are you pushing this, Mel?"

"Because, whether you know it or not, I complete you, J.J. You need a sounding board. Someone you can talk to. An Alexandrian white witch to answer your questions."

Now on the moving walkway that crossed under the airport's tarmac, I said, "Mel. Any commitment that I make would put you on a hit list. Why, Mel, should I embrace that future?"

Silence.

"You're afraid." She countered.

I sighed.

"No, I'm trying to be realistic."

"I see your point, J.J. But have you considered what I bring to the table?"

"I have, and you're right," I smiled. "In fact, we would make a terrific team."

"Yes, we would" she said as she closed the remaining gap between us.

"But there are a couple of things that I would like *you* to consider."

"Like?"

"Taking some self-defense at the Academy, specifically in lethal and defensive magic."

"You're serious."

"Yep."

"Why?"

"Because, Mel, if we're going to be a team, you have to become formidable. Especially now that serious stuff is going on."

"Like?"

"We're at war."

*   *   *

The panel on magic turned out to be one of many delivered at the University of Chicago's Oriental Institute. My particular panel had been placed in the James Henry Breasted Auditorium on the institute's first floor, since it could hold a larger audience.

When Melaina introduced me, I took the stage, arranged my script, took off my wristwatch, looked up to my audience, and began. Unbidden, in the back of my mind, flashed my first such presentation in San Francisco, delivered at a time that seemed decades ago.

Nine and a half minutes later I had finished, a full

five minutes early. After a spirited session of questions and answers, I stepped down from the stage and left the academic world. While no one else knew, I did, and so did Mel. It felt like a burden removed.

*   *   *

The Near Eastern magical cadre, led by my mentor, Professor Peter Glass, invited me to join them for dinner. Grabbing several taxis, we journeyed north to Chicago's Greek Town, where our reservation for dinner had been made. Seated in a lavishly appointed back room with floor to ceiling glass walls on three sides, our talkative group filled the long table that already had five bottles of Greek white and red wines placed along its center.

Once everyone had filled their glass, Peter, who had seated himself at the table's head, stood and said, "Welcome everyone, to Chicago!"

Several "hear, hears" responded. Glasses clinked.

"I wish to welcome a new face to our research band of ancient wizards and witches: Mr. J.J. Stone."

More raucous replies burst forth with raised glasses, further clinking, and deeper sips.

"As most of you already know, Mr. Stone is a graduate student of mine, whose MA has already garnered much interest from several publishing houses. It will become, in due time, required reading. Congratulations, Mr. Stone!"

While much of this adulation I could understand, I knew for a fact my thesis had yet to be signed off by the very man who had just praised it. I kept my lip zipped and went along for the ride.

From my seat, dead center, I could see nothing but

the brightest auras surrounding me, several I suspected were full witches and wizards from their distinctive glows. For a moment, I regretted my decision to leave academia. Here I sat among peers, accepted as one of them, made part of their tight little band.

Melaina, who sat to my right, must have sensed this conflict within me. She took my hand and said, "Relax, J.J., and just enjoy the moment."

As I have since come to realize, she was right.

*   *   *

That very evening, I called for the first time a very special number, one that I had saved for just this sort of thing. It was mom who answered.

"J.J.! Is that you?"

"Yes, Mom."

"*Daddy!* Your son is on the line!" Mom yelled.

A moment later, the conference call was complete.

"It's been so long, J.J. Are you all right, son?" Mom wanted to know right that minute.

"Yep. I'm fit as a fiddle. How about you all? Are you comfortable?"

"Yes, J.J., Daddy and I are safe and sound in a pretty little place near a lake. Why can't you come and visit?"

With tears running down my face, I choked out, somehow, "Because Mom, the bad people might follow me there and find you and Dad, like they did the last time."

Dad piped in snorting, "What bull-hockey! I've defended this household twice now. And you should see the new guns that I have …"

"Dad," I interrupted, "I am staying away not because I don't love you and Mom to pieces, but because I do. And let's face it, with those two instances, you were lucky.

"Mom and Dad, I called to share some good news."

"What, son?" Mom injected right quick.

"I'm calling to tell you that I met this wonderful lady."

CHAPTER 63
Stone 2.0

About six blocks away from my hotel in Santa Fe was an edgy, new age spa called the Bluffs. One of those places where the clientele wore sandals year-round, devoted themselves to yoga, pretended to flourish on yogurt, wore hemp clothing, and wore their long hair braided, oftentimes with beads.

This was the facility TIIIS had hidden Mr. Henry at over the past several months, ostensibly to speed the man's recovery from a variety of nagging ailments. Here the octogenarian struggled hard to get well and mend as fast as possible, because he couldn't stand the place.

That Tuesday morning, I managed to catch him at his exercises, bitching a blue streak at his trainer about this and that, wondering when he would get a full three squares, and yearning for a pint, pleading that even a cold Bud Lite would do. I could see that the man had reached his limit; if he was willing to drink Bud Lite, the desperation was beginning to set in. I couldn't resist intruding on this precious moment.

"So, my friend, how are you doing?" I said as I invaded the weight room.

"Ah! J.J., what took you so long, son?"

"Drove in late last night. Had to come out and look in on you."

"Careful, J.J., I'm in no mood for your pious solicitousness. I'm on a serious mission to get my shit together, so I can get out of this nut farm."

"Nut farm?"

"Yeah. That's all they feed you here. Twigs, nuts, berries, bark, and the like. I'm so jonesing for a rare steak that every cute little bunny or pigeon I see outside my window sets my mouth to watering."

"Then, I have some good news for you. I just finished talking with the staff, and they said we can go on a field trip tomorrow. We can have lunch wherever you please and even a beer or two."

A serious look and furrowed eyebrows now focused upon me as the man licked his lips.

"You're blocking your thoughts, J.J. Why is that?"

"Are you saying you don't believe me? That you don't want me to pick you up tomorrow, a Wednesday, at say nine in the morning?"

"Well, since you put it that way, I'll guess I'll be expecting to see you tomorrow, at nine, sharp."

*   *   *

The next day, Mr. Henry and I took off in my old red Colorado pick-up truck. He looked radiant, tanned, well-rested, and clear-eyed. Frankly, he looked marvelous. Maybe there was something to all that granola and nuts.

"You know, J.J., while I won't admit this to anyone else, one would think that by the time you reach eighty one's brain might actually function."

As personal assessments go, that had to be the most Mr. Henry had ever shared with me. I felt surprised and privileged he would disclose such a frank examination.

Then, "Where are you taking me? Some nice, dark, dive bar? Maybe with some pole dancers?"

"Nope, Mr. Henry. I thought it would be great if we paid a visit to the local ley line, the Silver Nile.

President Silver Moon thought it would be the perfect thing for us to do together. Are you up for it?"

"Capital idea. It's not far, as I recall. Besides, the scenery is to die for."

"That's what I'm told. The president provided me with directions and gave me these two flashlights to take along. Apparently, there's this cave."

"Yep. She's right about that."

After a pleasant drive along the southern limit of the Santa Fe National Forest, I pulled over at a scenic overlook next to a limestone monument. Getting out, we inspected its rough and weathered surface and read its engraved inscription.

> On March 28th, 1862, 51 God-fearing men of the Union Army stood and freely gave their lives to defend this most sacred land from the dark forces of the heathen. Remember always, stranger, when you pass this way, their mortal sacrifice.

Mr. Henry whispered, "J.J., do you know what this inscription is all about? Its context?"

"By its date, a battle during the American Civil War."

"That's correct, but only in part. Most folks think the sole reason for the Civil War had to do with the freeing of the slaves. While that's true, it's also part of a far more complex story. For that horrible Civil War took place because our country had developed along different lifestyles—agrarian versus industrial, states' rights versus federal, secessionist versus unionist, and southern versus northern nationalism. What is not widely known nor recognized is CMES' role in that conflict and their shadowy support of the South."

"You're kidding me."

"Not one bit, for the battle that this monument commemorates stopped the Confederacy dead in its tracks, and kept them from gaining control of the southern Rockies, and the New Mexico Territory in particular. Why, you might ask? Silver, J.J., CMES wanted control of this region's silver mines."

"And," I picked up on Mr. Henry's thread, "with control of the silver mines, any demonic opposition would be severely hindered."

"Bingo. And on top of that, check this out." As the white-haired man extended his arms out from his sides like a weather vane. "Do you see anything odd in the terrain along this approximate east-west line?"

As I sighted along his arms in both directions I saw it. A line of ridges, running in a straight line. "So this is the local ley line?"

"No, J.J. Not just a *local* ley line. It's *the* ley line of the entire American Southwest—the Silver Nile. About a half mile from here is that cave I think the president wants us to visit."

"You up to it?" I asked again.

"You bet."

*   *   *

Now on foot, Mr. Henry took the point, which seemed to invigorate the man as we passed through thickets of fragrant pine, breathtaking upland valley, and gorgeous red sandstone outcrops. Face it, the man liked to lead.

"J.J., it's over here." The wily ex-Marine pointed toward a rock face, and there, lo' and behold, appeared a fissure-like opening about eight feet high by four feet wide, two feet up the face. A gentle flow of water emanated from it. Grabbing a stick, I brushed aside an old spider web. We climbed up and entered with flashlights in hand. Mr. Henry naturally took the lead as tour guide.

As he turned on his flashlight, he said, "As you can see from that web, J.J., this particular cave is not well publicized."

The initial part of the cave narrowed, despite its generous looking entrance. I had to take care not to bang my head. After about sixty steps into the formation, Mr. Henry stopped, turned to me and said, "J.J. Can you feel it?"

At first I didn't know what he meant because of the loud rushing sound in my ears. I thought my excitement and blood flow had caused it more than anything else. I stood still in the darkness, relaxed, and reached out to lean against the nearby wall ...

The next thing I knew, Mr. Henry was kneeling over me wearing a ton of concern on his face.

"What happened?" I whispered, confused and more than a bit dazed.

"You've been out for a full minute. Boy, you gave me a fright. I even had to catch you before you cold-cocked yourself good on the floor. What cha' do?"

"I reached out to lean against that wall. I have never felt anything like it before. It knocked me for a loop."

"Oh," he said laconically, as he held the palm of his hand over where I had pointed.

"You're right, that's a pretty powerful hot spot there. No doubt a side branch of the Silver Nile."

Turning back to me, "Now, J.J., stop, before you get up, and take a good inventory. Are you okay?"

"I think so. But give me a hand, I don't want to touch any more walls."

Once up, I felt light-headed, but everything seemed to work.

"Mr. Henry, you're glowing. Your aura is really pumping it out."

Looking down at his hands, then at me, Mr. Henry corrected me. "No, J.J. It's not me, it's you. Your usual aura has gotten all sparkly somehow. I think you've been charged up. Now, as a test, read my mind."

And I did, as easily as if I were looking through a clear window pane into a beer cooler, and said so.

"*Well, now*, that's mighty interesting. I indeed had a frosty beer in mind, but I had my blocks on full and to the max. How hard did you try?"

"I didn't. I just did it."

"Well, son, I don't know what happened to you, but your psychic quotient just went from strong to god-awful powerful. I think we should carefully back out of here and find us some beers. What do you say partner?"

"Sounds like a plan."

*   *   *

On our way back to Santa Fe, I "spotted" the perfect place. A quaint highland gas station nestled in a pretty roadside setting. Mr. Henry and I each grabbed a beer from their full cooler, and sat down at an old wooden picnic table under the station's weathered silver wood awning.

We popped the caps, clinked the frosty long necks in salute, and took long delicious pulls. Mr. Henry asked me how I knew about this place. I said I didn't, but that it felt right. Then he said with a misty-eyed wistfulness that I had never seen before on his face.

"My boy, I do believe that you have survived your first evolution."

"What do you mean by 'evolution'?"

"You know how some caterpillars transform themselves into beautiful butterflies?"

I nodded my head.

"Did you know that spiders molt their skin?"

Now I shook my head.

"Well, when you accidently, or perhaps providentially, touched that hot spot in the cave, I believe you transformed like a butterfly, or molted like a growing spider.

"Consider: my Class Four Adept mental blocks seemed transparent to you, like the glass door of a beer cooler. Finding this perfect place, you did by feel alone. Now, my friend, I want you to look around yourself, reach out, and note what you now can sense."

By just looking around and probing with my mind I noted the following details. The level of the gas station's reservoir, a cavernous steel cylinder, sat half filled. The middle-aged attendant inside fought hard not to doze off. The family of squirrels living in the gas station's attic had four babies. I had to shake my head to clear it of all the clutter.

"Pretty awesome, isn't it?" my friend asked.

"Yes, it is. But it's also a bit overwhelming."

"Yeah. Ain't life a bitch. Like everything, J.J., you'll get used to it. But now you have reached another level. You've grown because the Silver Nile sensed you needed a long overdue software upgrade. By the way, today is a full moon and I need another beer, J.J. 2.0."

That beer came and went, and another.

"Mr. Henry, I've been thinking."

"Yeah, I know. I smelled the wood burning."

"How can a ley line sense anything?"

"Ley lines are like the aorta in your body. Big, powerful, channels of paranormal energy that like the earth's magnetic fields, surround and course through our planet like the veins and arteries of our body. In your case, you tapped into the Silver Nile by accident. As a result, you are now a part of it. Think of it this way: you are now an infinitesimal capillary of a vast interconnected system, web, whatever, of paranormal energy. It, the Silver Nile, has made you a part of it. It has accepted you and is willing to share its power with you.

"Now, and no one can say why ley lines do what they do, but without question, they are sentient, psychically sensitive, and do make decisions. I'm sure you heard at the Academy that whopper about a wizard tapping into a ley line and frying his ass."

"Yeah," I smiled at the memory, "Mr. Good did mention it."

"Well, ducky for Mr. Good, and as for the story, it's a crock. The immature wizard in question hadn't prepared himself for what direct contact with a ley line would mean. In his case, he temporarily lost some of his short-term memory, that's all. But he learned in the process not to fool with Mother Nature."

"That was you, wasn't it?" I asked with absolute certainty.

"Damn straight. And what a fool I was. But in your case, J.J., you blundered into contact. You didn't have it in your head to better yourself, in fact, quite the opposite. Up until that moment, you had a dark cloud over your head; you were troubled. Your aura said so, and I suspect that our dear president sensed that, too, when she suggested we come and make a visit."

We continued to sit there, talking, drinking beer, and eating some god awful microwaved hot dogs for a good three hours. We did deep dives about life, it's meaning, past loves, and the inherent loneliness of duty.

"Can you do it, J.J.?"

"Do what, Mr. Henry?"

"A young buck like yourself. You gotta meet someone you can open up to, someone to discover the rest of your destiny with."

Had he and Mel been talking?

"There's only one problem with that."

"What?"

"They all die … horribly, Mr. Henry."

"I know you think that, son, but it doesn't always have to be that way. Besides, you can't give up on yourself either. The world will be a far better place with J.J. 2.0, if he matures like I know he can. Take a deep breath and give yourself a chance, Marine."

CHAPTER 64
The Oracle

Valeria Costa, her forearms dusted with flour, kneaded a sizable lump of bread dough in her kitchen, when suddenly, the oracle slipped to her knees as if struck by a potent electrical shock. Her vision temporarily clouded, she sat stunned and helpless on the limestone flooring, her eyes tearing. After some time, her vision cleared, and the numbing sensation passed.

"It has happened," she whispered in awe. "Stone has made contact with the Silver Nile."

She sat there panting a moment.

"And that powerful source has accepted him as one of its own. *Mio dio*, there'll be no stopping him now."

ABOUT THE AUTHOR

This is W. J. Cherf's second foray into the realm of paranormal adventure literature and contemporary urban fantasy. *The First Soul*, the first book of the series, The Adventures of J.J. Stone, began the journey of U.S. Marine Sergeant J.J. Stone from his birth until he became a member in TIIIS. The book carries on the saga.

Cherf is also known for his works in historical science fiction. His award-winning five volume time traveling series, The Manuscripts of the Richards' Trust, takes place in ancient Egypt and early medieval France. They are full of adventure, intrigue, and vivid descriptions.

As to why Cherf writes in his retirement years, he says, "I always wanted to write a book without footnotes." This is an oblique reference to his treadmill "publish or perish" days as a professor of ancient history and archaeology.

To find reviews and free chapters to all of his works, not to mention a handy source for the latest breaking news in Egyptology, go to www.wjcherf.com.